KT-381-291

0749 904 64X 1 488 4D

Different Lives

Also by Connie Monk

Season of Change
Fortune's Daughter
Jessica
Hannah's Wharf
Rachel's Way
Reach for the Dream
Tomorrow's Memories
A Field of Bright Laughter
Flame of Courage
The Apple Orchards
Beyond Downing Wood
The Running Tide
Family Reunions
On the Wings of the Storm
Water's Edge

Different Lives

Connie Monk

PIATKUS

READING AREA

RR 1/99	RT	RC	RB
RP	RS	RW	MO6

Copyright © 1999 by Connie Monk

First published in Great Britain in 1999 by
Judy Piatkus (Publishers) Ltd of
5 Windmill Street, London W1

This edition published 1999

The moral right of the author has been asserted

A catalogue record for this book is available from the British Library

ISBN 0 7499 0464 X

Set in Times by Phoenix Photosetting, Chatham, Kent
Printed and bound in Great Britain by
Butler & Tanner Ltd, Frome and London

Chapter One

'I blame myself,' Cedric Sylvester repeated, his fingers drumming on the frame of the open door as in Kyneston's drawing room they waited, flinching at each cry from upstairs and yet straining their ears so that not a sound was lost. How else could they keep faith with their beloved Mary? 'You know why I agreed to young Clive Rochester marrying her, don't you?' Cedric didn't expect an answer. 'Because he was a neighbour, because he wouldn't be taking her too far away from her home.'

'And you did right,' Alice, his wife, assured him, 'Clive makes her happy. She wants this baby, she wasn't frightened. You'll see, a few more hours and all this will be forgotten, she'll have given him an—'

'Given him? Given him? This child is *hers*, it's she who has suffered for months, we've watched her and been helpless. It should never have been forced on her, she's been worn down to a shadow of herself and you say it's to give *him* an heir?'

Only Patience said nothing – after all, who would want to hear her opinion?

'Hark! Hush now!' At last Alice raised her head, listening expectantly. 'There's the bedroom door.'

Dr Saunders appeared on the gallery that overlooked the hall, then started down the stairs. His brows were drawn into a worried frown, he must have seen them waiting but couldn't bring himself to raise his eyes to meet theirs.

'News? Is it over?' Alice forced her voice to hold its note of hope.

The doctor nodded.

'A boy?'

'I did everything humanly possible. Her heart . . .'

'What are you saying?' Cedric cut in. 'Is something wrong with Mary?' He and Alice had brought her up as if she were their own child instead of a sister born when he was already a married man. What was the fool of a doctor trying to tell them? No . . . no, not that . . .

'Everything I could,' Dr Saunders repeated. He'd attended Mary Sylvester all her life. And that, of course, was the trouble. There were plenty of children who ran free, made the forest their playground, sat in the gutters of the local towns playing Five Stone or bowled their hoops along the roads; children who hung around the doors of public houses waiting for their fathers to come home – and sometimes their mothers too. Often they had little that was nourishing to feed on yet they had the stamina to fight off infection and, if they did contract any of the usual childhood ailments, chickenpox or whooping cough, they usually managed to recover without so much as calling for his help. Yet his visits to Hapley Court had been so frequent that he'd come to know Mary Sylvester well. He'd helped her through every childhood complaint even though he'd marvelled at any germ being able to get beyond Alice's careful guard. If, on a trip to Lyndhurst or Ringwood with Alice, some runny-nosed urchin should come into sight, Mary would have been taken firmly by the hand and made to cross to the other side of the road; yet every germ being carried on the wind had alighted on her.

'I think he's coming in,' Patience whispered, turning to the doctor, 'he must have seen you through the window of the gallery. Poor boy . . . Don't tell him in here . . . go out and speak to him on his own . . .' She was astounded at her own temerity. She never offered an opinion, who would have listened even if she had?

The doctor looked at her gratefully. What he had to do would be hard enough in the dark, but at least poor young Rochester would be spared the accusation he knew would be in Cedric Sylvester's eyes.

'The baby?' Patience followed after him as he went towards the conservatory and the garden beyond. 'What about the baby?' Normally she would have waited silently: years of knowing herself to be no more than a duty that had to be borne in her brother's household had taught her to know her place. But someone had to ask it and from the way Cedric was leaning

2

against the wall with his head buried in the crook of his arm and Alice sniffing into her handkerchief she knew their thoughts went no further than poor, darling Mary.

'A girl. Perfect in wind and limb.'

'You're overwrought. We all are.' Cedric forced compassion into his voice despite the anger that raged in him against the young man whose carnal appetite had robbed their beloved Mary of her life. So clearly did he recall the morning she had been born, the rising sun of May Day 1886 casting a golden beam of light on the tiny, helpless creature. His newborn sister, even in her first hour she had tugged at his heartstrings as nothing had before, not even his courtship and marriage to Alice. Now she'd been taken from them . . . yes, but she'd left a legacy, weak and vulnerable, with no mother to love her. 'We must try to be thankful we have her child, something of her. The day Mary was born I vowed I would care for her always. God forgive me, I handed over that trust.'

Clive didn't seem to be listening. Cedric and Alice had been up to gaze through their tears at Mary and the baby, Patience had wept as she'd hovered just inside the bedroom door. Only Clive had remained downstairs. He wanted them gone, their grief was for their sister, he had no part in it. Mary . . . how we talked about when it would be all over and you well again . . . remember? But you can't remember, you can't even know how frightened I am. You're gone. Dead. They're crying for you, Mary. Can you see their tears? A boy or a girl we'd wondered, Matthew or Melissa . . . but we never thought you wouldn't be here . . . there's no shape, no pattern, no reason. If there were, then you would still be here, if one of you had to die it would have been the baby. Melissa. It's a girl, Mary. I don't know what to do . . . Just make them go home, make them leave me alone.

Only after their carriage had rolled away down the gravel drive into the forest road could he let his features relax as, his head buried in his hands, he slumped forward in his chair.

'Here we are, Mr Rochester, sir.' The nurse too had listened for the Sylvesters' departure; now she stood in the open doorway, the baby in her arms tightly wrapped like a papoose in the shawl Mary had laid out ready with its first tiny robe. 'Just you look at her, I've never seen a lovelier newborn in all my days. That's it, Mr Rochester dear, nothing like tears for flushing out the misery.'

3

Clive hadn't cried since he was a child the unaccustomed tautness around his mouth, the burning sting in his eyes, was as unreal as everything else in the last hours.

'Here, take hold of her. Dear Miss Mary – for that's what she's always been to me – she's left you something of herself.'

'No. You take her. I can't . . .' as the nurse held the bundle towards him he pushed it away, he couldn't so much as look at it. 'Take her away from me—' Like a Jack-in-the-Box he sprang to his feet and rushed from the room taking the stairs two at a time.

Nurse Hume watched him, shaking her head helplessly. 'Never mind, my lovely, he'll feel better bye and bye. And there's love enough waiting for you with your poor mother's people. But what a crying shame, lovely young girl like Miss Mary. That's the mama you should have had. Ah, her and him too, always such a jolly young man. Crying like that . . . oh dear oh Lord, where's the Great Design You tell us to believe, if you can do this to a happy young couple? And there's those in the back streets, drop their babies as easy and as often as rabbits in the field and can't scrape together enough coppers to keep them nourished.'

It was after Mary's funeral that Cedric put his proposition to Clive, following him into the drawing room while Alice went up to the nursery, Patience three treads behind her.

'I don't know how much thought you've given to the child's welfare, Nurse Hume won't be prepared to stay above a month or so. What we are saying to you is this: Alice and I will make ourselves responsible for the baby. You had Mary for just one year, we had her for eighteen, we reared her, cared for her, loved her. I like to believe that if she had to be taken from this world, it is providence that the child she leaves is a girl. She will need a woman's care – and what more natural than that that woman should be Alice who was like a mother to her.' He raised a hand as if to stop Clive interrupting. 'No, just hear me out. I realize it lifts a burden from you, but it's not for that that we want the child. There is no feeling of duty on our part. Let us take her, let us do this for Mary. Another Mary for us to care for. History repeating itself.'

'Her name is Melissa.' The unfamiliar hard tone was lost of Cedric.

'Melissa? Nonsense, there has never been a Melissa in the

family. Mary, a gift of God, just as our own dear Mary was before her.'

'A girl Melissa, or a boy Matthew.' Clive wasn't arguing, he was simply stating fact.

'If that's what Mary wanted. What's in a name? Look Clive, my boy, we're not saying this without thought, we have discussed it thoroughly. A man on his own can't be expected to meet a child's needs. You can't deprive her of a woman's tenderness and understanding. For Mary's sake we shall love her as if she were our own – and for Mary's sake I'm sure you will want what is best for her.'

'She belongs here.' Clive felt trapped, frightened into a corner by Cedric's persistent reasoning. Clearly they considered him unequal to seeing the child properly brought up. Still the future had no shape, he knew nothing of children and had no inclination to learn. But their arrogance angered him, their suggestion that the year he and Mary had shared was of no more importance than any other – or was it fear at his own inadequacy that angered him? 'You are old enough to be her grandparents.' He took comfort from the cruelty of his words.

'You were brought up by grandparents yourself and, as I recall, you were none the less happy for it.' Cedric brushed the obstacle aside, determined not to let hard words come between them for that would be no way to win his point. 'Don't be hasty.' He made one more attempt at solicitude. 'Nurse Hume will look after things for a few weeks yet. Sleep on my offer, yes, that's it my boy, give yourself time. You're still in shock I dare say but soon you'll find yourself better able to listen to what Mary must be trying to tell you. Her childhood was a happy time, she'd want as good for this new Mar—Melissa.'

He was confident Clive would see the sense of it. They'd known him since since he'd been no more than a child himself and had always found him good humoured and agreeable.

From the first day, Alice Sylvester saw herself as guardian of Melissa's welfare. Sometime during each day she'd journey the two and a half forest miles that divided Hapley Court and Kyneston, sure that by the time Nurse Hume took her departure Clive would have come to his senses. It came as a surprise to her when the baby was a fortnight old to find a nursemaid in residence

5

as well as Nellie Hume, appointed to take control after the lying-in nurse left.

As she drove her trap down along the forest road towards home she met Clive out riding and at the same time exercising Hunter, his yellow labrador.

'I've come from Kyneston,' she greeted him, her voice commanding that they stop, there were things to be said. 'And what I've found is most worrying. Of course we must engage a nursemaid – and I dare say the one I met is as good as any – but these aren't things for you to concern yourself with. Domestic staff would have been Mary's responsibility.'

'Nurse Hume saw to things for me, she says this woman – Esme something – is right for the job.'

'I would have preferred the choice were my own.'

Clive laughed, but there was no humour in his handsome young face. 'We would both have preferred it could have been Mary's. However, I've made my decision, Esme has been engaged and I understand from Nurse Hume the baby is flourishing.'

'Esme "somebody"! Mary's baby should be cared for by family not by a paid "somebody". Don't be stubborn, Clive. We'd bring her up to call you "Father", we're not trying to steal her.'

'Her home is Kyneston.' His smile had vanished, this time he met her gaze squarely and she knew there was no point in trying to dissuade him. The sting of tears came from disappointment, sadness that she wasn't to be able to cling to this link with Mary – and a touch of anger too. He hated to see a woman cry, so he hastened to make amends. 'She'll soon grow big enough to be collected to visit you. I give you my word, Alice, she will see you as more than an ordinary aunt and uncle.'

She knew when she was beaten. Perhaps they'd misjudged him. He'd never been tested and tried, that's what Cedric always said. And it was true, of course. He must be twenty-five years old or more and he'd never done a day's work in his life: everything had fallen in his lap. By the time he finished schooling his grandfather had been his only relative, and what a fool he'd made of the boy: almost as if in him he was reliving his own youth, together they'd hunted, attended pheasant shoots, rowed out to sea to fish, swum from the beach at Milford, sailed out of Lymington. Life had been a round of pleasure. And when Henry Rochester had been thrown from his horse and killed leaving Kyneston and everything he had

6

to Clive, the young man had seen no reason to change his habits. And they'd played into his hands too, agreeing that he should marry Mary when she was but eighteen years old. Not tested and tried . . . but could they still say that now that he was facing life without her?

Watching her put her pony into a trot Clive felt no sense of victory. How much easier it would have been to let the child go to them. So why didn't he? He told himself it was because she was all that was left to him without Mary; but he was too honest to believe that that was the whole truth. The Sylvesters didn't approve of him, they'd never said so of course, for any criticism would have risked alienating them from Mary. Often enough he'd seen 'I know best, my boy' written on Cedric's thin face as clearly as if he'd spoken the words. And Mary, sweet, gentle Mary, would never say a word to upset them. Well, now they'd see he wasn't a man to jump to attention at their bidding.

A baby in the house . . . a nursemaid . . . Was his obstinacy making him a fool to himself? He sighed as he urged his horse to a gallop, Hunter barking with excitement and racing ahead of him.

The feeling that life had no shape lasted a few months. A conventional half-year of mourning excluded him from local invitations and he was conscious there were those who looked askance when he joined the shoot and when winter came donned his pink jacket and rode out with the hounds. What went on in his heart was his own affair. Certainly there were times when he was haunted by the memory of those first weeks of marriage, the time before a barrier of poor health had held her away from him. Mary had never overcome a fear of horses so last winter, as this, he'd ridden out alone from Kyneston. She'd never been amongst the party of ladies who ate lunch after a shoot, either, so there again there were no ghosts to touch him unexpectedly on the shoulder; neither had she come on the boat with him, nor sat by his favourite lake while he played for trout. But she'd been waiting at home, her blue eyes lighting with pleasure at the sight of him, never complaining at the hours she'd sat and stitched alone by the window ready to wave when he came into view.

Alice could find no fault with Esme Summers (as Esme something's name turned out to be). Melissa thrived, in appearance growing more like Mary as she developed from a helpless baby,

7

through the first dawning of intelligence and became a toddler with a will of her own. She might look like like an angel with her mother's golden curls and large innocent blue eyes, but she was quick to know what she wanted and to find that the surest way to get it was to scream and hold her breath. Usually she wasn't thwarted, usually that angelic smile was reward enough to make Esme, any of the household staff and certainly the Sylvesters, delight in pleasing her. Clive saw very little of her and he had no intention of looking for trouble by disciplining her; at the first sign of a tantrum he left her to other hands.

As soon as the accepted period of mourning was over, he was invited back into the round of local social events. At one time that would have been enough to satisfy him; but no longer.

It did occur to him that he might travel to Cornwall to attend the annual meeting of Wheal Creasey, the tin mine which brought him some of his income. His grandfather had invested in two sources: his first had been in thriving tea plantations in India, the profits had ensured a good income but at such a distance the work that went on there had meant nothing more personal than the annual report and the quarterly returns. His second investment and one nearer to home had been in Wheal Creasey and here Henry Rochester had liked to think of himself as more actively involved, always attending the adventurers' meetings. Clive had never accompanied him and, since he'd inherited the shares, he'd not taken his seat at the meetings. Perhaps he might enjoy the trip, it might be amusing to see at first hand where some of his money came from . . . perhaps he ought to interest himself . . . But would be really be interested? No, it wasn't worth the journey, all that way to end up listening to lists of dreary figures and with no better company than a group of tedious money-minded businessmen. So in characteristic fashion he turned his mind to more pleasant things, sorted his fishing tackle, loaded his luggage into the trap and set out for a few days trout fishing at his favourite haunt in Dorset.

He stayed in an inn where he found plenty of convivial company and for those few days he almost managed to put the clock back, recapture some of the youthful freedom he'd enjoyed before he'd lost his heart to Mary. For twelve and a half months he'd been married to her; now, for twenty-two months, he'd been a widower. Yet it was impossible to recapture the carefree zest for

8

life he'd known as a bachelor. The sort of adoration she had given him had left a wound that wouldn't heal.

It was as his trap bowled along the roads towards home that the emptiness of his existence threatened to darken his mood. Who was there to care whether he came or went? He was never short of invitations: bachelor or widower, a spare male was always a welcome guest. Yet, for all his acquaintances, he was alone, he mattered to no one nor anyone to him. Dwelling on his lonely state, his mood sunk lower.

That's when he heard the sound of music.

'Whoa, whoa. Hark,' as if the pony must be listening too. Drums, whistles, and surely a squeeze box . . . 'Walk on. Let's see what it's about.'

What it was about proved to be the annual Feast of St Peter, 29 June, a day when the local farm workers, maidservants and tradespeople alike who lived in the parish put down their tools and mops, locked their shop doors and came to join the fun. He was a stranger in their midst, but that didn't deter him. Tethering his pony and leaving his fishing roads and box of luggage unattended, he went to join the throng. To the accompaniment of the music children were dancing around a maypole, despite it being eight weeks beyond May Day; for tuppence a throw there was the chance of winning a pig and for only a penny he was given five balls to hurl at a row of coconuts.

'Well done, you got one, mister,' a small boy watching him jumped up and down with excitement.

'Here, you have a go.' Clive passed the child a penny. 'See if you can get one too.'

Like bees round a honeypot, more small boys attached themselves to him. Not his usual sort of company, but there was pleasure to be had in distributing pence and feeling himself part of their excitement in the day.

He wandered on, looking at the wares that were on display for sale, hand-pulled humbugs made from the sweet smelling confection that bubbled in a steaming cauldron, fruit pies, handmade lace, dried flowers, ribbons. On the far side of the green someone was trying (without success) to climb a greasy pole, someone else plaiting reeds and making baskets.

'Cheek o' the devil, see who's turned up!' One woman jostling with him for a view of the basketmaker whispered to another.

9

Whispered? In tone perhaps it was, but not in volume. His wasn't the only head that turned to follow her gaze.

'I heard a rumour she'd been seen in Ringwood. Fancy having the brazen cheek to show her face back here where she's known for what she is!'

'Well, she'll not get the time of day from *me*. Coming here with her load of trouble! No wonder her folk pulled up their roots and went off to make a new life without her.'

'Carries the brat like the gypsy women do.'

Disapproving of her presence or not, there was no doubt that the young woman added colour and interest to their day. As if unaware of the heads turned in her direction, the object of their attention was bearing down on a stall that sold dried flowers and ribbons. Clive watched her, fascinated. He couldn't guess her age, not that he consciously tried, but she was not a young girl. Tall in an age when women prided themselves on being petite, as dark as a Romany when fashion decreed beauty should be pale skinned. He couldn't take his eyes off her. Something in the way she walked, as proud as a queen despite the nudges and whispers she must have known she was attracting. Slung on her back, supported by a large scarlet shawl was a child, a girl who looked to be about Melissa's age. With her right hand behind her back the woman gave extra support to her 'load of trouble' and with her left she carried a large basket resembling an outsize trug. Instinctively he glanced at her ringless left hand and felt a tug of sympathy for her. As she came closer to the stall the locals moved away, but she seemed unaware or uncaring that she was being snubbed.

Giving his following of small boys a florin to share between them he too moved in the direction of the dried flowers and ribbons. Putting her purchases into her flat basket and her fourpence change into her chain purse needed both hands and that's when Fate stepped in. Without that extra support her 'load of trouble' started to slip, let out a loud yell of alarm, then found herself supported by two strong hands.

Georgina Hawkesworth craned her neck to look up at her rescuer. At barely two years old she knew what she liked, and she approved of the appearance of the smiling stranger.

'The shawl's come loose,' the tall woman turned to him grate- fully. 'She's getting too heavy for it, that's the trouble.'

'Then I have a better suggestion. Let her ride on my shoulders, we'll look at the Fayre together.' Seeing her moment's doubt, he added, 'I'm quite harmless I promise. I have a daughter about the same age at home.' Not that he'd ever carried her on his shoulders or any other way for that matter, but it seemed to satisfy the dark beauty. She untied the knot that had already slipped and let him lift the child high over his head to land astride his shoulders, from where she laughed with delight from her exalted vantage point. 'My name's Clive Rochester,' he introduced himself, 'I'm travelling home from a few days' fishing.'

'Home?' she asked.

'In the New Forest, between Lyndhurst and Lymington. And you?'

'I've been moving around. But I plan to find somewhere to settle in Christchurch. I'm Augusta Hawkesworth and this is my daughter, Georgina.'

With all the formality of an official introduction they shook hands, then he steered her away from the stall where she'd been buying to the other side of the green where the children had finished their dance and the ribbons of the Maypole were tangling in the breeze. He found himself enjoying the glances of the local gossips. A few people had gathered to listen to one of St Peter's male choristers who, having made free in the ale tent, was treating them to a rendition of 'Soldiers of the Queen'. One or two tut-tutted and muttered that it was disgraceful what drink will do to a respectable man, others egged him on for an encore. Clive and Augusta turned to each other at the same moment, their spontaneous laugh not at him, not at the reception given to his slurred entertainment, not at anything in particular except their sudden pleasure in being where they were. And, on his shoulders, Georgina threw back her head and shrieked with merriment, showing her pearly white milk teeth. Never before had she ridden so high, looking down on everyone around her. She shook her head vigorously from side to side, delighting in the feeling of the breeze in her gingery curls. Happiness lit her gingery-brown eyes – and her face raised towards the sky, it's likely that the sunshine added a few more freckles to those that already peppered her small nose.

For Augusta too the day was suddenly brighter. Just look at the way the local women were watching her: it was easy enough to guess what they were saying. Well, let them. Old crones the lot of

11

them, old crones or young ones, if whispering behind her back gave them any pleasure let them get on with it. She'd come to the Fayre to buy ribbons and dried flowers – and knowing the spiteful pleasure her presence would bring she'd made sure she looked her most flamboyant, even going to the length of wearing a large and striking straw hat she'd really made for Madame de Bouverie's salon but decided she liked it too well to let it go, a hat quite unsuitable to her station but one she was confident looked much better on her than it would on any of those able to afford to buy it from Yvonne de Bouverie. Yes, she'd known just how good she looked when she made her appearance amongst the stalls – and now, seeing the admiration in Clive's eyes, laughter bubbled up in her. She almost shared her joke with him.

'What would you do with a pig if you won one?' Clive asked, guiding her in the direction of another tuppenny throw.

'Live on pork until I hated the sight or smell of it I shouldn't wonder.'

The answer was no more serious than the question, which was as well since neither of them stood any chance of outbowling the local elevens cricket champion. They hardly knew each other, two strangers with no past and no future, nothing but the exhilaration they found in the unexpectedness of meeting.

The afternoon could have been marred had Georgina decided she'd had enough, but she was far too busy taking in the sights, sounds and smells of the Fayre. If they lingered too long in one place she would jog her small bottom up and down and urge her steed to 'gee-up' but, apart from that, occasionally holding her arms high in the air as if she thought she could catch the scudding white clouds or letting out a whoop of excitement for some reason known only to herself, she might as well not have been there. For Clive there was only Augusta, never had he been so aware of anyone's capacity for enjoyment; all around them people were cramming all the fun they could into the few hours of the freedom of the Festival, but Augusta's pleasure was different from theirs. He felt that it stemmed from something within herself, a radiance that came not from the transitory amusement of the Fayre but from her own joy of living.

They ate fruit pies, they drank cider. Georgina was lifted from her high seat and given a share of both. She bit into the plum pie with gusto, although her baby face did wince at the tart taste of scrumpy cider; but she was sensitive to atmosphere and although she was too young to reason, she accepted a nasty drink as part of the enchantment of this wonderful day. She looked at her mother's carefree expression, she heard the sound of this man's deep voice and his ready laugh. Once more hoisted to his shoulders she gave a shudder of excitement, she felt herself to be important, part of the reason they were all having such a lovely time. Had she understood that she was no more than Augusta's 'load of trouble', carried on Clive's shoulders but interesting him no more than did his own daughter, her balloon of happiness might have withered if not burst.

'How far have you to go? How did you get here?' he asked Augusta when the stallholders were busy packing, the Maypole had been taken down and only the serious drinkers in the ale tent had no thoughts of going home.

'For the time being I'm in a room in Ringwood. I walked.'

She knew she wouldn't be walking home.

It had taken more than an hour to walk from her lodging in Ringwood. The return journey went all too quickly.

'Thank you for today.' Clive's words banished the threat of gloom. The way he spoke them eradicated the last – and unacknowledged – vestige of hurt she had felt that not a single person from the village where she'd lived as a girl had had the courage or the inclination to welcome her amongst them. Not that she cared, she told herself. If she'd cared she wouldn't have taken such pains to make sure she looked so strikingly different from any of the village women. No, she didn't want their friendship . . . but keeping her thoughts on those lines built her anger, and happiness can't take root in anger. Now here was Clive speaking to her as if she were someone of status, a person he was proud to be with.

'No, I should thank you.' Her near-black eyes turned to him with honesty. 'That village is where I was brought up, you know. Did they see me as one of them? Not that I wanted to be. But there wasn't a single person who came to speak, to see Georgina. So it's I who should be thanking you. I shan't forget today.'

'We none of us will, and that includes Georgina,' Clive laughed.

Facing forwards, the little redhead sat on her mother's knee, her bottom bouncing, her hands before her as she held imaginary

13

reins. The rear view of the pony filled her universe, she wanted the ride to go on for ever. Her eyelids were getting heavy, she had to force them open. Against her will she lost the battle and collapsed backwards against Augusta, by the time they came through Rockford she was fast asleep.

'I assume there's just you and Georgina?' His question fell into the stillness of the summer evening.

She held up her ringless left hand.

'I've never had a husband, I thought you guessed that much. But I earn a living, enough to keep a roof over our head and feed us.' He heard a ring of pride in the words. 'Oh, not in the way those crones like to think. I earn my living by making hats for Madame de Bouverie's shop in Christchurch. "A salon" she calls it, not a hat shop. She likes to think her trade comes from the local wealthy. I design hats and make them. Sometimes I don't want to part with them.' Then, somehow looking younger, like a child hoping for praise, 'This one should have gone to her, but I couldn't resist it.'

'It would have been a sin for it to be on any head but yours. You look quite lovely.'

She'd wanted him to compliment her, now she felt she'd forced the words from him and wished she'd said nothing.

'Why I asked whether you were on your own, I was thinking of tomorrow. There won't be a Fayre to amuse us, but we could go somewhere, anywhere you like. Will you?'

And why not? Why shouldn't she snatch the opportunity? If he had a young daughter, then presumably he also had a wife. Perhaps she was as stuffy and boring as so many of Madame de Bouverie's clients . . . so where was the harm? Why shouldn't she have some fun?

'Despite what they must have thought when they saw us together at the Fayre – no. You're on your way home to a wife and child.' It wasn't the answer she'd meant to give. 'Today has been wonderful, let's leave it at that.' He knew she said it sincerely, the way she looked at him when she spoke set his pulses racing in a way he'd forgotten.

'And tomorrow can be better. Augusta, I lost my wife nearly two years ago. The thought of tomorrow, all the tomorrows, terrifies me. Please, we have no one to consider but ourselves. What shall we do? I have a boat moored at Lymington, what if I collect you and we spend the day on the water? Or Bournemouth? Do you fancy outshining the other promenaders in your so elegant hat? Anywhere you like, or nowhere in particular, just strolling in the forest. But say you'll come, say I may see you again.'

'A day on the water sounds like paradise. It's no place for a toddler, I'll see if I can leave her at home with Mrs Hodges – she's our landlady.'

Next morning even before consciousness fully returned Clive was aware of an unfamiliar feeling of eagerness for the day.

Georgina felt a glow of anticipation too, even though she hadn't the words to express it. From the safe anchorage of the high chair Mrs Hodges had at one time used for her own family, she watched her mother dress. There was something about the way she brushed her dark shining hair with such energy, something about the way she twisted and turned to admire herself in the long mirror, and particularly about the angle of her large hat and the purposeful movement of prodding her hatpin to keep it in place. In the little girl's young mind were a thousand images of yesterday, in her tummy was a fluttering feeling of excitement. It was going to be like that all over again! Yes, from her high seat she could see out of the window: that jolly man had come. She tried to clamber out of her chair and when Augusta lifted her free of it she put her arms around her neck and hugged her in gratitude and excitement.

But where were they going? The man was outside in the road, so why were they going into Mrs Hodges's dark kitchen.

'Here she is Mrs Hodges and here's the shilling we agreed. Be a good girl Georgina.'

And she was gone.

Kyneston saw very little of Clive during the weeks that followed. Neither Mrs Biggs nor the rest of the staff had any idea what took him off in such eager haste as soon as he'd swallowed breakfast. Any shopping expeditions they made were to Lyndhurst or Lymington, so whispers didn't reach their ears of what took him so regularly to Ringwood.

He gave no thought to Alice Sylvester and, if he had, it wouldn't have bothered him. Mary had been close to her family and now he knew their frequent visits were focused on Melissa. As for him, if he happened to be at home he welcomed them

15

cordially enough then absented himself. That Alice had a fondness for Ringwood hadn't occurred to him. She enjoyed bowling along in her trap, jogging over the unmade road of the forest, then turning through Burley and on towards the little market town. And it was here on a morning late in August that she noticed Clive with a tall, dark beauty on his arm – although when Alice reported the incident to Cedric she described their brother-in-law's companion as 'a swarthy-looking woman, dressed in gawdy colours. No wonder he did no more than doff his hat to me, she certainly didn't look to be the sort of creature I'd expect to be introduced to.'

For the next two months hardly a day went by when Clive and Augusta didn't spend at least part of it together. She often worked by lamplight when the late summer sun had set, determined still to fulfil her orders for Madame de Bouverie. As for Georgina, most of her summer was spent in Mrs Hodges's care. An extra shilling a day made a big difference to the landlady's income and at only just two years old Georgina couldn't describe how the time was spent, whether she was taken for walks by the river, strapped into a bassinet and told to be quiet while her carer chattered to friends they met in town, or was left to her own devices on the ill-lit brick floor of the kitchen where the most exciting thing she could find to do was to turn out the saucepan cupboard.

It was on the day when Alice first became aware that Clive was keeping company with 'another woman', as *anyone* who threatened to take Mary's place in his affections would have been seen, that Clive took Augusta to Kyneston. In the morning he drove her to Christchurch to take a case of hats to Madame de Bouverie (and no doubt collect payment, but that part of it didn't interest him), then to Lymington and to the Angel for lunch. It was after that that, instead of taking the direct road back to Ringwood, he set off through the forest.

Every inch of the way was familiar to him, but never had he travelled this road with Augusta at his side . . . Augusta who filled his every thought . . . Augusta who gave meaning to his days.

'Where are we going?' she asked, interested but not concerned.

'It's time I took you to Kyneston.'

She mustn't let her sudden insecurity show. Clive was different from anyone she had known in the past. Money seemed to be no worry to him yet he never talked of working – in fact he never talked of anything except the good times they had had together. There had been no time in her life to compare with these last weeks. Kyneston . . . his home . . . he had a child but no wife . . . he was young, perhaps younger than she was herself . . . was Kyneston his parent's home? She wished she'd been warned that she was to meet his family. They would probably hold it against her that he had 'wasted' his summer, for that's what they would call the way they had enjoyed each day together. As for her, she'd sat late into the nights stitching by lamplight; but Clive appeared to have no responsibilities.

'You're quiet,' he prompted her. 'Don't you want to see my home?'

'Of course I do.' Did her answer sound as forced to him as it did to her? 'Tell me about it.'

'What shall I tell you? Kyneston has been my family home since it was built by my grandfather at the turn of the century.'

'Family home?' So she was right. He was the son of the house. And what would his people think of her? If the people in her own village wouldn't acknowledge her, what would a meeting with his family do to the happiness she and Clive had found together? At that moment she would have given much to have pulled out of the air some good reason not to finish their journey to Kyneston. But she could think of nothing and the steady clip-clop of the pony's hooves brought the moment of truth ever closer.

One thing Augusta had never lacked had been self confidence. On the day Clive had first met her he had been struck by her beauty and by her bearing. Now, though, she knew herself to be gauche, frightened. Yes, most of all she was frightened; how much influence did his family have over him? If they didn't consider her a suitable companion, would he listen, would this be the end of these wonderful, joyous weeks? She'd hoped – sometimes she'd more than hoped, she'd believed – they were going to be lovers. They'd come to the brink, she'd been eager to be swept along by nature and love, she'd meant to draw him with her. Yet always he had found the strength to draw back. But why? If only they were lovers, then she could look his people in the face, sure that she had a place somewhere in his life.

'Will your parents be at home?' She must be something of an actress, she told herself, to sound so eager to meet them.

17

'There's no one, only Melissa, and she's not much more than a baby. I want you to see Kyneston.'

Her mind was darting in so many directions: no one at home except a baby and a nursemaid, was he taking her there because at last they were to be lovers? Why else would he want to take her to an empty home? Joy flooded through her.

They were turning towards a high wrought-iron gate, an open gate, for no animals could stray from the forest over the cattle grid that protected Kyneston's grounds. Almost immediately the drive curved and she had her first view of the house. Built of dark red brick, an early Victorian mansion, with three gables on the south-facing frontage, the sort of house she had never been inside in her life. It spoke of wealth, stability and no nonsense.

'You live *here*?' The words escaped her.

'Whoa,' he drew the trap to a halt. 'I wanted you to see it. I've loved Kyneston since I came here as a small child when my parents went to South Africa.'

'Are they there now?' As if it mattered where they were, she only said the first thing that came into her head while she looked around at the well-kept gardens planted with the hues of autumn, the mown lawns, the archway that clearly led to a stable block.

'In South Africa? No,' he answered. 'They died some years ago. I hardly remember them, my grandfather was my family. You would have loved him – and he, you.' He set the pony on in the direction of the stable yard – and it was from there that she saw that the grounds extended beyond to a paddock.

All this belonged to Clive!

Jumping down from the trap he walked round to help her. She held out her arms.

Listening to Alice's account of the couple she'd seen in Ringwood, Cedric set his mouth in a tight line. He felt genuinely hurt that Mary's husband – to him that's what Clive was, 'husband' not 'widower', a husband who kept her alive in his memory – could be seen out with another woman, let alone a woman of the sort Alice described. 'Perhaps he was doing a kindness—'

'And if he was, he was taking pleasure from it. Talking, laughing, not a care in the world between the pair of them. Mr Griffin from Tyler's Farm was in town for the market, he saw our

18

brief exchange. Now, listen to this and you'll not say he was doing her a kindness. Mr Griffin tells me they are often together, brazen as you please. A trollop, that's what she is, a trollop with a child to prove it. And that's the sort of woman Mary's widower takes up with! Mr Tyler made a point of telling me, thought we should be made aware of what was going on. It seems they're always together, he picks her up from some mean little lodging on Christchurch Road, and while she's off enjoying herself her land-lady minds the bastard brat. For that's what it is. He says he's been told she's always been a baggage, even as a girl. Plenty of men I don't doubt, but never a husband.'

'The young fool, getting himself in the clutches of a woman of that sort. I've a good mind to go and see him, tell him it's got to stop. Getting himself gossiped about! It's a slight to Mary's memory!'

'Yes. That would be the thing to do. His trouble is, his life has been one round of enjoyment – until he lost Mary. He's feather-brained, doesn't know how to handle unhappiness. He's running away from his grief, that's what it must be. He hasn't thought about what people are saying.'

'He's never thought about anything, that's his trouble. You said it yourself. Nothing but passing his days in pleasure-seeking.'

As good as his word, that same evening he presented himself at Kyneston. When the door was opened to his knock he told Doris, the maid, that he had come to discuss an important matter with her master.

'He has someone visiting, sir. I'll tell him you're here.'

She hovered, uncertain whether to take him straight to the drawing room or show him into the study to wait.

Cedric took the question out of her hands, he was close behind her as she knocked on the drawing-room door.

'Mr Sylvester has called to see you, sir.'

'Come in, Cedric.' Clive's voice was over-hearty, he wasn't going to let the visit mar these moments. 'Thank you, Doris.'

As the girl closed the door the three of them were silent. Both men had something to say, it was important not to approach from the wrong angle. Both men were aware of Augusta, the reason for Cedric's visit, the reason for Clive's elation. She was wearing a gown the colour of a russet apple ('Gawdy', that's what Alice said, and so she is, ran Cedric's thoughts. Not a lady! He wouldn't

19

admit to his awareness of her sensuality, it was easier to hang on to that disparaging 'Not a lady!')

Augusta didn't know who the visitor was, but she sensed his disapproval of her. This evening no one, not he, not even queen Victoria herself, could destroy her elation. In the beginning she and Clive had enjoyed being together, everything they did had been such fun, she'd felt for the first time in her life that she was really living. It hadn't taken long though for her to want more than their pleasure-seeking hours gave. She'd wanted Clive, not just as a friend, an admiring friend, she'd wanted him as a lover. She'd never expected more.

'I have ridden over to have a talk with you, a talk of some urgency,' the thin-faced visitor blustered, a sure sign that he wasn't happy with the situation, 'A private word.'

'You can talk in front of Augusta. Cedric, you are the first to share our news. Augusta has consented to be my wife.' It was the first time he'd known his brother-in-law to be at a loss for an answer. 'Augusta, this is Mary's brother, Cedric Sylvester.'

Cedric found his hand taken in Augusta's. Had he held it out to her, or had she reached for it?

'Marrying . . .?' Why hadn't he found out what the young fool was up to sooner so that he could have nipped the affair in the bud before it had time to bloom? How could he say what had to be said with those dark, sultry eyes on him, aware of his discomfort, seeming to laugh at him? 'You've been lonely,' he changed tactics and approached from another direction, uncertain of himself in circumstances he'd not envisaged, 'of course you have. Nothing can take Mary's place, not in your life and not in ours. Trying to replace her is only running away from your grief. You've got to face up to it, hold on to your memories—'

'Augusta isn't a second best for the wife I lost. She is my future.' He put his arm around her shoulder.

'I hope we shall learn to be friends, Mr Sylvester. I'm not replacing your sister.'

'By Christ you're not. Standing here in her drawing room, giving yourself the airs and graces of a lady!'

Clive had always taken the line of least resistance, steered clear of trouble. Now his change in manner took Cedric by surprise.

'You'll take that back,' he said, his eyes narrowed, his voice cold. 'Either you apologize to Augusta or you leave my house and know you won't be welcome in it again.'

Upstairs asleep in her cot was Melissa, Mary's daughter.

Stiffly, Cedric bowed his head in Augusta's direction. 'I apologize, I was overwrought.'

'Of course you were. I don't offend easily.'

Your sort can't afford to: he would love to have voiced the thought, but wasn't risking Clive's wrath.

'You say you aren't trying to replace Mary, but you are being brought in as mother to her child. Perhaps now, Clive, you will re-think our offer, let Melissa make her home with us.'

It was Augusta who answered. Until Cedric arrived she had been living a dream – no, even that wasn't quite true, for even in her dreams she had never allowed herself to imagine being mistress of a home like Kyneston. Now his unfriendly manner to her brought her feet firmly to the ground, gave her the confidence she'd lacked.

'I'm not replacing her mother, I'm not the world's most maternal. But I'm bringing her a sister, my daughter Georgina.'

Clive and Augusta were married in Ringwood, no one there except themselves, the rector, with Mrs Hodges and the sexton to sign the register, and Georgina struggling to free herself from the retraining straps of her basinnet and disliking the cold gloom of the church.

The ceremony over, the bridal couple were going to London for their honeymoon, but *en route* for Brockenhurst Station they called at Kyneston to deliver Georgina.

21

Chapter Two

'I was never happy about him!' Alice said 'And neither were you. For Mary's sake, because it was what she wanted, we accepted. But how could he do this? Another woman in Mary's place . . .'

With a little more understanding, although no more forgiveness, Cedric answered, 'He's still a young man, no more than twenty-seven or so, and you've seen the way the local girls always buttered up to him. Good looking I dare say, and with plenty of wherewithal. But his standards aren't ours, my dear. He was always a lightweight – yes, we had to accept for Mary's sake, I would never have said a word against him that would have hurt her. His sort is easy prey, we might have known he would take another wife. A woman of our own sort, that we would have had to accept – a bitter pill, but one we would have had to swallow. But this! You saw immediately the sort of person she was. To bring a creature of that ilk to be mistress of Mary's home, for Melissa to look on as mother, that bastard brat of hers as a sister—'

'That she never shall! Melissa has *us*. When she's old enough to understand, it's up to us to make her realise the situation. And I'll tell you another thing, nothing, *nothing*, is going to prevent me fetching Mary's baby over here for her day each week.'

It had been habit ever since Nurse Hume passed Melissa's care into the hands of Esme Summers that each Monday, Hobbs, the groom from Hapley Court, should take Alice to Kyneston and she should return with the baby in her arms, the impedimenta of its daily needs neatly packed in a wicker basket at her feet. Without realizing it, she had fallen in with Esme's choice of day. ('If you could manage Mondays, Mrs Sylvester m'am, I'd be glad to have those extra hours after the weekend, time to make sure all her little

22

things are kept as they should be' she told Alice eagerly, patently keen to please). Glad to see the girl so caring of her charge, Alice had fallen into the habit of leaving Esme with Mondays free to relax, see to some dressmaking on her own account, and walk in the forest with her sweetheart, Arnold Wilkins. Arnold worked for the fishmonger in Lymington and as no boats went out to sea over the weekend he was free until Monday's catch came in on the evening tide. The arrangement worked admirably for all of them.

It was the Monday after the wedding. Esme's second charge had been put into her care the previous Thursday, before Clive and Augusta were taken to Brockenhurst to catch the train to London on their honeymoon. With two small charges to look after she got them washed and breakfasted early, then looked out their clean clothes for their outing. Blow me, though, she thought, I can't find a decent rag to put on poor little carrot top's back, at least nothing half good enough to win her Mrs Sylvester's approval. First visit, it's important she looks nice. Oh well, Melissa's got enough for two – she's not going to notice if her new sister wears one of her frocks.

Georgina smiled with delight at the little red-head who beamed back at her from the mirror wearing a green taffeta dress with a lace collar and three frills in the skirt. She threw back her head and laughed for sheer joy in the moment. There was an inexplicable feeling of anticipation in the air.

'Now you just stay clean and good,' Esme admonished her, one eye on the clock to make sure they would be ready and waiting and she could wave them on their way and be free by ten o'clock as usual.

'My word,' she said as she tied Melissa's sash, 'don't you look a pretty pair.' No wonder she smiled, it was easy to smile on Mondays, a few more minutes and they'd be off her hands. 'Here comes Mrs Sylvester.' Then to the children, 'Who's this come for you then?'

Melissa's sweet face was a picture as she staggered towards her favourite aunt – indeed her favourite person. Georgina, sensing this person must be the reason for this morning's air of expectancy, did the same.

'Hello, my pretty one,' Alice lifted Melissa into her arms and was rewarded by a bearlike hug. Georgina waited expectantly, although she was less certain now what it was she was excited about. 'That child,' Alice drew away from her and looked accusingly at Esme. 'Am I right in thinking that dress doesn't belong to her?'

'Well, no, M'am, it doesn't. Her own things, well, there's nothing there fit to send her out visiting in. When they get back from London I'll have to have a word with the mistress, see about fitting her out in something better. All she's got is—'

'What she has doesn't concern me. You say visiting? And where is she going?'

'Why, I thought M'am they'd both be coming to you. I mean . . . well I never thought . . .'

'And there's no reason why you should, Esme. My arrangement has always been that I take Melissa home and that's what I shall continue to do.' Feeling a tug at her skirt she pulled away from Georgina. 'Take your sticky fingers off me, child!' They weren't sticky but that was lost on a two year old. What wasn't lost was the look of angry dislike.

Some children might have been frightened, some might have cried. Not Georgina. Instantly her expression altered, hope and expectation gone. ('I've never seen such a look on a child's face,' Alice reported to Patience when she arrived back at Hapley Court, 'spite, hate. And to think that is to be a companion for our little angel.') Georgina's lips were clamped tightly together, young though she was she knew that if they started to wobble she would be crying and the nasty woman would be pleased. She wasn't going to let that happen; instead she glared up at the stranger, then kicked her ankle with all her might. She put so much force into the kick that she lost her balance and fell backwards onto her bottom. Still holding Melissa firmly with one encircling arm Alice bent down and slapped Georgina hard, her aim intended for her shoulder but landing on her ear.

'Hate 'ou,' Georgina unclamped her lips just long enough to speak, then sat, her face flushed as she looked like thunder at one and all.

'An unpleasant child,' Alice observed, 'not a good influence on this one, I fear. We shall return about five o'clock as usual – and make sure you change her into something of her own. Melissa's clothes are not for common use.' The emphasis was on the word 'common'.

24

It was a bad start to Esme's day of escape, and not a good one for Georgina either. She was squeezed into the prettiest dress Esme could find in the poor selection, one that unfortunately she had outgrown and was too tight under her arms, then bundled into the bassinet and taken to the place where Arnold and his bicycle would be waiting, an unwanted third.

Each week Melissa was collected for her day at Hapley Court, each week at best Georgina was pointedly ignored, at worst was criticized for something that Alice saw as proof of her unsuitability as a companion for Mary's daughter: her breakfast porridge still on her pinafore (for Esme concentrated on getting Melissa dressed and prettied), her boots on the wrong feet where she had tried to dress herself, tangles in the mass of unruly ginger curls or, on one occasion, bringing a note of disgust to Alice's carping voice, a runny nose that she wiped across her rebellious face with the back of her hand.

Esme had hoped that when the honeymooners returned and Augusta realized that her daughter was left behind on Mondays, she might want to take charge of her herself. She soon found there was no likelihood of that. For the newly married couple life was far too full to have space in it for a reminder of previous relationships that Augusta would rather forget. For Clive, too, it was easier not to allow himself to think of Mary, he shied away from remembering her trusting adoration, his own boyish untried love. He wouldn't let himself compare the two, it would have been like comparing pale moonlight with the scorching rays of a summer sun. Dear sweet Mary, he was frightened to remember, frightened of his disloyalty in letting thoughts of those quiet nights of love be swept from his mind by the consuming passion that he and Augusta shared. Had there ever been a woman like it? Their nights were a glorious adventure. His mind spun at the thought of the hours of abandon, the need in him he'd never known he had, the need and the fulfilment. Neither of them wanted more children, he was careful of her and she was careful of herself. But lovemaking was a journey of excitement, even thinking about her set his pulses racing.

And if their nights were good, so too were their days. Augusta learned to crew his sailing boat, relished the feeling of the wind blowing her near-black hair and the tang of the salt spray on her lips; he taught her to ride and, although she'd never sat on a horse before, she took to it enthusiastically, so that by her second winter at Kyneston she rode with him to the hunt; she went with him to his fávourite trout-fishing lake in Dorset (and rightly, too, for he'd been returning from there the day he heard the music of the Fayre) and, as skillfully as any man she rowed the punt while he cast his fly for trout and sometimes they changed positions, he rowed and she cast; she went with him to the races, helping 'pick the winners', excited by any chance gains, discounting any loses with the same disregard as he did himself. The one thing she didn't do was instill in him what Cedric would have called 'a proper sense of responsibility for a man in his position'.

None of his erstwhile acquaintances invited them to visit, no calling cards were left. He realized that this was because the Sylvesters were part of the county set. But he cared nothing that he and Augusta were boycotted. All he wanted was to draw a line under his past and look to the future. He took her with him to his solicitors, Chadwick & Grieves, where he signed the new Will he had had drawn up. Then he arranged to adopt her fatherless child, changing her name legally to Georgina Rochester. In his eyes, and in Augusta's too, that put the past firmly behind them and set both girls on equal footing. That done, their future wellbeing could be left to Esme, Mrs Biggs or any of the staff who were on hand.

There was just one thing that right from the first Augusta had insisted, one hangover from the days before her marriage: she would continue to make hats for Mme de Bouverie. Clive saw no reason for it, she had no need to make pocket money ('pocket money', did he call it? – not so long ago it had been the sole income she and Georgina had lived on), but Augusta wasn't to be dissuaded, she enjoyed her work, she liked to think of herself as being responsible for fashion. So he didn't argue, instead he took pride in her talent.

For three years Arnold Wilkins and Esme both saved, counting as their pence became shillings and their shillings pounds, and patiently she stitched for her bottom drawer.

'I shall be leaving you by the end of the year, Mrs Rochester, m'am,' she said on one of Augusta's infrequent visits to the nursery. 'Me and Arnold, that's my sweetheart, we plan to get wed at Christmas. We've been promised since before I came here. Can't believe it's really happening.'

26

'How exciting,' Augusta beamed her pleasure, while secretly she wondered how they could have waited for more than three years, putting aside a safe nest-egg while she contented herself with making lace edging to trim her underwear and pillowcases. Patience had never been Augusta's strong point. 'What are you wearing for the wedding? Let me help you, Esme, I'd love to.' And so she would, she would take as much pleasure in seeing the nurserymaid start out with a pretty trousseau as she would one of her own family – if she'd had a family.

'Oh, m'am, thank you. I mean thank you for saying that about helping me, but mostly for not minding me going. I've been worrying about how to tell you. I mean, there's the girls to be taken care of. They've got used to me, I hate leaving them – leastwise I would hate it if it was for any other reason. You know what I mean.'

'They're not babies any longer, Esme. We have spoken to Reverend Carter. Beginning in January they are going to the rectory each morning. His sister has agreed to teach them their letters and their times table, and he'll instruct them when they are ready. Naturally we thought you'd still be here. But, never mind. How many five year olds have someone always watching over them? Did you? I know I didn't. Make sure they know how to wash behind their ears and dress themselves before you go, Esme. It'll really be good for them to learn to be independent.'

And with that Augusta put the problem of two unattended five year olds out of her mind.

Under the new system the children were woken each morning by Florrie, the housemaid, whose responsibility it was to see their clothes were laid out ready. She brought warm water to their room in an enamel jug and poured it into the washstand basin, made sure they were awake, told them to hurry, then left them to wash and dress as best they could.

'Your feet are in the wrong boots,' Georgina told Melissa.

'No, they aren't,' Melissa bristled.

'Yes they are. See.' She stood alongside so that they could compare their feet.

'Why's it mine have to be wrong? Why's not mine's right, and yours wrong?'

'Stupid! People's feet don't look like that. Sit down and I'll change them round for you.'

27

Melissa sat as she was told with her feet stuck out in front of her. Not for the first time since there had been no Esme to see they kept pace with each other she felt angry and frustrated. Always Georgina was right, *she* never managed to be the one to point out mistakes. Even at the rectory it was the same. 'Who can tell me what two and two make?' at their lessons Miss Carter would say and before there was time to start to think Georgina would shout the answer. 'Who remembers how to spell "tree"?' and in a flash she'd be calling out the letters and being told how clever she was.

And it wasn't just that Georgina could spell 'tree'. Melissa's silent resentment built, she could climb it too and call down from a high branch. Showing off, trying to make herself important and pretend she's better than I am. But she's not! Aunt Alice knows she's not! Aunt Alice says she doesn't even belong here really, this is *my* home. But Aunt Alice says that 'Mama' isn't *my* real mother, she's *Georgina's* so I don't see that I can belong here and she can't.

It was all a puzzle. And if Augusta, or Mama as they both called her, was mother to one and not the other, why was it that she didn't make a big fuss of Georgina? She certainly didn't. She didn't make a fuss of either of them. She saw they were both well dressed (for she loved clothes, from hats downwards), it was she who had suggested to Clive that he should ask the rector and his sister to instruct them in their lessons and tell Biggs to take and fetch them each morning, but as for spending special time with Georgina, or indeed spending time with either of them, she never did.

'There!' Georgina stood up, satisfied that Melissa's feet didn't look funny any longer. One thing they hadn't yet mastered was the buttonhook so, their kid boots on their feet, they took the tortoise-shell handled buttonhook down to the breakfast room where, quickly as anything, Florrie would fasten the buttons while Mrs Biggs was serving their porridge. Melissa didn't know whether to be angry with Georgina for being right about her having put her boots on the wrong feet, or relieved that they wouldn't know downstairs about her mistake.

Georgina concentrated on the way Florrie poked the hook into each buttonhole, caught the button and pulled it back through the hole with a quick twist. It looked so easy. Tomorrow she wouldn't bother to wash, she'd just get dressed quickly and have time to try

28

it for herself. Just imagine walking into the breakfast room with her boots all tightly done up. Melissa wasn't interested in the intricacies of buttoning boots, she sat with her feet straight out in front of her, smiling sweetly as Mrs Biggs told them that for a treat she'd put some strawberry jam on their porridge.

'Thank you Mrs Biggs. Say "thank you", Gina. You didn't say "thank you" to Mrs Biggs.'

She felt she'd straightened the score.

The jealousy wasn't all on one side. Melissa resented Georgina being the natural leader, but Georgina had cause to be jealous too. Now that they had started lessons Mondays weren't free, so the weekly trip to Hapley Court was changed to Sundays. Each week, almost as soon as breakfast was over, Cedric and Alice would arrive together to collect Melissa. Right from that first Monday, angry and hurt at being left out, Georgina had hated Alice. As months and years went on her hatred built to include Cedric – and even Patience, whom she never saw but heard about from Melissa who always returned from her visits to Hapley Court full of tales of the lovely time she'd had. Aunt Alice . . . Uncle Cedric . . . Aunt Patience . . . and sometimes Aunt Marguerite and Uncle Matthew who had been visiting there from their home in Cornwall and invariably brought 'dear Mary's little girl' a present. Georgina hated them all, seen and unseen.

Each Sunday she was aware of the bustle of preparation revolving around Melissa as she was made ready for her outing and, finally, examined by Mrs Biggs. Being collected by an uncle *and* aunt hinted at a much more exciting day ahead. If Georgina wished she were going too she made sure no one had the satisfaction of knowing it. Not that she did wish it, not *there*, not with precious Aunt Alice! Pityingly, she would say to Melissa, 'A nuisance for you, having to go there each week on a day we don't get lessons. Think of how much more fun you'd be having playing here, instead of having to be all dressed up and with no one but grown ups.' Had Melissa been that bit sharper she might have retorted that Georgina had no one but grown ups either! In fact Mrs Biggs organized Georgina's Sunday mornings, seeing that she was properly dressed to accompany Florrie and Effie, the tweeny, to church, thus keeping her occupied and out of the way for two hours. The children never joined their parents for meals so, on Sundays, rather than eat her dinner in the breakfast room alone, she had a chair at the table in the kitchen with the servants. If Augusta or Clive wondered where she was, they didn't enquire; as long as they didn't have any problems reported, they didn't go out of their way to look for trouble.

Sunday afternoon Georgina made her own amusement. Hunter was her constant companion and when the weather was good, even at that age, she roamed far beyond the grounds of Kyneston. They'd go out through the small gate by the side of the cattle grid, and she knew to be careful to close it behind her so that no forest ponies came into the garden. Then, once in the forest, they ran free. Without Hunter she might sometimes have been lost, but with the uncanny instinct of animals, no matter how far she strayed he unerringly led the way home.

It wasn't that she was neglected, neither she nor Melissa materially lacked for anything. In their own casual way Clive and Augusta were fond of them, praised them when any new skill was brought to their attention.

Augusta's workroom was 'out of bounds' for everyone, not even the maids were allowed inside to tidy. In Georgina's mind there was an aura of mystery and wonder that the pieces of velour or felt, the soft Italian straws, the lengths of silk and veiling she saw taken in there, should re-emerge in the shape of beautiful hats. But the aura of wonder went further and deeper than that, it had to do with the room belonging especially to Augusta. Sometimes on winter Sundays when it was too wet or too dark to wander in the forest, she would play private pretend games in the solitude of the nursery:

'Did you call me, Mama?' she would mime silently – silently, because even at that age she had no intention of being heard talking to herself!

'Oh, Georgina dear, I'm so glad you're here. I do wish you'd come and help me, if we work together we can make some really gorgeous hats.'

Or sometimes, she'd mouth:

'Am I disturbing you, Mama? May I come and watch?'

'As if *you* could disturb me. I just love working when we sit here together.'

And so on. Mama was *her* mother, that meant that she must

30

surely be special. On Sundays as her game unfolded she could almost believe it was true.

It was in the summer when they were six that Clive decided it was time they learned to ride and bought two New Forest ponies (a gentle, kindly breed if ever there was one).

'Come and see what I have for you!' In high humour he was waiting for them in the stable yard when they climbed down from the trap, home from their morning at the rectory.

Georgina looked – and jumped up and down with excitement; Melissa stood rooted to the spot, paralysed with fear. He remembered Mary's own terror of horses, a terror he had always blamed on the Sylvesters. They should have encouraged her to make friends with a pony when she was young. So thinking, he took Melissa's hand and went to lead her forward.

'No!' she screamed, standing her ground, pulling back from him with all her might. 'No. I won't come.' Beside herself, she fought, she hardly knew what she did as she kicked at him, her blue eyes full of terror and defiance.

He let go of her hand and turned to Georgina who was feeding first one pony then the other with handfuls of grass, holding her hand flat as Augusta instructed and apparently oblivious of Melissa's outburst.

'We'll try you first, then,' he lifted her to sit in the saddle.

All Melissa heard was the word 'first'.

'Come on, let me show you how to give your pony some grass,' Augusta held out her hand. 'What are you going to call him?'

'Nothing. Won't call him anything. Take him away, take him away! I'm not being put on him. Never.' So panicked, she felt she couldn't breathe, her tummy was full of trembles. If only she could run away indoors, but she mustn't, she had to make them know she meant what she said, she wouldn't go near . . . she *couldn't* touch it . . . Mama was coming towards her . . . All control lost she started to cry and when Augusta reached out to her, she grabbed the extended hand and bit it. Then she threw herself to the ground of the stable yard, rolled onto her back and beating her small heels and fists on the cobblestones yelled with all her might. Hearing the noise, Florrie came running from the house.

'Oh, m'am, whatever's the trouble. Has she fallen?'

'Take her indoors, there's no point in letting her spoil it for both of them.'

31

Florrie lifted Melissa for, six yeears old or not, she was an uncontrolled tornado when she was upset and there would be no chance of her walking. Her tear-stained face was dirty, and the misery of having wet knickers was as dreadful as everything else that had happened.

As far as Clive and Augusta were concerned that was the end of the matter: if Melissa didn't want to ride, there was no point in forcing her, and once she was carried out of earshot they put the incident out of mind. Up in the nursery, away from sight and sound of the stable yard, divested of her wet underwear and cuddled on Florrie's knee, still Melissa's little body trembled, she couldn't stop her hysterical crying – either couldn't or wouldn't try to control herself, Florrie wasn't sure which. Perhaps a sharp slap might stop her, she thought, but how could she bring her hand down on the poor little mite like that? So Melissa sobbed until finally she was sick, so often the end of her hysterical outbursts.

Outside, Georgina's happiness knew no bounds. Loving the feeling of the firm saddle under her and the motion of the pony, she was taken out on the leading rein, Augusta riding on one side of her and Clive, holding the rein, on the other. She wanted to look composed, but how could she when her face wouldn't stop smiling? That day at the Fayre had faded from her memory long ago, but the spirit was much the same as she skirted the paddock on her first pony ride. Father, Mama and her, all three of them together, all having a wonderful time. No wonder she beamed her delight at them as she leaned forward and stroked the pony's neck. She wished they'd let her hold the reins herself, just imagine all three of them galloping, not just here in the paddock but through the forest ... Father, Mama and her. Fancy Melissa being frightened! Probably she'd not been scared of the pony at all, more likely it had been because she thought she'd not do it very well – she'd lain on the ground and kicked and cried like that the other day when they'd persuaded Tom, the garden boy, to climb up and tie a rope to a high branch for them to climb up and she'd not been able to get more than a little way. Stupid. Of course it wasn't easy, but you just had to keep trying, getting a bit higher each time. Anyway, Georgina decided, this was much too splendid to be spoiled worrying about why Melissa had had a tantrum!

'Gee-up,' she urged for, as excited as she was, she just had to

32

say *something* and that seemed to her to be something the pony would understand.

That night Melissa cried out in her sleep, dreaming ponies were coming out of the forest, chasing her. Half awake in the darkness she knew Georgina was climbing into bed with her, cuddling her, keeping her safe.

On the flat, smoothly cut side lawn of Kyneston the croquet hoops were put out each summer. The girls often played, with all her might Melissa willing Georgina to mis-hit and send the ball into the surrounding bushes. Georgina didn't have to see it to know Melissa's expression as she watched her aim her ball through each hoop. The trouble was it was so easy to win, Melly had no eye for ball games; and when she lost she was no company at all, she would have a tantrum or sulk for the rest of the afternoon. So there were times when it was better to hit the ball 'accidentally' with the side of the mallet and lose lots of turns trying to get it out of the bushes and back on course. For the sake of a peaceful life that's sometimes what Georgina would do, knowing that would give her a sunny companion for the rest of the day. It wasn't that she minded losing the game, she even managed to tell Melissa 'Well done!' But she was disappointed. Playing your best was important, more important than actually winning; purposely playing badly was no fun at all. And how could Melissa be so cock-a-hoop about her victory, she must know it had been handed to her on a plate!

It was the same story with tennis. When the girls were too small to manage a racket they contented themselves picking up the balls and throwing them back to Clive and Augusta. But as they grew they were encouraged to play, sometimes by themselves, or occasionally with their parents. Usually Georgina and Augusta played against Clive and Melissa and, fortunately for the sake of peace, Clive was a good player so the two pairs were well matched. Trouble began when the contest was just between the two girls. Easily and for the sake of peace Georgina could have hit into the net or far outside the court, but sometimes she rebelled. Why should she always pander to Melissa's bad temper?

She was about fourteen when she took her courage in both hands and, almost silently, entered Augusta's holy of holies.

33

'I won't talk, Mama. Can I just watch you?'

'I don't see why not – as long as you're as good as your word and don't expect me to chatter.' Augusta threw her a quick smile then turned back to the more important job on hand with as much concentration as if she were still alone.

Fascinated, Georgina watched the skilled fingers working on a creation of pale lilac felt. She wondered at the way it was steamed, stretched into shape on the stand, the brim coaxed to just the angle to set it off. Conscious that she mustn't interrupt, she sat very still, asking no questions but missing nothing.

When Augusta had finished for the afternoon they tidied the work table together.

'You may come again if you want to,' her mother told her as they surveyed the cleared worktop. 'If you find it interesting, I mean.'

Georgina was so pleased she could actually feel her heart beating. How could Augusta not see the adulation in her expression as she answered.

'Oh, I do. Who taught you, Mama?' Every word was meaningful. Here they were, just the two of them.

'My grandmother never had money to spare,' Augusta answered casually, her mind on how much veiling was left on the roll she was replacing in the cupboard. 'She made all her own hats. Lots of people did in those days, but they weren't like hers. She had a flair. I watched, learned enough to put to the test when I was old enough to want smart millinery and had no means of buying it.'

'But you could go to Mme de Bouverie and buy the best hats in the place now.'

Augusta laughed. 'And why would I do that? The best designed hats in Mme de Bouverie's saloon are those I've made myself. And there's something else, perhaps you're not old enough to understand. Having money to spend, easy money I mean that you haven't actually earned, can't compare with the shillings you work for. Given the choice I know which I get more satisfaction from.'

'You must feel – feel – proud, really cock-a-hoop – that you can say what you did about Madame de Bouverie's hats and know it's true. People like that hateful Mrs Sylvester, she comes here all dressed up to the nines, how good you must feel to know you can look down your nose at her, she just *buys* the sort of hats she finds in the shop, she can't take a piece of material and make what she wants. Not that *she'd* know what she wanted and anyway whatever she puts on her head she looks ugly!'

Mother and daughter looked at each other, sharing their dislike of Melissa's doting aunt, Georgina knowing that her outspoken rudeness might be rebuked, Augusta knowing that she ought to rebuke. Instead she laughed, they both laughed. Perhaps in all their years that was their closest moment.

That was the start. Augusta didn't work every day and certainly not every afternoon, which was the only time Georgina was free. But on the days she and Clive hadn't other plans usually she could be found in her workroom, often with Georgina, elbows on the table, watching as trimming was added to the fashioned shapes, then with delicate stitches the silk linings sewn in. No two hats were the same, and not one of them was dull.

Melissa, still frightened of horses, had mastered a bicycle and was able to visit Hapley Court far more frequently than just Sundays.

Of the four of them, Clive, Augusta and the two girls, it was Georgina who loved taking care of Kyneston. It was she who, as spring gave way to summer, had learnt to mark out the tennis court on the lower lawn; it was she who hammered the croquet hoops into the ground; it was she who helped clean the stables and the yard, who learned to prune the roses and helped Jack Hopwood, the gardener, tie the bean poles. There was no need for her to do any of those things, there was no shortage of labour. She did what she did because she loved Kyneston and, in some unprobed way, she felt it gave love back to her. The thought was unprobed because she wasn't prepared to question; she was a realist, Kyneston was bricks and mortar, its garden filled with plants that would bloom with the same brilliance anywhere. But Kyneston was home, home surrounded by the magic of the forest.

That's where she loved to ride. In the beginning Hunter had come too, chasing wildly ahead of her, then back, then on again; as the years caught up with him he could only manage to plod along at her side. Now her rides were always alone, Hunter was with them no longer. Both of them with reddened eyes, she and Melissa had made a grave for him beyond the croquet lawn. He'd been their constant companion through their childhood days of freedom. In fact, although they'd never realized it, it was only

35

because Mrs Biggs trusted him to take care of them that they'd been allowed to roam where they wanted.

All that was behind them now. Hunter was gone, the girls thought of themselves as almost grown up. Sometimes, when the weather was right, Georgina would ride out alone to her favourite pond deep in the forest and far off the beaten track, a pond that was fed by a clear, babbling stream. There she would slip out of her clothes right down to her chemise and drawers and swim in the still water. The thrill of the outing was heightened by the fact that if anyone (absolutely *anyone* which included Augusta or Clive even though they never interested themselves in how either girl spent her time) were to see what she was doing, there would be trouble. Then, dripping from the cold water she would wriggle out of her wet underwear, dry herself in her petticoat, don her remaining dry garments and, feeling delightfully depraved and naked without her knickers, would hoist herself back in the saddle. She and Melissa had been about eight when first they had come upon the pond on a day when they'd persuaded Mrs Biggs to pack them some food so that they needn't come home until their new fob watches they'd had for their birthdays told them it was six o'clock. The eager way Hunter rushed into the water had been too much for Georgina. Throwing modesty to the wind she had peeled off all her clothes and waded in to join him while stockingless Melissa had paddled at the edge, frightened to watch them and sure they would both drown. That first day Georgina had done no more than immerse herself and take one foot off the bottom, but before summer was over she had learned to keep afloat and even move through the water, albeit with more splashing than progress.

'Come in too. It makes you feel all tingly,' she'd shouted.

'You shouldn't do it. Wait till they hear at home, you'll get a dreadful wigging – being all bare like you are. Aunt Alice says we ought not to come into the forest by ourselves, she says sometimes there are bad people, gypsy beggars.'

'Aunt Alice, pooh! We're not on our own, we've got Hunter. Anyway I bet a gypsy beggar would be just as good as *she* is – or better. If you tell *anyone*, even your precious Aunt Alice, that I go swimming' – my! but how good that sounded, not paddling or dipping in the water, but 'swimming'. Just you hear what I said, Melissa Rochester – 'I go swimming,' she repeated in case it hadn't registered the first time, 'you know what I'll do? I'll take

36

your birthday doll she gave you, Binkie all dressed in pinkie, and I'll take out every one of her teeth!'

'I won't tell. Don't do that. Pinkie's mine, you're not to touch her!'

'Then put your hand on your heart and promise you won't tell. God's listening to you, that's what Reverend Carter tells us, so if you break your word He'll know.'

'I won't tell.'

'Right you are,' Georgina had tired of the subject and was wondering whether she would sink into the water if she tried to lie on her back.

She did and came up spluttering, her ginger mop as wet as the rest of her. The quarrel was forgotten, the two girls looked at each other and broke into peals of merriment, while Hunter added a loud woof to let them know he was part of the fun.

Georgina looked for some word from Augusta that she was pleased to have her so regularly in the workroom, but she had to content herself with the thought that if she didn't want her she would tell her so. Not actually an invitation, but she liked to think it was a sign of acceptance of her presence that prompted Augusta to start putting off-cuts of material to one side, leaving pieces of trimmings to be used up, so that Georgina could practise her own sewing. Even a flat piece of felt gave her an exercise she could work on, edging it with ribbon, backing it with lining and trying to make her stitches as invisible as Augusta's. Her efforts were always carefully examined, faults pointed out and advice given. She was never put down by criticism, she meant to improve until no fault could be found.

'What would you like to see on this?' Augusta held up a finished hat, finished except for the final trimming. It was a bright cerise felt with a brim about five inches wide and, as yet, it was unadorned.

Georgina took it from her mother, eyes half closed she looked at it, lost in thought as she imagined.

'I know what I'd do. You'll probably think I'm wrong, but if I were making it I'd push the back of the brim right up tight to the crown, see it reaches to the top. But before I stitched it, I'd cover the back brim with deep cerise velvet that would be made to look as though it were knotted to hang down about eight inches below the line of the rim. The front brim would be down, then about here at the side I'd attach some of those pearl grey feathers so that they curled around the crown. But the trouble is, the lining is in now and the back would need to have been stitched before it was lined.'

Augusta was well pleased to see her training hadn't been wasted. Equally she might have been delighted with any apprentice, there was no maternal pride in her attitude.

'Over to you.' She passed the scissors, one tiny pair and one pair for cutting out. 'You'll have to unpick that lining very carefully. If you want help come and find me, your father and I are playing tennis at four o'clock and I have to get changed first. Go ahead, do as you think as long as you don't need to ask me anything.' Then, with a smile more in keeping with Georgina's fifteen years than her own forty-two, 'Make a good job of it and when we get paid you shall have your first earnings.' The expertise had been in cutting the felt and moulding the shape, but for Georgina it gave a spur to her ambition.

Two weeks later, from that one first step she had made a giant leap. Not one she would get paid for, but one that gave her a greater sense of achievement than anything she'd ever done before. From start to finish she had made herself a hat! When she cut the thread of the last stitch mother and daughter looked at each other with satisfaction, millinery brought them closer than anything else in their normally casual relationship.

That first creation was shaped after the style of a boater, but fashioned in cream felt, the wide brim curled at the rim and edged with brown velvet, the same velvet that formed its plain band. In appearance it was youthful, and yet there was about it an air of sophistication far removed from childhood.

'Look, Melissa!' Delighted with her success, she paraded into Melissa's bedroom, her head high, then turned slowly to show it off from every angle. 'What do you think of it? I made it quite by myself. I'm going to get good enough that Mme de Bouverie will take my work as well as Mama's? What do you think?'

'It's a nice enough hat. But I think it's all wrong for you to be doing it. I don't know why Mama messes about making hats, it isn't as if she has to earn her living. Supposing any of our friends actually bought millinery that she had been paid to make.'

'Wouldn't you be proud? I would.'

38

'Aunt Alice has friends who always go to Madame de Bouverie – and she says it would be humiliating if they knew Kyneston was being turned into a workshop.'

'Friends?' Sparks of anger flashed in Georgina's gingery brown eyes. 'You mean she actually has *friends*? Well, I'm jolly glad I'm not one of them.' Then for good measure, 'And it wouldn't matter who designed hats for *her*, she'd still look a hatchet-faced sight in them.'

The girls stood staring at each other like two cats waiting to pounce. For once Melissa felt that she had come out on top, for she was keeping calm, enjoying seeing Georgina lose her temper.

'Your hat is really quite nice,' she said with cool condescension. 'And, yes, of course Aunt Alice has friends, which is more than we do here at Kyneston. When does anyone ever call to take tea? When do our parents ever get invited to supper parties? Never. Aunt Alice says that long ago Father used to be part of the local social circle, that's how he and my own mother knew each other. They entertained a lot here, they were very popular. Don't you wish it was still like that? We'd be invited to parties . . .' Imagining how it could be with local swains vying for the chance to lead her into the dance, she was forgetting that she'd been meaning to put Georgina 'in her place' as they said at Hapley Court. 'I wondered whether we might suggest they gave a supper party here, that would start the ball rolling. I talked about it to Aunt Alice, but she says no one would accept. And to send invitations and have them refused would be humiliating. None of them want to be seen mixing with Kyneston anymore.'

'Then Kyneston is better off without them. And who do they think they are to look down their long noses at Mama – and at Father for bringing her and me here. That's what they don't like. If he'd married one of them, some prissy creature with a face like a wet Sunday, as long as she came off the same shelf as they did, then that would have been fine. You know why your precious aunt doesn't like her, why none of them include her? – I never told you this, but even when we hunt none of the women ever talk to her, or to me, although the men are friendly enough – it's because she can knock the lot of them into a cocked hat. She's beautiful, and look at the way she wears her clothes. They're jealous and I don't wonder.'

'You talk rubbish. I don't see how you'll ever be able to have

39

any fun. It'll be different for me. It's a pity you can never join in at Hapley Court.' And, in a moment of sympathy for her 'sister' she really meant it.

For almost fourteen years they had lived as sisters, they had grown up to accept the situation without question, even if on Georgina's part not without angry resentment.

'Perish the thought!' She had the last word. She turned for the door, her newly hatted head held high.

It was chance that sent Cedric to a business meeting in London on the same day that Clive and Augusta had taken the train up to discuss their plans with the shipping agent. It was chance too that made him almost miss the six o'clock train from Waterloo, the one he had instructed Hobbs to meet at Brockenhurst with the trap. That's how he came to fling open the first first-class compartment he came to as he hurried down the platform and the guard waited impatiently, whistle in mouth and flag poised.

With a deep sigh of relief he slammed the door closed behind him, not concerned that there were other travellers in the compartment. All he wanted was one seat and peace to read his newspaper.

'Why, Cedric. At home we don't see each other for months, now we meet up here in town.'

Young Rochester! For from his eighteen years' seniority that's how he still thought of Clive. And that Augusta woman! By Jove, she may not be out of the top drawer, but what a beauty she still was! His thought was instinctive, only to be stamped on firmly at the memory of Mary.

'Indeed,' he agreed. 'I feared I'd not get on the train. Never seen such chaos as there was on the approach to the station. One of those wretched new-fangled motor taxis had broken down on the roadway. The noise it made! Back-firing, sounding like canon fire. No wonder the horses jibbed at coming alongside the wretched thing. It's one thing to have motor cars on the open road, but the city is no place for them. Unreliable, noisy, stinking – I beg your pardon.' But from his expression as he turned to Augusta he did no such thing.

'We travelled everywhere by motor taxi today, didn't we Clive. We enjoyed it.'

'Humph.' Cedric opened his newspaper, his action implying that he would expect no better from anyone of her mentality.

'You were in town on business I suppose,' Clive said chattily. 'Ours was business too, business for the shipping agent, pleasure for us.'

'Shipping agent?' The newspaper was lowered.

'We are off to America – the New World!'

'You mean you're taking Melissa overseas?'

Augusta didn't intend to be ignored. 'We're not taking either of them,' she told him. 'They will be perfectly all right at Kyneston.' Then one jump ahead of him as she imagined the way his mind was working, 'The two of them don't need looking after. Even so, they are only nineteen and before we go we shall engage a suitable companion. It wouldn't be fair to leave Mrs Biggs with the responsibility of a pair of under-age girls as well as running the house.'

'That need not be, nothing would please us better than for Melissa to move into the Court.'

Too angry to think of the sort of the cutting retort his suggestion merited, she opened her mouth to speak but was silenced by Clive's restraining hand on her arm.

'You know that's out of the question. I thought I made that clear long ago,' Clive answered for her. 'Cedric, I want your word that while Augusta and I are on holiday you will respect the fact that Melissa and Georgina are *sisters*, they belong together at Kyneston.'

'Are you suggesting we can't see her in your absence? That's something I can't promise. It would break Alice's heart, she cares for Melissa as if she were her own.'

Clive's loyalty to Augusta – and after all, what was it but loyalty to her that had made him speak as he had about the girls? – gave her a warm glow of pleasure. She could afford to be generous.

'Things will continue just the same when we're away, I dare say the girls will hardly notice our absence.'

For a while they travelled in silence, rocked by the steady rhythm of the train. Sitting opposite them Cedric let his gaze rest on Augusta's ankles, trimly buttoned into russet coloured heeled shoes. Perhaps it was lack of breeding that made smart clothes so important to her . . . by gum though, she really was a looker!

41

'Is Patience still with you?' Clive asked. If they had to share a compartment all the way to Brockenhurst it was better to be civil. 'Despite living so close, I've not seen her for years and as far as I know Melissa never mentions her.'

'I suppose there's no reason why she should. But yes, we still give her a home. Who else would have her? Some women seem destined for spinsterhood. Here she is, pretty well fifty years old. If she couldn't find a husband in her youth we have no hope of getting her off our hands now.' With that he unfolded his newspaper and disassociated himself from them.

Augusta had neither known nor cared about the domestic arrangements at Hapley Court, but hearing how he spoke of the unwanted Patience the seed of an idea was sown in her mind.

'Just you and Father?' Melissa's turned accusing blue eyes on Augusta. 'But you'll not be going until after the winter?'

'We sail at the beginning of September,' Clive told her.

There was silence at the table as the girls digested the news of their parents' impending trip. They were already nineteen, and what had they ever done? Where had they ever been? Nothing and nowhere. The longstanding promise had been that in the coming winter they would have a month in London, see proper shops, go to theaters, live in an hotel.

'America!' Georgina's eyes were bright with wonder. 'And when you get there, where will you travel?'

'What about your promise? Only four weeks, that's all it was and you aren't even going to do that for us!' Neither Augusta nor Clive noticed the ominous way Melissa's tone rose. Only Georgina heard the warning sign. 'Aunt Alice says I ought to have had a season last winter, a proper season. Now it's to be *nothing*, the same as it was then, the same as always.'

Ignoring her Clive answered Georgina.

'We shall travel right the way across the continent. It'll be the trip of a lifetime. On the western coast it's warm in the winter, imagine Christmas in the sunshine.'

Georgina stretched her face into a smile.

'I shall have to see Madame de Bouverie tomorrow,' Augusta was saying. 'It's just a thought, Georgina, but I believe you're quite capable of carrying on by yourself until I get home. What do you say?'

She couldn't say anything, all she could do was nod her head; now her face smiled of its own accord, even if she'd tried she couldn't have stopped it.

'It's not fair,' Melissa heard the tremble in her voice, willingly, gladly, she let herself sink into her misery. 'You promised. Not that you care about promises, all you care about is yourselves.' By now she was sobbing, making no effort to hide her distorted face as she gasped for breath.

'They'll soon be home, Mellie. We'll go to London when they get back. Won't we?' Georgina looked helplessly at the others for confirmation.

'Of course we will. We'll be home again quite early next year. There'll will be lots of time before the weather starts to get too warm for the city.' Augusta made an effort to sound kind and caring although she could hardly make herself heard above Melissa's noise.

'Oh yes,' Melissa hurled at her, 'more promises—'

'Just leave the table,' Clive's voice cut in with unusual firmness. 'You're behaving like a spoilt child. Do you hear Georgina carry on like it? If you can't act like an adult you must expect to be treated like a child.'

Melissa took her spoon and hurled in somewhere in the direction of the middle of the table, got up from her chair with such force that she tipped it backwards to fall with a crash, then rushed from the room slamming the door behind her. They heard her running up the stairs, they heard the pitch of her crying getting higher and louder, then the slam of her bedroom door.

'She doesn't mean it,' Georgina spoke into the silence, 'it's just that she's disappointed. She can't help crying.' How could she hope they'd understand what she was trying to explain, when she couldn't understand it herself? In her heart she wasn't even sure whether it was the truth or whether Melissa's outbursts had so often given her her own way that she expected it always to happen.

'If you've finished you'd better go and talk to her,' Augusta said.

'Yes, good idea,' Clive agreed. They'd come home from London so full of excitement for this wonderful holiday, he wasn't going to let the girls cast a shadow.

Upstairs Georgina knew just how she'd find Melissa. Lying on her stomach, the cause of her misery forgotten, her whole being consumed by uncontrollable hysterics. It had happened so often, the treatment was as familiar as the storm. Five minutes later, a sharp slap having turned bellowing screams into healthy tears, she held Melissa in her safe hold. Gradually the demented girl quietened, she clung to Georgina, only her trembling gasps telling of the storm that had passed.

On the first Tuesday of September Biggs had their cabin trunks stowed behind the carriage. The girls waited by its open door as Clive and Augusta bid their farewells to the staff who congregated at a respectful distance.

Standing alone in the front hall Patience Sylvester watched the departure. Clive and Augusta were off to the New World, but Patience didn't envy them. Today she didn't envy anyone. She was free; she almost thought of herself as a person of consequence. After the way Augusta had been spurned by Hapley Court, to think that she could have offered her this opportunity, even made her feel she was doing them a favour to come.

Chapter Three

'A letter from America,' Patience took the envelope Florrie brought to the breakfast table. 'Addressed to *me*.' She tried to keep her voice level, but with such a monumental event it was difficult.

'Open it up,' Melissa said. 'Tell us what they say. When did they write it? It must be to let us know when they want Biggs to go to Southampton to collect them. Read it out.'

'It's dated 1 February, but according to the address they hadn't even left San Francisco. Perhaps they were just leaving. I'll read it.

'My dear Patience,' then, turning the page to see the signature, 'it's from your father. I expect he'll tell us when they're setting out.' She tried to sound as eager as she was sure the girls must be, but in truth she hated to look ahead to their return. She'd have to pack her boxes and go back to Hapley Court . . . 'I'll read what he says.'

My dear Patience,

I hope winter has been kind to you in England. Not as kind as it has to us, I fear. Augusta hardly ventures out without her parasol. From that you will gather that we are having a splendid holiday, delightful in every way. Tell Georgina and Melissa that we are bearing in mind that they are to have their turn when we return and will give them their month or so in London.

Now to our date of arrival. Our plans are very fluid as yet, having travelled so far it would be nonsensical to rush home especially as it seems prudent to avoid a stormy winter sea crossing. As long as there is nothing we should concern ourselves with at Kyneston we shall probably not leave here for a few weeks yet. However, if you have need to cable us in any

45

emergency you may use this hotel address for although we shall be sightseeing we keep our room here.

Another box of silks etc. (imports from the East which Augusta finds irresistible) is on its way. She says to tell Georgina she may open the crates and use anything that's necessary for Madame de B.

We both send our regards and trust you are willing to stay on at Kyneston beyond the time first suggested.

Oh, but she was willing! It was like being mistress of her own home. For the first time in her life she suspected that Alice was actually envious of her, for here she was looking after darling Melissa – and Georgina ('see you keep that girl in her place'), really there was something very likeable about the girl, almost loveable if she dared be honest. Although there was another side to her nature, there was no denying that on the occasions when Alice came to take tea – something she allowed herself to do now that Augusta was out of the way – the girl was far from polite, really quite insolent. So Alice never saw the generous, helpful person she really was. Oh dear, such a pity. Why it was people couldn't be nice to each other she couldn't think.

The days turned to weeks with no news of when they planned to sail. Perhaps they would send a cablegram when they arrived at the dock.

'It's spring already, they must come soon,' Georgina tried to ward off the threat of one of Melissa's difficult days. 'Let's make a list of the places we want to go to. You never know, Mellie, if they see there's such a lot we mean to do they may decide a month won't be long enough.'

'First we have to buy proper grown-up clothes. We can't be seen in London looking so unfashionable. So that must be the first thing we do, before we think of theatres. And as for balls, where are we going to find partners? You know what it'll be, we shall have to dance with each other or take turns if Mama spares Father to take us onto the floor.'

'Cheer up, do. It'll be wonderful. And even before we get our fashionable clothes there's one place we can go. The Zoo! Imagine, lions, tigers – we can even ride on a camel—' She saw her mistake. 'Or the monkeys, we can feed nuts to the monkeys.'

'They say it's smelly at the Zoo. I don't know that I want to go there at all.'

'Rubbish, of course you do. Anyway I read that they've planted lots of flowers and shrubs to kill the smells of the animals. What about Hampstead Heath? And Crystal Palace . . .' Georgina's list was growing.

'We'll travel everywhere in motor taxis,' Melissa was being infected by her enthusiasm, 'like *they* did the day they went up to book their passage.' Her mood had changed, she gripped Georgina's hand, unable to repress her excitement. 'Uncle Cedric detests their noise,' she giggled, 'oh, just think . . . it can't be long before they come, can it? A month in London makes that trip we had to Bournemouth seem like nothing.' Clive and Augusta had often been away, but the girls had had no part in what they did, so at nineteen their lives had been narrow, bordered by the forest and the small neighbouring towns. Even now Melissa was frightened to believe, frightened of the excitement that gave her a fluttering feeling somewhere in her chest. 'Suppose it goes on getting warm? If it feels like summer when they get home they'll say it's too late for London, we'll have to wait for the autumn.'

'No they won't. It's only April. I told you what I think – I think they will send us a cablegram to say they are sailing. Anyway, let's not waste a lovely day indoors. We'll take the trap and go to Lymington, perhaps there's something Aunt Patience wants from the shops.'

The word 'shops' took the frown off Melissa's face.

April was more than half over and still there was no news of the travellers' return. Disappointment was giving way to resignation, partly because the weather was unseasonally warm.

'I'm going out,' Melissa said as she trundled her bicycle out of the shed, a pout in her voice. No need to ask where she was going: most days she took her grievances to Alice at Hapley Court.

'Why don't you stay and help mark up the tennis court? It's easier with two of us. Jimmy gave the lawn its first cut yesterday.'

'No, don't you see? If they come home and see the court marked out they'll say it's too late to take us away. Like Aunt Alice says, all they think of is themsel—'

'Look! Melly, look! Here's the boy with a cablegram. Come on! Let's get it from him.' With no more dignity than a child half

47

her age, she hoisted her skirt and ran to meet the boy as he got off his bicycle.

'Overseas cablegram for Rochester,' he announced grandly.

'That's us. Wait while I open it then I'll get you something for bringing it.'

Georgina ripped open the brown envelope and pulled out the single sheet of paper, instinctively looking for the reassuring name of the sender.

'Do they say when?' Melissa prompted. 'Let's see. But who's Father O'Donnell? And look it comes from San Francisco. They would have left there long ago.'

'I don't understand,' Georgina whispered. 'What's happened? Melly . . . he must be wrong . . .'

But the message was clear.

REGRET AUGUSTA LOST LIFE INSTANTLY IN EARTHQUAKE STOP CLIVE ROCHESTER DIED SHORTLY AFTER OF INJURIES SUSTAINED STOP SIGNED FATHER O'DONNELL.

The boy who'd brought the message remounted and pedalled away; there would be no point in waiting for his promised tip.

Georgina stared out of the window to the garden, the colours of early spring a mockery. Mama, you're gone . . . never see you . . . too late now, you'll never know how important you were – *are*, yes, you still are – you'll never know how important it was to be with you in the workroom – why did I always pretend your occasional casual smile was all I wanted? If I'd shown you I needed you, would it have made you happy? Do you know it now? How can you? It's too late . . .'

'Melissa's isn't back yet,' Patience was saying. 'Of course they had to be told at the Court, but I thought she'd come straight back to be with you. Oh dear, I feel so useless . . .'

It was gone midday, three hours since the cable had been delivered.

'What's it got to do with *them*?' Georgina found it easier to vent her spite on the Sylvesters than face the aching void, the uncertainty. Afraid of her overwhelming misery – misery and fright too, but that was something she wouldn't admit to – Georgina rushed out of the room and upstairs, shutting herself in the workroom. On the table was a box of materials Augusta had shipped home, furs and fine feathers waiting for them to work on together. Taking a

48

pelt from the box she held it to her face, harsh sobs racking her body.

Without knocking Patience came quietly into the room. She'd never been more aware of her own inadequacy, yet she'd never wanted so much to say the right words. Melissa would take comfort from Alice and Cedric, but Georgina had no one, only her and what use was she? Tell me what to say to her, she pleaded silently, help me to help her. Perhaps it was an answer to her plea, perhaps it was something about Georgina's misery that took her back to the day when her own mother had died, her secret anguish, her terror of having no one. She hadn't been quite alone, not alone as Georgina was, she'd had Cedric, but he was so much older, he belonged to Alice who was jealously possessive about little Mary. Having no one, being uncertain . . .

Coming to Georgina's side she put her arm around her.

'I *do* know, dear, I *do* understand. I'm not much use, but you have me.'

'It's not fair,' Georgina croaked. 'Why them? They were so happy, every letter you could tell how happy they were. Was that a sin? Is that why they got killed? All her things,' with a sweeping movement she indicated the paraphernalia of Augusta's little millinery empire, the new treadle sewing machine Clive had bought her only a few months before. 'She won't do it any more. And I never told her how much I liked being here with her.'

How pathetic she looked, Patience thought, poor Georgina. Even in these few minutes her reddened eyelids were so swollen that her eyes were no more than slits in her blotchy, tear-stained face.

'She might not have known then, Georgina dear, but don't you think she knows it now? I'm sure she does. We mustn't cry for them, you said yourself they were having a wonderful holiday and this happened so suddenly they wouldn't have had time to suffer. They went together, and I believe that's the way both of them would have wanted it.' Patience had hardly known them, yet she remembered the impact of seeing them together, her (perhaps over-romanticized) certainty of their happiness in each other.

It took a minute for Georgina to digest her words, a minute while she fought for control and scrubbed her face with her handkerchief.

'Do you honestly think that, about her knowing?' she mumbled. 'Or are you just trying to make me feel better?'

49

'Yes, I truly believe it. And she's left you a legacy, a skill. Oh, dear, I do hope there won't be trouble with Cedric over your making the hats.'

'He can mind his own business,' Georgina sniffed. 'Nothing to do with him what I do.'

'It's just that he and Alice have always been so against Kyneston being used for working. He's my own brother and I know I have to be grateful to him – but he can be a difficult man. No, it's not Augusta and Clive my heart goes out to, it's not even dear little Melissa, for she'll always have Alice and Cedric. No, it's *you*.' Then, tentatively, 'You've got me. I may not be much use, but I do understand what it's like. When my own mother died I was hardly more than a child, I had no one but Cedric, he and Alice made themselves responsible for me. I've always had to be grateful for the home they gave me. Gratitude is a heavy cross to bear.'

To Georgina, the Sylvesters weren't important. She wanted just to cling to what Patience had said about her mother leaving her the legacy of her skill. That and the truth – for it was a truth – that if they had to die then it was right they should go together. Neither could have been happy without the other.

'Try not to feel hurt that they make so much of Melissa,' Patience's thoughts hadn't moved on from Cedric and Alice. 'It's not so much that they dislike *you* as it is that they love her too well. Because of Mary, you see, Mary was so special. They aren't *bad* people.'

'I don't care if they're good or bad. They're nothing to me.'

'Hark. There's someone knocking the door. Oh dear, not a visitor surely.'

'Not very likely,' Georgina spoke gruffly, spite feeding on misery. 'Who would call here? No one can have heard yet that Mama's dead and Kyneston isn't out of bounds any more. Oh, but it is, of course, there's still *me*.'

'Don't dear, don't sound like that.'

And if anything dulled Georgina's pain, it was the sight of Patience, her plump face creased into lines of anxiety, her pale eyes full of kindness.

They heard footsteps cross the hall to the door, then Effie's heavy tread on the stairs, then a tap on the door.

'Who is it, Effie?' Patience opened the door. Even that was

different. Mama's workroom, her sanctuary . . . now Effie was bringing a note up here as if it were no different from anywhere else in the house.

'From Alice, I know the writing,' Patience said as she tore open the envelope. 'She says Cedric rode straight to town to Chadwick & Grieves – they are his solicitors and, I believe, were your father's too. Mr Grieves is meeting them here at three o'clock this afternoon. They'll bring Melissa with them when they come.'

'If someone had to see Father's solicitor, it ought to have been us. We don't need your family's interference.' Purposely she needed to lash out and hurt. It was only as she saw the slope of Patience's shoulders as she went out of the room, leaving the note on the work table, that shame was added to Georgina's grief. She ought to run after her, to tell her she was sorry; but her legs were as leaden as her heart. Slumping onto the chair where she'd sat so many hours watching Augusta, she buried her head on the crook of her arm and cried.

They sat at the dining table, Mr Grieves at the top (in Clive's chair), Cedric at the bottom (in Augusta's), Alice and Melissa on one side, Patience and Georgina on the other. First he told them of his sorrow at hearing the news and assured them he would handle all the legal requirements.

'Before leaving for this trip, Mr Rochester made provision that in the eventuality of the demise of himself and his wife before the Misses Rochester attained their majority, responsibility for their welfare should be taken by Mr Sylvester.' He bowed his head in Cedric's direction as if he wanted the situation to be made doubly clear. 'This, of course, with Mr Sylvester's agreement. Indeed it was at his suggestion that I persuaded Mr Rochester that some sort of provision should be made before they embarked on such a journey. Although none of us could have foreseen a tragedy of this magnitude.'

Georgina stared at him with eyes as wide as their swollen lids allowed. To be made a ward of the odious Uncle Cedric! Father couldn't have done that to her! Mama would never have agreed! But then they expected to come home, they never thought this would happen. An earthquake . . . an Act of God . . . an Act of the Devil, a wicked evil spirit . . . but if God was so Omnipotent, why didn't he stop it happening? There was no God, that's why. There

51

was no pattern, no sense in anything. All you got was what you fought for. Well, she'd fight, she'd fight hateful Cedric Sylvester . . .

Mr Grieves had moved on to the disposal of Clive's estate. She made herself listen.

'This Will was drawn up at the time of my late client's marriage – his second marriage – and had he pre-deceased his wife his entire estate would have passed to her. However, in the event of her not living to inherit, Kyneston, the house and grounds, and all his monies and possessions are to be divided between his daughter Melissa and his step-daughter Georgina when they reach their majority, their share being of equal proportion. Now to his investments. That in the tea plantations in India is to pass to his daughter Melissa, and in the Cornish tin mine to his step-daughter Georgina.'

'Are we to understand these investments bring approximately the same income?' From the way he asked it, it was clear Cedric already knew the answer.

'Sadly, the income from the tin mine has declined,' Mr Grieves answered. 'The peak of the tinning industry is long since over. Indeed, over the last year or two the dividend has been negligible.'

Without looking at Cedric, Georgina could feel his eyes were on her, she knew the triumph in his expression. She was aware of that, and of her own stiff and swollen eyelids as she fixed her gaze on the far wall of the room, seeing nothing, full of fear she wouldn't acknowledge. What was 'Mr Always Right, I Know Best' planning? If he'd expected that he'd be lumbered with *her* he wouldn't have agreed to take responsibility any more than Mama would have let them make the arrangement. None of them could have anticipated this happening. He'd probably only suggested it to make Father appear irresponsible in front of the solicitor for not planning ahead for himself. Well, she didn't care what he said. If he expected to take her to Hapley Court (like poor Patience, being put up with, slighted at every opportunity) then he'd have to have her tied up and carried there. Yes, and even then she wouldn't stay. If he closed Kyneston until they came of age, perhaps Madame de Bouverie would give her more work, enough that she could afford a room in Christchurch. But what about everyone else here, what about Biggs and the horses, Mrs Biggs, Florrie, all the others? Her miserable imaginings cut her off from the sober scene around the table until Cedric's decisive voice cut across her thoughts.

'The income will continue, I shall use it on my charges' account so that there need be no changes here to Kyneston. And you, Patience, I'll be obliged if you will remain here. Until Melissa – both of them – attain their majority there should be a woman with them.'

A few minutes before, Georgina had held herself in readiness to fight and win; now there was nothing to conquer. So why did she suddenly have to clench her fists in an attempt to stop her hands trembling, why did she feel as if her arms and legs had turned to jelly?

Cedric and Alice were shaking hands with Mr Grieves. With her arm around Melissa's shoulder Alice drew her forward to say goodbye too. They must have expected that to be the end of his visit, but instead he leant across the table to where she and Patience stood side by side.

'You know where you can always find me, Miss Rochester.' In his voice she believed she heard all the deference he would have paid to an adult or an important client. She longed for her mother's easy confidence, hating the knowledge that her face flushed as she felt her hand taken in his. 'If ever you wish to talk to me I shall be glad to see you. This must be a sad day for you and your sister.' Georgina murmured her thanks, ashamed that she couldn't find something worthwhile to say in appreciation. Then he gave a cursory handshake to Patience – and even that was more than life had given her cause to expect – and was ushered to the door.

All through the winter the girls had talked about the promised clothes-buying trip to London, had imagined the gaiety of the month of sightseeing, theatre-going and dancing. There had been no substance to the dancing part of their dreams, for to dance required a partner. At the back of their adolescent minds, though, was youthful trust that once they were wearing their soon-to-be-acquired finery a new world would be opened to them.

After Cedric saw Mr Grieves out, tea was brought in. Had Georgina not disliked Alice so thoroughly she might not have been aware of what she meant to do but immediately the tray was placed on the small table she realized. Just as if Patience didn't

53

exist, Alice was moving towards it as if this were *her* home, it was *her* place to pour the tea.

'Aunt Patience, come on. Tea time. Do your job.' Georgina's voice was unnaturally bright, far removed from the silent message her eyes fixed on Alice.

'Oh, yes, of course,' poor Patience twittered, looking at Alice as if for permission. 'Is that all right . . ?'

Ignoring the tentative question, Georgina moved ahead of both of them. 'Unless you'd rather Melissa or I did it for you?' Then, when Alice reached for the heavy silver teapot, 'Please don't do that. If Aunt Patience is too upset by everything, we can manage. We don't ask our guests to wait on themselves.'

'Impudent young miss,' Cedric was glad of the chance to 'put her in her place' and, by Jove, that's what she needed! 'It's quite time you learned some manners, young lady. I should have expected the years you've been given a home here to have instilled some sort of grace in a child whatever her inherited breeding—'

'Or lack of it,' Alice added, breathing down her pointed nose.

'I beg your pardon,' Georgina answered with dignity but no humility, 'but I had always supposed that a guest waited to be offered. Come on, Aunt Patience, you'd better pour Mrs Sylvester's first, she seems to be impatient for it.'

Cedric's face was flushed with anger, Patience's with embarrassment, Alice's expression was inscrutable and Melissa burst into tears.

'Now see what you've done!' All Cedric's dislike of her was in his tone. 'If you were a year or two younger, my girl, you would be sent to your room.'

'Mellie, don't cry.' Turning her back on him she dropped to her knees in front of where Melissa sat on the sofa. The others were forgotten as she took the trembling hands in hers. 'Don't cry, you've always got me. We'll be all right. Think how much worse it would be for them if only one had been killed. They're to—'

Melissa snatched her hand away.

'It's not fair!' She wasn't answering Georgina, she wasn't speaking to anyone in particular, it was a cry against life's injustice. 'I knew something would happen. If they hadn't gone – but they didn't care – they promised—' By now she was so sunk in her own despair she gloried in the sound of her own wild crying.

54

'No,' more to herself than to Melissa, Georgina whispered, 'please, Mellie, no.' Surely today they could share their unhappiness, help each other.

But Melissa was beyond being checked, it was as if some devil had possession of her egging her on, her voice getting ever more strident. She didn't even notice the way Georgina drew back as if she'd been hit by the impact of what she said. 'All they cared about was their *own* holiday, never mind about us. They *promised* – when we get back, they said – oh yes, that was easy – push us to one side like they always did – have all the pleasure themselves—' Her tone got higher, she was bordering on hysteria.

Georgina knew the signs all too well. 'Stop it!' She brought her hand down hard on Melissa's shoulder, then shook her. Experience had taught her that sometimes – sometimes but not always – a shake or a sharp slap would make her gasp for breath and turn that dreadful tormented sobbing into the sort of crying that could be comforted.

Tea was forgotten. Georgina found herself pushed from where she knelt, to lose her balance and sprawl on the ground as Alice sat at Melissa's side and took her shaking body into her arms . . .

'Oh dear, oh dear,' Patience couldn't interfere, Alice was in command of the situation. 'Oh dear, oh dear, poor little Melissa, she doesn't mean what she's saying. I can't bear it when she gets so wild, it makes me feel quite shaky.' But shaky or not she bent down to help Georgina to her feet; not that her help was needed, but it was a silent way of showing whose side she was on.

'They had *promised* – you remember, Aunt Alice,' Melissa gulped, 'I told you what they had promised. Now none of it will happen. They said they'd have their holiday first, but once it was over they'd make sure we'd have *our* turn.'

Patience and Georgina looked at each other, scarcely believing what they heard.

'London, that's where they were going to take us. New gowns, they said we'd go to theatres – I told you, I told you all about it – we'd dance. All the time they've been away we've made plans, all the places we would go to, the things we'd see.' Any control she might have been finding was lost as her voice escaped upwards to a high squeak. 'None of it's going to happen. It's not fair. It had to be *them* first . . . if they'd taken *us* first none of this would have happened. But we weren't important . . .'

55

'Hush, dear, hush, don't cry so. Hush, now. When have your uncle and I ever failed you? You shall have your pretty gowns just the same, you shall have your season in London. Nothing will be different.'

Georgina met Cedric's gaze, she looked at Alice, such a different Alice in her tenderness for Melissa. And she knew that things would indeed be different.

It was a morning early in May, Georgina was planting the young geraniums in the urns in the conservatory when Melissa came to say goodbye to her.

'They're here, the carriage is almost at the door. Oh I do wish you were coming too, it would be so much more fun if we were both getting new things together. I'll be home this evening and I'll tell you all about it. Amais Pilkington isn't like an ordinary seamstress, a lady of talent and taste, that's what Aunt Alice calls her—'

'Be careful then, if she has your aunt's kind of taste.'

'Don't be horrid. You're trying to spoil it for me.'

This time Georgina laughed and put out her hand.

'Careful! Don't touch me,' Melissa drew back, 'your hands are all soil.'

'You'd better go, you mustn't keep them waiting.'

'Please,' Melissa's rapped her clenched fists together nervously, 'please Georgina, say you're pleased I'm being taken, don't try and spoil my day.'

'As is I would – or could. Off you go.'

'Just think, if you were coming . . .'

'I shall be cleaning out the stable – preferable to enduring a day of the Blessed Lady Alice.' She put an end to the conversation by turning her back on Melissa and digging her trowel into the earth in the urn with more vigour than the job merited.

And that's where Patience found her a few minutes later.

'It's not right,' she said without preamble, 'taking one and not the other. I never did approve – not that it would have been any use my saying so – but that was when your parents were alive. To do it *now*, she ought to be ashamed. I'm not holding Melissa responsible, Alice has always wanted to be the one to buy her things. But it's not right,' she repeated, her kindly face pulled into a worried frown, 'she ought to have taken you with them.'

'I'm sorry she didn't invite me too,' but there was no sorrow in her voice, only hard, cold anger. 'Yes, Aunt Patience, I would have liked her to ask me. Then I could have told her I wouldn't go if she paid me.'

'Oh dear, oh dear,' Patience twisted her fingers together helplessly, the poor girl must be so upset to speak like it. 'If I had the money I'd buy you fashionable gowns, you could look just as nice as she will.'

This time there really was mirth in Georgina's laugh.

'A likely thing! Melissa is the prettiest girl I've even seen, she'll look really beautiful. But I'm not going to sit and weep about it, neither am I going to dress in last year's gowns for ever.' Brave words and she hoped they had the ring of truth.

Patience wanted to put out a hand and touch her, give her a hug, something she'd never done to anyone – or not since she'd been a girl and her mother had died. Instead she picked up the watering jug and moistened the soil around the freshly planted geraniums.

While Melissa spent so much of her time at Hapley Court, Georgina shut herself away in the workroom. Patience would like to have disturbed her, gone in to see how she turned out such beautiful hats. So often she listened from the passageway outside the door, surprised to hear the treadle machine. It wasn't up to her in inquire (that would be breaking Georgina's ruling that she wasn't to be disturbed), but she'd imagined all the millinery was stitched by hand.

It was one September tea-time when Melissa returned from Hapley Court, her eyes shining, her face wearing an expression of such happiness that Patience was uneasy. No one should show their feelings so clearly, especially poor Mellie who could so easily get cast down.

'Listen, just you hear what I have to tell you.' Her news was so momentous she couldn't even wait to take off her hat. 'You know Aunt Marguerite?' Then to Georgina, 'Well, *you* don't actually know her but I've told you about her when she's stayed at the Court. She's there now, she arrived today. Fancy, Aunt Patience, none of you ever mentioned to me about her house in London. Imagine being able to go there just when you want!' No one answered, but then she didn't pause for breath long enough to give anyone a chance. 'I'd seen her lots of times, she's visited the

Court as long as I can remember, but I thought – if I thought about it at all – that she lived all the time in Cornwall, because that's where she always came from. I never paid much attention to her or to Uncle Matthew – he was her husband, Georgina. He's dead now.' It appeared she didn't notice Georgina's exaggeratedly disinterested expression. 'She says that she and Uncle Matthew used to go to London a lot, and she still has friends there, people they used to socialize with, people with families about our age I mean. Although she doesn't stay in town as often as she did when he was alive, she still keeps the house. It's in a smart part, not in a working-class suburb. I didn't know any of this until today, I just thought of her as Aunt Marguerite from Truro. But listen! She going to take me to stay – not in Truro, in London. It seems this is what Aunt Alice has had in mind, why she has been buying me such nice things.' Then she looked at Georgina and some of her excitement evaporated. 'I wish you could come too, Georgina. I *did* ask if you could, honestly. I tried really hard to persuade Aunt Alice to say you could, told them about how we had planned it all, all the things we'd been going to do together. But she wouldn't listen to me. It's not fair, Father and Mama getting killed like that. If they'd done as they promised and come home at the beginning of the year instead of just wanting to go on having a good time by themselves, they would have been here with us when that beastly earthquake happened, they would have read about it in the *Times*, it wouldn't have mattered a jot – not to any of *us*, I mean, not to our plans. Honestly I did my best, I begged Aunt Alice, I even told her it wouldn't be as much fun for me without you – but she wouldn't listen.' She was riding high in her bubble of excitement – a bubble that could so easily burst.

'I'd rather you'd saved your breath. Don't you ever understand what I say to you? It wasn't your place to beg your precious Aunt Alice on my account. I wish you hadn't suggested it. Anyway, I wouldn't have gone.'

In a second Melissa's volatile mood changed. 'You are mean! Mean and hateful! You're just being nasty because you want to spoil it for me,' she yelled. 'Aunt Alice is right, you're never a bit grateful! I knew it would make her cross that I wanted you to come, but I didn't let that stop me trying. First *she's* horrid to me because I tried to persuade them to take you too, now you're beastly and spiteful because I'm going and you aren't. It's wicked to be jealous, and that's what's making you so mean-minded. Because you can't come, you're trying to spoil it for me too.' Even before the tears, her voice was shrill; hearing it willingly she let herself take the single leap which was all it needed to carry her from wild and joyous excitement to hysteria.

Did she expect Georgina to comfort her? If she did, she was disappointed.

'Of course you'll have a good time, your precious hatchet-faced aunt will see to it that you do. Yes, I do wish she'd invited me, given me the opportunity of refusing.'

'Jealousy is a sin. Yes, it is, it's as wicked as cheating or lying or – or—' Choking on loud and unchecked sobs Melissa slammed out of the room.

'Oh dear, oh dear,' Patience twisted her fingers together, a sign that she didn't know what to do but was sure she ought to do something. 'I'd better go and talk to her. When she cries like that you know what happens, she'll go on until she's sick. She won't be able to eat her food, it makes her quite poorly.' Helplessly she looked at Georgina, as out of her depth with one girl as with the other. Upstairs she knew she'd find Melissa hurled across her bed, beating the pillows with clenched fists, by now beyond remembering what she was crying about, unable to stop; and there stood Georgina, tight-lipped, unapproachable. 'Oh dear, oh dear . . .' it appeared to be all she was capable of mumbling as she turned for the door.

Left alone Georgina's expression relaxed, anger gave way to – what? Drawn to the window she looked out across the terrace to the lawn, as familiar to her as her own reflection, yet she felt removed from it. Her eyes burned with the sting of tears. No! This was self-pity, she hated self-pity! She leaned her forehead against the glass of the window pane, the cool contact with something outside herself helping her fight down the threat of weakness she wouldn't allow. What she'd told Melissa was true: if they'd asked her she wouldn't have gone. They thought she wasn't good enough for them, *not good enough* for that hateful woman who'd considered herself so much better than Mama. Well, she'd show them! She had no idea how, but somehow she'd make sure that one day they looked *up* to her, not *down*.

She clamped the corners of her mouth between her teeth. She hated them, she hated all of them. Even Mellie. Oh no, that was

59

dreadful, she couldn't hate Mellie. But in all her excitement, didn't it matter to her at all that this was the holiday they should have had with Father and Mama? More than anything that was what hurt. It would have been so easy, such a relief, to give way to the tears that stung her eyes.

Instead she went upstairs to the workroom, closing the door firmly behind her. There was no better antidote for the blues than work. Yet, instead of sitting at the table and taking up her needle as she'd intended, she opened the cupboard where hung the result of her summer's work. Gowns that used to be Augusta's, seams unpicked and the material pressed then remodelled. She would like to have shown them to Melissa – but she couldn't. In her mind she could hear Melissa's voice: 'They're really quite nice, fancy you doing all that work. Wait till you see the gown we're collecting tomorrow from Amais Pilkington . . .' or, even worse, 'You'd truly hardly know they weren't new . . .' No, she couldn't show them to Mellie, she wasn't strong enough not to mind if that's what she said. And that was another thing that hurt: they'd always shared everything. If it weren't for wretched Alice Sylvester and her rich sister with a London house, they could have worked together – well, she would have done the sewing, but they could have pinned and fitted together – on making 'something out of nothing' as Mama used to call it. Georgina gave up the fight and felt the first hot tear roll down her cheek. She wanted to think she cried just for her mother, but she knew that was only half the truth and the knowledge brought her self-esteem to its lowest.

On the last Tuesday in September Hobbs arrived in the carriage from Hapley Court and Melissa's boxes were loaded. She was off for two months? three? four?

'Will you be lonely?' She bit her lip, tears brimming in her lovely deep blue eyes, genuine affection for Georgina casting a shadow on this most exciting of days. 'Oh, I do wish we could have been going together.'

'I shall miss you, but I shan't be pining I promise you. Anyway, you're never home these days, I shall hardly know the difference.'

Melissa's mind had jumped ahead, she wasn't listening.

'You know what they say, Georgina? They say that for some girls it only takes one social season to find a rich and handsome husband. Do you expect I shall do that? Just imagine, I may come home on the arm of a baronet or even a lord!'

'Why stop at that,' Georgina chuckled, egging her on, 'you'll look pretty enough to capture a real live Prince Charming. Off you go, Mellie, have a wonderful, wonderful time. You'll be the belle of all the balls.'

Any temporary shadow had disappeared, Melissa's happiness was restored.

Chapter Four

When Marguerite Chadwicke heard about Melissa's longing for a London season, she entered wholeheartedly into the scheme. She and Matthew had led a very social life but his death had brought a change: things were very different for a woman on her own. Opening up the London house, arranging dinner parties and once again receiving invitations gave her a new purpose. It was as if here at last was the daughter she'd always wanted – and what a beauty too!

Melissa's first letter arrived at Kyneston when she'd been away a week.

'I never knew life could be so thrilling. I just wish you could see me, all my lovely new garments – right down to my chemise everything is new and silk, the feel of it on my skin is – oh, I can't think of a word, luxurious, precious . . . Georgina, it's so *grown-up*. I know you get cross when I say it, but I *do* wish the aunts had said you could come. I just can't imagine how dull it must be for you with nothing to do but make those wretched hats.'

No mention of anything at Kyneston in that first letter, nor in any that followed it. Descriptions of the gowns she'd had made not just by some local dressmaker but by a fashion house, the House of Duprès; descriptions of various young men she'd met, some more attractive than others but always 'I could tell he was very taken with me'; how her programme was filled and she danced the whole evening with partners who were 'like bees around a honeypot' – and, in a rare moment when Georgina felt the letter was really meant for her alone and not just a written report: 'You'll think me vain, but honestly G. it was a wonderful feeling, there wasn't a person there who looked even a quarter as good as I did.'

Some names were mentioned more often than others: Archie Blachford ('a shame he has such a spotty complexion, his father is a judge, and his sister is married to a lord, but it would be hard to fall in love with someone with a spotty face although he is nice apart from that and I can tell he is quite smitten'), Anthony Meldrake ('quite good looking and he dances divinely, but he's so shy, sometimes I find he's looking at me, and his look says volumes, but when he actually speaks he blushes. Perhaps he'll grow out of it'); and John Derrick ('he's the most handsome person I've ever seen, very dark but with light blue eyes that seem to look right into you. Quite thrilling. Have you heard of Northney's? I hadn't, but then I'd never heard of anything until I came to London and started really to *live*. Anyway Northney's are *the* national firm for antiques and he is the great-nephew of Sir Edmund Northney and works in the family business. Not that he works in a breakfast-until-evening sense, not in the boring way so many people do. He is an expert on porcelain and that sort of thing, goes all over the country buying. Isn't that a romantic way to earn a living. I think he is interested in me, no, I *know* he is, he looks quite put out when I dance too much with other young men.')

Patience wished things were different for Georgina. Hour after hour she worked on the treadle machine.

'I hear you working so hard on that sewing machine, dear. I always thought those lovely hats had to be hand stitched,' she said as Georgina came down from a longer than usual session in the workroom.

'They do, Aunt Patience. When you hear me it's *me* I'm sewing for, not Madame de Bouverie. I've done enough to start wearing some of the gowns now. Come upstairs, I'll show you.'

Patience had always respected the sanctuary of the workroom, this was the first time she'd entered it since the day they'd heard of Clive and Augusta's death. Georgina led the way then, like a conjuror producing a rabbit from his top hat, opened the door of the hanging cupboard.

'Gowns? But where did they come from? Where did you get the lovely materials?'

'I wanted Melissa to be settled before I said anything – I don't know why—' But she did know why. Melissa's reaction would have touched her on a tender spot, it wouldn't have been pleasure at the results of Georgina's labours but sympathy for what she would see as second rate. Augusta had loved clothes and Clive had loved to indulge her; the cupboards in her dressing room were bulging. So Georgina had unpicked seams, pressed yards of material and restyled the garments for herself.

'Didn't you wonder why I kept making excuses not to get rid of Mama's things? Look – what do you think?'

Patience looked at her in wonder as one by one the results of her work were held up for inspection. 'To think you made lovely outfits like this, fashionable – and more than that, you designed them – to think you can do that . . .' In the pier glass she caught sight of her own reflection. Here she was, fifty years old, dowdy and dull: life had passed her by. What if she'd had Georgina's spirit – and her skill – instead of taking Cedric's charity and learning to be grateful? Nothing will hold Georgina down. She'll battle, she'll work, she'll be honest and courageous – and, please God, came a silent plea as she watched the girl hanging the new garments away, she'll find happiness.

Lost in her own thoughts she didn't notice Georgina's contemplative expression and was surprised by her remark.

'Come and look at Mama's things, Aunt Patience. I could alter something to fit you. She'd like that, I know she would.' She saw the way Patience's face flushed – with embarrassment that the sparsity of her wardrobe, her few gowns either black or serviceable grey, had been noticed? 'You wouldn't be offended, surely?'

'Offended? Never that. But why should you do that for me, Georgina dear? None of us at Hapley Court ever made any overtures to you or your poor mother.'

'Call her "poor" and I might withdraw the offer,' Georgina tried to make a joke of it. 'We're the poor ones that she isn't here to help us. She'd be thrilled to see what I'm doing, I know she would. My things may not be House of Duprès,' – she tried to keep the note of envy out of her voice, but how hard it was – 'but Mama told me once that anything you did for yourself was better than having things handed to you. It's the way she always used to dress herself, she'd told me so, before Father came onto the scene. Making something out of nothing, she called it. She had *style* – she could knock all the others into a cocked hat. Come on, let's see what we can find. There's a pale violet velvet you'd look pretty in—'

'What nonsense!' Patience interrupted, laughing, unfamiliar excitement welling up in her, try as she would to hold it down, 'I could never look pretty.'

'That's not true. You wait until I've finished with you.' She ought to have been able to share Patience's unalloyed pleasure, she kept the smile firmly on her face. How hard it was not to imagine Melissa's description of the elegant rooms of the House of Duprès, the drawings of gowns, the plush fitting room . . . Well, let them have it, she'd show them! She'd never be lovely like Mellie, but she knew about dress. She'd show them!

As autumn gave way to winter with still no word of Melissa returning home Georgina was as good as her word. Never had Alice's down-trodden sister-in-law had gowns such as Georgina created for her. She had dreamed her youth away, always trusting that one day her Knight Errant would come. But by fifty her dreams had turned into a mockery – until she saw the bright-eyed woman gazing back at her from the looking glass. Here at Kyneston, with Georgina as her friend and champion, who was to say the best of life wasn't still to come?

Christmas came and went, 1906 gave way to 1907. If Melissa's hope had been to acquire a husband during her season, she made it clear she only had to choose. The most frequent name to crop up in her irregular letters was that of John Derrick. 'I have told you all about John haven't I,' she wrote, 'he isn't just handsome, he's – don't laugh at me, promise you won't – he looks like I always imagine the hero when I read, Heathcliffe, Mr D'Arcy, Edward Rochester . . .' Georgina's picture of the wonderful John became less positive, for three less similar characters she couldn't imagine, but her picture of Mellie was clear and she smiled tolerantly as she read. 'And even if you are laughing, you wouldn't if you met him. Perhaps you *will* meet him one day, perhaps . . . no, I mustn't say it or it might be tempting fate.'

Sometimes Georgina gave Patience the letters to read, but that time she didn't. Confidences like that were for her alone. Instead she slipped the envelope into her writing case, then saddled Samson and set off at a brisk canter along the winter hard forest tracks. She told herself she was happy for Mellie, yes of course she was. So why did she have this feeling of melancholy, of such

65

empty misery? Father and Mama gone, Mellie gone – gone in spirit already and soon she'd be gone altogether with so many admirers eager to snatch her up. It wasn't jealousy (or was it? Could she honestly say that jealousy had nothing to do with it?), it was a sudden feeling of uncertainty, not knowing which way to steer her own future, knowing that she was alone . . . She put Samson into a gallop.

The sound of his pounding hooves, the wind loosening her ginger hair from its pins and sending curling tendrils to blow about her shoulders, the crisp air on her face, all these things helped raise her spirit. Then, coming back towards Kyneston, through the winter bare trees she could just glimpse the roof of the house, the welcome of the smoking chimneys. She reined in and stopped, leaning to rest her hand on Samson. Her heart was beating hard, not from the ride but from something she had no words for. Kyneston . . . She couldn't remember the time before it had been the background of her life. See its chimneys, its gabled roof . . . shut your eyes and you can see the gardens, smell the peaty soil, feel the cobblestones of the stableyard under your feet . . . Kyneston . . . and Father made it half yours. Nothing can ever take that away. How can you ever feel sorry for yourself or hard done by? Kyneston is your anchor, more than that it's your heritage. A picture flashed into her mind of the story of Paul on the road to Damascus. Suddenly he had known a certain truth with blinding certainty. And this was her truth . . . wherever she went, whatever she did with her life, always there would be Kyneston.

Half way through March Melissa returned home. She wouldn't have come then, but Marguerite insisted that she wanted to be in Truro for Easter.

'I've a million things to show you – and to tell you,' she said as she and Georgina sat together on her bed half an hour after her arrival. This was just as they'd always shared confidences. 'Just wait till the railway wagon brings my trunks. I'll have to throw out half my old things to make room in the wardrobe.'

'Do you like this?' Georgina stood up and turned slowly to show off her latest creation.

'Yes, I do. It's really stylish.' It was a statement and a question rolled into one. The gown hadn't the look of the local dressmaker.

'I made it.'

66

Melissa laughed. 'Honestly? I feel awful. Just think of the hours it must have taken. While my days have been so full of going to places and seeing things, all you've had is Kyneston and stitching – and poor old Aunt Patience for company.'

'I expect my company was as good as yours,' Georgina bristled.

'Anyway, never mind that. I want to tell you ... Last week Uncle Cedric and Aunt Alice came to stay for a few days and we invited John – John Derrick, you remember I've told you about him, he's the great nephew of Sir Edmund Northney – we invited him to dinner. He's in love with me, I'm sure he is. He's not such a boy as most of them, some of them weren't much older than us. He must be quite twenty-five, very worldly, sure of himself. I keep running away from the point – that's because I'm so excited. He said he hoped one day to visit Kyneston, he asked Uncle Cedric and Aunt Alice if he would have their permission to call here. And do you know what the outcome of it is? He's coming to stay, actually to stay. It was Uncle Cedric's idea, he said it would be quite proper because of Aunt Patience living here.'

Georgina tried to show the right amount of pleasure, she tried to tell herself that she was being mean-minded to dislike this so handsome visitor before he even arrived, simply because he was part of the London scene she'd not shared and because the Sylvesters so obviously approved of him.

'You'd better be sure to get on well with him,' Melissa chattered on. 'He might be going to be your brother-in-law. Truly Georgina, he's not told me so, but I know he is head over heels. I'm sure that's why he wants to come here, so that he gets to know them at Hapley Court, so then Uncle Cedric will agree to his proposing marriage to me.'

'It's up to you who you marry, not your uncle. In two months you'll be of age, he won't have any say.'

'Don't start being beastly about them as soon as I come home,' Melissa pouted. 'Anyway, you're not going to make an argument. Just sit still and listen ...'

The train wasn't due at Brockenhurst until midday. Even allowing for the journey from Kyneston to meet him surely Melissa didn't need to start titivating at nine o'clock in the morning! Called to her room to give an opinion on her third change of gown, Georgina's patience was wearing thin.

'If he's so besotted with you, he's not going to care what you're wearing.'

'You wouldn't understand. You don't know anything about young men. Why do you think he fell in love with me – doesn't that sound wonderful? Fell in love with me – it was because I looked pretty. And what about you? You mustn't let me down. If my clothes fitted you I'd lend you something, but I'm smaller than you. You've got those things you make from Mama's old gowns . . . Anyway he won't have eyes for anyone but me! By now he'll be at Waterloo. What do you think, which one do I look prettiest in?'

'You look pretty in any – and you know it.'

'You're cross. What have I done? Oh Gina, don't be cross. Help me to make everything as perfect as I've dreamed.'

Georgina relented and helped her dress, even brushing her hair for her and pinning it into a golden crown almost too lovely to be covered with a hat. By half past ten, and far too early, Biggs took her on her way to meet this perfect man.

Could Melissa really be in love with him or was she swept off her feet by his apparent adoration? He wasn't such a boy as the others she'd met: had that something to do with her infatuation too, the fact that he was looked on as an authority in his profession? Georgina watched the carriage disappear round the bend in the drive, her sandy brows pulled into a frown. Melissa's discarded gowns were thrown on the bed, the room was heavy with the perfume of oil of violets. Turning her back, Georgina went out and shut the door on it. A clear spring morning, the call of the outdoors couldn't be ignored even though she had work to do for Mme de Bouverie.

She decided to clean out the stables. Reacting to the last hour spent perfecting Melissa's appearance, a perverse streak in her made her don a brown calico dress and stout boots; so might many a labourer's wife go to work in the fields. Taking shovel and stiff broom she filled a bucket from the yard pump and put her abundant energy into her chosen job. This morning it suited her mood, the earthiness, the pungent smell of warm hay and straw, the scraping of the shovel and finally the rhythmical swish of the stiff bristles across the stone-flagged floor were therapeutic. When her task was done she took the saddle and bridle down from the wall and went to the paddock, shared between Samson, her own pony,

Cleo and Juno who used to be ridden by Clive and Augusta. She wouldn't part with any of them and these days their exercise was her responsibility. She'd brought Augusta's saddle so first she had to catch Juno and get her ready, then raise herself to her side-saddle mounted position – not an easy task with no one to give her a hoist. Then she was off, her wide and, by this time, none too clean skirt lifted in the spring breeze. Melissa's visitor was forgotten.

Working in the stable she hadn't worn her watch so when, with Juno again turned loose in the paddock, she returned the saddle she was surprised to find the carriage put away. It must be later than she'd thought – except that she knew she hadn't thought at all. Suddenly aware of her dishevelled state, her dirty hands and mud-spattered boots, she took a bucket outside to the pump for the second time that morning. Childhood training died hard, Mrs Biggs had never let them back into the house until they'd rinsed off traces of garden or scrubbed off traces of the stables. Next came her boots, unlaced and left in the back porch. Then she meant to go through the hall and up to her room unnoticed, but as luck had it the dining-room door was opened at just that moment so that Effie could carry out a laden tray.

'Oh there you are dear,' Patience saw her. 'We waited a long time but in the end we started without you.'

'I left my watch indoors, I cleaned out the stables then I went for a ride. Time just flew. I'm sorry.'

'Never mind. Now Effie knows you're back she'll bring your food, they've been keeping it warm for you. Come and meet Mr Derrick, Melissa's friend.'

'Like this?' She pulled the scarf off her head and exposed the ginger curls that were winning their battle with the hairpins.

'You look awful, you can't come to the table like that!' Melissa spoke to Georgina but she looked at John, worried at his reaction to her sister presenting herself looking no better than a scullery maid.

Georgina looked at him too, and saw the laughter in his light blue eyes. Her response was immediate, instinctive.

'Hello Mr Derrick. I'm cleaner than you'd think, I scrubbed at the pump before I came in. Anyway, it's from good honest toil.' Then, screwing up her freckled nose, 'I don't smell of stable, do I?'

'More likely you smell of fresh air,' he told her.

Her preconceived ideas of Melissa's so-handsome Romeo were knocked askew. Yes he was smart, she found herself thinking, then changed her mind. Smart? No, that's wasn't the right description, he looked as though he ought to be an artist or a poet or even a composer. Not what she expected. She wished she'd got through the hall without being seen so that she could have put on clean clothes and brushed her hair. And stockinged feet did nothing for her self-assurance. Melissa's obvious displeasure at her untidiness hadn't bothered her, yet at his smiling 'More likely you smell of fresh air' she felt gauche.

Too late to retreat now, her warmed and unappetizingly dried-up food was being brought in for her. And after her morning's exertions she was hungry enough to enjoy it despite its appearance.

'Do you ride, Mr Derrick?' Patience asked, doing her best to keep the conversation going rather than leave Georgina to eat her meal alone.

'Oh no, Aunt Patience,' Melissa cut in. 'John hasn't come all this way to help exercise horses. I don't know why Georgina insists we keep them, they'd be much better off where they were needed.'

'I'd enjoy exercising them. Since I've lived in London riding is something I've missed.' In fact he hadn't sat a horse since he was a boy but this sister, so different from Melissa, interested him.

Georgina felt rather than saw Melissa's pout. Quickly she swallowed the mouthful she'd been chewing so that she could take up his offer before it got laid to rest.

'Then Kyneston is just the place for you, Mr Derrick—'

'John please,' and to Patience, 'both of you, John not Mr Derrick.'

She beamed her acceptance. 'That's good. That's what we think of you as, that's what Mellie calls you, so we'd have trouble in remembering the Mr. But, about the horses. This morning I rode Juno, she belonged to Mama. Her saddle isn't right for Cleo – she was Father's mount and it's not the easiest thing to ride astride in a skirt. But I try to see poor Cleo gets fair shares. She's a big mare, but a darling, no trouble at all. It's just I'm more comfortable side-saddle.'

'Then I'm your man. What about you Melissa?'

Melissa looked at him, wide eyed, timid – and utterly beautiful.

'I know it's silly to be frightened, it's no use your telling me. I just can't help it. I'm not like Georgina, she can never see danger. She's lucky not to have my imagination, that's what Aunt Alice says it is.' Then, her face lighting into a smile aimed especially at John, 'But I could dance all night – you know I never tire of dancing and music and – oh, all the lovely, beautiful things you taught me.' Nothing else was said about John riding, and that evening he and Melissa dined at Hapley Court.

'Don't go to sleep yet,' Melissa crept into Georgina's room after the house was settled for the night. Closing the door quietly she tiptoed in the dark to sit on the bed. 'You've not told me? What do you think? Can't you see he really is taken with me? Aunt Alice whispered to me how happy she and Uncle Cedric are, so you see they have noticed the way he looks at me, they can see. It's so disappointing, do you know what Aunt Marguerite has persuaded them? They're going off tomorrow to stay with her in Cornwall, they'll be there ages I expect, at any rate until after Easter. And you know I told you why I was sure John wanted to come down here – so that they got to know him, so that he could talk to Uncle Cedric about asking me to marry him. Now it's all spoilt, they won't even be here.'

'Well, he's here, that's the main thing. How long can he stay away from Northney's?'

'I've no idea. Sir Edmund was glad he was coming down here.' To Georgina it was no answer at all but it seemed to satisfy Melissa. She gave a contented sigh then let her mind drift back to the evening at Hapley Court. 'When Aunt Alice told us they were going off tomorrow, I hoped he might have spoken to Uncle Cedric this evening, but I expect he thought they needed longer to know him. But he asked lots of questions.'

'Questions?'

'Things about *me*, about Kyneston and my father, things he wouldn't have cared about unless he was really interested in me. He knew Uncle Cedric was my guardian so I suppose it came from that – you know the sort of thing, how lucky I was that they lived so near and we were able to stay in Kyneston until we come of age. But listen to this: he asked what would happen if I decided to live in London, whether Kyneston was entailed or anything. Obviously if he is going to marry me he wants to know how I stand. Of course he knew we were step-sisters, I'd told him about you. He seemed surprised that Kyneston belonged to both of us. But it's *him* I came in to talk about, not us and the house. He really must mean to make a good impression, he was nice as pie to poor old Aunt Patience, and to you.' She chuckled, thoroughly happy with the situation. 'If it ever happens to you, you'll understand how thrilling it is to know someone is so eager. Aunt Alice was delighted, I could tell.'

'What about you, Mellie? Is he the person you want to marry. It would mean you'd have to *live* in London I expect, that's different from a month of two having fun.'

'Phooey, a month or two indeed. I was there six months and I'd go back tomorrow. Honestly Georgina you don't know anything about anything, buried here in the forest.'

The words stung.

'I know one thing: spending the rest of your life with someone can't be the same as the thrill of knowing they're in love with you. You haven't said . . . do you want to be Mrs Derrick, spend the rest of your life with him?'

'Don't you think he is splendidly handsome? Of course you do. Oh Georgina, don't be jealous and horrid. You can be my Maid of Honour – and if Aunt Alice argues I promise I won't listen. Then you can come and stay with me. I'll introduce you to people, I'll help you make yourself look attractive—'

'Jolly good!' Could Melissa hear the heavy sarcasm? 'Put a lemon in my mouth like the prize pig in Mr Haynes butcher's shop window, why don't you?'

Melissa giggled. 'Can I get in bed, my feet are cold?' Without waiting for an answer she pulled back the covers and wriggled in by Georgina's side. 'Coming in like this to talk is nice. If we marry, do you suppose we'll be expected to sleep in the same bed? Father and Mama always did. But Aunt Alice and Uncle Cedric have separate rooms, that's so much nicer.'

'You wouldn't marry anyone you didn't want to share a bed with.'

'I know what you have to do to get babies, I wasn't meaning that sort of thing. That's not like having someone actually in your bed, going to sleep there, waking up there. Even *we*, you and me, we've never done that. This is nice though isn't it, lying all snug and talking. But bedrooms are private places.'

It was Georgina's turn to laugh, spontaneously taking Melissa's hand in a firm grip.

'About riding,' Melissa went on. 'He really means it, he wants to exercise Cleo.'

'You don't mind? He's your visitor, not mine.'

'Silly, of course he's mine. But I shall quite like you taking him off for an hour or two, I've so many exciting things to think about. Especially if you go first thing in the mornings, then I can be all dressed and ready to impress him when you come back and we shall still have the whole day ahead of us.'

John had arrived during the third week of March. Then came Easter. A week after that there was an auction sale he was to attend for Northney's in Winchester. So the time went and he seemed in no hurry to return to London.

'Sir Edmund Northney thinks a lot of me,' Melissa told Georgina complacently, 'so does Lady Northney. They won't push him to get back to the gallery, not if they know he is paying court to *me*. It's what they hope for. I could tell.'

But Sir Edmund and Lady Northney didn't know of the hours their great-nephew spent with Melissa's step-sister. It had started with the early morning exercising of Cleo and Juno. Of the two Georgina was the better horseman, that, John readily admitted; he hadn't sat ahorse for ten years whereas a day seldom passed when she didn't ride.

'They enjoy their morning gallop,' Patience observed to Melissa, saying it casually yet watching keenly for the girl's reaction. 'It's nice to see them getting along so well.' There now, that should open her eyes without putting it into words. For Patience was worried. He was a charming young man, why he even treated *her* as though she were important to him. Couldn't Melissa see the way Georgina's eyes lit up when she spoke to him? Couldn't she see how he responded? No, she probably couldn't, she was too blinded by stardust. 'You don't mind them going off together? You don't wish you were going too?'

Melissa laughed. 'Silly question. Going early in the morning is ideal, it gets it over and doesn't spoil our day.' And more than that, she liked it when they came home flushed from their ride and from attending to the horses and found her looking cool and elegant. 'And today John is going to view the contents of a house sale just beyond Ringwood. He wants me to go with him.'

73

'You'll enjoy that dear,' Patience said with more conviction than she felt.

'Oh look, they're back. They're coming up the drive now. I hope John remembers we have to leave just after breakfast, he won't have time to mess about with the horses this morning.'

John rode into the stable yard ahead of Georgina, dismounted first then raised his arms to lift her to the ground.

'I wish I were an artist,' he told her. 'The sun making your hair glint like fire, your cheeks glowing from the early morning air . . . Georgina, I wonder if you enjoy our outings half as much as I do.'

His eyes held hers, she couldn't look away. It wasn't just the early morning air that made her cheeks glow. What was he telling her? Or did young men expect to talk like that? She didn't know. Did he mean what he said? She didn't know that either. For those seconds she forgot Melissa, she wanted to hold onto this precious moment for herself, for herself and for him. She slid down from the saddle into his arms as he helped her to the ground. Then sanity returned, she remembered Mellie who wanted them to be friends, Mellie who was so certain of his love.

That morning was the first time she let herself believe she was something more than the sister of the girl he loved, the girl he would soon make his fianceé and then his wife. His mouth was only inches from her, something outside themselves seemed to have taken hold of them.

'I've come to fetch you, John.' Melissa's voice interrupted them. 'You'll see to the animals won't you, Georgina. We're out all day, did John tell you?'

'I can't leave them both to her,' John answered. 'We'll not be long.'

'Of course you can leave them both to me. I'd forgotten today's the day of the sale. Off you go, leave Cleo to me.'

She saw how Melissa took his hand as they walked away, she saw how he turned to her to speak but they were too far away to see what it was that made Melissa smile up at him so sweetly.

That morning Cleo and Samson were groomed with more vigour than usual. She longed to relive those few precious seconds but she shut her mind to the memory; perhaps he'd thought he was being charitable to Melissa's dull and plain sister, she told herself, yes that's probably what had made him say what he had. '. . . hair shining like fire . . .' 'Little carrot top', that's what Biggs used to

74

call her when she was small – and that was nearer the truth. She felt humiliated by John's words, humiliated at how close she'd come to making a fool of herself. Because that's what she would have done if she'd let him know the strange, wonderful, terrifying sensation that had made her arms and legs ache, her heart beat a wild tattoo as her mouth had come close to his. Had she imagined the way he'd looked at her? Yes, of course she had, she'd imagined it because that's what she'd wanted to see. He belonged to Melissa . . . he was friendly to her because she was Melissa's sister. No, that wasn't true. It wasn't something that had happened just in those seconds, it had been growing and strengthening each time they were together, it hadn't happened in just those seconds when he'd said that about her hair . . . no one had ever spoken to her like that before, well of course they hadn't, who had she ever known? Mellie was right, how could she know anything about young men? Her thoughts jumped first in one direction, then in another. She dreaded being alone with him again . . . no, she longed to be alone with him . . .

He found her in the paddock feeding the horses with carrots she'd brought out with her earlier.

'Oughtn't you to have gone by now?' she greeted him with her best 'sisterly' smile.

'Yes, Biggs has the trap almost ready. Georgina, I couldn't just walk away. What I said to you – it was nothing compared with what I'd like to say. Our mornings have meant something to you too. They have, haven't they?'

Her gingery eyes stung with tears of joy. 'You know they have.'

'An hour on a horse, that's not what I want. Didn't you say you have a boat?'

She nodded. 'On the water at Lymington. Do you sail?'

'Do you?' he counter-questioned.

'Not well enough to take the boat out alone.'

'You wouldn't be alone.'

A letter arrived from Alice telling Melissa that she and Cedric would be returning to the Court the following Friday. 'We hadn't intended to be away so long, but Marguerite had a nasty bout of influenza and we felt we couldn't leave her to no one's care except the servants. By now Mr Derrick will have gone back to London of course. I do so look forward to hearing about "things".'

75

But John hadn't gone back to London. Apart from attending two sales, purchasing a Chinese vase, some Italian glassware and various small items of antique silver he had done nothing. The vase and the glassware were carefully boxed and sent by carrier to Northney's Gallery. The silverware, for reasons known to himself, he brought back with him to Kyneston and stowed in his own trunk for safe keeping.

Except for his morning rides and a few visits to Lymington with Georgina he spent most of his time with Melissa, who saw his keen acceptance of her invitation for him to extend his visit as sure proof of his feelings. Georgina spent most of her days hat making, escaping from them and, in work, trying to escape from what was happening outside her control. But there was no escape. She laid her sewing on the table in front of her and sat, gazing unseeingly. To think of his marrying Mellie was impossible. Did Mellie have this dreadful aching, empty feeling, something that no one and nothing but John could satisfy? No. She might think she was in love, but remember what she said about not wanting to go to sleep by his side, wake up by his side. Georgina closed her eyes, she gave up the battle and let her imagination carry her. Sometimes I'm sure he loves me. But he doesn't want to hurt Mellie, he must know why she's asked him to stay on here. Wouldn't it hurt her more if he married her but loved me? How could he choose me, though, when he could have her? She's quite the loveliest person I've ever seen – and I'm not thinking that just because she's Mellie and I love her, well, most of the time I love her. How good she's been lately, perhaps she's outgrown all her dreadful storms. Has John done that to her?

Georgina opened her eyes and took up her work. But there was no escaping this nameless ache. Sometimes she wished he'd never come to Kyneston, but those thoughts never lasted. The truth was that nothing could ever be the same as it had been before he came, he'd woken feelings in her that she'd been unaware were there lying dormant. But they'd never be dormant again. Once more she pushed her work away from her. Elbows on the table she cupped her face in her hands, moving her fingers on her cheek. If only they were his hands, his fingers . . . An April shower sent silver needles of rain to run down the window, from downstairs she heard the sound of John playing the piano then Melissa's sweet soprano voice.

Shutting the door on her work she ran down the stairs, collected a rubberized waterproof, changed into thick boots and strode down the drive and through the gate into the forest.

On the Thursday Melissa rode to Hapley Court to leave a note to greet Alice and Cedric when they arrived home and inviting them to dinner at Kyneston on Friday evening. 'Please come, even if you are tired after your journey. John is returning to London this weekend.' She knew they'd understand the underlying message.

'Why don't we all go to the boat,' Georgina suggested at breakfast, knowing very well that Melissa was even more terrified of boats than she was of horses.

'You two go if you don't mind getting a drenching. It looks like another showery day. I've got lots to do, I want everything to be really welcoming and perfect for them this evening.'

'We'll take waterproofs. And we'll take something to eat too, then we don't need to watch the clock all the time. We're really getting quite proficient, aren't we?'

'We manage to keep afloat,' he agreed, laughing.

It was already raining when they left the trap at the coaching inn on the High Street and set off towards the boat. Then down the cobblestone hill to the water. From there they were on soggy grass all the way to where *Cork's Crew*, as Clive had named her, was moored, one of a desolate row. Long before they reached the moorings the rain was lashing, they were running, John with his arm around Georgina's shoulder as if that way he gave her protection.

'Do you think we're mad?' she laughed as she clambered aboard.

'Anything but. Get inside, under cover. There, now tell me,' with a hand under her wet chin he raised her face to look straight at him, 'tell me, if this is being mad, would you rather be sane?'

'No. No, I wouldn't be anything but what I am.'

'And would you rather be somewhere else?'

'No.' All her laughter was gone now, the sides of the little cabin seemed to be pressing in on her, there was nothing but this place, this time, themselves. Outside the rain beat a tattoo on the cabin roof, the wind had whipped up the water, it splashed against the sides of the boat as they rocked in their own isolated world. Blood was racing through her veins. 'No,' she repeated, her voice hardly more than a whisper, 'I want to be here, like this, just with you . . .'

His mouth was so close . . . closer, she could feel the warmth of his breath . . . his mouth was on hers as she clung to him. He'd wanted this almost since that first day when he'd told her 'You smell of fresh air'. She was natural and unaffected, yet even as she'd eaten her dried-up food with such hungry relish he'd wanted to watch her. Untidy and work-soiled some people might have called her; John had seen her as sensual and earthy. And as the weeks had passed he had become more certain that behind the shield of her friendly manner there was an animal passion waiting to be stirred. He'd never wanted any girl as he did her. Now here she was clinging to him, her lips parted as her mouth moved under his, her fingers in his hair, the only sound a repressed moan that told him more than any words.

'Take off these wet things,' he whispered, even though he didn't want to loosen his hold on her. 'You won't be cold.' And that was true enough, their body heat and the damp waterproofs gave the confined space an atmosphere more like a Turkish bath. A sudden flash, followed by a loud clap of thunder only emphasised the intimacy of their haven. Today they wouldn't be raising *Cork's Screw's* sail. They closed the cabin door.

'I've got to go back to London. All the times we've been together. Yet not together.' Disjointed sentences, so unlike his usual confident manner. Was he treading on unfamiliar ground just as she was?

She raised her hands gently to his face, touching him as though he were precious. Oh, but he was. He loved her, his eyes told her he loved her.

'We're together now. There's no one but us,' she leaned against him, pressing herself close, joyously aware of his heightened passion, proud and exalted that she was the reason, 'only us in all the world'.

'You know what'll happen? Georgina, you drive me wild, I think of you, I want you.'

'And me.'

This time when they kissed they both knew it was only the beginning. Already their waterproofs were on the floor, soon other garments were taken off and thrown across a table where the sextant was fixed. They weren't torn off in one abandoned rush, undressing was part of their ritual love dance until they stood naked. This time he pulled her gently into his arms, flesh against flesh she leaned against him. When he knelt before her she felt no surprise at what he did, she drew his head towards her. He was carrying her with him to another world, new, rich, a world where every sensation was a part of their love.

Later they lay close together – very close, for the bunk was narrow. 'Those whom God has joined together . . .' The words sprang to her mind. And He had. If God was Love, then He had. She never wanted to move, she wished they could stay like this for ever.

Then another thought nudged at her. Melissa. This evening Cedric was coming, Melissa was so sure why John had stayed on at Kyneston. But she was wrong. He had stayed to be with *her*. Another picture: John talking to the miserable Cedric, asking permission to propose marriage to *her*. Fleetingly she was sorry for Mellie, but she was too happy for the thought to take root.

The carriage had already arrived, downstairs the Sylvesters were gathered in the drawing room with John, Melissa and Patience (for in Georgina's mind Patience didn't count as a Sylvester). Tonight it was important to look better than her best. She knew that she could never be beautiful like Melissa, but she had inherited something of her mother's flair for style and tonight she meant to make the most of it. She knew Alice would look down her long nose and consider she was overdressed for a dinner party at home, but let her think it. This was no ordinary evening. She was John's woman, 'you drive me wild' came the echo of his words. Those isolated and beautiful hours divided her past from her future. This evening John must be proud of her. Oh but he would be, every time he looked at her he would remember. She wanted to tell the world – but she could tell no one.

Satisfied with her appearance she decided it was time to make an entrance. Coming along the gallery she could see there was only one door open leading onto the hall, that was the study. Her heart missed a beat. Standing still she listened. Yes, John was talking to Cedric. Quietly she walked down the carpeted stairs reaching the hall just as Cedric looked her way. He gave no sign of having seen her and she would have gone on to make her entry

79

in the drawing room, but she was sure he was speaking loudly for her benefit. Drawing nearer the door but keeping out of view she listened.

'Yes, it's a fine house. Of course the upkeep, the staffing and so forth is heavy. Until the girls reach majority I attend to that from capital left by my brother-in-law.'

'A difficult arrangement for them, looking to the future. A house owned jointly, I mean.'

'The house may be in joint ownership, but not the income that goes with it. Melissa will find herself very comfortably off, indeed if she looks to the other one to supply half the outgoings for this house she will be whistling in the wind.'

'I don't understand?'

'A worked-out tin mine – that's Georgina's inheritance – hardly compares with tea plantations in India – Melissa's. It's those that provide the wherewithal for this establishment. No, half a house of this size and a poor purse is a mixed blessing.'

'More of a liability than an asset,' John agreed cheerfully. 'I'm glad you managed to get back before I left, sir. I've not spoken to Melissa yet, although I'm sure she knows my intention but I felt it only courtesy to see I have your approval first.'

Chapter Five

She had walked down the stairs full of confidence, the glimpse of John and Cedric together in the study adding to her certainty.

Now she leaned against the wall, out of sight yet no more than feet from the open doorway. Georgina's nature was to rush wherever instinct directed; now it prompted her to rush to John, to stop what he was doing before it was too late. But there was another emotion that struggled in her, struggled and won. He must know he *wasn't* in love with Melissa, he'd given her no more thought than Georgina had herself in the sanctuary of *Cork's Screw*'s small cabin. But it was Melissa who had an ongoing income which, even in little over a year since the earthquake had taken their parents, must have built into a sizeable sum, an income which would bolster their future. Surely it was impossible . . . John couldn't marry for money . . .

'If Melissa cares for you – and I saw how happy she was with you in London – then you both have my blessing. And Alice's too, of that I have no doubt.' There was a rare ring of warmth in Cedric's voice.

Across the wide hall behind the closed door of the drawing room were other voices, Melissa's and Aunt Alice's. Georgina didn't need to hear what they said to know where their conversation was carrying them, both anxiously awaiting the sound of the study door, both confident of why it was John had asked to talk to Cedric.

Glancing across the hall, Georgina caught sight of herself in the gilt-framed mirror. The image mocked her. Half an hour ago she'd been thrilled with her appearance as she'd pinned up her fiery curls, threaded with Augusta's 'second best' pearls which she'd not taken with her to America. The ivory satin gown had looked as elegant as anything Melissa had had made in the London fashion house she talked of; now it appeared just what it was, cut down and remodelled from something in her mother's wardrobe.

Carefully stepping out of her satin slippers she picked them up, then in her stockinged feet crept back up the stairs and along the gallery to the shelter of her own room. The oil lamp cast flickering shadows, there was no sound except the soft ticking of the clock on the mantelpiece over the empty grate. Preparing for the dinner party her mind had been filled with the memory of those hours on the boat; it still was, yet now there was no joy in remembering. Surely he must have felt the same as she had, or none of it would have happened . . . or was that the way men behaved if they found a woman who was willing? Willing? Oh but she'd been more than that. She closed her eyes, holding her folded arms across her chest, reliving the moment when their last garments were stripped from them, the overwhelming sense of rightness in what she knew was going to happen. Only now she realized just how naïve she'd been, she'd imagined love had come to them both with the same blinding certainty. More than that, she'd taken it for granted that for both of them loving was a new and wonderful experience. But think back, she told herself, if he'd been no more worldly than you were yourself he wouldn't have acted like he did. Would a callow youth have knelt . . . no, don't think of it! Then a new alarm bell sounded in her mind, one that deafened her to all else. Pregnant! No! It's not possible! But it *is* possible! Could he have made me pregnant? I never even considered it, I just knew I wanted what we did, nothing else mattered to me. If I am, if he finds that I am expecting his child – his, mine – then he'd not marry Mellie . . . but would I want that? To know that I was no more than a responsibility he had to shoulder. No! Mama had no husband, when she talked to me about how she made a living to keep us I always knew she was proud. And so will I be. I'll not be married out of necessity. How hateful Alice would love it. But making love once – twice, she corrected herself remembering their hours in the humid warmth of the cabin – wouldn't have made me pregnant . . . would it?

She couldn't go down, she couldn't bear to feel his gaze resting on her, his mind going back just as hers was. Such a short time ago she'd looked forward to the moment when she would face him across the dining table, know his eyes were on her and that he too was remembering.

'Miss Georgina,' Effie rapped on her door, 'Didn't you hear the gong Miss Georgina? Miss Sylvester sent me up to see if you wanted any help dressing.' She was in the room without waiting for a 'Come in'. 'Oh, you're all dressed ready. Oh, Miss Georgina, you look real lovely. Begging your pardon Miss, not for me to tell you, but the words just hopped out before I could stop them.' That was what so often happened with Effie's words, at any rate when they were directed at Georgina. Their relationship had stemmed from those days some fifteen years ago when on Sunday mornings Mrs Biggs had wanted them 'off from underfoot' and sent them to church where they would be out of harms way and hers too.

Georgina laughed.

'Don't apologize, you've cheered me up. Does my gown look all right really?'

'Now you're fishing for more compliments,' poor plain Effie beamed. 'Can't put a finger on what it is, isn't as if you've got her colouring, no and not her tall build either, but sometimes I can see a look of the miss'us in you – and I can't say fairer than that. None of us ever saw her anything but right beautiful. Come on now, Miss Georgie, put your feet in your pretty slippers and down you go. Not like you to be late to table when there's a feast prepared like there is this evening. Anyway, what kept you? The others have been down there this last half hour.'

Georgina's slight shrug was her only answer.

'Ah well,' Effie chattered on, 'I doubt you missed much. From what I heard – passing the door on the way to the dining room you know – Mrs Sylvester was doing the bulk of the talking. Now though it's different. The gentlemen have joined them and the dinner's being taken through.'

'Then I'd better come down,' Georgina smiled warmly at the gossiping maid, sure that in her she had a ally. Effie said she looked 'real lovely' – something Georgina was sure was an exaggeration – and that was enough to breathe life back into her fighting spirit. At dinner John would see Melissa and her together, he would remember the boat and know how impossible it would be to marry Melissa.

'Good evening.' She greeted the party assembled around the dining table, an over-bright smile held in place. 'I'm sorry I'm late, Aunt Patience. I hadn't realized the time until I heard the gong.' She slipped into her place. On her instruction the table had been set with Patience at the head, John on one side of her and Cedric on the other. Next to John sat Melissa. Facing them, next to Cedric was Alice and then her. She had taken a fiendish pleasure in the seating arrangement knowing that Alice would consider Cedric, who still controlled the purse strings, should sit at the head of the table whilst she, herself, should face him at the foot. This evening there had been another reason for Georgina wanting it this way: although Melissa would be next to John, it was she he would look at across the table. Taking her seat it hurt to remember her excitement as she'd set out the place cards. She held her chin high, she wouldn't let anyone – and certainly not John – guess how hard it was to keep a smile on her face.

She attacked the steaming Windsor soup with more gusto than genuine appetite.

'We were on the boat when the storm broke – and what a storm!' Did everyone hear her voice as unnaturally loud and spirited as she did herself? 'It was so exciting. Did John tell you about it, Mellie?'

'Please, don't. You know how I hate storms.' Her eyes wide as she remembered how frightened she'd been as she'd hidden in her bedroom with the blind down and the curtains closed. 'You don't think it'll come back tonight do you?' She looked first at John, then at Cedric and Alice for reassurance.

'No, my dear,' Cedric reassured her. 'It was a dirty morning right enough, but there's nothing of it left. Nothing but a steady rain. There'll be no more lightning and thunder to worry you.'

'A dirty morning?' Georgina laughed, her eyes on John. 'Perhaps if you hid away indoors that's how it seemed. We found it exhilarating. It had been brewing for days. You can feel a good storm in the atmosphere, can't you, it builds up till it can't contain itself.' She willed him to meet her eyes. 'When it breaks all the tensions snap. Like the starting pistol at a race – or like a fat lady unlacing her corsets—'

'Enough!' Cedric bent forward to glower at her across Alice's soup bowl. 'If you've no civilized conversation to offer then I suggest you keep silent.'

'I *do* beg your pardon,' her tone belied her words. 'I dare say any mongrel in a kennel of thoroughbreds makes the occasional escape to sniff around the gutters. But I apologize, this evening we have guests. So let's see if we can make intelligent conversation, shall we?'

'Sometimes I despair . . .' Cedric muttered under his breath.

Georgina wasn't asking herself what she expected of John, nor even what she hoped for; her own emotions were too confused for clear reasoning. Did she imagine the secret laughter in his eyes as he looked at her, laughter she felt held them apart from the others at the table? He wasn't committed to Melissa yet, perhaps even now he would realize how impossible tying his life to hers would be. And what of Melissa? Georgina's pity was genuine as she looked at her. She thought she was in love, but Mellie hadn't even started to know what love was.

The meal over there was no suggestion that the ladies should retire to the drawing room while the men sipped their port or brandy. It seemed that this evening everyone was aware that what had to be said between them had been said already. Whispering something to Melissa as they moved from the table John steered her towards the garden while the others moved across to the drawing room – all except Georgina. She escaped upstairs, took off her satin gown, put away Augusta's second best pearls, then donned the calico workaday dress she wore for gardening, threw a cape around her shoulders and in stockinged feet went back down, along the corridor to the side door and the lobby where her rubber boots were kept.

It was no longer raining, occasionally the moon showed itself through a break in the clouds. On her own and led by instinct and habit Georgina crossed the cattle grid to the open forest. The air was heavy with the smell of wet earth, last year's damp rotting leaves. It was balm to her spirit, it never failed her.

By now he'll have asked Melissa to marry him. Half a house and not enough money even to pay the staff let alone repair the roof. If John took Melissa to London to live, as he undoubtedly would, she might even want to get rid of Kyneston. Surely she couldn't. Imagine strangers in Kyneston. Yes, but Melissa had never been interested in it except as a place to live; she'd never so much as pulled up a weed; it had never been she who'd marked out the lawn and put up the tennis net; it had never been she who'd swabbed out the stable (Just imagine it! Even this evening the image of such a

85

thing brought a flicker of a smile to Georgina's mouth); it had never been she who'd entwined the bannisters with holly and ivy dressing the house up for Christmas. '. . . stuck here in the forest . . .' Georgina could almost hear the contempt in her voice.

Rather than resent Melissa for her power over both their futures, her mind was filled with images of so much they'd shared, times they had turned to each other when things had gone wrong. How they'd cried together when Hunter had died and Hopwood had dug a deep hole near the hedge that divided the garden from the forest so that they could bury him; how they'd partnered each other as they'd danced in the hall, their only music supplied by their own voices as they'd waltzed and polkaed; the many, many times she had shaken or slapped Melissa out of a hysterical storm of tears when minor calamity had grown to major proportion in her mind, then held her close as the weeping subsided. Would John understand her? Would he have the patience loving her demanded? How could he have? He didn't love her. He couldn't possibly love her, today there had been no shadow of Melissa, not for either of them. But Mellie deserved better than a man who married her for her inheritance.

Tramping unseeingly through the wet leaves, following the familiar path unerringly even though the moon only occasionally appeared from behind the clouds, Georgina's mood gradually changed. How dare he use Mellie like it! Oh yes, he'd dare. Hadn't he used *her* for his own pleasure too? She mustn't be pregnant. It was Friday, her period should come by Monday. Supposing this time next week nothing had happened – no, don't suppose any such thing, even considering the possibility might be tempting fate. Just think of Melissa believing he was madly in love with her ('head over heels' Mellie called it), while all the time he's been holding her on a string and steering me towards making a fool of myself as I did today. Supposing Father had left a different Will, and I'd been the one with the income from the plantations piling up, by now he would have asked *me* to marry him, it would have been *me* who would have been living in a fool's paradise. So I should be thankful. Yes, thankful that I know what he's really like. And I will be thankful. I *am*. Melissa might be engaged to him, but it's *me* who can see him for what he is . . . a no-good gold digger. She's welcome to him. No, that's not true, Mellie deserves better than him.

86

Following the known paths and bridleways she took a circuitous route bringing her back at last to the cattle grid and the grounds of Kyneston. She hadn't realized how long she'd been out, the house was in darkness except for a strip of light telling her she'd not quite closed the curtains in her own room where she'd left the lamp burning. The day had been momentous for her and for Melissa too. She thought it was over, but it hadn't finished with her yet.

'Wherever have you been?' A starry-eyed Melissa was sitting up in bed. 'Fancy going out when we had visitors! Really Georgina you do the funniest things. Anyway, never mind that. I've got lots to tell you. I got into your bed, that's all right isn't it? Hurry up and get undressed.'

'To tell me?'

'Not till you're in bed. I want all your attention. Oh Georgina you know what I'm going to say, you must know.'

'You are betrothed to John.'

'Don't say it like that, as if it weren't the most thrilling thing in the world. How did you know? Did he tell you on the boat that he was going to ask Uncle Cedric's consent this evening.'

'We didn't mention you. As I came down the stairs I heard them in the library, your uncle was explaining your legacy – yours and mine too.' As soon as she'd said it she felt sure that Melissa must remember how she'd been late coming to the dinner table, and would know that after hearing them talking she had escaped back to her room. From that it would be only one short step to realizing what she'd been running away from. But no, Melissa's mind was on other things.

'You saw how he took me away after dinner. Georgina it was so romantic, better even than I'd dreamed it would be. We walked in the rose garden. It's a pity the flowers weren't in bloom yet – well only the odd one or two – but it was getting dark so they wouldn't really have shown up. Anyway, I want to tell you . . . He said he was glad it had been raining, no one else would come outside,' she laughed happily as she said it. 'As if they were likely to when they must have known why he'd taken me out there. You know what he said? He told me that all his life he'd be drawn to beautiful things and I was the most beautiful person he'd ever known. When he told me he'd spoken to Uncle Cedric – oh, I can't tell you. Well you wouldn't understand, you've never been in love.

When he asked me to marry him I said he'd have to ask me properly, down on one knee,' and remembering she chuckled as if so much happiness couldn't be contained, 'even though the path was wet that's what he did. You've never really said – don't you think he is the most handsome, dashing young man you've ever seen? Not that you've seen many so how can you know? Tell me you're happy for me.'

'If he truly loves you then of course I am. But Mellie, would he still want you if you had no fortune? You've got to be sure. I told you, your uncle was telling him everything about your income. And would you love him if, oh I don't know, if he had an accident, wasn't handsome any longer?'

'That's just stupid. Of course he'll go on being handsome. And of course he talked to Uncle Cedric about my inheritance. After all, once we're man and wife (doesn't that sound grand!) man and wife,' she repeated for good measure, 'he will have control of my affairs. Here's your nightgown, do hurry up. Then we can make plans for the wedding. I wanted it to be in June. It'll be the most wonderful day of my life and I wanted it to be the longest day of the year. But Aunt Alice said that is too soon, she said I'd need longer to see to having a proper trousseau made. So she is going to send out the invitations for the third Saturday in July. She said she saw no reason for me to have a Maid of Honour, but I insisted – I just wouldn't listen to any arguments, you would have been proud of the way I stood up for you – so in the end it was agreed that you're to be my Maid.' She held back the covers and Georgina got into bed by her side. Her voice rattled on. 'Aunt Alice still has the wreath and veil my own mother wore. She said she was the most beautiful bride and that I'm just like her. I want everything white, all the flowers in the church, everything. You're to wear white too.'

'Maids of Honour don't dress like brides, of course I can't wear white.'

'Of course you can. White is pure, I'm not having any colour at all. But your gown will be quite different from mine of course, very plain and you won't have a veil or anything. We'll have to see your hair is covered with a cap of some sort, it's so vivid it would spoil the effect if it showed. Mine will look right showing, being so fair. You will carry a posy of white rosebuds, and I shall have a bouquet of white blooms. Aunt Alice says she can remember everything about my parents' wedding. My mother had everything white – but she carried a white prayerbook and she passed her bouquet to Aunt Alice in the front pew – there was no Maid of Honour. That's what she wanted me to do. But I *insisted*. Don't you think it sounds just perfect?'

She seemed set to talk all night.

Early in the week when John told them of his intention to return to London he had said he'd take the train from Brockenhurst just after midday. But a lot had happened since then and Georgina wasn't surprised when, the next morning, there was no sign of him saddling Cleo for their daily ride. She told herself she was relieved, but there was no running away from the scenes that had forced themselves into her imagination: John telling her that already he knew he'd made a mistake, one that he meant to correct before it was too late; John telling her that she was the only woman he could ever love; John begging her to listen. And her reaction? Turning the knife in the wound she'd pictured herself telling him that she too had made a mistake; yesterday ought never to have happened and all she wanted was for both of them to forget it. As for his plea for her love, it would salve her pride if not her hurt to scorn him.

None of that happened. She rode alone. Returning round the bend of the drive she saw the carriage was already at the foot of the front steps, John about to climb aboard.

'You haven't seen John to congratulate him,' Melissa called, excitement and pride helping her overcome her dread of Cleo coming too close. 'Do come on, he's just going.'

'Oh, but I do congratulate him. I knew his intention before you did yourself, Mellie, I told you I heard him talking with your uncle.' No one could take exception at her words, and only John saw the mocking contempt in her eyes as, without dismounting, she leaned down to hold her hand towards him. 'Treat her well or you'll have *me* to reckon with.'

'Oh, what a thing to say. Of course he'll treat me well. Georgina always manages to put a blanket of cloud over any exciting thing that happens to me.'

John ignored Melissa, his gaze fixed on Georgina.

'It's been good, our riding, our sailing ...' He sounded friendly, as if he meant his words to set the tone for a future fraternal relationship.

89

Leaving them to say their farewells (and surprised that Melissa wasn't driving with him to Brockenhurst) she walked Cleo round the side of the house to the stable yard. In those next minutes two things imprinted themselves indelibly on her mind: one, the sound of the carriage moving away along the drive, then the rumble as it crossed the cattle grid onto the forest road; the second, a confusion of emotion as she lowered herself from the saddle certain without a shadow of doubt that two days ahead of its time her period had started. She was thankful, of course she was thankful she told herself. And yet what could have drawn a final line under the last few weeks more firmly?

'He was anxious to get back to London, he didn't even wait for a proper breakfast.' Melissa told her later. Anxious to get away without seeing *me*, Georgina answered silently, unwilling to delve into why she should find satisfaction in the thought. 'He'll be wanting to see his uncle and tell him. Sir Edmund and Lady Northney will be delighted, I told you I could see it's what they were hoping. And it's not just me who'll have things to organize, John has to find us a home. I want it to be right in town, some-where central where I can entertain. Just imagine it, Georgina,' she giggled like an excited child, ' "Mrs John Derrick will be At Home . . ." You must come and stay. I'll find a young man for you too, I promised didn't I? I'm off to Hapley, I want to talk to Aunt Alice. Don't be surprised if I'm not back until this evening.'

During the following weeks Melissa was away more than at home. The two aunts escorted her back to London, where she was in seventh heaven choosing material, having fittings, going with John to look at houses. Despite it not being as large and grand as she had dreamed, she was delighted with the property they found to rent. The time would come when they would move into some-thing more substantial and befitting to the status of Sir John and Lady (how wonderful it was to dream!), but in the meantime she could be proud of her new London address, it wasn't in some dreary suburb. Willingly she left John to organize the interior: curtains, rugs, furniture, right down to the last silver teaspoon their home was a show case of his taste. For herself she delighted in being certain that anything he (or his Great uncle Edmund) chose must be correct and was content to concentrate on herself, her wedding day, her wardrobe, her plans for making a reputation as a hostess. Her trousseau, and that included her bridal gown, was being fashioned in London so she grudged any time she spent at Kyneston during those weeks leading up to her Big Day.

Miss Dunkley, a local seamstress, was sent to Kyneston to measure Georgina.

'I'm to work from this picture,' she told her, 'that's the instruction I've had from Hapley Court. All in white, I understand, bleached white cotton. Not like any wedding I've sewn for before, but if that's the way Miss Rochester wants it, then who are we to argue. It's *her* day.'

The design of Georgina's gown was simple: none of the high shoulders of fashion or leg-of-mutton sleeves, her white cotton gown was exaggeratedly plain with a stiffened high neck. It wasn't shaped but back and front cut to hang from the shoulders, then held by a white sash made of the same white cotton plaited to resemble a cord so that it fitted her slim waist. Her hair was to be completely hidden (for no colour must be allowed to spoil the effect of virginal whiteness), and to this end she was to wear something that resembled a nun's wimple. Melissa – or Aunt Alice! – had had another thought on the subject of the Maid of Honour. No longer was the idea for her to carry a posy of white rosebuds; the decision that she should hold a white prayerbook no doubt had its roots in the nunlike outfit. Her role was to emphasize the purity of the bride.

'I shall look ridiculous, it's like fancy dress,' she said on one of Melissa's short visits home. 'I've a good mind to say I won't do it.'

'Oh, don't spoil things! You're always doing it. But I'm not going to let you. No one will notice you anyway, that's the whole idea of having you dressed plainly. Please Georgina, this is *my* special day. Anyway you won't look ridiculous, it would be stupid to dress you in something as gorgeous as my gown. This is plain and simple. It'll be *me* everyone is looking at. I don't think I've ever been so excited. Well, of course I haven't, this will be the most thrilling day of my whole life.'

'I hope it isn't!' Georgina stamped down her natural irritation. 'This is just the beginning.' She took a sadistic pleasure in torturing herself. 'Imagine the day you have your first child, when they allow John into your room to see you and the baby—'

'That won't be for ages. I'm not a bit keen and he's never hinted that he is either. To be honest, Georgina – and I wouldn't talk about – well, all that sort of thing – to anyone but you – but I do hope he doesn't expect me to have children for ages. Aunt Alice told me . . . I think she was embarrassed, but she made herself do it. I don't feel ready for us to face all that sort of thing. Anyway, we shall be having far too much fun with our friends. Let's think about the wedding. Have you got my mother's prayerbook safely?'

Georgina opened the drawer of her chest and handed it to her, surprised at Melissa's quick frown.

'Will it look white enough? It's starting to go quite yellow.'

'No one's going to look at me so you needn't worry.' This time Georgina didn't bother to hide her irritation but it was lost on Melissa.

'I expect you're right. And I can't upset Aunt Alice by saying I want a new book, she really meant me to carry it like my mother did. But I persuaded her. Oh Georgina, I hope all this happens to you one day, it's so thrillingly exciting. I'll find you a husband, just wait until I get to London.'

Georgina kept her back turned as she hung up her 'fancy dress' and covered it with a white sheet. In that moment she came near to hating Melissa. Yet was she being fair? Poor Mellie, she believed John was prompted by no motive except love. 'And perhaps he is, perhaps I'm the only one he deceived.'

It was the morning of the wedding, Georgina already in her nun-like outfit, was helping Melissa to dress.

'It's a secret really, so promise you won't tell anyone. When we come home from our honeymoon John will tell Sir Edmund, but until then we're not telling a soul so you mustn't either.'

'What?' Georgina's imagination took her back to the cabin of *Cork's Screw* and for one wild moment she expected to hear that Melissa had something the same to tell her, even that she was pregnant. What else could it be?

'Once we are settled in our new home, John is going to leave Northney's. He's going to open his own gallery. Promise – word of honour – you'll not breathe a word. He's wanted to do it for ages but you can't stock a Gallery without capital.'

'You mean you are giving him the money? You mean he asked you?' Georgina's last trace of respect for him melted.

'You wouldn't understand. It's for my sake as well as his. One of these days his name will be known, he's an authority already but all his knowledge is used for Northney's. He exports goods to the New World – nothing to do with Northney's, this is a business he's been building for himself. But it's still small, he hasn't the money to invest.'

'You mean he exports in his own name? But when he goes to buy its for Northney's.'

'That's what they all think,' Melissa laughed. 'everyone knows he bids for Northney's. But he doesn't use Sir Edmund's money, not for things he buys for himself. Of course he buys for Northney's and, as he says, he always pays a fair price. But some of the small things, small but easily exportable, he buys for himself. Can you bring my hair forward a bit more, I want some curl to show in front of the veil.'

'If he has no money how can he buy good pieces for himself?' He was a cheat, a rotter. Georgina wanted the pain of hearing the worst.

'That's what I thought. But he explained. He travels to many a sale, sale of contents of houses, that sort of thing. Not big enough to attract a lot of attention, but houses that always have at least a *few* things worth having. Because he comes from Northney's the auctioneers look up to his knowledge. And when he sees something he knows is right to ship out to the New World he starts the bidding very low, he lets it be seen he isn't terribly interested – and that gives a clue to other bidders. He's able to buy well. But he doesn't do the sellers down, when he bids for Northney's he always pays a fair price, even pushes the bidding high. So he isn't really cheating.'

'No? Anyway, that's before you came into the picture. So now he will use your money – oh Mellie, don't let him use you as he has those poor souls who have been selling up their homes.'

'You're being stupid, melodramatic. I've told him I want him to use anything I have. Don't you see, he has to stock a new gallery, Derrick's Fine Arts, that's what it's to be known as. And it will be *known*, all over the country, just like Northney's is.' She hugged herself in her excitement, then turned back to the mirror, only throwing in a final, 'But you're to forget I told you. And about the export business, his uncle doesn't know anything about that.'

What Georgian heard surely took away any last vestige of respect she might have harboured for John.

The third Saturday in July had dawned with the promise of a perfect summer day. John and the Northneys had all arrived on the Friday and were staying at Hapley Court. Alice was delighted at playing hostess to Sir Edmund and his wife, not for the world would she have agreed to their suggestion that they should all lodge in the coaching inn at Lymington. As Melissa was to be given away by her uncle, he had to collect her from Kyneston to escort her to the church.

Biggs drove Patience and Georgina, then, having deposited them at the lychgate of the church, turned back towards Kyneston to collect Mrs Biggs and any members of the staff he could crowd into the carriage, meeting them as they walked the mile of forest road. With Patience already seated in the front pew on the left hand side of the aisle, Georgina waited alone in the porch. And that's where John found her when he and his cousin Rupert arrived.

'I hardly recognized you,' was his friendly greeting, just as if their last day together had never happened. 'For one moment I thought you'd taken Holy Orders! This is Georgina, Rupert, Melissa's step-sister. It's a sin to cover her head like that, she has the sort of hair men write poetry about.'

Rupert took the hand she held to him, but she felt she made no impression on him.

'Yes,' John enlarged. 'Hair the colour of deep amber'.

'Or carrots.' With her head high, Georgina's smile was brittle. It was pride that made her turn his compliment into a joke. 'Depending on whether you happen to be a poet or an honest man.'

'Go on in Rupert, make sure you still have the ring and everything is in order. I'll stay and keep Georgina company until I see Melissa's carriage coming.'

'There's no need. I'm perfectly happy on my own.'

But Rupert had gone.

'Of course you are. Georgina, we've always been friends, we mustn't let anything alter that. You must have known I would marry Melissa?' Was it meant as a statement or a question?

'I know just what you hope to gain from marriage to her if that's what you mean.'

He ignored her inference. 'You're blaming me for what happened on the boat. Is that why you're angry? You were as keen as I was. If I'd refused to let it happen would you have felt any more kindly towards me now?'

If he'd hit her she couldn't have felt more shocked. For one unguarded moment they looked at each other in silent misery.

'But I couldn't refuse,' he told her, 'any more than you could – any more than I can forget. For both of us it was an hour of madness, a glorious hour.'

She wanted him gone. No that wasn't true, she wanted him here with her. Before she could hold it back her imagination leaped ahead, she cold almost feel the pressure of his hands on her shoulders, she had no power to turn away from him. Only in the secret silence of her mind she heard him telling her there could never be anyone else for him except her. Another scene rushing in before the first had played itself out: they were facing the congregation, telling them the wedding couldn't go ahead, already they were lovers joined together body and soul in that 'glorious hour of madness'.

He didn't reach out to touch her. She pulled her imagination into check, remembering Melissa.

'Glorious?' she question him. 'You profess to love Mellie . . . she's my sister . . . I'd never been disloyal to her . . . do you call cheating her glorious?'

They could hear the sound of a carriage approaching along the lane to the church.

'You blame me.' This time he did take her hands in his. 'I had no more power to stop what happened than I did to still the storm. I must go inside, here are Mrs Sylvester and my uncle and aunt.'

And he was gone, walking purposefully up the aisle to take his seat next to his best man.

'Dearly beloved brethren, we are gathered here in the sight of God and in the face of this congregation to join together this man and this woman in Holy Matrimony . . .'

Just look at Melissa . . . how could he not be in love with her when she is so beautiful, so trusting? An hour of madness, that's what he called it, yes but a glorious hour, something he'll never forget, something he was powerless to prevent . . . If he'd been in love with Melissa it could never have happened . . . all that I am I gave him . . . gave him? . . . give him? . . . every inch of my body, every secret of my soul . . . and wasn't it like that for him too? Wasn't it? He can't marry Melissa, he could never love her with all that he is . . .

The Rector's voice boomed on: '. . . if any man can shew any just cause why they may not lawfully be joined together let him now speak or else hereafter for ever hold his peace.'

John and Melissa were standing half turned towards each other by the chancel step, Georgina only feet away. The church was full and yet the words the Rector spoke seemed to echo and vibrate as if in an empty hall. Even now it wasn't too late. Yes, I do, her heart screamed. Had she made some sound, or did only John hear her silent cry? Turning his head his gaze held hers, she felt that he defied her to speak.

Melissa passed her her bouquet; the moment was lost.

'Wilt thou have this woman to thy wedded wife . . . wilt thou love her, comfort her . . . forsaking all other, keep thee only unto her . . .'

'I will.' John's response was firm and clear.

The perfume of the white roses was overpowering. All around her Georgina was aware of the satisfaction and happiness of the 'happy couple's' families and friends, even Mrs Biggs was shedding a tear of rare and happy emotion.

'With this ring I thee wed, with my body I thee worship, and with all my worldly goods I thee endow . . .'

Worldly goods! What worldly goods? 'With all your worldly goods thou me endow' that's what you should be saying, her heart screamed out to him. Here in church you can make solemn vows, sell your soul and your freedom, and all these people are looking at you and thinking what a splendid fellow you are. Well, I'll make a solemn vow too: I vow that I'll put you right out of my head. You are Mellie's husband, that and nothing more. And you'd better be good to her too.

The service had gone ahead, Rupert was leading her forward to follow the bride and groom to the vestry to sign the register while twelve angelic-looking choir boys entreated 'God be in my Head and in my understanding . . .'

* * *

96

'I wish you were coming too,' Melissa told Georgina, holding her in an unusual and fierce hug. 'It was different when I went just for a little while at a time, but now I'm going for good, I hate to think what a dull time you'll be having.'

Georgina's answer was more for John's ears than for Melissa's.

'If you think that, you think wrong. My life is never dull.'

Perhaps John heard her, Melissa certainly didn't. Already she'd turned to say goodbye to her favourite aunt.

'May I kiss my new sister?' John had taken her place in front of Georgina, who coolly proffered her cheek. 'Friends?' he asked in a whisper.

'As long as you are good to Mellie.' She noticed the way he looked at the party gathered around his new wife, the buzz of their farewells evidence that his conversation with a mere Maid of Honour wasn't interesting them.

'You think I won't be?'

'I think it doesn't take much to distract you.'

'That's not fair,' still he whispered, 'and it's not true. I'll never forget those morning rides, nor our trips out in *Cork's Screw*. I'll not forget a single moment—'

'Anyway, whether we're friends or not isn't going to be important. Once Melissa has her home in London she may even decide to sell Kyneston. You'll probably show her ways she'll prefer to use her income rather than the upkeep of a home she doesn't use. With half a house and virtually no income – what was it you called it? A liability rather than an asset, that was it.'

'All ready, my boy?' Sir Edmund interrupted them, a tall man, age and a slight stoop robbing him of none of his dignity.

Georgina moved away. Standing aside from the gathering she felt isolated. Many of the guests were friends of the Sylvesters, people who had gone out of their way to ignore her mother. She looked at them with contempt, there wasn't one she would want to call her friend. Friends . . . was that what he really thought they could be? If he and Melissa were to have a happy marriage that's what she must make sure they became.

She watched him hand Melissa into the carriage, Melissa with stars in her eyes and transparent faith in him. All her resentment was aimed at John, handsome, confident, no doubt pleased with himself for the financial gains the day was bringing him.

As soon as they'd gone she changed from her nun-like outfit and no one tried to dissuade her when she said she was going home.

She pretended it was because she'd eaten too much at the wedding breakfast that she didn't want her supper that evening, but once she was in bed and the lamp out there was nowhere to hide from the truth. Nothing would ever been quite the same again, it was as if part of herself had been lost. Where would Melissa be now? In her mind she followed them. If she'd tried to turn her thoughts away it would have been impossible, but as it was she took sadistic pleasure in punishing herself. It wasn't right to pile all the blame on John, she had been as eager as he had himself . . . as powerless to stop herself.

There was more pain than pleasure in remembering, in imagining. In the secrecy of her lonely bed her hands moved over her slim body, with her eyes tightly closed she relived that moment when he'd knelt in front of her drawing her close, the first electric thrill that had set every nerve in her body tingling . . . What had he done to her that she had no more power to stop herself now than she'd had when they'd rushed headlong into such wild and wonderful love. Imagine this were him, imagine the warm pressure of his mouth, the caress of his tongue, imagine how my body ached to be part of him, imagine . . . Catching the sheet between her teeth she clamped it hard to stifle any sound. In her mind she heard her voice cry out, hers and his too. Body and soul they were one, she'd been so sure. Those whom God has joined together . . .

She lay breathless, her cheeks were wet with tears, joy had gone and all that was left was a lonely dark room. Her pounding heart mocked her as she faced the truth. John was no raw novice, she was probably just one of a whole host of women; but Melissa was his wife.

Turning on her side Georgina buried her head in the pillow. She felt debased by her own actions.

Chapter Six

Melissa wanted the day never to end. Not one single thing had disappointed her. Friends of her uncle and aunt, family she hardly knew and, some of them, who had made long journeys specially to be at her wedding, Sir Edmund (she would have to call him Uncle Edmund now – it seemed a shame to waste a title) and Lady Northney (Aunt Kathleen – another waste), all John's family; she'd been aware that every one of them had looked on her with admiration and approval. More than that, how simply wonderful it had been to see the proud and loving way her uncle and aunt had gazed at her. Even Georgina hadn't made horrid remarks about the 'precious aunt' as she often did. No, every single thing had been perfect.

Her mind had been so caught up in its own whirl of excitement that she hadn't noticed how quiet John had been. Even as the train sped them on their way to a honeymoon in Bath her happy chatter needed no help, his monosyllabic replies were enough to keep her steady flow going.

'Isn't this splendid!' Arriving at their hotel late in the evening she looked admiringly around their room. More than a room, it was a small suite: apart from a fourposter bed and the normal bedroom furnishings, their elegant room contained a chaise-longue, a Queen Anne table and two chairs as beautiful as any she'd seen. Three doors led from it: one to the corridor; one to a small dressing room furnished with an enormous walnut wardrobe with fitted drawers, a chair and a long mirror; and the third to a room containing a bath even more splendid than the one they had been so proud of when Father had had it fitted at Kyneston, an enormous enamelled tub standing on four tall, claw-like gilt feet.

99

At Kyneston the warmth of the water depended on the heat of the fire in the kitchen range, she wondered idly what sort of inferno could supply water for a hotel like this. Not for long did she dwell on it, like a butterfly her mind flitted on to the next attraction. The drapes on the bed were white, how utterly perfect! That she would have to curl up for sleep next to John and, worse, wake up tousled next to him momentarily cast a shadow but it was driven away by the arrival of two waiters wheeling a trolley with their supper. This time she looked at John with open admiration that he could have organized everything so well and so extravagantly. How was she to guess that the honeymoon was a gift from Sir Edmund?

Only once had Melissa stayed in a hotel – and that in Bournemouth where she and Georgina had shared one room and Clive and Augusta another – never had waiters attended her in her room with the silver service. They called her 'Madam', John referred to her as 'my wife' as if he'd had a lifetime of experience. She was almost too excited to eat.

If she wanted the day to last for ever, it seemed John didn't. As soon as they'd finished their meal he rang the bell to have the plates removed.

'This has been the best day of all my life,' she told him, her lovely eyes wide with the wonder of it all. 'Isn't it a pity we have to get tired. Where are you going to take me tomorrow? You said there's so much to see here.'

'Today isn't over yet.' Taking her hands he pulled her to her feet and held her against him. How nice he smelt. She was glad she'd married him. Imagine if she'd been here with Archie Blachford, his pimply face rubbing against her hair.

'Bedtime,' John whispered.

Really she wasn't a bit tired, but perhaps he was and anyway Aunt Alice had always told her that if you wanted to look your best in the morning it was important to get a good night's sleep. She'd said that to Georgina once, she remembered, and Georgina had scoffed that 'precious Aunt Alice must have some jolly disturbed nights'. Thinking of Georgina she was suddenly scared. They used to talk together as they'd started to grow up, sharing anything they learnt about what she thought of as 'babies and all that sort of thing'. But there was no need to be scared, she told herself, as she'd said to Georgina it would be years before she and John wanted children – 'years and perhaps never' was her secret hope – so she wasn't going to spoil the ending of this perfect day by worrying about the half-understood and wholly uncomfortable sermon she'd had from Aunt Alice.

Instead she hid herself in the ornate bathroom, carefully closing the door behind her, and changed into her specially made white silk nightgown. How pretty it was with its frill at the neck and around the cuffs, she felt like a bride all over again. She was torn between getting into bed so that she could have the covers pulled around her shoulders before John emerged from the dressing room or taking time so that she could see his look of admiration as he watched her sitting in front of the mirror brushing her hair. Still undecided she was standing before the dressing table when John came back, a stranger in dark red silk pyjamas and with his heavily embossed long brocade dressing gown draped around his shoulders as she'd often seen him wear his evening cape.

His dark, brooding expression was unsettling. Where was the look of admiring adoration she'd expected?

'Don't you think it's pretty?' Like a child in a party dress she twirled in front of him.

'Too pretty to crumple.'

'I'll be careful. Anyway, I never toss and turn very much.' She caught her lower lip between her teeth, but there was no way of catching her fast ebbing confidence. Not sure what made her do it, she lowered her eyes to the tied cord of his pyjamas, then to what made her raise them again with a start. 'I must brush my hair.' She said the first thing that came into her head, then added, 'Or do you want to do it for me?' She had a romantic notion that brushing her golden glory would be the ultimate joy to end his day. If she could have seen into his mind, known the anger that raged in him – anger against himself, against Georgina for the scorn she showed him, against Georgina too that what he'd intended to be no more than a brief interlude was impossible to forget, against his own body's disregard now for the confusion that raged in him as it sent the blood pulsing through his veins in anticipation, and against Melissa that she understood no more about desire than if she'd been a beautiful china doll.

What have I done? I've sold my soul for a handful of silver. Silver, brittle, cold silver. Dear God, if this were Georgina . . . but it isn't. Melissa is my wife . . . forsaking all other. She's beautiful, her body is probably as perfect as her face. Probably? A sleeping beauty . . . I can wake her . . . I can turn her from a lovely child into a warm, passionate woman . . .

He was aware of the sudden tension in her body as he took her into his arms, with one hand exploring the gentle curve of her small, firm breast. His mouth sought hers. She didn't draw back, so how was it he was so sure that she surrendered to him from dutiful obedience.

'My lovely wife,' he murmured, changing his hold on her so that even though one arm anchored her as firmly, his hand moved down the length of her spine. Determined that she should relax, that he would find a way to awaken the passion that surely must be waiting to be stirred, the hand that had aroused no response from her small breast moved on, raising the smooth silk of her long nightgown.

'No,' she whispered, suddenly electrified into action as she tried to push her skirt down. She had been alarmed and embarrassed when, through the delicate silk, his hand had found her breast. Now it was more than fright that made her try to force him off, it was revulsion. She was ready for him to touch her face, her arms, even ber throat (in fact in her more romantic moments she had imagined herself – fully clothed of course, not like this in nothing but a thin nightgown – cradling his head to her breast), but to have his hand trying to explore – no, it was disgusting! Her body was her own, it was private. She and her aunt had been as embarrassed as each other as Alice had done the dutiful thing in an attempt to ensure that she knew how she might expect to conceive a child; she hadn't delved into anything she hadn't properly understood, after all if the time came that she and John wanted a family she would have to succumb to his doing that hard to imagine and, as she thought of it, 'disgusting' thing to her. But that would be for a purpose. And it wouldn't be *yet*. Children had no place in the lifestyle that awaited them. Now it was as if he was a hungry animal trying to devour her. As he loosened his hold on her she stepped back, but his movement was quick and she was unprepared.

He dropped to his knees in front of her. Only minutes ago she'd delighted in her exquisite new nightgown, now the material was unceremoniously pushed almost to her waist, his face pressed against her. Humiliated and unable to escape from his hold, she looked down at him. There was no tenderness, no reverence in

102

what he did. She saw him as driven by something outside himself, something evil. Could she but have read his mind she would have known his angry despair, have known that his imagination was taking him back to that first moment with Georgina. Melissa heard a strange, suppressed moan, but how was she to know that he heard it not as his own voice but Georgina's.

Just as suddenly as he'd dropped to his knees, now he knelt back on his heels, letting her nightgown fall.

'. . . beastly thing to do,' she whispered, appalled. 'Get up. Don't say anything.' Any fear she'd felt at his first touch had been swamped by angry disgust. Her voice was small, the anger was hidden, only the disgust was there for him to hear. She *had* to say it. It couldn't be right. Her body was private . . .

'I frightened you, I shouldn't have.' Still kneeling he looked up at this cold, beautiful girl who was his wife. 'I didn't mean to frighten you. You're so lovely.'

Ah, that was better. She even managed a smile as she held her hands to raise him to his feet and when he held her close against him she raised her face to his as a sign that she meant to forgive him for his uncontrolled lapse. They mustn't end their wedding day – this day that had been so perfect – under a cloud. His mouth covered hers, feeling his tongue reminded her of what she wanted to forget. Stiff as a ramrod she stood held tightly against him, understanding the one thing that had remained a mystery from her Aunt Alice's 'little talk'; the thing that, fearing Georgina might laugh at her, she had never liked to talk about.

'I'll try not to hurt you,' he whispered, his mouth moving only far enough for hers to form the words, as he eased her backwards and pressed her down to lie across the bed.

Too late she struggled, there was no chance of escape. Unerringly he steered himself into her. She tried to move away, this was beyond her worst nightmare. Was this how Aunt Alice had know it would be when she'd said he would plant a seed from his body into hers? Her aunt's embarrassment and her own had made it impossible to delve into the details. But Aunt Alice had said that was when they wanted a family . . .

Clenching her teeth she lay as still and unyielding as a log, hardly daring to breathe, except that this time when he touched her breast she pushed his hand roughly away. How long would she have to lie like this? It was hateful, surely it must be hateful for

103

him too. It was as if he was running a race, making a last final effort to reach the finishing post with a triumphant cry of exaltation. She opened her eyes, hating his contorted expression, hating *him*.

Then he rolled off her still gasping for breath. 'I wanted it to be good for you too,' he panted. 'truly I tried not to hurt. Next time will be easier.' (Again he was on that narrow bunk on the boat. 'I mustn't hurt you . . .' 'Yes, hurt me, hurt me . . .') He turned his face away from Melissa. His heart still pounding, his body sapped of strength, he was filled with self-loathing. When his breath caught in his throat, he clenched his jaw.

Melissa's perfect day was over, there was nothing of the excited child who moved across to the dressing table and sat down to brush her hair. Even in the mirror she wouldn't look at him.

Far into the night sleep eluded Melissa. 'Making love', that's what John called it as they had lain side by side in the large fourposter bed, and 'next time' as if it were something they did for pleasure. He had talked to her gently, kissed her goodnight tenderly and with none of that greedy uncontrolled passion. 'Making love' . . . but where was the love in it, it was bestial, disgusting, it turned him into a stranger. Memory took another leap and she was in the study of the rectory having lessons from Reverend Carter. He used to start each morning with a reading from the Bible. It must have been during Lent, a time when the readings had always been miserable, that his warnings had been against fornication and lusts of the flesh. Georgina had been good at remembering difficult words so they had looked up 'fornication' in the dictionary when they got home but they hadn't been much the wiser any more than they'd known what he meant by 'lusts of the flesh'. Now she understood. John called it loving, but lusting was the real name.

She felt she'd never be clean again. Chasing sleep she tried to think of other things: of the home that waited for her in London, of the lovely furniture Sir Edmund – no, Uncle Edmund – had given them. Perhaps it wouldn't happen again like last night, that might have been because having a wife was new and exciting for him. She must close her eyes tight and make herself sleep or she would have shadows under them on their first full day of being married.

* * *

104

Back in London in the house John had rented (a good address, as she'd stressed when she'd given it to Georgina), those first weeks held as much as she'd hoped. A middle-aged widow rejoicing in the name of Esmerelda Wilmott had been recommended to her by one of the Northney cousins. In her turn Mrs Wilmott had vouched for a young niece of her own, Jessie Simms, who could come in daily and 'would be licked into shape in next to no time.' As for other staff, there was a woman to collect the washing and bring it back ironed, another to do the scrubbing, chop the wood, clean the drains. The housekeeper was given a free hand. Esmerelda – or Mrs Wilmott as Melissa always called her – proved to be an excellent cook and nothing pleased her more than to have a dinner party to cater for, which was fortunate for in those first weeks they were rarely alone in the evenings.

Sir Edmund and his wife were amongst their first guests; Melissa blossomed under their obvious admiration.

It was a morning towards the end of August when Sir Edmund sent for John to come to his private room at the gallery.

'Good morning, Uncle.' John had no suspicion how soon his confidence was to be toppled. 'I have a message from Melissa, she hopes you and Aunt Sarah will—'

'I want an explanation – indeed I deserve it and I demand it young sir.' There were occasions when Sir Edmund's arthritis made his mood peppery; John, his cousins and his uncles too had all suffered the consequences. 'You attended Milbourne Grange last month, I have here a list of the porcelain you purchased – and I might say purchased at a higher price than I would have myself.'

The first of John's alarm bells rang, but he gave no sign of it.

'It's a long time since you attended a sale, sir, you probably still think in terms of a few guineas—'

'I'll thank you not to tell me my own business.'

The bells rang louder.

'I beg your pardon, Uncle, that certainly wasn't what I meant to infer.'

With narrowed eyes the elderly man considered him.

'I'd been a visitor at Milbourne Grange. Perhaps you weren't aware that I was familiar with the items in the catalogue. There was a particularly beautiful garniture of vases, Sèvres, personally I considered the gilt jewelling to be the work of Erienne-Henri Le Guay.'

105

'My opinion too, sir. They were quite exquisite. But if you complain about the prices I paid, I can only be glad I fell out of the bidding for the Sèvres vases.'

Sir Edmund said not a word. John's heart was hammering, his alarm bells deafening him.

'Is something worrying you, sir?'

'Worrying me? No. Sickening me? Yes, young sir, *you* are. I dined with Archibald de Vere last night. Let me refresh your memory. Archibald de Vere inherited Milbourne Grange from his bachelor uncle and sold the contents before putting the house on the market. Imagine his surprise when I asked him about the vases. Imagine mine too when he told me who had bid for them – bid for them after giving his opinioned reasoning why they weren't decorated to Erienne-Henri Le Guay's standard. Out of step with today's prices, you call me? One thing I know: de Vere was cheated. Cheated in the name of Northney's, cheated by one of my own kinsman. No,' as he saw John about to sit in the leather chair facing him, 'I want you standing if you please. Understand one thing, no man can serve two masters. If you didn't buy the Sèvres vases for Northney's, then for whom? And I want the truth.'

'You shall have it. I didn't buy them for Northney's, I bought them for myself.'

'For Melissa? But why couldn't you have told me?'

'I said for myself. You've asked me, so I'll tell you. They aren't the first items I've bought – not with *Northney's* money but with my own. All right, I'm recognized as bringing Northney's expertise, but this firm has never been cheated. For years I've had two masters, the first is myself, the second is Northney's.'

'And where might I ask do you place the goods you buy?'

'Not in London. I ship them to America. Prices are good there. When the money comes in I buy more. Would *you* have been content to spend your life buying and selling for someone else? Of course you wouldn't. And neither am I.'

All the cards on the table, the two men glared at each other, Edmund with anger, John with defiance that hid a new sense of freedom.

'All you know you owe to me,' Sir Edmund might have been talking to a wilful child. 'Is this how you show your gratitude?'

'You've had your pound of flesh. All right, it was you who

106

awakened my interest, gave me a thirst for knowledge. But this profession isn't one that can be learned from any master, it comes from reading, yes of course it does, but more than that it comes from experience, it comes from instinct and from an inner eye, from love of craftsmanship—' He broke off. The driving force in his life was his work, his love for the things he handled. Often enough he talked about the items themselves – but never about how deeply he loved what he did, how humbled he felt when he held a piece crafted perhaps 200 or 300 years ago, crafted with patience and dedication into a thing of beauty. So now he broke off mid-sentence, wishing he could recall his words.

His outburst had been lost on Sir Edmund, who still looked at him with the air of a headmaster looking for a fair punishment to mete out on first-former found cheating.

'For years you've deceived me, you tell me so with no feeling of shame—'

'Shame? What shame should I have? In these last years, Northney's has gained a reputation for expertise in porcelain and pottery. And who has been responsible for that? I have. But no more. From now on, I'm on my own. Give me a few months to get established and I'll give Northney's a run for your money.'

He'd done it! The die was cast, now it was up to him to carve his own future. John's relief was twofold: in part it was a feeling of freedom, and it part it was thankfulness that Melissa's money gave substance to his plans for a gallery of his own.

He was late home that evening, but his day hadn't been wasted. Leaving Sir Edmund's room he had collected his hat and cane and walked out of the door of Northney's without a backward glance. The day was put to good use: he'd known of a nearby property to rent, all that had prevented him previously was that last and final decision. But now that was behind him and before he returned home in the evening he had seen the landlord, agreed the terms of a lease, and engaged decorators to start work as soon as the legal work was done.

Melissa was delighted. Now he wasn't just an employee of Sir Edmund, he was his own man. In her mind Derrick's was on a par with Northney's already. That the money behind the project was hers didn't interest her, her sights were firmly on the future.

With a new business to set up and so much to fill his mind, she

107

felt sure he would have better ways of tiring himself than putting
her through the nightly degradation she dreaded. John called it
making love, he expected her to be eager, sometimes she even
suspected he'd be pleased if she pretended to get as excited and
uncontrolled as he did. Hating what she had to endure was only
one stage from hating John himself. All her life she had given way
to outbursts of rage and despair that had appeared out of all
proportion to those who had had to suffer her moods. But this was
different. This time she was like a prisoner with no hope of
escape. As the next weeks went by tension built in her as if a
spring was being wound ever tighter until one day it must surely
snap. But if it did, what then? What of all her dreams of the future
when the Derrick Gallery would be as recognized and respected as
Northney's, what of the place she was certain she would hold in
London society? If that was to be her reward, she had no choice
but to grit her teeth and endure. So she steeled herself to accept
John's 'love making' or, as she thought of it, 'his bestial lust'. The
spring tightened, it strained and quivered . . .

'Why don't we invite your Sir Edmund and La—I mean your
uncle and aunt – why don't you call and arrange for them to visit
us one evening? Mrs Wilmott thrives on cooking for visitors and
now that we're settled I'd like them to see how well we do things
even if our home is only small.' She misinterpreted his quick
frown. 'I'm not complaining about the house, John. One day,
when your gallery is well known like his, our home will be as
grand as theirs.'

'They won't be coming for the time being. I don't think he's too
pleased that I've left him.'

'How silly. He ought to be glad. After all, everything you know
you learned while you were working for Northney's, He ought to
be glad he'd taught you so well. I'll call and see him, leave him to
me.' She had no intention of falling out with her only claim to the
nobility.

That same day, having taken even greater than usual pains over
her appearance, she presented herself at Northney's Gallery only
to be told that Sir Edmund regretted he was engaged and unable to
see her. It was as she turned to come out she saw the printed notice
placed on a table bearing items of exquisite porcelain:
'Northney's Gallery wish it to be known that they have no associ-

ations with the gallery recently opened by their previous employee, Mr John Derrick . . .' No association with John . . . But why? Because he wanted to open his own establishment? Wasn't that what Sir Edmund had done himself?

As a hostess Melissa blossomed; this was the life she'd dreamed of. John had a wide circle of friends, she delighted in enchanting them all. One evening at the end of September they had been entertaining an ex-colleague of his from Northney's, middle-aged Harold Rogers who had been employed by Sir Edmund since long before John had been taken into the firm and whom John meant to prise away from the family business to join him at the new gallery. No matter where a conversation started, it seemed to Melissa that it always found its way back to the same subject: a Ming bowl John had found only that morning . . . a salt-glazed stoneware tankard . . . English delft from a house sale in Huntingdon . . . Meissen ware put into everyday use in a farm kitchen in Dorset. Melissa had to be content to talk to Harold's dowdy wife. But it was second nature to her to be her best in company so even though she privately thought Harold and Virginia Rogers a singularly dull couple there was nothing in her manner to hint at it. Clearly John was pleased with the evening; she was amazed that two grown men could get so excited about a few 'old pots'.

At last the guests had gone. She had meant to be in bed by the time John came from the bedroom across the corridor, the room he had adapted as a dressing room. Instead she was still brushing her hair.

'I've been thinking,' she said, hoping to steer his thoughts away from what she supposed must be their usual track. 'If I were to sell Kyneston we would have a lot of money. You could stock the gallery really well, really fill the shelves and cases. We shall never want to go and stay down there in the forest – and if we did we could always stay at Hapley Court.'

It was something she'd been tossing around in her mind for some time, but her reason for making the suggestion when she did was to drag his thoughts away from where she was sure they were heading. Sell Kyneston . . . of course Georgina would be difficult, but that was because she'd had such a narrow life. They'd have her to stay, help her find a husband. Aunt Patience would have to go back to Hapley Court, they'd never see her without a home.

Her suggestion wasn't having the desired effect. But then she couldn't know how his imagination leaped to Georgina, the girl with half a house and almost no income.

'You seemed to enjoy your evening,' she smiled sweetly, 'but, my goodness, I'm tired.' To prove it she gave an exaggerated yawn.

'No you're not.' He moved to take hold of her and trying to pull away from him she stepped back too far and lost her balance to fall onto the bed with John, still gripping her, thrown almost on top of her, whether by accident or design no one but he could know.

The spring had been tightening in her for weeks. It was then that it finally snapped. With clenched fists she struck him.

'Leave me alone, why can't you? I'm not your plaything. You know I hate you touching me. But you don't care, you don't care. What do you expect? That I'll enjoy being treated like – like an animal? Well, I don't! I don't want to be touched . . .' She heard her shrill voice, she gloried in the sound, she didn't care if Mrs Wilmott could hear from her attic bedroom, she didn't care if all the world heard her; it was like listening to someone else, someone outside herself. Just as if it were someone else's drama and she the spectator, she heard her hysterical screams and had no power to control them even when he shook her. Then he brought his hand sharply across her face, making her catch her breath in dry, trembling sobs.

Without speaking, he picked her up, pushed the covers out of the way and dropped her to lie in bed. Then turned out the gas and, still without a word, walked around to the other side of the bed and climbed in.

She had shed no tears, yet even now her breath was catching in her throat. She'd never been able to imagine what would happen if she let the spring snap; now she couldn't look ahead, not to tomorrow, not to next week or next year. What had she done?

'. . . told you I was tired,' she hiccuped, sounding more like a miserable child now than a hysterical woman.

'Go to sleep. I'm not going to touch you if that's what you're frightened of.'

The abyss between them widened with each day. John treated her with a combination of courtesy and cool disinterest. Melissa ought

110

to have been relieved, so why was she so miserable? Why did she feel so wretched?

'You ain't had not a scrap o' that nice breakfast, Mrs Derrick m'um.' Scrawny little Jessie Simms looked at her mistress, her huge dark eyes filled with compassion. 'Same every morning.'

'I'm not hungry.' Melissa shook her head, tears welling into her eyes at the sight of the child's (for at seventeen Jessie looked no more) concern. She had a lump in her throat too large to swallow and when a single tear escaped she let it roll unheeded down her pale face. At the back of her mind she knew she ought not to encourage Jessie's familiarity, at Kyneston she wouldn't have let even one of the maids who'd known her all her life talk to her like it.

'Well, likely a cup of tea isn't to your fancy, I've known times when my mum can't look a cup of tea in the face first thing in the morning, makes her sick as a parrot. How about I boil up a drop of milk and make you a nice milky cocoa. What d'you say?'

At the thought of it, Melissa's believed her inside turned over.

'Couldn't . . .' A second tear joined the first, falling onto the damask tablecloth as she sat with her head bowed.

'Nothing really up with you is there, m'um? I been thinking these mornings lately that it must be you're in the family way. It's just the way mum is when she's like that, but get the first few weeks behind her and she eats like a horse. Oh, come on, now, m'um, don't cry like that. I didn't mean to go upsetting you. Trouble with me is I talk too much.'

Coming close to Melissa, she put her skinny arms around her and cradled the head, with its beautifully arranged golden curls, to her flat chest. It didn't enter her kindly young head that this wasn't the normal way to behave. She'd put Melissa on a high pedestal from the first, what she felt for her was a combination of genuine love and hero worship.

'You think that's what's wrong with me? Jessie, how can you know?'

'Well, come to that, I suppose I can't – not for sure. Are you late? You know what I mean.'

Melissa nodded. But why hadn't she thought of it herself? She'd had just one period since her marriage and that had been in the middle of August. Now it was the beginning of October. Lately she'd been so relieved that John had wished her a cool,

111

polite goodnight and turned his back that she'd forgotten the possibility that she might already be pregnant.

To John's satisfaction, Harold Rogers came to join him at the new gallery. Harold's knowledge was on a par to his own, but he'd always been an employee, he always would be an employee. He lacked the confidence and the personal ambition (or the capital) to strike out on his own. But once he was installed John was free to travel, following up house sales where he expected to find pieces of interest. So it was that he was often away from home, leaving Melissa to her own devices; leaving her, too, with too much time to fall prey to fears even worse than the truth of her condition which with each day became more certain.

'John, about Kyneston,' she said to him one evening when he returned from a trip to Somerset. 'I must talk to you – about that and about me.'

What was she going to tell him? For one wild moment he expected her to say she was leaving him, returning to Kyneston. Ashamed of his momentary, instinctive relief, he wasn't expecting what he heard next.

'I've mentioned it before. I want to sell my half of the house. Georgina will have to agree, she can't afford not to. Anyway, the money will be useful to her. So it will to us. We are going to need money, we shall have to move to somewhere bigger.' Sitting very straight she looked at him, her expression that of a tragedy queen. 'You will need extra staff. For you won't have me.'

So he'd been right. She wanted to leave him.

'What are you trying to tell me? You mean you're leaving me?'

'Not as you mean. But I shan't be here.' Her lovely face was a mask of grief, her mouth quivered, silent tears spilled.

'What is it?' He came to kneel at her side. 'Have you hated being married so much? Friends come here, they all see you as happy – you can't pretend I ask much of you—'

He might as well not have spoken.

'When I was born my own mother died. Everyone says I'm just like her. You wouldn't know, you're never here, you don't know how unwell I've been. Don't you understand even now? You and your horrible, greedy pleasures, you've given me a child. You don't want it! I don't want it! And it needn't have happened.' She gave in to the storm of tears. '*You* did this to me, you with your

112

perverted sense of enjoyment. Wasn't what you promised when we were married. With my body I you worship, that's what you said,' she screeched. 'Worship? All you wanted was to make a plaything of me. Now look what you've done with your – your – *wicked lust*. And I shall die. I know I shall die just like my mother did. And you'll have killed me.'

In the passage outside Jessie pressed her ear to the door.

'Come back here,' Esmerelda Wilmott hissed, 'come along now.' Then when Jessie came near, 'I'll not have that, my girl.'

'The poor missus, she's that upset.'

'And none of your business if she is. Let me catch you at that game once more and you'll get your marching orders. Now, get the last of the dishes seen to then off you go home. And another thing, young lady, don't you dare breathe a word to anyone about things you see and hear in this house.'

'I wouldn't tell them at 'ome, Auntie, but it's not right him making her cry like she is. He ought to be taking care of her, but you know what 'e did. Screaming like anything she was and he took is hand to her, slapped her so she had a job to get her breath.'

Mrs Wilmott sniffed. In her opinion . . . but it wasn't up to her to have an opinion, she corrected herself. And even if she had one, she wasn't going to share it with a bit of a chit like young Jess.

'Get your coat and get off home. I'll see to these last few dishes.'

With her head bent Jessie hurried along the gaslit streets. In time it took her no more than half an hour, but the difference between the respectable middle-class terraced house where she worked and the squalid, overcrowded terraced cottage where she lived put them poles apart. Washing lines were strung across the narrow cul-de-sac and, although it was nearly nine o'clock at night, her mother was unpegging the family's well-worn underwear that had hung there since the previous day, while Maud Dorey, her next-door neighbour, was leaning against the wall, arms folded, all the time in the world for a gossip. Beyond them, hours after children were in bed and asleep in the sort of home Jessie had left, those of her neightbours' were still in the street playing 'tip and run' even though the only light came from uncurtained windows.

'Get shot of one and the bugger's at it again, dipping 'is wick, putting another in its place,' she heard Maud saying. 'If he belonged to me, Cynth, I'd take the carving knife to it, that'd put paid to his tricks.'

Jessie hung back in the shadows. Were they saying her mother was pregnant again, with young Vic only four months old. Jessie was the eldest of the Simms' brood followed by six brothers at regular intervals, then a gap representing her mother's two miscarriages, and finally Vic.

'That's one way of looking at it,' she heard her mother answer. 'On the other hand, I'd rather know he came home to me for his comforts than looked about him for some young floosie like some of them.' They both knew she alluded to Maud's husband. Jessie knew it too.

'Not so sure *I* would.' Clearly Maud understood the inference. 'Here comes young Jess.'

'About time too,' Cynth turned to her daughter. 'Your dad and the boys will be back from the market and I'm all behind. Get your coat off and see about getting the bloaters on to fry. I suppose that woman they pay you to wait on has had a busy day,' her voice was heavy with sarcasm and spite, 'a fitting or two for a new gown perhaps, or a stroll into town for a new hat. Well I'm not paying you, I'm telling you, so cut on indoors and get the heads off those bloody fish.'

Without a word Jessie did as she was told. Her mind was still on Melissa as she gutted the fish, the screaming that echoed in her head wasn't her mother it was the scene she'd left behind her. She felt weak with love for her poor, beautiful, gentle, ill-used mistress.

'You know what I'm going to do?' John was saying to Melissa at about that same time, 'I'm taking you down to Kyneston. I'm away such a lot at the moment buying—'

'But I told you, I've decided to sell Kyneston. When the baby comes – and I won't be here to look after it, I know I won't – you'll have to have space for a nursemaid, a nursery. You can't bring a child up in a little house like this.'

He made a supreme effort.

'Melissa, you are not going to die. And families live in houses half this size.'

'Not our sort of families.' He heard the pout in her voice. 'Anyway, I've decided. If I want advice I'll ask Uncle Cedric.'

114

'We're keeping Kyneston – and that's final. There isn't any question of selling. I'll send a telegram to them in the morning and I'll take you down the day after tomorrow.'

It wasn't until much later that either of them realized how little interest he'd shown in hearing that he was to become a father.

The next morning Jessie heard the plans when she went up to the bedroom in answer to the bell.

'You going to have your breakfast in bed then, Mrs Derrick, m'um? Likely you'll feel better that way, let it settle before you start to move about. What do you fancy?'

'Jessie, I want to talk to you. I'm going away tomorrow, going home.'

'Oh, Lawks m'um. I heard you and the master having a ding-dong . . . oh, m'um, you don't mean you're running out on him, with the baby coming and all?'

How was it that Melissa wasn't offended by the the girl's honest, outspoken concern? She certainly wouldn't have taken it from anyone else, not Aunt Alice, not even Goergina. All the same she preferred to ignore the girl's reference to 'a ding-dong'.

'It was his idea that I should get out of London until I feel better. At first I didn't want to agree, it doesn't seem right to leave him here with no one to entertain his guests, no one to keep him company.'

'Oh, get along with you, m'um. Aunt Esmerelda – Mrs Wilmott I mean – she'll see he's looked after and I'd bet my last three-penny bit that he'll have his cronies here with him. Good excuse for them to get out without their women I wouldn't wonder. Nothing the chaps like better than a "men only", that's what my dad calls it. But I shan't half miss you, the house'll be dull as the tomb.'

If her thoughts hadn't already leaped ahead to the next stage, Melissa would have heard the quiver in the girl's voice.

'I want you to get my trunk down from the loft. If you can't manage, ask Mrs Wilmott. Then we'll go through my things, you can help me pack.' Returning to Kyneston might be quite exciting, she'd a lot to tell Georgina. And what a comforting thought it was to know that Aunt Alice would be so close, always ready to listen and understand.

It was later, as she sat on the edge of the bed watching Jess pack

115

for her that she realized how much she was going to miss the girl's almost childlike honesty.

'Jess, I'm so frightened.'

'Frightened, m'um? About the journey? But isn't the master journeying with you?'

'Not that. Jess, it's the baby. I shall get fat and ugly, and I'd been so looking forward to living in London. But not with a baby! And probably I'll go on feeling ill. I don't want a baby. I want to go on living, everything to be happy . . .' Like an old and worn rag doll, she drooped, her face crumpling unashamedly as she cried.

Jess knew nothing of protocol, she only knew she hated to see Melissa miserable. Coming to sit on the bed she put her arm around her. 'Come on now, ain't so bad now is it, it'll soon all be over. Let's talk about after the baby gets born, that'll cheer you up.'

'No,' Melissa felt herself taken in the girl's arms, 'oh Jess, why did it have to happen?'

Why? Jess thought of her mother's acceptance of producing one child after another. It happened because men were all the same, that was her youthful opinion, greedy and selfish. And the poor missus, her so sweet and lovely, made miserable just to keep the master happy. Men!

Chapter Seven

'Well, has she come?' Mrs Biggs followed her husband into the coachhouse wanting a first-hand account out of earshot of kitchen gossip.

'Ah, the train came in on time to the minute. Three of them there were.'

'She's brought a guest?'

'Come to help her get unpacked and settled, that's what Miss Mellie said. Calls her her personal maid. Rum sort of personal maid if you ask me. Cockney sparrow, fledgling sparrow at that. Looks like she'd be more in place behind a school desk – and sounds as though she could use a bit of schooling too.'

'Miss Melissa's not silly, the girl must be useful or she wouldn't have brought her,' Mrs Biggs defended loyally.

'Likely you're right.' Biggs dismissed Jessie, it was Melissa they were interested in. 'I thought Miss Mellie looked peaky, lost her roses and can you wonder, summertime in the dirty city. Nothing a good blow of forest air won't put right I dare say, that and a few weeks of your cooking, eh m'dear? And Mr Derrick, Lord alone knows what he's got in that crate he had lifted off the train so careful. Watched over it, he did, like it was the Crown Jewels. Had me help him carry it into the old wash-house, then put a padlock on the door if you ever heard of such a thing. What does he think we are? He might get prowlers in the city helping themselves, but I tell you for two pins I'd have told him what I thought, coming here and treating us as though we can't be trusted.'

'I'll make her a nice bramble and apple tart for this evening, she was always fond of that. I oftentimes worry about her, wondering who's making her meals. She always was a fussy eater – not like her sister. Still, she's home now and we'll see if we can't keep her here for a while. Soon as news that she's home reaches Hapley Court, that Mrs Sylvester'll be over, you may be sure of that. Not a sign of any of them all the weeks she's been away – not to see Miss Patience, not even a word for Miss Georgina's birthday. And for that I shan't forgive them, stuck-up lot that they are. Well, I mustn't let you waste my time out here gossiping. There's some of us got work to see to.'

'Jessie's unpacking my things so I've come to talk to you.' Melissa – presumably believing that her married status gave her privileges previously not permitted – came unannounced into Georgina's workroom.

'Have you enough space in the wardrobes? I've been moving Mama's things into the spare back room,' Georgina stabbed her needle into a pin cushion and turned to Melissa prepared to give her all her attention. 'At least, all her things I haven't already taken,' she laughed. 'You know, Melissa, I really enjoy remodelling her gowns, it's such a challenge. Better even than making hats.'

'That's because you do them to wear yourself, not for women who can afford to buy.'

'Probably that's it. Anyway, tell me about *you*. Have you been too busy to write?' For, except for Georgina's birthday, in all the weeks Melissa had been away she had only sent one brief letter and that addressed to both Georgina and Patience. Taking a sadistic pleasure in the thought, Georgina supposed that now she had a husband she wouldn't want to share secrets any more.

'I entertain a lot – friends or clients of John's.' Why did she say it with such defiance? Georgina was uneasy.

'Is everything all right, Mellie? You're not homesick?'

'Homesick?' Her surprise at the question was genuine. 'Not a bit. We must have a talk about Kyneston, I shall never live here again. I told John I want to get rid of my share – but he said I'm to keep it.' Her voice broke. 'It's *my* house not his, it's for *me* to say. Aunt Patience would have to go back to Hapley, but I suppose he thinks it would mean putting you out. But Georgina, you'd have enough money to buy somewhere – or you could come to live with us—'

'Don't talk nonsense,' Georgina promptly slapped that idea down.

118

'But you get on well with John. And you don't know how miserable and lonely I've been. I'd made up my mind I wouldn't tell you . . .' She made no attempt to hide her tears, looking at Georgina her face crumpled as she cried.

Immediately Georgina was at her side, dropping to her knees by her chair. 'Whatever's wrong? You said you weren't homesick.'

' 's not that. He's made me pregnant. You've no idea about being married . . . even my body doesn't belong to me any more. He does things – can't tell you – so horrid. It wasn't that we wanted a baby. We didn't – we don't. If we'd meant to have a baby I know I would have had to let him – oh Georgina, you've no idea how beastly it all is. It's making me hate him – and we've got all our lives ahead.' Then she stopped, as if she'd realized what she'd said. 'No – I shan't. Now I shan't have a life. Georgina I'm so frightened. I shall die just like my mother did—'

'What rubbish you talk! Mellie, a baby is wonderful news. Stop crying and just think: perhaps a little girl, perhaps like you, perhaps like John. Don't be frightened Mellie. They say the first weeks are the hardest, stay here until you are feeling quite well again.'

'That's what he says. He seemed to like the idea, he said he'd come down quite often.'

Georgina was ashamed of the way her own thoughts jumped at Melissa's words: John liked the idea, said he'd come down often. No, don't be a fool, of course he'll come often, he'll be anxious about her.

'I don't know anything about his business,' Melissa was saying, 'but he's gone into the village to send a telegram to someone saying that he's here. Probably something to do with the crate he brought down with him.'

Her tears seemed to have done her good. She was sufficiently recovered to let her mind wander to the half made hats on the table.

'Do you still need to work? You're twenty-one now. I know that old mine isn't worth much to you, but Father left money too, you have half of what he left.' She had never interested herself in the pounds, shillings and pence of their legacy, her uncle dealt with everything until her birthday and after that the responsibility would be John's.

'I need that to cushion me against the outgoings on Kyneston. The income from the mine has been getting less each quarter.'

'How do you know? I've never talked about money to Uncle Cedric.'

Georgina laughed. 'And you may be sure I haven't. When Mr Grieves came to read us the Will, remember he said always to go and see him if there was a problem. So I went. He showed me all the figures. I know exactly how I stand.'

'You really are funny. Fancy doing a thing like that – and not telling Uncle Cedric. Not very polite of you.'

'May I ride with you in the morning?' John turned a brotherly smile on Georgina.

'There's no need. I treat them all fairly. If you're only here for a day or two you don't want to waste time away from Melissa.' Only John heard beyond the honeyed tone.

'I'm better just with Jess,' Melissa made the decision for both of them.

Looking on, Patience felt her old stirring of unease.

When morning came Georgina was resolved to beat John at his own game; if he could look on her as a sister, then a sister she would be. They rode one behind the other along the track. The leaves were taking on the first golden hues of autumn, occasionally a rustle would proclaim another cluster of sweet chestnuts falling. Did it mean nothing to him to be here with her? And what did she want it to mean? Nothing! She answered the question almost before she asked it. For the rest of their lives they would meet each other, have contacts just like all families do. Her imagination leaped ahead. Perhaps Melissa will ask me to be Godmother to the baby, Godmother to John's child. Melissa isn't really miserable, she's just frightened. That's why she is trying to put the blame on John for making her pregnant. Once she feels better, once the doctor tells her she is normal and healthy – and she *is*, all that's wrong with her is in her mind, over and over I've seen it happen – ought I to try and explain to John. Talk about Mellie to John? No, I can't.

'Georgina.' They were coming out into a patch of open forest when she could tell from the way he said her name that he had things on his mind to tell her.

'Come on, let's give them their heads!' She knew it was cowardly. Perhaps raking the ashes wouldn't stir them to flames in

120

his heart. She put Cleo into a gallop, suddenly exhilarated by the pounding of hooves on the hard ground. Forget what's gone before – don't think of what might lie ahead – let *this* be all that matters.

He must have taken his mood from hers. They rode much further than usual, neither of them thinking of breakfast waiting for them back at Kyneston. When at last they came through the little gate at the side of the cattle grid and rounded the bend in the drive, there was an empty hansom cab outside the house.

'We must have been longer than I thought, I asked Steven to come early, but I hadn't expected him quite so soon.'

'Steven?'

'You could say he's a business colleague. Come and meet him. Leave Biggs to see to the horses.'

Inside the house they found Patience, flushed with excitement and delight at finding herself so unexpectedly playing hostess to a dashing sea captain.

'I wondered whether you might have forgotten Captain Howard was coming, John dear,' she twittered. 'I've looked after him for you, in fact he joined me for breakfast. Melissa isn't down yet, poor little soul, so I was glad to have company. The man who drove him is in the kitchen, I told Mrs Biggs to take care of him.' It was a sure sign of Patience's excitement that her words tumbled out so freely.

'We rode further than usual.' To her own ears Georgina's remark sounded abnormally casual, as if she were trying to pull Patience back to earth. 'John didn't tell me he was expecting a visitor.'

Having warmly shaken Captain Howard's hand, John turned back to Georgina.

'I had no idea we'd been out so long.'

'Think how far we rode and you'll soon see where the time went,' she laughed. 'Aren't you going to introduce your friend?'

'Steven, this is my sister-in-law, Miss Georgina Rochester. She and I usually ride together when I'm at Kyneston. Georgina, Captain Steven Howard, master of the vessel that carries goods for me to America.'

She was ready to treat the handsome sea captain with the scorn she felt for what she thought of as the shady second trade Melissa had confided in her that John had been carrying on unbeknown to

121

his great-uncle. But, instead, when she felt her hand taken in their visitor's firm grasp the idea of being unwelcoming melted.

'And what better way to start the day than a gallop in the forest?' he smiled. 'It's a pleasure to meet you Miss Rochester.'

Patience said nothing, and yet Georgina was aware of her standing close, watching them all – particularly watching Steven Howard. She looked at the stranger more closely, trying to see him through Patience's eyes. Age? Probably forty, perhaps more, perhaps less, it was hard to tell with a man of his sort. His complexion was weather-beaten, a crow's nest of lines around his eyes; but she suspected they had more to do with scanning far horizons in bright light than with the passage of years. His hair was the shade of ripened corn, but even that owed much to the sun and wind that had bleached it to that colour, with a different lifestyle it might have been nearer the auburn of his brows. His eyes were a light, gingery brown. His physique was magnificent: he must have been over six foot tall; if 'slim' meant having not an ounce of excess weight then he was slim, yet not slight. She was aware of his power in his broad shoulders, his strong hands . . .

'Not in a rush are you?' John was asking him.

'Except for my cab I've nothing to hurry for. The crew are in home port, they must have time to indulge. Most of the cargo will be taken aboard Wednesday and Thursday of next week. I plan to set out on Friday, a week today.'

'Well, Georgina and I haven't eaten yet. Come and keep us company why don't you.'

Patience watched the three of them go towards the dining room, her own moment of glory over. Or was it? He had been so courteous, so charming. Never in all her life had she met anyone who had made her feel like this . . . almost attractive. Oh, but it was nonsense. Here she was, fifty years old, dull and dowdy. In the hall she glanced in the mirror just as Georgina had on the evening she'd heard John and Cedric talking in the study; unlike Georgina the face in the mirror didn't mock her; on the contrary it smiled back at her, it's pale blue eyes shining like a girl's. She glanced down at her morning gown and, not for the first time, was grateful to Georgina. The pale grey suited her, she felt feminine and – dare she say it? – she felt attractive. Almost running, she went up the wide, shallow staircase and into her bedroom. There she peered again, this time in the long mirror. Then, sitting on the edge of the bed, she hugged her arms around herself and gave way to dreams she thought she'd succeeded in putting out of her head.

Never had she seen such twinkling brown eyes. And when he'd drawn her out to talk to him, surely he couldn't honestly have wanted to hear all about the husbandry of the New Forest, the verderers and the people with grazing rights. Yet he'd given her every bit of his attention, no one else had ever made her feel that what she had to say mattered as he had. Then it had been his turn, and think of the tales he'd told of his journeyings, the ocean storms, the cargoes he carried. She believed she would surely remember this day for the rest of her life, 7 October 1907, the day touched with magic.

Going to the dressing table she carefully took the pins out of her hair, let it hang loose and straight, then brushed it. Not a sign of grey . . . not that it had much colour of any sort, just a pale ratty shade . . . but if she didn't pin it up so austerely . . . Was she making a fool of herself? Georgina would say she wasn't. That's it, think of Georgina and her spirit, *she'd* never let herself be crushed. So wake up, Patience Sylvester, if the Lord has seen fit to give you another chance (another? when was the first?), then grasp it, grasp it and say thank You. Oh, but I do. He *did* seem to like me, You must have made them late home purposely, if the others had been here I wouldn't have had a chance. Thank You, thank You. If I try and do something not so plain with my hair, please don't let them laugh at me – and please help me to do it properly.

Strand by strand she twisted it around her fingers then pinned it up. It would have been easier if she'd put it in rags at night, but too late for that now. Did it look better? Did it make her look younger? Or did it look silly?

Hark, they were out in the garden, she could hear John and Steven talking. ('Steven, please call me Steven, not Captain Howard. In this half hour we seem to have come to know each other too well for formalities.' Fancy! No one had ever said anything like that to her before. 'And I'm just Patience,' she'd told him.) So now looking down from her window she felt possessive towards him. If only there were someone she could confide in. There was Georgina, but even Georgina might not understand.

'There's Alice arriving,' Patience was the first to see the trap. 'She must have got word that you're home, Melissa.'

123

'I sent a note, Effie took it on her cycle,' Melissa told her. 'I hoped she'd come.' At the thought of an understanding ear, her troubles swamped her.

Patience wasn't brave enough to carry off her new hairstyle in front of her sister-in-law. Perhaps it didn't look so very different, though, for Melissa seemed not to have noticed.

'I expect you want a nice quite chat with her, dear. I'll go and help Georgina, she's picking the Blenheims, I'll carry them and lay them out for storing.'

Hurrying to hurl herself into Alice's arms Melissa neither listened nor cared how Patience was going to occupy herself.

'How long are you here for, dear? Can John spare himself away from his new gallery? Oh, but it is so lovely to see you.'

'I'll tell you all about it. John won't be able to stay many days, but I shall be here for a while.'

For a while? Even if she didn't feel so wretched, what John had done to her had shattered her dreams of a gay, social life. Frightened and miserable, she turned to the aunt who never failed her.

Having been brought a tray of Madiera wine and Bath Olivers and said they weren't to be disturbed, she told her tale of woe. Alice was the audience she craved. Jess gave her affection, warmth, devoted care; but Jess had had no experience, what could she know about marriage?

'You were so young to face marriage,' Alice's voice was rich with sympathy, her memory carrying her back to the night of Melissa's birth. 'It was the same with Mary, poor Cedric felt ridden with guilt that he had consented to your father marrying her when she was little more than a child.'

'I'm so frightened Aunt Alice. Suppose I die, as she did.'

'Oh, but you won't, we learned our lesson, we won't let that happen to you,' Alice was quick to reassure her. 'All the months she waited for you to be born she was living with him – as his wife, I mean. It's not right to criticize the dead, but you're grown up now, you understand what I mean when I say he was a man of carnal appetite. I remember suggesting to her she should have a room to herself, but Mary could be very stubborn, she wouldn't hear of it. She was besotted with him, unwell though she was. You say John is going back to the gallery and leaving you here. You'll miss him, of course you will, but we must say thank God he has the wit to know it's here you will get strong. Now, dear, I'm going to pour us both a glass of Madeira, and you're to eat a good wholesome Bath Oliver.'

Looking trustingly at her aunt, Melissa did as she was told.

The last of the apples to be harvested were the Blenheims and in the orchard picking was in progress. Georgina had been staggering in that direction carrying one end of the long, wooden ladder while Jim Neil, the garden boy, held the other.

'Here, let me take that.' Coming to join them Steven had taken the ladder and effortlessly raised it to carry it across his shoulder.

'Where to?'

'Over there. I'm going to pick the Blenheims. I've put the boxes by the trees ready.'

'Then I'm your man. What better way to spend an October morning?'

'But have you time? What about your cabby?'

'I've sent him on his way,' John answered her as he joined them. 'Georgina, Steven is going to stay a night here.'

'Wait!' Steven held up one hand, balancing the ladder with the other. 'What I should be saying is, have I your permission to accept John's invitation?' There was laughter in his voice, and had she ever seen eyes shine with such merriment?

'From your present performance, I'd guess you'll be an ideal guest. Prop the ladder against this tree, can you? This is as far as I got yesterday.'

'Oh, we can't have this, John. We'll climb up and pick, then hand them down. How's that?'

Apple picking had always been Georgina's job, she loved the smell of the orchard, the occasional rustle and thud as a bruised fruit was dislodged and fell through the branches to hit the ground. It surprised her to realize that her eager acceptance of his offer had more to do with Steven's presence than John's. From that moment when he balanced the ladder amongst the branches and started to climb, the exercise ceased to be an annual labour (even one she enjoyed), it became a morning of pure fun.

So when Patience came to join them the first thing she heard was bantering laughter, a shout of 'Well caught!' She quickened her pace.

'Another pair of hands to catch what they drop,' Georgina

greeted her. 'Come and join the team, Aunt Patience.' Not a word about the new hairstyle, but Patience was sure that this time it hadn't gone unnoticed, and sure too that it met Georgina's approval. With an agility she hadn't known she was capable of she leaped to catch a large and lush fruit that tumbled from the top of the tree.

'Hooray!' Like children on an outing the shout went up.

'You've got twigs in your hair,' Georgina laughed, her hand touching Patience's affectionately as they went back towards the house, leaving the men to carry the baskets of picked fruit to the upper room of the carriage house where she would lay them out later in the day.

Patience bit her lip, her nervousness returning.

'My hair – does it look silly? I can't think what came over me to make me do such a thing.'

'It looks very nice. When we get indoors let me brush the twigs out for you and pin it back up. May I?'

'Oh Georgina, you must think me a silly old woman.'

'You're not silly – and you're certainly not old. Anyway, even if you'd lived enough years you still wouldn't be old. That's funny isn't it? Some people can be old even when they're young.'

'Funny girl you are,' Patience chuckled. But somehow, her pinned-up hair didn't feel as out of place on her middle-aged head now.

John had enjoyed having the right to issue his invitation for Steven to spend the night at Kyneston and had been pleasantly surprised when the suggestion was accepted with such alacrity. Melissa was poor company at the moment and Georgina – he wasn't ready to examine his thoughts on Georgina. When he'd been here before, he had found her attractive and, even more important, he'd seen behind her façade of friendship, believing that she understood the rules and played the same game as he did himself. Then had come their hours together in the cabin of *Cork's Crew*, a situation that had hurtled them out of control – a situation he wasn't ready to remember yet was unable to forget. And worse even than that was the memory of the nun-like bridesmaid, the scorn she'd made no effort to hide.

He felt he had problems enough with a difficult wife, without

126

undercurrents in the relationship with his sister-in-law. In truth, although he may not have fully realized it, that was one reason behind the invitation to Steven. Three was a much more comfortable number than two, hiding behind Steven the ghost of those hours on *Cork's Crew* might fade. It was essential that he built up a casual, friendly relationship with Georgina, theirs was to be a lifelong association. If Melissa followed the pattern of her recent days she was unlikely to act as a cheerful third, so Steven's presence couldn't have been better timed. It wasn't in John's nature to run away, but it occurred to him that the following morning he might accompany Biggs when he took Steven back to the dock, then catch the London train from Poole. Melissa wouldn't be sorry to see him go, she could give herself up to being fussed by that strange child she'd taken such a fancy to.

Georgina took time coaxing Patience's hair, using over twenty 'invisible' pins, and pulling the front hair forward to soften the line of her brow.

'Perhaps we ought to get Melissa to see it before I go downstairs,' poor uncertain Patience held her thumb between her teeth as she viewed the end result. 'Supposing she says something about me having it done differently – in front of John and his friend. Oh dear, I don't know . . .'

Georgina knew it wasn't beyond the bounds of possibility.

'Stay there. I'll get her. I heard her coming upstairs just now.' And before Patience could think of anything else to worry about she'd gone.

'It's only me,' she tapped and entered Melissa's room just as she always had, forgetting Jessie's presence. Standing behind the dressing-table stool, the girl was massaging her mistress's shoulders and neck.

'Didn't 'arf give me a start, charging in like that without so much as a knock. Don't make a noise, the poor missus has got a blinder of a head.'

'Jess knows just what helps,' Melissa opened her eyes long enough to see who the visitor was. 'I try and keep my mornings quiet lately, but today I've had Aunt Alice here.'

'Enough to give anyone a headache!' was Georgina's opinion. 'Aren't you coming down to the table? John has invited Captain Howard to stay overnight, did you know?'

127

'I've not even met him yet. Is he nice?' Something seemed to have taken her mind off her headache, whether it was Jess's ministrations or the thought of a guest it was hard to tell.

'A swashbuckling sea captain, no less. Mellie, come with me a second, I want to show you something.'

Jessie watched resentfully as Melissa was taken away from her.

'Listen,' Georgina whispered, the bedroom door closed. 'I've been doing Aunt Patience's hair for her, it looks really nice. Come and see – and *please* Mellie tell her it suits her. You know what she is, she needs us to boost her up.'

'She's not harbouring hopes of the handsome captain?' Melissa's giggle was for the impossibility that Patience – poor, boring, on-the-shelf Patience – might still have dreams of a Knight Errant.

'Chump!' Georgina laughed too. 'Come and see how nice she looks. And for goodness sake *tell her so*.'

Melissa was suddenly and inexplicably happy. What fun it was to be home, whispering secrets with Georgina, even giving old Aunt Patience a boost, with Mrs Biggs and all of them making a fuss of her, with Aunt Alice to be her prop.

'When Biggs takes Steven back to Poole in the morning I shall go too,' John announced that evening. 'But I shall have time for our ride first.'

'I wish I could persuade him to let me take his place,' Steven smiled across the table at Georgina.

'No need for that,' she answered. 'There are three mounts, we shall all go. No slacking though, I like to be all saddled up by half past seven.'

Melissa shuddered, giving the guest her sweetest smile.

'How I envy you.'

'I'm not taking your mount?' Steven let his gaze rest on John's exquisite young wife.

'Indeed no. Even a walk is more than I feel able to contemplate just now. John has brought me here to build my strength. I shall listen to you all setting out at first light and, as I said, I shall envy you your robust good health. But John, what about Jessie? I'd expected you to see her safely home.'

'Let Biggs put her on the train when you've done with her.'

Georgina sent him a scathing glance, disappointed in him that he could be so careless of the spirited Cockney girl who seemed such a child – and glad that his casual disregard was yet more evidence of his selfish character.

Riding out next morning, the presence of a third person held the balance and it was almost possible to imagine she and John were brother and sister-in-law, that and nothing more. It had been his idea that a third person would help, but Georgina's intuition told her that just *any* third person wouldn't have done. Steven Howard was important, she knew it quite certainly as they galloped across the wide expanse of open forest, the thunder of the horses' hooves music in her ears.

'A morning to remember,' he said as, returning home, he reached her side before John and lifted her from her saddle. Usually she rode alone, usually she dropped effortlessly to the ground – they both knew she was capable of dismounting unaided.

'Have you things you have to do in Poole? If not, can't you stay on a few days while you're in dock?' She kept her eyes firmly on Steven, but she spoke clearly enough for John to hear the warmth of her suggestion.

'Are you inviting me?'

'If you wouldn't find us too quiet. After weeks at sea you may be looking for more in the way of entertainment than Kyneston has to offer.'

'I can think of nowhere I'd rather spend my time on shore than here. But I'll need to pick up a few things from Poole.'

'Wonderful!' John approved the plan. 'We'll go across this morning. Come with us Georgina—'

'No, I have things to do.' She thought she'd done well, her friendly invitation to Steven must surely have carried the right message to John. But she wasn't ready for a morning in his company, there were limits to how long she could play the role of a casually friendly 'sister'.

Hidden away in the New Forest, what did Georgina know of men? In Melissa's opinion: nothing. But there was one thing Georgina was sure of and that was that she was the reason Steven accepted her invitation so readily, keen to stay at Kyneston, not just for a single night but for all the days he could spare until his *Seahorse* took on its cargo the following week.

129

It didn't need words to alert her to the way he watched her, listened to her. And she was glad, she wanted John to be as aware of it as she was herself. Steven was charming to Patience, gentle kindly Patience with her pinned-up curls that were now the outcome of her inexperienced nightly efforts with strips of cotton torn from a worn-out petticoat; he showed all the appreciation Melissa's loveliness merited. But he was drawn to Georgina like iron filings to a magnet.

On the next two morning the three rode out together, both Georgina and John determined to established a basis for a lifetime relationship: Melissa's sister and Melissa's husband.

John heard that the contents of a large house in Bournemouth were to be on view the following Monday morning prior to the commencement of the sale in the afternoon. Tempted by that and by the fact that Steven would still be at Kyneston, he decided not to return to London until after that.

'Almost a return to summer,' he said as, home from their gallop on the Monday morning, they attacked their breakfast, 'why don't you come with me to Bournemouth for the outing? If you don't want to come to the house, you could walk along the undercliff. Melissa, what do you say?'

This morning Melissa had emerged in time for breakfast. Whether the colour on her cheeks was entirely natural he didn't question, certainly she looked delightfully pretty in an up-to-the-minute day gown of cornflower blue, the skirt hanging straight from the waist in front with all the fullness at the back, the taffeta underskirt rustling provocatively as she moved. The fussily trimmed corsage was loose, draped over a self-coloured sash that accentuated her small waist. She looked enchanting and she knew it, something that helped her join the returning riders with a smile on her face.

'Drive to Bournemouth? Oh John, I'd be frightened. Today I feel so much better – but let me rap on wood quickly or I'd be tempting fate. No, I'll be quite happy here. Why don't you two go with John? Not to some boring house sale looking for china pots, I don't mean that,' she added laughing, 'I mean why don't you go to the sea. Or do you see more than enough of it?' she added to Steven.

'I'd no more tire of the sea than John here would of what you call his china pots. What do you say, Georgina, shall we have a day out?'

She ought to say 'No', she ought to say 'You men go, I'll stay with Mellie.' But already her imagination had jumped ahead. She knew exactly the game she meant to play and, in playing it, protect herself from the hurt she was frightened to contemplate. She would let John see her encouraging Steven – and where was the danger in that? In days Steven would be gone, her ploy would have succeeded in that she would have made it clear she had no interest in John.

So instead of 'No', she said 'Yes, we can all squeeze into the trap if we take a big breath.'

And it was that squeeze that set the mood for the day.

'Why don't we go to the sale, have a look at what it is John is interested in?' she suggested as, Christchurch behind them, they bowled through Boscombe, almost at journey's end. 'It wouldn't interest you.' John knew how Melissa viewed his love of 'old pots', 'old china'. Her view put a barrier between them. It wasn't simply that she had no knowledge of the things he loved, what held her so distant was that she had no conception of what his work meant to him no wish to learn, no feeling of wonder. He would rather Georgina remained outside this part of his life than know that she scorned the things he found so exciting – and more than exciting; to hold an item of beauty that had been crafted by loving hands perhaps hundreds of years before, how else could he feel but humble?

'I know I'm ignorant – but I'd be interested. At home we have a Minton tea service, that's what Mama said it was, she always called it Grecian – the design I mean – but the flowers on the panels are very English. You know it John? Then in my bedroom there's a vase – quite different, almost drab. No, that's not true, it could never be drab. But it looks like plain eathenware, it's not glazed. It's the decoration that makes it really lovely. Not paintings, but wonderful white modelled flowers. Even they're not glazed, it's plain . . . what's the word? Sort of pure. Mama said that was Minton too. But I can't see how it can be, it's so different from the tea service.'

She hadn't been talking to impress him, indeed had she been she would have made sure she had a better knowledge before she started, been able to tell him what the markings were on the

131

bottom of the vase. All she had done was voice a genuine curiosity.

'I know the tea service,' John told her. 'Beautiful and certainly Minton, dating from the very early years of the last century. As for the vase, I've not seen it. But I'd like to. If your mother told you it was Minton she was probably right. From what you say I'd guess it to be around the middle of the century. I'd be interested to see it.'

She imagined the vase standing on her wide window ledge; she imagined taking John to her bedroom to see it; she imagined—

'I don't want to stay for the sale, but I'd love to look around. What do you say Steven?' Referring back to him helped pull her thoughts together.

'I'm no connoisseur of fine arts, but I'll pander to your whims for an hour or so. My home is on board ship remember, furniture has never been of prime importance.'

Sitting between the two of them, squeezed onto the bench seat, Georgina was suddenly and inextricably happy.

Chapter Eight

Georgina liked to think herself mistress of her own fate. She had her own reason for encouraging Steven's attention; she wasn't even distracted from her objective by Patience's ragcrimped hair nor the shy, hopeful smiles bestowed on their visitor. In a few days he'd be gone and that must surely put an end to whatever secret dreams were stirring under the newly pinned curls just as surely as it would put an end to the use she meant to make of him herself.

That was what she intended as, making a play of treating John with the casual friendliness she would have shown to whoever Melissa had married, she fell in with whatever the exciting sea captain suggested. Over the weekend she had walked with him in the forest; while John and Melissa were visiting Hayton Court she had taken him to the lake where she'd so often secretly bathed; she'd pointed out the tree she'd scaled and the branch where she'd attached a rope for climbing (loyalty prevented her from telling him how, with the rope firmly tied, Melissa had refused to take her feet off the ground). Could he really have been interested in these tales of youthful innocence? One thing was certain: talking to him brought alive so much that had been happy in her years of early freedom, it was almost like understanding the child she'd been – the roots of the person she'd become.

On the Monday, after they left John at the sale they returned to Boscombe and walked on the clifftop. Then she enjoyed the rare (rare? Unheard of in her narrow life) treat of eating lunch in an hotel while she encouraged him to talk to her of his travels – and, hardly realizing what was happening to her, with every hour she came nearer to forgetting that her intention had been to use him for her own ends.

133

'I'm being a poor host,' John said as they made for home on that Monday. 'But tomorrow I want to come back to the second day of the sale. There are some good pieces coming up.'

'Don't worry,' Steven assured him, his eye enquiringly on Georgina.

'I've an idea,' she was quick to turn the knife in the wound. Her own? John's? 'On your way to Bournemouth in the morning, drop Steven and me off at the bottom of Lymington High Street. What do you say Steven to our taking *Cork's Crew* out? She's not your sort of boat, just a tiny cabin—'

'You don't need to ask. You know what I say,' he told her. As for John, he said nothing. Her heart raced. She knew her message had gone home. How was it Steven could be unaware of the tension as he took her hand lightly in his. 'We'll take our lunch, have a day's sailing then meet John as he comes through Lymington on the way home.'

'Don't bank on it,' John warned. What was he thinking? She wouldn't let herself look at him. 'It's blowing up, I shouldn't be surprised if tonight sees the last of this good spell.'

'This is a sea captain you're talking to, John!' Georgina laughed mockingly, 'He's no fair weather sailor. Anyway we have rubber waterproofs, don't you remember?'

Oh he remembered, she had no doubt. A quick glance at the set of his chin told her just how well he remembered. John, John, why did you do it? Why did you marry Mellie? But I know why: you married her because you wanted her money. I don't think you even try to make her happy. I ought to hate you . . . you used *me* . . . you use *her* . . . but if you were free, even now I'd want you . . . I do want you . . . How can I love you when I despise the way you've behaved? Anyway, you are Mellie's husband, I'm not going to think of anything except *that*.

Sailing with Steven was thrilling. Her own expertise was limited, John's had been even more so. Under Steven's hand the *Cork's Crew* skimmed across the Solent, he the skipper, she his crew. Watching him she felt a new emotion stirring in her. He was strong, he was one with the elements, his straw-coloured hair blowing in the wind, his eyes half closed against the glare on the water.

'All right?' he called, turning to her with a smile of pure enjoyment.

134

She nodded, catching her bottom lip between her teeth. Oh yes, she was all right, she'd never known such joy in being alive, being part of nature. Her imagination ran riot, she saw them sailing from the Solent into the Channel, sailing on . . . where? To what? She had no idea, only a half-understood yearning for escape and a feeling of the rightness of Steven being at the helm.

'There are sure to be items I know will find a better market in America, but whether or not I'll have a shipment ready for your next trip I can't say. I have my own home market now,' John told Steven as they sat at breakfast on the Wednesday morning, their last ride behind them, only an hour or so left before Biggs would bring the carriage to take Steven to Poole Harbour and John on to the railway station.

'You'll let me know?' Steven answered.

'I'll write to you at the Harbour Office,' John told him.

This morning one of Patience's curls refused to be held in place with its pin, it stuck out at a right angle from the side of her head. Perhaps it was that that touched Georgina, perhaps it was something in the way she looked at Steven; or probably she used Patience as a comfortable excuse for her suggestion.

'If you've nothing any better to do with your time ashore, why don't you come to Kyneston again when you get back. If John's left a crate here, all well and good; if he hasn't, you'd still be more than welcome. We've enjoyed having you here – haven't we?' She looked at Patience for confirmation of the invitation, Patience whose round face was flushed with pleasure and hope.

'Indeed, Steven, you are always most welcome.' She tried to make her voice as cool and prim as Alice's would have been.

'There's nothing I'd rather do,' Steven told them. 'It won't be until after the turn of the year. Between now and then don't forget your invitation, for I certainly shan't.'

'Oh but we won't forget.' Patience's words jumped out before she could stop them. The situation was saved for her by a timid tap at the door, then the appearance of Jessie.

'I been sent with word from the missu – Madam – Mrs Derrick—'

The girl's confusion at being the focus of four pairs of eyes restored Patience.

'Yes dear? Do you need one of us to come up?'

135

'No, t'ain't that. That's what she don't want.' Her message was patently meant for John. 'She said to tell you, sir, she'd say goodbye to you down here. I only got to help her finish off, she's almost done. So you just wait down 'ere for her, she'll not be more than a few shakes.'

'Tell her we're leaving at half past. If she's not down by twenty past I'll come up to say goodbye.'

'Best you do as she says. She's been more herself this morning, like. Don't want to go upsetting her do we?' There was no criticism of Melissa in Jessie's tone.

By the time the carriage was brought to the front steps the day that had started bright was changing; already clouds were gathering, the early morning breeze had gathered force, singing through the leafy branches with the promise of autumn.

'I hope the seas are gentle and the wind always with you,' Georgina said as she held her hand to Steven. She meant what she said – yet even as she felt her hand taken in his she couldn't shut out the image of John taking Melissa into his arms any more than she could close her ears to his assurance that he expected to return to Kyneston at the end of the following week.

'I've never set out on a journey so keen for it to be over,' Steven spoke quietly, with his back to the others so that only Georgina heard him.

Releasing Melissa, John came towards them.

'I'll take care of Mellie, you needn't worry,' Georgina told him, hearing her voice as brittle with cheerfulness. Wasn't that what he expected from a sister-in-law? 'Perhaps next time she'll be feeling well enough to go home with you. Poor John, you'll be lonely without her.' She said it, knowing that purposely she was trying to hurt him and herself too. Yet it was the truth. Of course she'd look after Melissa; of course he would be lonely without her; of course Melissa would want to be with him; that's how it was, that's how it must be.

The days found a pattern in some respects not unlike the one before Melissa's marriage, although now she was conscious of her wedded status. Here she was, a married woman with a home in London and a lady's maid in attendance . . . yet sometimes it was easy to slip back into her old relationship with Georgina. Pampered by Mrs Biggs, waited on and cared for with untiring solicitude by Jessie, fussed over by Aunt Alice, at this precise time Kyneston was just what she needed. By the Friday of the following week, the day John was expected, she had begun to feel sufficiently better that for hours at a time she could forget her miserable predicament, the wretched outlook of the months ahead of her.

The morning dawned clear and bright. Knowing that later in the day she would be glad to shut herself away in her workroom, Georgina was busying herself with one of her favourite autumn tasks in the orchard, raking fallen leaves and fallen rotten apples alike, scooping them into the barrow and wheeling them to the compost heap at the back of the kitchen garden. This morning she needed the exertion. Scratching her rake into the earth, she breathed deeply. She loved the outdoors at any time of year, spring was filled with hope and promise, in summer the air was heavy with the scent of flowers; but this, the rich, decaying scent of autumn was best of all.

So engrossed was she that she didn't notice the sound of footsteps shuffling through the leaves.

' 'Scuse me,' came the piping tone of a young voice. 'Scuse us, but we've lost Simpkins.'

She turned to see that her visitors were two young girls. To her inexperienced eye at a first glance they looked about the same age although there the similarity ended. Surely children ought to be at school.

'Have you seen him, Miss?' Despite the second voice being deeper, she saw looking at them more closely that the speaker was in fact the smaller.

'Simpkings?' Their minder? Their brother?

'He's white, well almost white. You see, we only moved in yesterday. He won't know where he is.' This from the slightly taller, her unchildlike face puckered with anxiety.

'White, 'cept he's got one eye that's black. If you'd seen him you couldn't miss him. I keep telling Vicky, he's so 'spicuous if we ask everyone, someone will know.'

'Is he your dog?'

The elder one – she must be Vicky – looked even more worried that anyone could ask such a stupid question. The little one's face broke into a smile.

'Our dog's called Bluff. He belongs to me. He's safe at home.

137

Dogs know. Simpkins is Vicky's cat. Mrs Griffin put butter on his paws, but he just liked the taste I 'spect.'

'You haven't seen him, Miss?' Vicky was in no mood to waste valuable hunting time making small talk with a stranger.

'No, but we'll go into the house and ask if anyone else has. You say you moved in yesterday? Where to?'

As they went together to the house they told their tale. She had heard that old Mr Hubbard the veterinary surgeon was giving up before winter but she hadn't known he was going so soon. Apparently the girls' father had taken the practice, their new home had a plaque on the wall proclaiming its name to be 'Kingsbury', but for miles around it was known simply as 'The Vet's'.

'My name's Vicky – Victoria really, Victoria Graves. I'm eight.' Apparently being the elder she felt it her place to honour the conventions and introduce them. 'This is my sister, her real name's Rebecca but we call her Becky. She's—'

'I'm seven,' announced Miss Gruff.

'Only just. She was seven the day before we moved.' It was important Georgina should appreciate the gap between 'seven two days ago' and 'eight approaching nine'.

'So we are going to be neighbours. And I'm Georgina Rochester.'

Even Vicky let some of her cares fall from her shoulders. If this lady with the red hair and friendly smile was going to help them, they'd find Simpkins in no time.

He proved to be more elusive. When the children went home for their dinner Georgina promised to call for them and help in the search in the afternoon. She didn't dig into her inner self to ask why she was so willing.

'But John comes this afternoon,' Melissa complained, 'and if you don't take the trap that means I have to get Biggs to drive me. I'd looked forward to the two of us going. You can't be going to put some old cat before *me*. Anyway, why doesn't their mother go with them if they can't look by themselves. Remember when we were little, we never needing a grown up.'

'As well we didn't,' Georgina laughed, remembering.

'So you'll come with me?'

'Mellie, they've lost their cat. They're in a strange place. Anyway, I hadn't even considered going with you to Brockenhurst.

John won't want a reception party. You really ought to handle the trap—'

'You know I can't. Just thinking about it upsets me.'

Georgina wasn't to be dissuaded. She called for the children expecting to introduce herself to their mother – Mrs Graves. Instead as she reached the house she met a tall stranger about to climb into his trap.

'Are you wanting me?' he asked her.

'You must be the new veterinary . . . Mr Graves? Has Simpkins come home?'

'Ah, you're the lady who kindly helped my daughters. No, regrettably he is still missing. He may be anywhere, cats have a homing instinct and this, I fear, isn't yet home to him.'

What a 'buttoned-up' man. That was Georgina's first impression and, even while she thought it, she looked again at her new neighbour. He was tall, his face was long, strong boned, with a Roman nose, firm chin and dark, bushy eyebrows, He didn't attempt to shake hands with Georgina, but turned to climb into the trap. She noticed his hands – long, bony.

'Then I've promised to hunt with them again this afternoon.' She ignored what she considered his unneighbourly behaviour, or perhaps it was nearer the truth that she had been ignored by local society all her life and had come to look for nothing more. 'I know the area like the palm of my hand, they'll be quite safe with me. And I've written a notice for Mrs Holmes to put in the window at the shop in the village. If we don't find him, I'll take it over to her.'

'You are extremely kind.' Friendly enough words, yet spoken without the vestige of a smile. 'I have visits to attend to, I'll bid you good day.'

As she went up the path and tugged at the bell-pull outside the front door, her reaction to her meeting with the new vet was one of sympathy for the as yet unknown Mrs Graves.

'We're ready,' she heard the gruff voice call even before the front door was opened. 'We're just getting our hats.'

Then she was face to face with an elderly woman who immediately brought to mind the word 'comfortable'. Over her outdated grey gown – such as not so long ago Patience would have worn – she had pulled a full-length overall over her head, a shapeless, sleeveless garment. Perhaps she wasn't as elderly as Georgina had

139

imagined at first sight, rather she was ageless and dateless, there was nothing distinctive about her plump face and figure, nor yet about her grey hair pulled to be anchored on the top of her head in an austere bun that was out of keeping with the kindly expression. A normal cap and apron would have given her an identity, but this was no ordinary servant. So could she be the wife of that unsmiling man? Or perhaps his elder sister – or sister-in-law, she thought, her mind immediately jumping to John?

'You're the lady the girls told me about,' she greeted Georgina. 'Poor little souls, they're that upset about their cat.'

'If he's still about, we'll find him. Yes, I'm Georgina Rochester from Kyneston, the house back along the lane. You've just moved in they tell me. I hope you and Mr Graves will be happy here. You're not from the Forest?'

'I'm sure he'll settle. As for being happy, poor soul, what sort of happiness can there be for a man with a family and no wife?' Then, turning to call up the stairs to the children, 'You'll need warm coats, the wind's got a chill in it. And hurry along, Miss Rochester hasn't got all day.'

A clatter of feet as the girls raced down the stairs, their coats unbuttoned and their Breton berets pulled well on. Before she let them pass, she fastened their coats, checked with them in a loud whisper that they'd 'both paid a visit' then deemed them fit to go out.

Georgina had brought a few enticing pieces of food which she had left in a bag outside the door: a fish head, a piece of cheese and some scraps of beef. Vicky had the meat, Becky the lump of cheese ('How did you know? Simpkins loves cheese') and she carried the fish head still in its wrapping. For more than an hour they wandered, calling. They went to what few cottages there were, sheds were looked in. Then when there seemed nothing for it but to take the notice to the shop in the village Miss Carter, the rector's sister, lifted their hopes.

Of all the local people, she and her brother had always been kindest to Georgina, she because teaching her had been so rewarding and he because he felt it his Christian duty.

'A cat, you say. Not an hour ago I chased one off. I wouldn't have, mind you, but for Arthur's asthma. Cats do him no good at all. Big white creature it was, shot off like a dart over that way amongst the trees.'

140

Hope was restored. Clutching Becky and a bag containing a fish head in her left hand and Vicky's hand in her right she led them into a thickly treed area of forest, to them strange and eerie, to her as familiar as the garden of Kyneston.

'Aren't you scared?' Vicky whispered. 'Poor Simpkins, he must be frightened.'

Georgina laughed. 'More likely he's hungry. As for scared, I'd never be scared in this forest. My sister and I grew up knowing it like our own garden. You'll learn to love it too.'

'Are there hobgoblins?' Even the gruff voice was uneasy.

'No. There are squirrels, rabbits, sometimes even hares. Then there are other animals, not amongst the trees but in the clearings, pigs to eat the acorns, cows, deer, hundreds of lovely ponies. No one could be frightened in the forest. It's pure magic.'

One pair of worried blue eyes, one pair of wide brown ones looked up at her from beneath the well pulled-on berets.

'Tell you what,' Becky pronounced, 'I'm jolly glad you were in your garden. Suppose we'd knocked on the door and someone cross had answered— '

'They might have just said no, they didn't know anything about Simpkins.' Imagining how it might have been, Vicky's voice sounded ever more worried than before. 'How long do you think before we find him?'

'Hush . . . listen . . .'

They listened. Silence. But Georgina was sure she'd heard a faint mew.

'Simpkins. *You* call him,' she whispered, unwrapping the fish head in readiness.

In minutes the hunt was over, but not the recovery. The fugitive was on a high branch. He'd found his way up there, it must be possible for him to find his way down. But with feline obstinacy he stood poised, probably enjoying being the centre of attention.

'You spread the food out on the ground,' Georgina told them, 'and if he comes down hang on to him. I'm going up.'

Nature had given Becky wide brown eyes, but now Vicky's pale blue ones too were opened in wonder as the children stood at the foot of what, to them, looked an impossible climb. Georgina's tree-climbing expertise had developed over a childhood when she had gloried in impressing Melissa. Now she hauled herself to the first branch and from there on up. When she was about to clamber

141

onto Simkpins' level, he made a wild dash back to the trunk of the tree then ran down, to him the vertical presenting no more problem than if he'd been coming down a flight of stairs.

By the time Georgina was back on the ground the fish head had nearly disappeared, his loud purring partly a sign of appreciation for that and partly pleasure at being with his adoring owners. So that was the end of the incident, or would have been except that on being delivered back to 'The Vet's' Vicky remembered her manners and thanked her for her trouble just as they'd been taught.

'Yes,' Becky nodded her agreement. 'See how pleased Simpkins is. But – there's something else – um—'

'What's that?'

'I was thinking . . . if we came to call for you when Mrs Griffin says we can go out, would you come out and play? Show us the things you used to do in the forest? Would that be all right?'

Georgina knew nothing of children, she'd never thought much about them, but at the little girl's suggestion she found herself looking forward to showing them the haunts that had always been 'special places' to Melissa and her.

Arriving back at Kyneston she found Patience dead-heading a late flowering of roses.

'All's well, we found the wanderer.'

'I'm so glad. Poor little girls, with no mother to care for them. Mrs Biggs was telling me. It seems the blacksmith told Biggs all about them. The veterinary is a widower it seems, they have a housekeeper. But it's not the same, not for the children.'

'Perhaps that accounts for him being so po-faced,' Georgina said, trying to think of their new neighbour more kindly – trying without a lot of success.

'I came out to do a scrap of gardening, I thought it would give Melissa and John more space.'

'I'll get a rake and gather up some leaves. I ought to be seeing to Madame de Bouverie's order, but I'll work twice as hard this evening to make up for it.' And be glad of an excuse to escape too. Going off to collect the rake she raised her eyes – but not her head – towards the window of the drawing room, rewarded by the sight of John gazing onto the garden and sure that it was she who held his interest.

Always she enjoyed raking leaves, but that afternoon they gave

142

her double the pleasure. Without looking again towards the house, she worked with vigour. Did she imagine she still had an audience? Perhaps subconsciously she did, but even to herself she wouldn't admit it. Her pile of leaves wheeled away to the compost heap, she went indoors and up to her room to put away her hat and coat. Only as she passed the door of the room that used to be Clive and Augusta's but which had been taken now by Melissa and John did she slow her pace and instinctively tread quietly. Voices . . . quiet voices . . . Melissa's laugh . . . John telling her something, something just for the two of them to share . . .

Georgina remembered the way she'd wielded her rake, the conscious grace of her movement. She felt belittled, ashamed. And worse, she felt alone. Into her memory came the image of Steven, she saw him standing at the tiller, his hair tousled in the wind, his light brown eyes dancing with pleasure as he smiled at her. America was such a long way away . . . it would be weeks, months, before he came back. Walking purposefully she went back along the corridor, passing Melissa's closed door without slowing her pace, and into her workroom.

The evening was heavy with good intentions: Georgina's that she would be good humoured, friendly, full of sisterly camaraderie that embraced both Melissa and John; Melissa's that she would be welcoming to John, just as charming to him as she always was to their dinner guests in London; John's that he would be all things to all men (or in this case to 'all women' which included Patience), while at the same time setting the scene for a new start with Melissa. She had been hysterical and difficult in London, but she hadn't been feeling well – 'poor darling' he consciously made himself add. For more than a fortnight she'd been resting at Kyneston, already the colour was back in her cheeks. In fact he'd never seen her look lovelier. From now on things must be right for them . . . it *had* to be. They were still at the beginning of their lives together. The gallery was making a promising start, professionally their future looked bright; she'd have this child, perhaps she'd have others, they'd become a family.

There was a feeling of stillness in the room. John sat swirling his brandy in its goblet, Patience worked at her embroidery, Georgina read the *Times* (or made a pretence of reading it), while Melissa was apparently content to do nothing.

143

'You were going to let me see that vase, Georgina. You said your mother told you it was Minton. Remember?'

'It's in my room. I'll fetch it.'

'Go up with her, John,' Melissa suggested, fearing the evening would develop as she'd so often seen when John climbed onto his hobby horse. She'd been bored all too often while the conversation carried him and his cronies down the path of Minton, Meissen, Coalport, the Sèvres influence, to her a foreign language.

'A good idea,' he needed no persuading, 'I imagine it might be quite heavy. I'd hate you to drop it.'

By the time they reached the gallery at the top of the curved staircase they heard the first tinkling notes; Melissa was playing the piano – apart from looking beautiful that was the one area where she'd always shone. Georgina was glad to hear it, the sound travelled with them, a reminder of Melissa.

'Ah!' Hardly audible John breathed, it was an expression of his delight in what he saw. 'Is it perfect?'

'It's not damaged, if that's what you mean. But was Mama right do you think?' It was easier to concentrate on the vase. When he carried it nearer the lamp, sitting on the edge of the bed to examine it, there was just one moment when she allowed herself to watch him, impressing the image on her mind, holding it to be relived. Then came reality in the sound of a tinkling piano.

'Exquisite,' he whispered. With one hand on the base, the other inside the rim, he turned the vase looking at each modelled flower, each projecting stamen and drooping bud.

'Well?' she prompted. 'Is it Minton?'

'Yes, made early in the 1850s. Cherish it, Georgina.'

She nodded, too unsure of herself to speak. Carefully he carried it back to the wide windowsill then re-drew the curtain, took her hand and somehow she found herself sitting by his side on the edge of her bed.

'I've hardly seen you. Always there are other people. Georgina – we *are* friends, aren't we? You've forgiven me.'

'Yes, we have to be friends. Perhaps a devil got into us, but not for long. I just want you to make Melissa happy. As long as you do that, then of course we're friends.' Did her words sound as forced to him as they did to her?

'I want to make her happy. Whether I have up to this point is another matter. Has she talked to you about how things were in London?'

'She's talked about your home, she's enjoyed having your friends to visit. Apart from that I've gathered that almost from the start she was feeling unwell. I think she's frightened. Be gentle with her John.'

'She seems better – like she used to be.'

'I don't know about having babies, but I believe it's the first weeks that are often the worst. Perhaps she's ready to go back with you now. Jessie watches over her like a broody hen.'

'I'm out so much, it's lonely for her. But of course I shall try and persuade her.'

'We must go down. I'm glad Mama was right about the vase. It was always one of her favourite things, it used to stand in her workroom – my workroom now – but I brought it in here because I wanted it for myself.'

'It suits you . . . true, steadfast like the clear earthenware of the vase, a basis for the perfectly formed flowers, white, pure . . .' His hands were on her shoulders, her knees ached with weakness. But she had to be strong. Anyway, she told herself as she pulled back from him, he'd made a fool of her once, she'd not give the chance to do it again.

'Listen, Mellie's playing "See Me Dance the Polka", we used to sing that when we were children practising to dance in the hall.'

And she was out of the bedroom.

One thing about working for Madame de Bouverie, Georgina had a ready excuse for escape whenever she needed it. So for the rest of that weekend she hardly saw John. Watching him with Melissa she made herself believe she was glad to see the relationship between them was easier, less strained. She tried not to remember the way Melissa had cried as she'd told her how she hated the intimacies of marriage.

'May I ride with you?' John asked when he met her in the hall on the Sunday morning.

'Too late,' she laughed, 'some of us get up in the morning! But Cleo hasn't been exercised, if you feel like a ride why don't you take her.' Not a hint that she'd stolen quietly down the stairs an hour ahead of her usual time and before it was properly light so that she would be away before he stirred. It was cowardly of her,

145

she knew it was. The time would come when she'd accept his companionship with all the ease she pretended – but it hadn't come yet.

It was on his third visit that she saw Jessie carrying his clothes to hang them in the room that used to be Melissa's.

'What's happening, Jess?'

'The mistress, she doesn't sleep that well, she needs the quiet of being on her own. She needs her rest. Mr Derrick, 'e told me to take his things and put them along here.'

'Does Mrs Derrick know?' She stamped on her stirring emotion.

'I checked with her. It's her I look after – not him. I wouldn't do nothing unless she said. But it was her what told me this was the right room. This is her room she says.'

'Yes, that's right, it always was. Make sure you put hot bricks in the bed, Jessie, it's not been slept in since the spring.'

'Do this, do that,' Jessie grumbled silently as she went on her way. 'My job's to look after the missus, not to be at the beck and call of her man. Any road, I ain't even sure he's *that*. Looks to me more like she's given him his marching orders.' This brought an appreciative twitch to her lips. 'Kicked him out of her bed – and good luck to 'er, I say. I suppose it's different for the rich ones. Back 'ome, wouldn't be no good Ma telling my Dad she wanted the bed to 'erself. From what I see of 'em, they're all alike, men, the lot of 'em. Don't give a bugger whether a woman wants it or not, think because they pay the bills she's there for them whenever they have the fancy. Look at the times I've seen our Mum drag herself off to bed, tired out with looking after that lot back 'ome, but it's no good her saying no thank you. Not likely. Not in bed five minutes before I 'ear 'im at it.'

Home seemed a long way away from well-managed Kyneston, yet she thought of it with no trace of regret. Sleeping head to toe with her younger sisters in what was little more than a cupboard with a window, hearing the rough and tumble of the boys across the narrow landing where they occupied the best bedroom, one with space enough for a double and a single bed – and worse, far worse, trying to block her ears to the sounds from the adjoining bedroom used by her parents.

'You won't find me ever getting married, buggered if you will.

146

Not a shred of difference between any of 'em, that's one thing that money don't alter. Suppose they think a poor fool of a woman must be glad to oblige, same as she's glad to scrub 'is shirts an' 'ankies or put the heels back in 'is socks. Well, no one's going to catch me fool enough. And summut else too, come what may I'm not going back home again, not to live. Go and see them, that's one thing. Poor ol' Mum, no chance of her slinging her hook. Well, I'm luckier and this is where I shall stay – here or wherever the missus is. She likes having me taking care of her, and she'll come to need me more all the time as the months go by, just see if she doesn't. And me . . . I need her right enough. Can't imagine not being with 'er, not now.'

She bit her lip, turning from the wardrobe where she was hanging John's suits to gaze onto the autumn colours of the garden. 'Oh, but I never knew this sort o' feeling. It sort of fills me right up, so I can't think o' nothing else. She's that lovely, sometimes I just want to look at her – to touch her. Remember that night Dad fetched me up to see to Mum, just before our Ern was born. Snowing like Ol' Harry it was, the brick path like ice, Dad said come and see to her 'cos she felt rotten and she couldn't go off down the yard to the "houses of parliament". Remember how I got the bucket and waited while she was sick as a dog. Poor ol' Mum, that's what I thought. But I made myself think it, 'cos I was ashamed that I could have felt like I did. But I hated what I had to do for her. Felt rotten that I minded 'cos I was sorry as anything for her. But I 'ated it, turned me right over, listening to her throwing up then having to empty the pail and swill it out. Even when she'd done, I hated touching her to wash her face. Poor ol' Mum. But being sorry for someone doesn't mean you can do rotten, dirty jobs for them. But I never felt like that when the missus has been so bad. I've just ached with loving her, there isn't a thing I wouldn't do, I've just wanted to be part of what she's feeling. And when this baby gets itself born, I'm not going to let any ol' midwife come bossing about, telling me to wait downstairs. I reckon I could see to the missus myself, that I do.' She looked at the bed where John would be sleeping. 'I bet *you* never felt like I do about her. No, you with your pots and ornaments and such, if you loved her anything like as much as I do you'd have behaved yourself and you wouldn't have been given the elbow. Makes me sick just to think of him getting at her, pounding away

147

like I used to hear Dad at it at 'ome. She's not like Mum, she's –
she's like a princess – or an angel. Fancy 'im being inside the
same bed with her, just think of it. Cor . . . I'd hold her so gently,
soft and warm she'd be, smells all scenty. But 'im! Can't tell me
he comes all the way from London for a cup o' tea. Dirty bugger.
I seen love bites on her when I been helping her in her tub. Banged
into the corner of this or that, she'll say. But I know it ain't the
truth, I know it 'cos I love her, that's why.'

Her silent voice had no need for care, her 'aitches' flew in all
directions. Yet she always tried to 'speak proper' to Melissa, the
effort was an expression of her respect and adoration.

It was apparent Melissa wasn't going back to London until after
the birth of the baby. Beyond that point she was frightened to let
herself look, afraid to face the premonition that her destiny was to
be the same as her mother's – and afraid to imagine a time beyond
the birth lest she might be tempting some cruel fate.

So she lived from day to day, hating any physical change in her
appearance. Alice took her to Winchester to have suitable gowns
made by Amais Pilkington and, although she revelled in her
aunt's ceaseless care and watchfulness, she resented the reason for
it. As the weeks went by she was ashamed of her body. Always
slim and slightly built, she had assumed any child she would bear
would be the same, easily camouflaged; but in that she was wrong.
By the time she felt the first movement of life her waist was but a
memory. Only her face was still as beautiful.

'There you are, Miss Mellie,' Jess greeted her when she came
to her room at bedtime. 'Now, just tell me, didn't they think you
looked pretty as a picture?' Melissa was wearing a gown received
that day from Amais, the blue accentuating the colour of her eyes.
The staff at Kyneston hadn't changed the old habit of calling her
Miss Melissa, and before she'd been there many days Jess had
followed suit. Then, liking the way Georgina so often said
'Mellie', she had altered her form of address to Miss Mellie, tentatively at first in case she was overstepping the line. Apparently she
wasn't.

Without answering Melissa let Jess undress her and slip a volu-
minous nightgown over her head.

'Down you sit. Let me give your hair a good brush. You didn't
tell me, didn't they all say how pretty you looked?' For this

148

evening Alice and Cedric had been dining at Kyneston and Jess was sure they would have given all the praise Melissa craved. What she didn't expect was to see those lovely blue eyes swim with tears that spilled to fall as she put out a hand to draw Melissa towards the stool in front of the dressing table.

'I don't look pretty. I'm fat and ugly – and I get worse all the time. So ashamed . . . don't walk anymore . . . waddle like a duck.' Melissa's face crumpled as she gave way to her misery.

'That you never do. Oh, Miss Mellie, don't cry like that.'

There was a difference of four years in their age and until these last few weeks Melissa had thought of the maid as no more than a malnutritioned child. Scrawny and underdeveloped she may be, but Jess knew more of life and its troubles than Melissa. From personal experience she knew nothing of men, but she'd seen plenty. From sophisicated mistress and naïve maid, the tables were turned. Standing before her, her face contorted as she cried, Melissa might have been a little girl with a pillow under her night-gown.

'Come on now, Miss Mellie, you're tired I wouldn't wonder.' She guided Melissa to sit on the stool then started to unpin her hair. Obediently Melissa accepted her ministrations, but the rhymthic brushing did nothing to stem her crying. Instead it grew louder.

'I planned a lovely winter in London,' she sobbed, making no attempt at control. 'Dinner parties, theatres. Like last year – but better because I'd be in my own home. Now look at me! Last year I was just *me*, I belonged just to *me*. Soon as you get married, everything changes. First you belong to *him*, he can do what he likes with you. Now look, look what he's done. I *hate* it!' All her life it had happened: tears took possession of her, the louder she sobbed the stronger she became. Pulling away from Jess she pounded her swollen stomach with clenched fists. 'You hear me? I do, I do. I *hate* it.'

'Come on now Miss Mellie, you're just tired.' Jess put her arms around Melissa's heaving shoulders.

Neither of them heard the door open – indeed, with the noise Melissa was making they wouldn't have heard Georgina enter even if she'd been wearing hobnailed boots.

'Stop it, Melissa!'

Jessie stood with her mouth open in disbelief as Georgina

149

brought her hand sharply across Melissa's cheek making her catch her breath.

'You didn't oughter do that to 'er. She can't 'elp it.' 'Aitches' were the last thing on Jessie's mind as she saw the marks of Georgina's fingers on her beloved mistress's face. 'Leave 'er alone, can't you. It's me what looks after 'er.'

The slap had had the desired effect, no longer was Melissa glorying in the sound of her uncontrolled hysterical crying. Still she wept, weakly, helplessly as she felt Georgina's strong young arms around her. Her panic was gone, she felt safe, the reason for her outburst almost forgotten.

'You can go to bed, Jessie. I'll attend to Mrs Derrick.'

'But there's things I do for 'er you wouldn't know about. When she's in bed I give her back a good rubbing, it helps her to sleep. She needs me.'

'I'll look after her. You get to bed.'

Life had taught Jess to accept, she didn't anger easily. Now her heart was hammering with helpless rage. Who the 'ell does she think she is, coming in here making herself more important to Miss Mellie than what I am? Her look said it all as she turned in silence to the door.

Georgina didn't even notice her going.

'Hush, Mellie, it's all over. You're all right.'

'But I'm not. Every day I get worse – and all the time it gets nearer. So frightened . . .'

'Be proud Mellie, not frightened.'

Sniffing convulsively Melissa turned to her, not understanding.

'Proud? Proud to look this sight! You wouldn't understand. Do you know what my waist measured when Amais Pilkington put the measure round me? Thirty-five inches!' She almost spat the words out. 'By the time the baby is due I shall be as fat as I am high. Doesn't matter if the hateful creature does kill me, I shall be glad to die. I look so awful I can't go out, I hate even going to the Court. So what is there to be proud about? If you're so clever, tell me *that*.'

'You ought to be proud that you're having John's baby. *You're* the woman he loves, the woman he wants to have his children. That's what you should be proud for the world to know.'

'. . . don't want it. Easy for you to talk. You don't know anything about being married. Wasn't *me* he wanted, it was just a

150

woman in his bed. And me being pregnant, did that stop him?' Her voice was growing ominously loud, she was working herself up for another scene. 'No! What do you think he came here for? I'll tell you—'

'No! Stop it. I don't want to know. You're behaving like a spoilt child. Why can't you grow up? What sort of a wife are you. And it's not fair of you to say that, anyway. He comes all the way from London every weekend even though he doesn't share your room.'

Melissa's answer was unexpected.

'Who says it's me he comes to see? Look at the time he spends with you, riding, walking, showing you the things he's storing here ready for that shipping man.'

'And what do you expect him to do with his weekend? You don't stir yourself to enjoy his company.'

The atmosphere was charged with emotion.

'He never loved me, he could never love anyone,' Melissa sounded like a tragedy queen. 'He loves beautiful things – and I *was* beautiful. But he didn't cherish me as he would some beautiful vase, oh no. He used me, he did this to me. Oh Georgie, all I wanted was to be loved,' again the tears spilled, her mouth worked, she looked utterly wretched.

'And so you are loved, Mellie. Of course he loves you.' Did he? Did he?

Kneeling outside the door Jess pressed her eye to the keyhole. She missed nothing, not a word, not a gulp or a hiccup from Melissa and not the way she buried her face against Georgina's shoulder – nor yet the unfathomable expression on Georgina's face. It was as if her emotions had to find an even balance: against the love she felt for Melissa had to be weighed spite and hate for those who hurt her, for John and for Georgina.

Chapter Nine

The day on the boat was still alive in Georgina's mind: waking and sleeping, she was haunted by John. But their relationship was moving on, encompassing far more than the physical magnetism that had drawn them. For surely it had drawn him too? He'd told her that he couldn't forget, even on his wedding day he'd said it. But since then he'd had a wife, soon he would be a father. Only Georgina was left with nothing but memories to taunt her. During days of activity she could run away from them, only alone in the quiet of night was there no escape.

Willingly she encouraged their friendship to develop, determined to keep it on platonic lines. In building the blocks of friendship she trusted that one day she would learn to be free of him. She never failed to greet him with the sort of ready smile to be expected from a sister; she was sure she never failed, for she knew the effort it cost her. Each weekend he came. She told herself that Melissa must look forward to Fridays with eagerness; but if she did there was little evidence of it. For herself, though, even though in the beginning she over-emphasized the casual warmth of her welcome, yet as the weeks went by she found herself waiting for his arrival with something more than the bittersweet pain of being with him. He would talk to her about his week and, if he brought items to await Steven, he would show them to her and appreciating her interest and willingness to understand, would teach her to recognize their origin. She was a natural pupil but, more than that, learning to love the things he loved brought them close.

'Why don't you bring Sir Edmund for the weekend – and Lady Betsy of course. Perhaps they could stay a few days, Melissa would like that. I wonder she hasn't suggested it herself.' Her breath hung on the air in a cloud of vapour as they rode side by side over the frost hardened forest one morning in late January.

'They've not written to her, have they?'

'No. I wish they would. They seemed so fond of her at the wedding.'

'They were. I expect they still would be – except that being fond of her would involve them with *me*. He kicked me out, you know. But I didn't tell Melissa that – I've not told anyone until now – I don't know why I've told *you*.' How silly it was that she should feel this flutter of excitement at his words. 'The trade I do in America, that had always been my own affair, nothing to do with Northney's.'

'I know. Melissa told me. You mean he found out you'd been buying in your uncle's name?' She dreaded his answer.

'I suppose that's what the auctioneers thought, but no. I didn't use Northney money. I was tempted, very tempted in the beginning I don't mind admitting, but anything I bought to ship out of the country I paid for myself. When the money came back to me I didn't look on it as profit, I ploughed it back. When my uncle got to hear, you'd think I'd been embezzling the firm the way he behaved. Fortunately it all cropped up when I was ready to sign up for my own gallery.'

'Why didn't you do that sooner? You could have been selling at home as well as abroad . . .'

He gave her a quick glance. She'd realized from the start that he'd married Melissa knowing the extent of her wealth, but hadn't she known that he had nothing of his own, nothing except what he was paid at Northney's.

Her words drifted into silence as she waited for him to reply, despising herself for setting a trap and encouraging him to concoct some plausible excuse, and despising him that he was about to lie to her.

'I had no capital, nothing at all but the salary I earned. It was Melissa who put up the money for the gallery.' His honesty was unexpected. 'Don't pretend you didn't know.'

'I knew you needed money, but not that you had nothing.' Instinctively they reined in their horses coming to a halt, then silently they looked at each other. 'I wonder whether Father did her any favours, leaving her the plantations.'

'Georgina, you think I'm a rotter. Perhaps you're right. But I mean to make our marriage work.'

'And so I should hope.' Then, letting the veil fall and speaking honestly, 'I really do hope so, for your sake, for her sake – and for the baby's. And for mine too. We're learning to be friends, you and I. That's what I want for us.'

She knew just how narrow was the line she walked, emotion was dangerously near the surface, even after all these months the ghost of her mistaken certainty was ready to catch her.

'I may be a rotter, but what we have is important to me. You do believe me?'

She told herself his friendship was all she wanted.

Not even Georgina knew how, at every sound from the drive, Patience would glance hopefully from the window. After nearly four months' practice she had become quite adept at tying her nightly rags and pinning the result on top of her head. But sometimes she wondered if her efforts weren't a waste; perhaps her hero had forgotten his promise to spend his time ashore at Kyneston.

Then on Thursday of the first week in February she looked out at the sound of wheels on the gravel – and there he was! Just as handsome . . . just as thrilling . . .

'My word, what a surprise! It's Captain Howard – Steven.' she corrected not able to keep the flutter out of her voice, 'How the weeks fly by, I hadn't realized he was due back so soon.'

'A visitor! Whatever do I look like?' Melissa's glance in the mirror only showed her head and shoulders – just as lovely as ever – but imagination did the rest. 'A lumbering elephant. I can't let him see me. I'm going upstairs. Get rid of him as soon as you can Aunt Patience.'

'Don't be stupid,' came Georgina's tart answer. 'He's come to stay, he'll be here until he reloads the *Seahorse*.'

'Who invited him? John, I suppose.' The dangerous rise in Melissa's voice was all too familiar. 'It's not his place to say who—'

'I invited him,' Georgina told her. 'Go and welcome him Aunt Patience. Tell him we've been expecting him.' Patience knew that what she meant was: Keep him outside until Melissa calms down, we don't want a scene. She almost ran across the large, stone-flagged hall and down the steps to the drive.

'If you're so ashamed of carrying John's child, then I've no

154

patience with you,' Georgina told Melissa, aiming at stopping her threatened loss of control before it carried her away on a torrent of hysteria. 'You spend a fortune on attractive clothes, lots of women have to make do with things that don't even fit them. And you look pretty, you know you do.'

'You've got no business to invite people without seeing if I want them too.' Melissa clutched at the nearest straw.

'I've as much right as you have. Steven is your husband's friend and colleague and it's up to you to behave yourself and make him welcome.'

'You don't understand ... I'm not well ... ugly ... fat and ugly ...' With her face contorted she turned to go back upstairs. 'No one understands ... no one cares ... when it's too late you'll all be sorry ...'

Georgina held out her arms to the retreating figure, then let them drop to her side. Looking up the stairs she saw the door of Melissa's room open and Jessie come to meet her adored mistress.

'Oh Miss Mellie, you mustn't cry like that. What've they been doing to you?'

Irritated by the increasing volume of Melissa's crying and the way the girl drew her into her ever-ready arms, Georgina turned away. Outside Patience was enjoying the role of hostess. With his bag off-loaded and the cabby paid and dismissed, Steven was admiring the snowdrops and early crocus she pointed out to him. With no one to share his attention, her cup of happiness was full. Even so she greeted Georgina with a smile.

'There you are, dear. See who's arrived! Isn't it nice to have him safely back. Is Melissa with you?'

'She's upstairs resting. We won't disturb her to tell her she has a visitor. Welcome back, Steven.' She held both her hands out to him, feeling them taken in his warm, firm grasp. For weeks the thought of him hadn't crossed her mind, and it surprised her just how glad she was to see him.

And just as she had on his last visit, so she encouraged his attention. A little less self interest and she would have been aware how, for weeks, Patience had kept eye and ear open for his coming; and, even though the idea of her day-dreaming and homely 'aunt' capturing his interest was so unlikely, Georgina would have acted differently, tried to play matchmaker. On his first visit she had used him as a weapon to hurt John. This time she soon found that

155

her reason for enjoying his attention had subtly altered: there was something comfortable and right about being with him, it was as if Fate had brought him into her life for a purpose. More scarred than she'd realized by the treatment meted out by Alice and Cedric, by the local society, and even by John who had thrown her aside for Melissa, Steven gave her confidence and self-pride.

On the surface that weekend followed much the same pattern as the days of his previous stay; yet there was a difference. There was no doubt in her mind that Steven had come to Kyneston because of *her*, when he'd left last time she'd known it was she who would bring him back. And yet she'd let her mind focus only on John. This time it wouldn't be like that, when he sailed away this time she would be looking forward to his return. Her experience of men was narrow (wasn't that what Melissa had told her?), going little further than her father, the Rector, Biggs and the gardeners – and of course John. Steven wasn't like anyone else, he was the epitome of manhood, a pillar of strength, master of his ship. He'd travelled the world, battled against the elements and not been conquered.

Confused and out of depth with her emotions, that weekend she watched the two men together. Her heart cried out to John – but she wouldn't listen to it, she *mustn't* listen to it. It was a relief when she saw two small girls trudging up the drive followed by Bluff, the terrier mongrel their father had taken in as a puppy when it's elderly owner had died.

'Well, I'll be—' Jess watched from the window of the bedroom.

'You'll be what?' Melissa chuckled. 'What am I missing?' She lay on the bed, stripped of all but her chemise and drawers, the body she considered unsightly hidden from view by the counterpane and eiderdown. Both of them enjoyed the two hours of her afternoon rest, it had a quality of intimacy, no one – not John, not Georgina, not even Alice – would disturb them.

'Miss Georgina and those two girls she hangs around with. They just turned up for her and bugger me – beg pardon Miss Mellie – but guess what. Instead of the three of them going off like normal, that man what's staying, he calls after them, says something to your Mr Derrick and I'm blowed if the lot of them ain't gone off together. But is she walking with the girls? Not likely! Laughing away they all are, you'd think they were off on a real jaunt, her with one arm linked through Mr Derrick's and one through that other one's.' Under half closed lids she stole a glance at Melissa to see the effect of her words. 'That Miss Georgina, she entices them, you know, Miss Mellie. Not my place to tittle-tattle, but I'm not going to sit by and watch her and her capers. I seen it before, not just with her, with some of the women round our way at 'ome. Draw men like moths to a flame – and it ain't their looks that do it. Oh Miss Mellie, I didn't oughta say such things to you not with you like you are. But I'm not going to stay quiet and watch, I've seen too many of her kind.'

'I'm no company—'

'You're all the company *I* want and that's God's truth. I'm glad he don't want to, but wouldn't you think he'd want to kick me out and sit here with you. Like all the men, don't stop to think how tired you must be starting to get. And months of it ahead of you yet too. There I go again! Why don't you stop me, Miss Mellie? Now I've got you upset.' Dropping her sewing she came to the bed, half sitting and half lying on it she gathered Melissa into her arms. There was no tormented hysteria in the quiet tears, simply terror beyond words. 'Time'll soon go, Miss Mellie, soon it'll be over. He's just one of those young men what's scared of sickness. That's what frightened him away to the other room. And that's why he hangs around with Miss Georgina, her what never has so much as a cold in her head. Once you've had the baby, he'll be back sharp enough then.'

'It's not that,' Melissa sobbed. And out poured her fears, her terror of having the baby, her morbid certainty that the birth would kill her. There was no reason, no logic – just a black wall of misery.

Jess drew the counterpane and eiderdown over them both. Holding Melissa's trembling body close she ached with tenderness. How could she know such deep happiness while her beloved mistress was wrapped in despair? Not even believing that her hints about John and Georgina had fallen on stony ground could spoil the wonder; she had never realized loving someone could make you feel like this. If only she could have borne Miss Mellie's pain, but there was nothing, nothing she could do except hold her. She felt humbled and thankful.

That afternoon the seeds of gossip might have seemed to have landed on rocky ground, but there must have been soil enough for them to germinate.

* * *

157

'Father is going to buy us ponies. One for Becky and one for me,' Victoria announced as the five of them followed Bluff's lead towards the open forest.

'And guess what?' Becky's deep voice took up the tale. 'We've 'suaded him that he will take us to the sale to find them and – guess what? He says we can ask you to come too Georgina.'

'He said we might ask you if you'd be kind enough to come too,' Victoria, the well-mannered, corrected.

'I'd love to, if you want me. What fun. We'll be able to go much further once you learn to handle your ponies – and soon you'll have wonderful adventures.'

'Like you and Melissa,' Becky's said with satisfaction.

'I rode mostly on my own – but it didn't stop me making friends with the forest. Tell Mr Graves I'm delighted to accept the invitation. The sale is on Thursday, I saw the notice.'

'I'm very 'cited,' Becky announced. 'We have to learn how to groom them. Father never has time to teach us.'

Georgina heard the unspoken request.

'If he likes, I'll help you.' If she was good for the girls, so they were good for her. They behaved with such naturalness, she knew they came to her for one reason only – they liked being with her.

But before Thursday there were days to be spent with Steven. Was she being naïve to imagine he was in love with her? She'd made that mistake once before and was still suffering the bruising. But Steven was different, she absorbed every word he told her, descriptions of the ports he'd visited, storms he'd ridden. She almost heard the bustle of the docks and tasted the tangy salt on the spray. More than that, though, she felt part of what his life had been. Yes he was falling in love with her, she was sure he was. That he was too old for her, too experienced, counted for nothing. When, on the Wednesday morning that he was leaving, they came back together from their morning ride and led the horses into the stable, she knew the moment was important. She was ready for him, eager for him as his mouth covered hers. For a second that other memory flooded through her but she pushed it away, she wanted Steven's lips to take away the impression she believed John had left to be with her for ever.

'You'll be with me every mile of my journey,' he whispered. 'You know what you've done to me, don't you. I want to be with you always. Be here for me when I come back.'

She nodded. Within her, pain fought with joy. She was being given a second chance; but there was nothing second best in Steven, he was king of the jungle, a man in a man's world. Travelling the world he must have known many women, probably even now there was someone waiting for the *Seahorse* when it tied up in America. That didn't matter. Georgina wasn't looking to the future. Here and now was what mattered. With her eyes wide open she hurled herself into love with him, he was salve to her wounded spirit.

Travelling to the horse sale with Alex Graves and the girls, she thought of Steven again – and again. If he'd been taking them to the sale the outing would have been an adventure. How different he was from her dry and sober companion. Steven would never be old; Alex, she suspected, had never known how to be young.

'Are we nearly there, Father?' Becky wanted to know after no more than a quarter of an hour, while Victoria looked at him expectantly.

'Not for some miles. We have to go beyond Ringwood.' His tone was patient enough, yet somehow he implied the journey was no more than something to be endured, not part of an exciting morning's adventure. Looking at the girls Georgina was prepared for them to appear as deflated as he had made her feel. But she was wrong. With their eyes fixed on him trustingly they nodded their understanding, then seemed to settle further into their wooden seat as if that way they wouldn't fidget with anticipation. Oh no, Alex Graves wouldn't expect any fidgeting.

When they arrived selling had already started.

'We ought to have come sooner,' Georgina said. 'I hope we haven't missed—'

'Those I'm interested in haven't come up yet,' he cut her short. 'Nearer the end of the sale, I understand.'

'How do you know?'

The children looked from one of them to the other. Friend and father, both important to them. Victoria didn't like the edge she heard to their voices, her brows were pulled down in that anxious look that was all too frequent. Becky felt a tension too, but she put it down to the fact they might be too late for the ponies they wanted so she tugged urgently at Alex's hand.

'I know because I was at Old Hatch first thing this morning

159

attending a pig. Mr Holt' (the name made a stranger of the farmer known to everyone as Old Silas and who had appeared unchanged in Georgina's eyes since as long ago as her memory stretched) 'had sent over two young ponies from his forest grazing, he assured me they'd make safe mounts for the girls. Too late to take them off him at the farm but he told me he'd keep them back until he saw I'd arrived.'

'Suppose you don't like them? You ought to look at the others too.'

'Mr Holt is an honest man.'

Georgina felt herself flush with anger. Was he inferring she doubted Old Silas? But perhaps the girls would lose their hearts to other young ponies who were being trotted around for inspection.

'Ah, he's seen me. Here we are then girls, these will be your mounts.' Old Silas hobbled forward, a rope in each hand as he led the animals out for inspection. Both young, unused to being restricted, they tossed their head, their manes flying. Becky giggled and jumped with excitement, Victoria looked less certain but she held her chin up bravely. Both ponies had the thick, shaggy coats demanded by a harsh forest winter.

'They're darlings,' Georgina whispered encouragingly.

'I'm calling mine Squibb. That's a good name isn't it, Father? Squibb's that one that's trying to dance.' In her mind Becky was astride him already. Then her jaw dropped as someone facing them on the other side of the cordoned off sale ring shouted out his bid.

Silence. Oh but surely their father couldn't disappoint them. From further along came another call. Then silence. The two men bid against each other, then the first appeared to drop out. Only then did Alex enter the bidding. Georgina's sigh of relief was as heartfelt as the girls'. She let herself watch him as he went forward to hand over his money. Never had she known such a stony-faced, expressionless, buttoned-up man. Left alone with her the children could hardly contain their excitement, yet when he returned they took on a cloak of dignity almost akin to his own.

'Thank you Father,' Victoria's gentle smile had lost some of its former anxiety. 'We'll look after them and I expect they'll soon learn to quieten down, don't you?'

'I don't want Squibb to change one scrap, I think he's perfect. And Vicky, they know the forest already, won't they be glad when they see where they're going to live.'

160

'I haven't been any help in the choosing,' Georgina observed as the children clambered into the governess cart, and she and Alex secured Squibb and Honey, as the second was to be named, to trot behind. 'You knew before you came what you meant to buy.'

'The children were insistent they wanted you to be there. And this has presented me with the opportunity to thank you, Miss Rochester, for the time you spend with them. I am out a good deal, Mrs Griffin cares for them wonderfully, but I appreciate the interest you have shown. It's two years since they lost their mother, it hasn't been easy for them. But they are good girls.'

'If I hadn't wanted to I should never have got involved with them. I don't need to be thanked.' She was appalled, she sounded as gauche and gruff as he did himself. So she softened her words with what she hoped was a relaxing smile which she aimed at extending to her voice as she added: 'I know your own spare time is limited, but I shall be happy to help them to ride. They know *that*, I don't need to tell them.'

The smile was apparently lost on him and her friendly offer met with a formal inclination of his head.

'You are most kind. However, I have already arranged riding lessons for them.'

Just for a moment she felt rebuffed, then she looked at him afresh. Tall, unbending, aloof, fiercly independent and, she suspected, frightened of being the object of sympathy in his care for his daughters.

'Lucky girls,' she laughed. 'My parents taught me the rudiments – then nature took over. So it will with them, you know, when they're a bit older. They'll come to know and love every forest track.'

'You may be right. There, the ponies are secure. If you care to climb in with the girls, we'll start for home.'

The ponies were everything she would have chosen. As she'd just said, learning to ride them would open new vistas for Victoria and Becky who already were watching them not so much in awe as with pride.

'Do you expect they wonder where they're being taken?' Victoria whispered to her.

'I believe animals have an uncanny perception, they probably sense they're going towards the forest.'

'That must make them glad.'

161

It was Becky who put into words the thing that mattered most to them, more than the prospect of galloping across the open forest or sitting high while the ponies picked a delicate track through the treed enclosures.

'They look so big, bigger than us. But it's *us* they will look to, we're the ones to take good care of them.' She sighed, but there was no anxiety in the sound, only huge satisfaction in the responsibility. For Georgina the years rolled away, again she was six years old, filled with joy she could hardly contain, joy that came only partly from the fun waiting for her when she could ride properly. She remembered the wonder of feeling the firm saddle beneath her, of leaning forward and, for the first time, running her fingers through the coarse hair of Tinker's mane, the mixture of pride and humility that here was a living creature belonging to her, depending on her.

Unexpectedly the image of Melissa sprang into her mind. How would she react when the baby was born? To have a living person, small and helpless, depending on her, might give her the purpose her life had lacked. Poor Mellie, always looking for something, never knowing what. Marriage had frightened her just as everything had always frightened her. But things would be better once the baby was born, it would bring a new meaning, a child that was hers and John's would bind them ... So often Georgina played this game of torturing herself and, now as always, it ended by tipping her thoughts towards Steven; she'd remembered the strength of his arms, the feel of his mouth on hers, the sound of his voice. In the place of her self-inflicted misery came something akin to peace. Being with Steven was right, there was no make-believe in the hold he had on her.

As the governess cart rattled its way over the rutted forest road she was lost in her own thoughts, but so were the girls so they didn't notice her silence. As for Alex, there was no way of knowing what went on behind that expressionless face. A po-faced sobersides, Georgina had thought him, and the hours in his company had done nothing to alter her view.

'Is John coming as usual?' Georgina asked, knowing full well that he was, but hoping to coerce Melissa into the right mood to welcome him.

'You're the one who ought to know.' It wasn't so much what

162

she said as the way she said it that warned Georgina. Melissa was spoiling for a fight. In fact it would have made little difference whom she fought, her bitterness was against life, against things outside her manipulation – like the change in the baby's position that made her back ache, gave her the shape of a bow window and warned her that her latest gown was already too tight. 'Not likely he wants to see *me*! Not that I blame him! Who'd want to look at such an ugly lump!' Heaving herself off the sofa she glared rebelliously at Georgina. 'Do you think I don't know what goes on between you and him? I've seen the way you butter up to him. Just like you used to before I married him. You've always been the same. Like Aunt Alice says – whatever I've done you've always wanted to do better. And now that I look like this you even try to steal my husband.' Did she even know what she was saying? Her tone crept higher, her voice rasped.

'Damn your Aunt Alice. You know it's not true.'

'I ought to be watching you, that's what she says.' Like an out-of-control canoeist caught in the rapids she rushed on. 'Jess knows too. I expect the maids all know – all know and all laugh at me that *I* have to be so wretched – ugly, ill, miserable—' Oh, the relief of scorching tears, rocking backwards and forwards on her feet she screamed the words. Tears and misery needed a background of noise, noise that filled her head as she rejoiced in her own bellowing. 'And *you*, doesn't matter that you were never even pretty, you can run and ride and – and – be there for him.'

The accusation came as a shock. All these weeks Georgina had battled against her own feelings, hiding the truth from John, from everyone she'd believed, even trying to hide it from herself. She recognized the truth in all Melissa said. And she recognized something else too: even though Melissa seemed concerned only in herself, yet she was jealous of the time John spent with anyone else. Memories crowded back, John vowing his marriage would be a success, her pledging to be his friend, his sister, that and nothing more.

She held out her hands to Melissa and spoke gently.

'Mellie, John is your husband, my brother—'

'Not what you want though, is it? You want him in bed with you – you're like your mother, that's what she says—'

'If I'm like Mama, then I'm grateful. How can you listen to your mean minded aunt talking like that about her.' Reason told

163

her that Melissa didn't know what she was saying. But reason had no more place than honesty, the honesty she'd shunned when she's said that John was simply a brother. Like two cats on a wall they glared at each other, Melissa living in a hell of her own making, her once-slim bosom heaving, her fists clenching and unclenching.

The door burst open. 'Jus' leave 'er alone, why can't you?' Like an avenging angel Jess was there.

'Get out until you're sent for,' Georgina snapped without taking her eyes from Melissa. Only afterwards did she realize how surprised she must have been that Jess obeyed (probably to wait in the corridor with her ear to the door.), now she was conscious only of the rift that had opened between herself and Melissa. No matter how they had argued or vied with each other over the years, the bond had never broken. Until now. 'Mellie, stop that noise. Stop it, you'll make yourself sick.'

'Want to be sick . . . want to be dead . . .'

With a stinging blow Georgina's hand came sharply across the tearstained cheek. Melissa gasped . . . again she gasped . . . and always in the past this would have been when she would have felt Georgina's arms around her, giving her courage, driving away the devils. But not this time. They looked at each other in misery, neither able to bridge the chasm.

Georgina was shocked not at Melissa, for after all scenes like this were nothing unusual, but at herself that she could feel so remote from Melissa's trembling form slumped now on the sofa, that she felt no compassion for the wild panic in her bloodshot eyes. She turned away and walked to the window, frightened by the confusion of her own emotions. Look at the daffodils, their trumpets dancing in the spring breeze – remember how we used to cut them for the house, Mellie and me. Mellie and me . . . Mellie and me . . . all the make-believe games we used to play . . . and remember the secrets we shared when we started to know about being grown up. Then you met John . . . remember how he vowed he would make his marriage work. And so it must. Why can't she grow up! Why can't she stop play-acting? They've a lifetime ahead of them, why can't she try and make him happy instead of thinking just of herself? John . . . beloved, greedy, probably selfish, so much in him that I can't respect, but what has that to do with what's between us? If he were free – no, be honest, if he were

164

free he'd be looking for a wife who would help him up the ladder of his ambition. Well, that's the sort of wife he has, please, please God, if you can do such wonderful things, surely you can help them. Make things work for them, make Mellie behave like any other woman having a baby. John . . . a lifetime of marriage to Melissa ahead of him, father of the child she so resented . . . John . . .

In her fervent plea for them she found her own courage. A minute ago she'd not been able to look at Melissa, now she went back to her and dropped to her knees by her side.

'Yes, I've talked to John about you, Mellie, of course I have. Each week he comes, but do you ever let him close to you? He's worried about you, he can't get near you—'

'Can't touch me, you mean,' she hiccuped, a remark that Georgina ignored, 'Can't use me as if I'm just here for his pleasure.'

'You've been married less than a year.' Somehow she had to seize this moment. She took Melissa's hands, holding them tightly and not letting them be snatched away. If the chance to help John, to help both of them, had been put her way then she would grasp it. She was their sister, part of their family . . . that was the only silent voice she would listen to. 'You've all your lives ahead, you'll share everything with each other and with your family – your children and his. Mellie, be kind to him—'

'There you are!' And unable to free her hands, Melissa kicked with one foot almost unbalancing herself. 'I said it was *him* you cared about him. About him – not about me—'

'About both of you. You make things hard for yourself. If when John comes you'd show him you're pleased to see him, talk to him, if you're frightened and miserable then let him be the one to share it with you. And ask him about his week.' Seeing she was getting nowhere she loosened her hold and stop up. The calming effect of her heartfelt petition was wearing thin. 'Stop thinking just about yourself and you'd find you'd both be happier.' Still giving the occasional trembling snort Melissa kept her gaze lowered.

So often the thought of Steven braced Georgina. It did now. She knew exactly what she was going to say – and it's true, of course it's the truth, she told herself – she felt like someone about to dive into deep, icy water, confident that she could swim, but knowing

165

it would take her breath away. 'And, as for me, you're talking rubbish. There's someone else.'

'How can there be? You don't know anyone. Who?' It had the desired effect, Melissa had stopped crying although she looked at Georgina with suspicion. 'Tell me who.'

'Steven.'

Suspicion gave way to laughter, mirthless laughter that was as unnerving to hear as her crying had been.

'Does Aunt Patience know?' Hysteria was only just below the surface, Georgina could hear it in the uncontrolled way she giggled. 'All the hours she must have wrestled with her curling rags and you sweep him for under her nose. You tried to take John from me, now you're playing the same game with poor old Aunt Patience.'

'With a mind as twisted as yours, no wonder you're miserable! Aunt Patience has made her hair look very pretty. There's more to life than chasing after men, you know.'

Without waiting for an answer she left, colliding with hovering Jess and still hearing the echo of Melissa's words. Was it true? Did Patience harbour dreams of a romantic sea captain? But she hardly knew him, to her he was no more than a charming visitor.

At a mere twenty-one Georgina couldn't be expected to understand the lonely longings of middle age.

Chapter Ten

Not long after Melissa's stormy scene, a box arrived for her: two
gowns made for her by Amais Pilkington. Cheered by those and
by Jess's never failing support, she presented a picture of patient
suffering when she'd raised her cheek for John's greeting.
Whether or not they spent the evening together, whether she
encouraged him to talk to her about their home or his week at the
gallery, Georgina had no idea; for as soon as their meal was
finished she made the excuse that she was behind with her work
for Mme de Bouverie and shut herself in her workroom.

Sitting near the lamp she worked, listening to the sound of the
piano, conscious of the silence when at last it stopped, then hearing footsteps on the stairs. Not Melissa retiring alone; that was
John's voice, then the click of the latch as Melissa's door closed
and further along the corridor of John's. Minutes went past as she
worked, Jessie must have settled Melissa for the night, she was on
her way up the attic stairs to her own room. Then she heard something else, a sound that took her to open the workroom door just
far enough that she could see. Melissa, barefoot, wearing a volu-
minous silk nightgown, walking as lightly as she could down the
corridor. A light tap at John's door – and she vanished from sight.

Back at her work table Georgina took a roll of pearl grey
veiling. Work, that's what she must do. Measure the veiling . . .
cut it . . . twist it . . . set it like this . . . pin it in position . . . thread
the needle . . . That's when she pricked her finger. Hardly enough
to draw blood, but more than enough to make her thoughts take
wing. Pushing the hat away she had no power to stop them, they
carried her where they would.

* * *

167

'Melissa!' Already in bed, John threw back the covers and was instantly on his feet, coming to meet her.

'I wanted to talk to you. Not downstairs with Aunt Patience hearing every word.'

Was this the miracle he'd once hoped for? This evening she had been more relaxed, gently friendly. She had talked about their home, enquired about the gallery and Harold Rogers. Now this! Could this be a new beginning, a sign that she wanted to put these troubled months behind them? She was his wife, after all his visits when she avoided being alone with him – even fully clothed and in broad daylight she had treated his as though he were her arch enemy – now she had come to him like this. John read her message as having only one meaning. He was human, and despite the tender way he came to her, putting his arm around her, that one meaning was uppermost in his mind.

'Darling,' he mustn't frighten her. She didn't pull away as he held her with as much care as if she were made of the delicate porcelain he loved. She even raised her face and brushed her lips lightly on his cheek. This was the way she wanted a husband to behave. And this evening she was thankful in the confidence that he couldn't expect anything of her now, at least she was safe from the humiliation she used to suffer; wearing just her nightgown her swollen body made her see herself as a pitiable sight. He'd be ashamed that it was the way he'd behaved had done this to her.

'I didn't say anything to you downstairs, not in front of Aunt Patience,' she repeated. Why did she instinctively whisper?

'Say it now,' he spoke quietly too, seeming aware that she could easily be frightened but never doubting what it was she'd come to tell him. The early months were the worst, didn't everyone say so? And that other thing he'd heard too: pregnant women were more passionate, more demanding. His pulses raced.

'Georgina told me this afternoon,' her words came as a shock. 'She's in love with Steven Howard. Did you know? Had she told you?'

No! Why's she telling me this? Does she know how I feel about Georgina, does she know that if I'd been half a man it would be Georgina in my arms, Georgina, warm, loving and glorying in love, understanding, wonderful . . .

'Is that what you came here for, to tell me that?'

168

There was something different in him, the gentleness had given way to a repressed strength that frightened her.

'Let go of me. You can't touch me—' Oh but he could, the strength he had been holding back found uncontrolled release. Was this how men committed murder, with no more will to stop themselves than he had as he pushed her back onto the bed. She fought him as he pushed her nightgown out of the way, but she had no chance against him. 'You'll hurt me, you're wicked, you can't do that, not now—'

'You're my wife. "Don't touch me" ' he mimicked. 'Was that your duty, letting me make you pregnant?'

She struggled, but she had no chance. There was nothing gentle in the way he entered her, his movements were violent, convulsive. If she hadn't been so revolted by physical contact she might have been exhilarated that he desired her so desperately.

Little did she know the devils that plagued him. Georgina, you can't love him, you belong to me. I let you go – for this . .

'Stop it,' Melissa gasped, 'when I'm gone you'll wish you'd—'

Whatever it was she was so sure he'd wish, he didn't hear. There was no joy in what he did, only the demands of a passion that had only one outlet. In hardly more than seconds it was over.

Next morning, an hour before her normal time, Georgina crept out, leaving a note on the table near the foot of the stairs where it was bound to be seen:

'John, I've had to start the exercise routine early as once I've been back for breakfast I've arranged be out for the rest of the morning.' A white lie, backed up with no hint of where she had arranged to go. 'If you feel like giving Juno a gallop, she'll be pleased to see you.'

Her ruse worked. Coming home for breakfast she found he'd already gone riding. Was he following their usual tracks, looking for her? Lifting the lid of the warming dish she viewed Mrs Biggs's special weekend offering (a vast quantity compared with other mornings, for she came of the school who believed a man needed abundant fuel) of bacon, mushroom, eggs, kidney. Fresh air usually gave Georgina an appetite but this morning she closed the lid leaving the food untouched, then ate one slice of toast, a token breakfast forced down out of respect for Patience's worried expression. Then she went up to her room as though she meant to

169

change out of her riding habit. In truth what she did was watch and listen for John's return, only when she heard him safely in the breakfast room, going quietly down and letting herself out of the side door and making once again for the stables.

It was better for John and Melissa if she were out of the way, that's what she told herself. But she knew she was taking the coward's way, using the children as a means of escaping her own thoughts. Their pleasure at seeing her was apparent, to go out on their ponies on a Saturday was a treat they hadn't anticipated.

'You'll let us go, Father? Please. We'll be right as rain with Georgina.'

'Can you manage two of them, Miss Rochester. And, girls, I'm not sure that I care for you calling Miss Rochester by her Christian name.'

'What nonsense!' Georgina laughed, her smile hiding her irritation. What a stick the man was! 'And of course I can manage, I watched them the other day, not just them but their mounts too. They are doing splendidly.'

'If you are confident, then I'm obliged to you. I have calls to make, I shall be out a good deal of the day. If you have time to spare, why don't you let me tell Mrs Griffin you will come back and have lunch with them.' Then, with a half smile that might – just *might* – be held back by shyness, 'I'd be most grateful.'

'That sounds like fun, doesn't it girls? Come on, then, if your father says you may come, run upstairs and get ready. I'll start saddling up.'

Feeling lighter-hearted than she had since her session with Melissa, she watched them race up the stairs.

'We're having our riding lessons after school two days a week now. Tuesdays and Fridays Mr Holmes comes to take us out,' Victoria told her.

'We just have time to have a glass of milk and a slice of cake and get changed. We hurry like anything,' Becky added her contribution.

'And you're doing jolly well. I'm sure he's pleased with you both, isn't he?'

Being with them did more than anything else could to clear her mind of its tangles and the heartache she wouldn't acknowledge.

'Go down this track to the right. If you're not getting tired I'll take you to the place Mellie and I often used to come to play. It was our make-believe castle when we were little, she was a beautiful princess and I was a gallant knight.' Those were the days she wanted to remember, the freedom, the carefree hours with nothing more to worry about than whether Reverend Carter would like what they'd written for him about William the Conqueror or the wicked slave trade, or whether they'd get their spellings right when Miss Carter tested them.

She liked it too that Bluff usually came with them, somehow in him she felt the spirit of Hunter who'd been the constant third in their own childhood adventures.

There was no sign of Alex's return when, having shared a lively lunch with the children, she set off home. It was still only Saturday afternoon, she had another twenty-four hours to keep herself busily out of the way without it being too obvious. And why was she doing it? Would John even notice? That was just *one* of the unanswerables in her mind as she rode along the familiar track. With no Victoria and Becky to protect her, she couldn't prevent her mind going where it would. If yesterday evening were any indication, Melissa must have taken my words to heart. I should be glad, I should be saying 'thank You for listening to me'. Instead I just want him to be waiting, watching for me to get bck. It's Melissa he wants, Melissa he is determined to make a good life with . . . what sort of a sister am I? For *her* sake, for *his* – yes and for my own too – I must act the way that's right, make a future that's good. I don't need John Derrick any more than he needs me . . .

Yet as she came round the curve in the drive she couldn't keep her eyes from the drawing-room window. The afternoon was blustery, no one would be in the garden. When he heard the sound of hooves on the gravel drive he would look out . . .

There was no movement, no sign of him.

'All alone Aunt Patience?' she asked brightly as she came into the drawing room where Patience was painstakingly embroidering a dressing-table runner.

'Mellie's having her rest. Where have you been dear? I was getting anxious.'

'Riding with the children, then I stayed there for lunch.' Then, steering back to her original question, 'If Melissa's resting, what about John?' She had to ask.

171

'He went back as soon as he'd swallowed his breakfast, back to London. I wonder he went. I hate to criticize, but I do feel that today his place should have been here.'

'If he's as busy as all that I wonder he came.'

'Busy or not, his place was with Mellie. Jess tells me she fetched her down last night, after we were all in bed and asleep. Poor little Mellie, and she's seemed so much better yesterday. I told Jess she ought to have called us, but to be honest I expect she'd had more experience than either of us, her being the eldest of a large family.'

'She should have called John.'

'Oh no, dear. No place for a man. And Mellie wouldn't have liked to let him see her with one of her sickness attacks. Yesterday she seemed so bright, so calm. Usually when she has one of those bouts it's when the poor child has upset herself crying. I sent a note for Alice. She has been with her most of the morning, she always manages to cheer her.'

'Did John know she was unwell?'

Patience nodded.

'She sent the message by young Jess that she wanted to be left alone, that she didn't want him to come up to see her – and he took her at her word. Jess told him about what a bad night she'd had. You know, and I know, how it is with Melissa. This morning she probably wasn't looking as pretty as she'd like him to look on her. But did he argue? I couldn't believe it. He packed his valise and called for Biggs.'

Georgina remembered watching Melissa go to his room the previous evening. None of it made sense.

'I must go up and change.' She put an end to the conversation.

Instead of going to her own room to change from her riding habit, she tapped lightly on Melissa's door and went straight in.

'Miss Mellie's trying to have a quiet rest.' Jess was as protective as a guard dog.

'And so she shall. You may go, Jess, I'll call you if she wants you.'

Standing her ground, Jess looked at Melissa. She only took her orders from one mistress.

'I kept you awake most of the night, Jess. You go and have a nap too. When I'm ready for you to help me get my clothes on, I'll send someone to wake you.'

172

'I'm not that tired. I don't like leaving you.' Then, looking accusingly at Georgina. 'Miss Mellie wouldn't let me wake Biggs and send for the doctor. But that's what I wanted, awful lot of pain she was having. Worst I've seen her, she was.'

'You should have called me, Jess.'

'You? You don't know nothing about having babies.'

She stopped herself answering that she knew a lot about Melissa! But the girl's honest concern prevented her.

'Go and rest, Jess,' Melissa urged. 'I'll wake you if I need, I promise I will.'

'As long as you promise.' The girl's retreating glare at Georgina made it clear that there was only *one* person's wishes that meant anything to her.

'Come and sit by the bed.' Could this be the same girl who had been spoiling for a fight twenty-four hours earlier? 'John's gone back to London.' Melissa sounded casual, but she was watching the effect of her words of Georgina.

'I know. Aunt Patience told me. He must have hated leaving you feeling poorly.'

'Huh!' came the sulky grunt. 'And who made me poorly? *He* did. Yesterday evening was so nice, we were friendly, he was gentle and kind. It was almost like it used to be before we were married.'

'How long are you going to hold it against him that you're having a baby? It's not fair. It happens to married people for goodness sake.'

As soon as she'd spoken Georgina wished she could recall her words; the last thing she wanted was to bring on another storm of self-pity. Instead Melissa was watching her with an expression it was hard to fathom. Triumph? Cunning?

'I went to speak to John in his room after we came up to bed.'

'Mellie, you oughtn't to tell me.' No . . . I don't want to hear . . . Don't look at me like that . . .

'In just my nightgown. Without even my corset he could see just how fat and ugly I am. Just look at me!' She pushed the covers out of the way. After her bad night, today she hadn't attempted to get up and dress. 'I went into his room, he got out of bed and came to meet me. He can be so gentle. When he held me against him I could tell how thankful he was.'

'Don't Mellie. All this is between you and him.' Georgina

173

moved away from the bed, looking out of the window she tried not to listen. But what she heard surprised her.

'Men aren't like us.' This time there was neither triumph nor cunning in Melissa's voice. 'You know what he did to me? I never thought – I mean, it's not right, it's disgusting to do what he did when I'm like this. Almost threw me onto the bed. Like a madman he was. I feel bruised all over. Look!' She pulled down the neck of her nightgown and exposed the tell-tale marks. 'I couldn't move, couldn't get away. An animal! That's what he is. After, I managed to get up to Jess's room ... almost crawled ... so frightened. What could he have done to me?' And more tears.

'He didn't mean to hurt you. You said you knew he was thankful you'd come back to him.'

'I didn't know *why*, I thought it was just me for myself. I told him "No". I did. I told him it was wrong – unnatural. He didn't even seem to hear me.' This wasn't the stormy tornado of yesterday, today Melissa's quiet crying brought Georgina back to the bed to take her gently in her arms. 'Wish I'd never got married, even being stuck in this dreary place is better than what *he* expects,' she sniffed. 'Aunt Alice came this morning. I didn't tell her about last night. You know what she says? She says that when my mother was expecting me, she always "slept" – you know what I mean – with my father. She says that was what hurt her, why she died having her baby. And now look what he's done to *me*. Last night I felt so ill. I wish I'd lost the baby – I wish – I wish—' With her head buried against Georgina there was no way of knowing just what it was she wished.

Over the next weeks John didn't come again to Kyneston. He wrote saying he was travelling north, buying; the next week he wrote that the gallery was busy, he felt now that it was beginning to make a mark he ought not to leave what amounted to each Friday and Saturday to Harold; another gap and then he wrote that he looked forward to hearing from Melissa that she felt fit enough to come home.

'He's begging me to leave here and go back to London,' she crowed, enjoying her married status at this safe distance.

'And why don't you, dear?' From kindly Patience's viewpoint this was a time when any husband and wife ought to be together. She knew now that only in her imagination had Georgina been turning what should have been a family circle into a triangle; she knew it because Melissa had told her that Georgina's affections belonged to Steven. And she was thankful – of course she was, she told herself repeatedly. It had become habit for her to be prepared for her own dreams to mock her. A silly woman old enough to know better – repeatedly she told herself that too.

'Why don't I go to London? Like this?' This was in March, there were still two months before the baby was due. 'Neither of you understand. How can you when you've never been beyond this dull, miserable place. Aunt Alice understands. Life in London is so different, we receive invitations, entertain guests. I can't do any of that – and at least here no one sees me.'

'Oh dear,' Patience's brow puckered, 'such silly conventions. Why should you have to hide yourself away? And you always look so pretty, too. Mrs Turnbull, from the blacksmith's you know, she is further gone than you are and doesn't have new gowns keeping pace with her, she was in church on Sunday '

'I'm not the blacksmith's wife. And I'm surprised even she would go out in public view. I agree with Aunt Alice, it's not decent for a woman to flaunt herself in front of strangers. Anyway, I'm not going back to London. If John wants to see me he must come here. But he won't.'

And in that she was right.

She replied to his letter. How she couched her refusal she didn't say. It might have been supposed that having put the idea of leaving Kyneston out of the way she would have settled down to her final weeks of waiting, enjoying Jess's never failing devotion and the undemanding routine of her old home. But it wasn't in Melissa's nature to let life flow along unchallenged. Fear for what was growing ever closer, resentment that patience and kindness only set her further away from those around her whose lives had no black cloud threatening: both contributed to her resentment.

'You spend more time with those children than you do with me,' she whined to Georgina early in May.

'I want them to learn to love the forest as we did. And they are too. Yesterday I took them to the hide, down the track from our secret castle, remember? Of course, first light is the right time. I thought I'd ask their father if they could come here for a night so that I could take them ready for dawn.'

'If he knows about my condition you don't expect him to let

them come. It wouldn't be right. They wouldn't understand about what's wrong with me—'

'Nothing's wrong with you! You are having a baby. It's happening all the time with the ponies. Oh, Mellie, I wish you could have seen. We came upon one yesterday, she had just dropped her foal, it wasn't even on its feet. It was the most beautiful thing. We were quite near, but we stood absolutely still and the mare must have known we wouldn't hurt them. She was still cleaning it – it was so beautiful—'

'You're cruel – you don't care—' Like a tragedy queen Melissa swept out of the room – or as near to sweeping as she was able – slamming the door behind her.

'Poor little Melissa. She takes everything so hard, she always has,' Patience did her best.

And two days after that Steven arrived.

It was partly Alice's influence and party the hangover of Victorian middle-class convention that convinced Melissa that it was unseemly for her to be seen in public. So she spent the first hours after Stevens's arrival in her room while Jess borrowed her bicycle and took a note to Hapley Court. The outcome was that, without encountering the guest, she, Jess and their luggage were collected in her aunt's carriage.

'It's not right, driving the poor girl out of her own home,' Mrs Biggs grumbled. 'Miss Georgina ought to have put her foot down and told this Captain Howard that with a baby due Kyneston was no place for him.'

'Not Miss Georgie's fault. The captain's a friend of Miss Melissa's husband. They ought to be grateful to her for taking him under her wing as she does.' Effie wasn't going to let her Miss Georgie shoulder the blame for that other one always acting up; she'd been like it all her days, and usually getting her own way too. Well, let her hatchet-faced Aunt Alice have two pennorth of her showing off. More than likely she was to blame for the way the girl behaved. And nice to see Georgina looking so happy. She and that captain seemed thick as thieves, and what a joy it was to hear her, she sounded as though there was a laugh always bubbling up and looking for a way to escape. Pity he wasn't a few years younger – but it wasn't the length of years that counted, it was whether you let them grind you down and take away your sense of fun. And watching the two of them together she smiled her approval. No number of years would do that to them.

Steven had never looked forward to arrival back in Poole as heartily as he had this time. He'd had plenty of women waiting and watching for him through the years, he'd enjoyed their company, taken what they offered but been sure to stay free of commitment. Not one had tugged at his heartstrings as Georgina did. An hour from the port and thoughts of lady friends would have vanished – until now. Like some lovelorn youth he had let his mind be filled with the sound of her voice, the feeling of her hand on his arm. And more than that, her easy, graceful movements, her slim waist, the curve of her breast: waking or sleeping these things haunted him. In the night he'd be woken from a dream where he'd been holding her; he'd cling to the dream like some adolescent on the verge of awareness.

The dawn visit to the hide was her idea.

'I've been thinking of taking the girls to a hide to watch for deer at first light. I've often done it, but it'll be new to them. Let's go while you're here, shall we?'

'As new for me as for them. I've watched the day breaking plenty of times, but I've never seen the forest coming to life.'

That same day Fate threw her into the path of Alex Graves whom she waylaid in the lane, he on his way to a neighbouring farm, she and Steven to Ringwood. In the past she'd always been alone when she'd called for the children, or delivered them home full of chatter and excitement.

'You are most kind,' like a parrot repeating his party piece he said it after hearing her suggestion. 'You say you and your friend are inviting them. Won't you introduce me, Miss Rochester?' I don't hand my daughters to just *anyone*, his unsmiling tone implied.

'Forgive me,' she meant her smile to encompass them both, hiding her irritation at his manner. 'Captain Howard is a house guest at Kyneston. Steven this is Mr Graves, Victoria and Becky's father.'

Watching them together only reinforced her opinion of the stiff-neck vet.

'Well, at least he agreed,' she said as Alex rode away from them, 'and to their staying the night too. You'd think, with a father like that, the girls wouldn't know how to enjoy themselves.'

177

'You misjudge him. He's a sound man.'

'Humph.' No more than a grunt, but it said it all. 'Anyway, let's not waste our morning worrying about Mr Po-Face Graves. Let's get on to Ringwood. Walk on.' The trap moved forward, the incident seemingly over until, with a chuckle, she had a final word before it was laid to rest. 'Graves! If ever a man was aptly named!'

The dawn outing held its own magic for all of them. For the girls there was the thrill, for the first time, of being out while the world still slept; for Steven, who'd spent all his adult life at sea and who had served through every watch, yet never looked on the pale colours of morning through the outline of ancient branches, never felt himself to be a part of this sort of stillness as if the world held its breath – and never been more aware of Georgina than as she shepherded the children almost silently up the wooden ladder to their high lookout; for Georgina too this hour was awesome, she didn't ask herself why.

When finally the sun was up, the silver mist lifted and the forest once more the place they were beginning to know, the girls were taken home.

'Thank you very much for taking us, Georgina, and for having us to sleep.' Victoria recited what she had promised she'd remember to say, her words seeming to cast a long shadow of their father.

'Yes,' came the echo, excitement in the gruff tones. 'It was 'stroadinary, it was – was—' Lost for words she looked at Georgina.

'It was a memory we'll keep. Perhaps we'll do it again.'

Becky shook her head. 'No. Again wouldn't be the same.'

She was learning young.

That was on the Saturday, midway through Steven's stay, and the only occasion during eight days that the children were with them. Mostly they spent their time together: on Wednesday, the day they'd met Alex, they took the trap to the street market in Ringwood; on Thursday they rode to Bucklers Hard; on Friday they took *Cork's Crew* out on an almost becalmed Solent; Saturday was the visit to the hide; on Sunday they hammered the hoops into the side lawn and played croquet. The way they spent their time was immaterial, the joy came from doing these things together. And each day Georgina threw herself more cetainly in love with him. When John found a crack in her defences and pushed himself into her mind she forced him out again. John hasn't been here for weeks, she reminded herself, and if he came it wouldn't be to see *me*, John belongs to Melissa, he wants her in London with him. Anyway what he wants is nothing to do with me. Once the baby is born Melissa will go back there with him. They'll engage a nursemaid, everything will be like it was in the beginning for her. I hope it will be – of course I do, that's what I must hope. Occasionally when she had to pull her thoughts sharply back into line, she would look at Steven and be thankful. So different from John, he wouldn't know a vase of the Ming dynasty from a Meissen, but he was vital, he was male. The excitement he stirred in her was real. Put the two of them together, she told herself, glorying in belittling John, would be like comparing a man of the woods with a man of words, a miner and a musician. Steven was as strong as stout oak, that was what she loved, what she'd always dreamed of; but more important even than that, he had the same zest for life that she had herself. Yes, she was in love with him. When she woke in the morning if the image of him wasn't waiting for her, she was quick to conjure it; last thing at night as she lay drifting between wake and sleep, if her thoughts strayed away from him she pulled them back. In words he hadn't told her his feelings, but she didn't need telling. She knew that he loved her; she clung to the knowledge.

On his last morning they rode to the pond where she had learned to swim and had so many secret dips through the years.

'I wanted you to come here. Of all my special places this is the one I love best. We used to walk here when we were little – I learnt to swim here. And later I'd come alone. No one ever comes here, no track leads to it. I know the way so well, it's as if it was put here to be my own private garden.' What was she telling him? She could feel the pounding of her heart . . . her gaze was locked in his . . . her own private garden, isolated. 'Hark! Not a sound. Nothing. Just us.'

As if to prove her wrong a skylark rose high above them, it's song piercing the still air. But she heard it as a sign that they were part of nature. Knowing exactly what she did and yet with no will to try and stop herself, she moved towards him. He loved her, he wanted her. As she'd led him on their mysterious and circuitous route between the trees and bushes until they came to the pond surrounded by mossy grass, had this been what she'd meant to happen? Reason was being overtaken by desire. Soon he'll be gone, but not yet, not yet. It's right for me, I know it is, if he makes love to me I'll know I'm his.

Minutes later, her eyes wide open as she gazed upward into the high blue sky, she was torn between joy, thankfulness and something even stronger – a desperate need to wipe out the haunting memory of that stormy morning in the cabin of the *Cork's Crew*. And afterwards, still sure of the rightness of what they'd done, she felt his warm breath on her cheek as he cradled her close, heard something akin to reverence as he whispered.

'How can I leave you? You're like part of my very being . . . soul of my soul . . .' Yes, yes, her heart cried out, say it again, we belong, I'm like a part of him and he of me. 'When I come back, tell me you'll marry me. Come with me wherever I go.' Then rolling a little away from her he gave a strange cry, a whoop of joy? Of amazement? Of satisfaction? Perhaps all and more too.

'Me! A wife!' He carried her hand to his lips, caressing it with his mouth. 'Fancy free, that's all I've wanted – until now. Say you'll marry me, say you'll share my world.'

'Yes. It's what I want, to be with you, to love you.' Half dressed and dishevelled they finally got to their feet from their none too dry, springtime mossy bed.

By afternoon he would be on his way back to Poole, by the end of the week he would be heading south, for this time when he left Poole the *Seahorse* was bound only for Spain and North Africa. He expected to be back within a month. While he was away she would get her papers in order, make the necessary arrangements so that they could be married at the end of his trip.

'I'll tell Mellie and Aunt Patience when you've gone.' Would he understand? 'This morning belongs just to us – I don't want to talk about it to anyone. Secret, like the pond.'

The pressure of his fingers was the answer she needed.

Biggs took him to Brockenhurst for the train. John's waiting crate was left at Kyneston until his next visit, the visit that would change Georgina's life. The high pale sky of morning was still cloudless, she answered the call of the newly dug earth. There was no better place to enjoy her newfound anticipation than in the solitude of the garden. Today, because of Steven's afternoon departure, they had eaten their main meal at about one o'clock, so with a feeling of freedom she donned her calico gardening dress, tied a scarf around her mop of curls and came down stairs prepared to plant the sweet pea seedlings.

'I sent a note to Hapley Court this morning, dear,' Patience told her, 'telling Alice that Captain Howard was leaving. I've been anxious about Mellie being away, her time is getting close, she ought to be at home where everything is ready for her. Effie cycled over with the note and brought a message back that they would be home by this evening.'

'That's good. I thought they might have hung on to her, I'm glad she said she wanted to be here.'

'It's weeks since Jessie got the room laid up ready. That's where she'll be comfiest, there in her own old bedroom. And – but never breathe a word of what I say – I would have been frightened for her to be confined in the room she uses now, the one she was born in, the one poor Mary died in. But mind what I say, don't breathe a word. The poor child is frightened enough without me and my silly superstitions.'

'You say the room's ready?'

'Has been for these last two or three weeks. You can never be sure when labour will start. So Jess put rubber sheets on the bed, put everything to hand that will be needed . . . oh dear, oh dear, I just dread the thought of her having to go through all that. Will she be able to manage? She is as she is, she can't help it, bless her. But will her nerve break? Oh dear . . .'

It wasn't a question Georgina cared to consider.

'So it's not John's room any more?' she changed the subject. Then she wished she hadn't. He must come soon, would he want to be here when the baby arrived? She shied from the answer to that too.

'Aunt Patience, I've got something to tell you.' There, now she was going to say it. Now it wouldn't be a brilliant dream, it would be reality. 'Steven will be back in three or four weeks—'

'So soon? That's nice, dear.'

'And when he comes I'm going to have everything arranged and ready. I am going to marry him.'

One look at Patience's face and she remembered Melissa's cruel laughter as she'd mocked about the nightly rag-twisted hair.

181

So she had been right. But how could Patience have harboured dreams of Steven? She only knew him as an agreeable house guest – that and an excitingly striking-looking, thoroughly masculine seaman. Georgina pretended not to notice the momentary look of distress.

'Georgina, dear Georgina,' with loving arms stretched wide Patience came towards her. 'When did all this happen? I had no idea, you seemed just happy friends. Oh dear, why do silly women cry when they hear good news?' She took out a large and practical handkerchief, wiped her eyes and blew her nose as if to put an end to emotional nonsense. 'Is he going to give up his boat?'

'Lots of boat owners take their wives with them. I shall travel the world, Aunt Patience.' She heard a ring of bravado in her voice. 'But we'll always come back here. Kyneston will always be home.'

Early that evening, while Georgina worked neatening the edges of the freshly cut grass, a pale-faced and weary Melissa was brought back – and not a day too soon in Patience's opinion. Not that she'd had any experience. Often over the past months Georgina had been irritated by Melissa's tempestuous moods and self-pity, but now her sympathy was sincere as she laid down the shears and went to help her step down from the carriage.

'I'm glad you're home,' she hugged her with unusual fervour, touched by the contrast between the heavy form and thin, palid face.

'Miss Mellie's going straight up to rest, she promised Mrs Sylvester that's what she'd do,' Jess put herself in change.

'I'll give you ten minutes, then I'll scrub my hands and come up and talk to you,' Georgina told her.

'Knock before you come charging in,' again it was Jess, the faithful guardian with no conception of status.

And when she knocked it was to be told that 'Miss Mellie's gone out like a light, poor darling, soon as her head touched the pillow. Cor, but I won't 'arf be glad for her when she gets it over with.'

The express purpose for Georgina's suggestion of coming up to talk had been to tell Melissa about her engagement. Barred from entry by Jess, relief flooded her before she could stop it, and hard on its heels the image of her news being passed to John. But

182

immediately she had her thoughts in order. Nearly six o'clock . . . where would Steven be? What time would the *Seahorse* set sail? And . . . on the next voyage, as Poole receded into the distance, she would be aboard, the world before her.

The day had been a foretaste of summer, but even before the light started to fade the wind had gathered force bringing clouds and the threat of rain.

Too restless to stay indoors and despite it already being late Georgina took a lamp and, instead of following Patience up the stairs to bed, went out to the stables. This afternoon she had planted three rows of sweet peas, seedlings Hopwood had brought on in the greenhouse. In the morning she meant to erect sticks then attach netting for the plants to climb up; that's what took her to the stable loft where the sticks had been stored through the winter.

Cleaning and counting them, she suddenly became aware of a moving shadow. Someone was downstairs, she heard the carriage door being closed, then footsteps.

Chapter Eleven

It wasn't fear of an unknown intruder that froze her to the spot, still holding a bundle of canes. No stranger could have made her heart pound like this.

'I saw there was a lamp,' he said unnecessarily,

'It might have been Hopwood.' Empty words, but reason seemed to have deserted her. Why should he follow the glow of the lamp, sure that it would lead him to *her*? Before the question was formed, the answer followed. 'You want to find out how Melissa is? To talk to me about her before you see her?'

John took the canes from her hand and laid them on the ground.

'I want to talk to you, yes. But not about Melissa. About *us*, about what a fool I was.'

'A fool? To marry a wife who can set you up in your own fine gallery?' Sarcasm and mockery protected her.

'And you? What sort of a fool are you being? You know why I've stayed away? Of course you do. Why did you tell Melissa you were in love with Steven Howard if it wasn't because that way you knew I'd hear?'

'Why should I care what you hear?'

Standing in front of her, his hands on her shoulders, she felt trapped. Trapped yet exultant. Every pulse in her body throbbed with the hammering of her heart.

'She told you the truth. I love Steven. I've never felt so happy – so *myself* – with anyone.' Even though she made herself say it, yet it was the truth. If only he could walk in now, push John away from her, take her in the shelter of his strong arms and protect her from herself.

'You lie. Georgina, darling Georgina, how can you even pretend?'

184

She tried to move backwards, to put more space between them. At least, she believed that's what she tried to do. But his hold was like a vice, her willpower gone; there was nothing in her world except this moment. The future would be waiting for them, the shadows of the past would fall on them, but as John crushed her against him there was nothing but the present.

If reason had had any power over her, or over him either, would they have sunk onto the bed of straw piled by the back wall? Surely as long as she lived the pungent smell of straw would carry her back to this moment. Nothing held her back, all her wild longings and dreams were drawn to culminate in this. When, through the thick calico of her workdress she felt his hand shaping the contour of her breast, of their own volition her quick fingers unfastened the buttons, pressed his warm flesh against hers.

'I want you so . . . I want you so,' his words were barely audible as his mouth moved on her breast, warm and demanding, his lips drew on her. For weeks they'd been determined to build on their growing friendship, this was the man who'd talked to her about his gallery, who'd exalted in the freedom of riding with her in the early morning air . . . It was as if she'd slipped off a high precipice, nothing could stop her fall. This wasn't a dream, it was real. Conscience whispered that these minutes were stolen, but conscience had no place in this wild and glorious moment. 'I want you so,' he'd told her and she felt a rush of thankfulness and mindless joy at the urgency of that want. Her body strained towards him.

Yet at his next movement, cold reason took hold of her. Only hours ago she'd lain like this with Steven, Steven who loved her, Steven whom she loved and would share her life with. She'd longed for him to make love to her, to drive away the memory of John. What was she doing? She must be mad. John's need wasn't just for *her*, it was for her warmth and willingness. For months Melissa had rebuffed him . . . he was a sensual, passionate man . . . no, don't think of that, just remember Mellie . . . he's using me just as he did before, he thinks I've no resistance . . . and have I? In less time than it took to blink, all these thought crashed into her mind, but not before his hand homed in on her and there was no hiding from him how she yearned for his loving.

So he was unprepared for the convulsive movement as she thrust him away.

'Don't! Get up, get off me.'

Trembling with rage and passion, with his left arm bent to anchor her shoulders to the ground, his right hand possessed her.

'If you tell me you don't want me, you're lying,' he said through clenched teeth. 'That's where I belong, deep, deep . . . you want to devour me.'

Breathing heavily she pushed his probing hand off her, then in one swift, violent movement struggled to her feet. That she was putting up a fight did nothing to douse his passion. She'd thought the battle was won – but it wasn't even over. Coming nearer he locked her gaze with his, as if she were hypnotized she couldn't look away from him. But he couldn't control her mind: into it flashed something she'd read in a book so long ago that the story was vague, but clearly remembered was a woman who was paralysed with terror and who found the strength to withstand it by clutching the cross she wore around her neck. Georgina wore no cross, what she clutched with all her might was the image of Steven, the sound of his laugh, she pictured him before the mast on *Cork's Crew* – no, don't think of *Cork's Crew*, think of this morning, my secret place, *our* secret place, his and mine.

Without warning John was on his knees before her, her skirt and petticoats forced out of the way. Once before this was what he had done. Then it had driven her into a frenzy of desire; now with more strength than she knew she had, she pushed him to send him sprawling back onto the straw while her skirt fell back into place.

'You could never love Steven Howard,' he panted, struggling to his feet.

She stood tall, her head high, trying to ignore the humiliation of feeling her white drawers slipping ever nearer to her ankles.

'I shan't mention this to Mellie. I prefer to forget it.' She clutched at dignity even though her heart pounded so hard she felt he must hear it.

'You know you can't forget. I made you mine once and so you always will be.' Recovering from the ignominy of being so inelegantly disposed of, he was on his feet again. 'As for Melissa,' he said her name with such scorn, 'she's not likely to care how many women I have as long as she's not one of them.'

. . . how many women! So that's what she was, just one of the many!

Her attempt to turn his thoughts to Melissa had done nothing to divert him. His mind was on Georgina and himself, Georgina and Steven. Steven was something of a womanizer, that much he knew. But then what else could you expect of a man who spent months at a time at sea?

'Steven will be back in about four weeks.' The thought of being one of those 'many women' helped her find the cold disdain she sought. 'When he comes we're going to be married. Then I shall travel with him.'

He looked at her in . . . what? Horror? Disbelief?

'You can't!'

'A brother-in-law can hardly stop me. Steven's my lover. And I'm glad. You hear me? I'm *glad*. I wanted him to make love to me. Yes, and it was wonderful. You hear me?' Her brown eyes flashed fire, her voice was unnaturally shrill. 'Every time he touches me I'm more sure.' She turned and ran down the wooden steps, or as near to running as she could manage with her drawers at half mast. She knew every flag on the floor of the stables, she needed no light. With one backward glance, half expecting that he would be following her, she went out into the yard and made for the side door of the house. It was late, even the servants were in bed, but the lamp had been left burning on the hall table ready for when she came in.

John sank back onto the straw, sitting with his head in his hands, her words echoing in his brain. 'I wanted him to make love to me . . . it was wonderful . . .' Imagine her lying in Steven's arms, imagine the joy of her sensuality, imagine how it might have been . . . I could have persuaded her to sell her half of Kyneston . . . no, she loves Kyneston . . . damn and blast Melissa's money . . . money isn't everything, I know that now, now that it's too late . . . Steven will have the joy of her, she'll be there to cheer him when things go wrong, to encourage him, to laugh with him, to love him . . .

The window of the loft was set in the eaves. From where he sat, when John raised his head he could see across the yard to the house. There was the glow of a moving lamp, through the window at the bend of the stairs he could see it move upwards, darkness, then the light appeared again on the first-floor landing. She was going to her room, in his imagination he was there with her. What if he followed her? Just the two of them, the door closed, the blind down, nothing and no one to come between them?

187

Her sudden rejection had only enflamed his passion, now he let his thoughts run unchecked. But he knew the difference between fantasy and fact; he knew that following her to her room was impossible. Taking the lamp he went down the wooden stairs, his feet less certain in the shadowy light from the lamp than hers had been in the darkness, then he crossed the stable yard to the side door of the house just as she had.

At the head of the wide shallow flight of stairs instead of turning to the left to the room he knew was hers, he went to the right, the direction of the bedroom to which he'd been exiled. Here at least he would find solitude, privacy. But what had they done to it? On the bed were piles of towels, old sheets; on the floor there were two buckets; the bedside table had been cleared then covered with a plain white cloth.

In that misty area between waking and sleeping Melissa lay gazing at the ceiling. Her eyes had become attuned to the darkness, and even though there was no moon and, after such a glorious spring day the wind had increased, bringing rainclouds that gathered with nightfall, yet had she woken up sufficiently she would have been able to recognize the familiar dark shapes of the furniture. But her lids were getting heavy, her eyes were closing. Only her thoughts weren't quite ready for sleep.

Something's happened, I know it has, one fear chased another through her mind even while it became increasingly difficult to hang on to reason. All day it hasn't moved – and I've been thankful not to feel that beastly squirming inside me. Perhaps the baby's dead. If it's dead how will they get it born? I knew, I always knew something would go wrong. Please help me, I'm so frightened. Don't think, don't think of anything. My back's been aching – yet the baby doesn't move. Ought I to tell someone? Shall I call Jess? Please help me to know what I ought to do. Perhaps when it's as near to being born it sleeps like a person does, perhaps by morning it'll be moving about again. Perhaps . . .

Whatever terrifying scenario was trying to push its way to the top of her mind, sleep was winning the battle, sleep and even a feeling of security as she half heard a footstep on the corridor. She wasn't on her own . . . Georgina must be coming up to bed . . . Aunt Patience, Jess, the Biggses, Effie, Florrie . . . everyone was safely in the house with her . . . all of them loved her . . . Melissa slept.

When she felt a body warm against her she whimpered, she stirred. No, no, it couldn't be happening . . . it must be a nightmare . . . naked, his mouth covering hers, stifling her, stopping her shouting. He couldn't do this to her . . . he was so heavy . . . no, he was hurting her . . . hurting . . . he was mad, like an untamed devil he rushed on until he reached a climax that left him crushing her, a dead weight.

'You're wicked,' she wept. 'Vile.'

Rolling off her he turned away, deaf to her words and to her misery. She lay very still, she felt bruised and torn, her thighs knotted with cramp. What was that? Biting her lip she listened to him, his head buried in the pillow to smother the sound as he sobbed. She never doubted that this was his punishment, even through her own pain she felt angry triumph that his shame could have brought him to this. Neither of them spoke, they were both wrapped in their own cocoon of misery. Gradually he was quiet and soon exhaustion carried him into a deep sleep, there was nothing but the sound of his regular breathing.

Melissa lay there, as far away from him as she could get, uncomfortable and miserable. The night wrapped around her like a black blanket, there was no chink of light, no hope, nothing but this dreadful aching pain. Minutes, hours, time had no meaning any more than the future held any promise.

Then something woke her: seering agony that was terrifying beyond anything she'd known. It was like the days she'd dreaded each month in her early adolescence, like it but a thousandfold worse. Then it eased, she lay still hardly daring to breathe. He'd done this to her, he with his bestial greed. It had nearly gone, don't move, pretend to be asleep, fool it into thinking you're asleep.

It – whatever she imagined 'it' to be – wasn't so easily fooled. When the pain came again it was worse, it tore through her groin, it sent echoes to her legs, arms, beads of sweat rolled down her face (or was it tears that touched the corner of her mouth?), the palms of her hands were clammy. It was instinct rather than reason that prevented her crying out, calling for help – Jess, Georgina. It was instinct that told her to cry would only wake John. It was like lying next to the devil, a movement from her and he'd be awake, ready to pounce. She didn't ask herself what she

189

meant, questions and answers were beyond her. At the back of her tangled mind was something that through these months she'd never been able to imagine, yet now she saw it clearly: there would have been life for her after the birth of the baby, but John had stolen her future. The thought of being as she used to be, her body not gross and ugly, taunted her. In the chaotic way her mind was working, she even believed that that's how things would have been again had he not forced himself on her. In the moments after the first violent contraction eased she remembered how ill she'd been all night after she'd gone to his room to tell him about Georgina and Steven. But that had been nothing to *this* – help me, please, please, if there's a god at all, then please help me. It's coming again, no, I can't bear it. She bit her lip so hard that she tasted her own blood. Get away from him, that's what she had to do. Get away, run free from him, free from the agony that tore her . . .

In his sleep John turned over, throwing his arm across the bed. A natural enough movement, and for one who usually sleeps alone what was so strange in the other side of the bed being empty? So why did he wake?

'Melissa . . .?' he whispered urgently. Where was she? There was no lamp burning. 'Melissa?'

Memories of the night crowded on him. He'd raped her! Against her will and with the child due he'd forced himself on her, he'd done it purposely as if hurting her would salve his own misery.

'Melissa . . .'

Surely she couldn't have preferred to sleep on the floor rather than near him. Moving across to her side of the bed he put his feet carefully onto the floor half expecting to find her there. But already his eyes were getting used to the darkness, he could see she'd gone further. Could she have started labour? But surely, even after what he'd done, she wouldn't have left him sleeping while she'd gone for help. Going onto the landing he looked both ways towards the other rooms to see where a shaft of light showed under the door. Nothing. Upstairs perhaps where that young girl Melissa seemed to set such store in slept. Nothing. The whole house slept.

Back in the bedroom he lit a candle, aware of his nakedness he threw on his clothes, then went downstairs. That Melissa should have chosen to spend the night on the sofa seemed unlikely, but where else could she have gone? If that's where she was, he'd send her back to bed, he'd promise to use the sofa himself if that was what she wanted. This was *his* fault.

The sofa was empty. Outside the night had turned ugly, clouds that had gathered in the evening being driven by sudden gusts of wind and heavy showers, he heard the rain tapping against the window pane, heard it without interest. Where could she be? Georgina – yes, she must have gone to Georgina, there was room for two in her bed. Georgina . . . Steven . . . no don't think of that now, concentrate on Melissa. You've done this to her, in your spite you've frightened her as if hurting her would do anything except make everyone unhappy. What a bloody mess . . . and all of it my doing. Georgina loved me, I know she did, I knew it even when I married Melissa. Now she doesn't, now she despises me – and isn't that what I deserve? But to marry Steven – she *can't*. But she can, and she will. Nothing wrong with Steven. Please God make them happy, that's what I should be saying. And please God when I look into her room I'll find Melissa there with her, I should be saying that too. And I am. Isn't Georgina the one person she would have run to?

He meant to open the door quietly and only far enough that the light from the candle fell across the bed. Once he was satisfied Melissa was there he'd close it again, neither of them need wake. No more scenes, not tonight. As he turned the doorknob he was conscious of something he'd not given a thought to until that moment: his face had that strange, tight feeling that comes after tears, his eyelids stung, he knew they were swollen. It was years since he'd cried, and childhood tears left no aftermath, they were over as easily as they came.

The flickering glow fell across the bed and in the silence Georgina, lying there alone, looked back at him. For a second he saw only her – and then the empty pillow at her side.

'Melissa,' he whispered. 'I can't find her. I thought she must have come to you. Not in bed – not downstairs – where else?'

In a second Georgina was on her feet and reaching for her dressing gown.

They lit the lamps, they looked everywhere downstairs, then they woke Patience and finally, realizing she couldn't be anywhere in the house, they woke the staff. Everyone must help in the search.

'Miss Melissa, not indoors you say?' Sitting up in bed, her head totally covered in a far from becoming night cap, Mrs Biggs stared uncomprehendingly at Georgina.

Helplessly Georgina shook her head. Every road her thoughts took led to her fear, a sense of failure that Mellie could have come to this and she hadn't known, hadn't even considered the recent hysterical outburst had been anything different from the tantrums they'd all grown used to. 'Will you help us look for her? It's been raining, you'll need to dress, boots and things.'

'But why would she go out?' The housekeeper's brain didn't wake easily. 'Here, Claude, wake yourself up won't you, hear what Miss Georgina tells us. Miss Melissa's run off somewhere. Poor child, there's no running away from what ails *her*.' Fear made Georgina suddenly shiver, she read Mrs Biggs's thoughts, they both knew that Melissa's troubles went back long before her pregnancy, 'what ails her' had been with her all her life.

'Perhaps she's taken shelter in the stable,' Biggs suggested, already climbing out of bed although he did make sure his night-shirt was pulled well down out of deference to Georgina.

'No, she wouldn't. She wouldn't go near the horses.'

'Oh dear, oh Lor! You go and wake the others Miss Georgina, we'll have our clothes on in a couple of shakes.'

So in minutes the household was roused. From one to the other the story was passed, the pieces falling into place but making no understandable picture. John had woken to find her gone . . . none of them mentioned that when they'd gone to bed they hadn't even known he was expected. That is, none of them questioned his presence except Jess.

'Wot 'appened then? She never said nothing to me that you were coming.' Even Jess didn't tell him he had no right to intrude in his wife's bedroom. 'Tired as anything she was when she went off to bed. Don't understand it. Is there something you ain't told us?' She took the lamp he passed to her, not surprised that he didn't answer the question. She glowered at him, hating his right to be with her beloved Miss Mellie, hating him for all the pain and grief he'd caused.

'We'll all go different ways,' Georgina said, 'in pairs if any of you are afraid of getting lost alone. I'm all right alone. Aunt Patience?'

'So am I dear. There's more to worry about than a few trees. Oh poor little soul. She's been so frightened . . . all her life she's scared so easily . . . poor little soul.'

At the gate they parted company, spanning out in different directions. Mrs Biggs went with Effie, Claude Biggs with Florrie, Jessie (who knew nothing of the forest but wanted to escape the others, imagining herself to be the one to find Melissa, the only one amongst them who loved her above all else), John, Patience and Georgina by themselves. They held their lanterns high. None of them acknowledged the dread they couldn't drive from their minds, but as they looked through the trees there was no running away from the the image conjured by their fear – the ray of light from their lamp falling on her, the horror of finding her hanging from a branch by the cord of her dressing gown. None of them stopped to question how Melissa, who even as a healthy child had never had the courage to climb a tree, could have fixed the cord to a branch as high as they imagined. And if John had checked her bedroom more thoroughly he would have known that her dressing gown was still where Jess had put it across the back of a chair.

Wearing only her nightgown, her bare feet cut and bleeding, she blundered on. Where she was going wasn't important, her only goal was escape – from the house, from the pain. She didn't even know she was crying as she stumbled along the narrow track, stopping only when each blinding onslaught took away her power to do anything but cling to the nearest tree, her nails bending and breaking as she gripped the bark. Now it never more than partially receded, even when the intensity grew less violent, still she knew nothing but pain.

She'd known the forest all her life, normally she couldn't have got lost. Now she had no idea where she was, but it was of no consequence any more than was the rain-soaked nightgown that clung to her shivering body. The track came to an opening, instead of ground carpeted with last year's dead leaves and pieces of broken twigs or bracken, under her feet she felt the wet mossy grass. She must have felt it, but it no more registered than the cry of an owl that flew overhead. On she went, perhaps heading to another track, perhaps to a wall of trees. She might not have noticed the call of the owl, but the background sound, like the deep bellowing cry of a child, travelled with her. It was part

193

of the hell that enveloped her, her own crying like her pain isolating her.

Suddenly she stopped quite still, silenced beyond tears or cries, hardly able to breathe. For months she had been full of terror, sure that she would die in childbirth, yet now that the moment had come she had no thought of death. Indeed she had no coherent thought of anything. Wet and bitterly cold, she felt something warm trickling down her inner leg. She couldn't walk, she had no strength to stand and nothing to cling to, not so much as a tree. Sinking to her knees she fell forwards, her head on her folded arms like a pilgrim reaching a shrine.

That's how it was she didn't see the yellow glow of a lantern coming from the trees behind her.

'Oh you poor darling,' Patience took off her cloak and draped it over Melissa's wet form. 'It's going to be all right, dear, you mustn't cry like that.' For her presence had pierced Melissa's wall of isolation, now her screams and cries rent the air. 'Help! Help!' Patience added her own yells, surprising herself with the volume of her voice.

John was the next on the scene, then Claude Biggs and Florrie. There was no quietening Melissa, her eyes were wild, she flailed her arms, beating her fists on the ground.

'We must get her home, oh dear, oh dear, we must. But can she walk?' Patience talked more to herself than anyone in particular.

'It's no good Miss Sylvester,' Florrie had never felt so helpless. 'She can't walk like she is. She's already started with the baby. Oh thank God, here comes Miss Georgina. She'll know what we have to do.'

'What if I try and carry her?' John suggested.

'Too late for that. Look at her nightgown, covered with blood it is. Baby's on its way,' Florrie tried to sound practical, tried to hide her fright.

Georgina took in the scene, feeling as helpless as any of them. She dropped to her knees by Melissa's side.

'You're going to be all right, Mellie. We'll make a bed for you under the trees where it's not so wet. John, can you and Biggs carry her. Carefully.'

At seeing John bent over her, Melissa's scream was enough to

194

raise the district, but ignoring it he and Biggs lifted her gently and carried her to where Georgina had laid her own waterproof cape.

'You'll get drenched. Here, put your arms in here.' He took off his jacket and held it for her.

Another moving light coming closer, then Jess arrived.

'Oh Miss Mellie, wot you come out 'ere in the wet for? Why didn't you call me? 'strewth – you started on the baby, out 'ere without so much as a drop of 'ot water nor nothing. Oh Miss Mellie love, just look at the state of you. Never mind, Jess'll look after you. Clear off you men, she don't want a lot of chaps gawping at 'er, now does she? How far away does the doctor live? What about *you*,' to Georgina, 'doubt if anyone else'll find their way out of this place, can you go – fast as 'ell – and bring him?'

'He's miles away. We'll have to manage. Jess, you've seen babies born before – I've seen foals – we'll have to help her ourselves.'

'Babies don't pop out like a cork from a bottle, she might be like this for hours. Enough to kill 'er, out 'ere in all the weather. There, love,' she gathered Melissa into her thin young arms. 'Now what you have to do is push the baby out. When the pain comes real bad don't fight it, just push, push like 'ell.' Then to Georgina, her 'aitches' as surely lost as her confidence, 'Oh, I dunno, 'elping ol' Mrs Bradley see to my mum is one thing, this ain't the same. We're going to need some 'elp.' But hadn't she been telling herself for weeks that she could see the baby born without outside interference? Somehow, out here in the chill night with rain dripping from the trees her courage was ebbing away.

It was then that Georgina thought of Alex Graves. He wasn't a doctor, but surely a veterinary surgeon was the next best thing. If she took the far track it wasn't more than half a mile to his house, she'd go and knock him up. Not that she'd tell an urban creature like Jess she was bringing a vet!

Carrying her lantern high, wearing John's jacket, her ginger hair a cap of tight auburn curls in the rain, she left the others. The last she heard was Jess dismissing John.

'She don't want you here, no more than she wants Biggs. It's all right ducky, that's it, squeeze my hand tight as you can when the pain comes, go on, 'arder than that . . . Go on, you blokes, just bugger off can't you, she don't want men standing there gawping at 'er.'

'That's it. Not right having men at a private time like this,' Mrs Biggs put her foot down. 'And when you get to the house just make sure the fire is burning well so there's hot water in the taps, put on plenty of kettles.'

'I shall stay,' John answered. 'We must get her home as soon as she can be moved – but she won't be able to walk.'

'She'll take a bit of carrying,' Jess viewed him doubtfully, she's always seen him as something of a dandy, it would take better muscles than his to carry Miss Mellie. 'Well, if you must wait, you must. But she don't want you staring at her struggle, keep back out of the way. There ain't nothing any of you can do. No, I'll tell you what. Go 'ome and find something we can carry her on, don't matter what you come up with, an old door, even one of those deck chairs you got cleaned up ready for the summer. Only make sure it's strong, don't want the canvas tearing. Off you go, just leave Miss Sylvester and me with her till Miss Georgina turns up with the doctor.'

'Poor child,' Mrs Biggs rang her hands helplessly as Melissa fought against the pain, her piteous cries eerie in a forest where there was no sound but the dripping from the trees. 'If only I could be going through it and sparing her.'

'Left things a bit late for that sort o' caper, Mrs Biggs,' Jess answered, not taking her eyes off Melissa. 'Now, all you lot get off back 'ome, find something to carry her on and see everything's ready for when we get 'er 'ome. Hope that doctor's not going to bugger us up, this baby's not going to hang about. Sooner it gets itself born the better for poor Miss Mellie.'

Patience marvelled at the girl's ability.

Walking ahead with his lantern high Biggs led the procession back to Kyneston while John backed away to the grass, then across it to the trees beyond. No one watched which way he went and, sitting far from the aura of their lanterns on the thoroughly wet trunk of a hewn tree, he was soon forgotten.

Coming at last to the lane where the night seemed less dark, Georgina's flagging courage took a boost. Jess had tried to sound confident, but what could a girl like that know if anything went wrong? Alex Graves would help, he *must* help.

For the moment the rain had stopped, the night was still. In daytime she'd never noticed the click of the garden gate, at night it was enough to rouse the household. It didn't do that, but it did rouse Bluff who played his part as guard dog with gusto.

Above her the curtains were opened, she could see the flickering light of a candle. Mrs Griffin must have known that Bluff wouldn't bark in the middle of the night for nothing.

'Who's there?' With her iron grey hair tightly secured in two thin pigtails, she pushed up her window.

'Mrs Griffin, it's me, Georgina Rochester. We've got trouble, I've come to fetch Mr Graves.'

'Best I can do is tell him when he gets back. They fetched him to Meadsfoot Farm just as he'd got into his bed. Can it wait till morning? He's had not a wink of sleep.'

'. . . in labour . . .' Mrs Griffin must have misheard, as far as she knew the only animals at Kyneston were the horses.

'Hark, I hear him coming.' They both listened to the sound of a horse approaching.

Thank You, Georgina began her silent plea, You've brought him home, now *please* make him come with me. And make him know what to do. Help Mellie. Take care of her, make her be all right. *Please*.

Mrs Griffin watched as Georgina spoke to Alex. Out of earshot she was still left without knowing why he was wanted at Kyneston. And why had Miss Rochester come on foot? Well, it seemed he wasn't going with her, he was leading his horse round to the stable. But why was she waiting?

Then, of course, the final and completely unfathomable mystery: wherever were they going, setting off in the opposite direction from Kyneston and on foot?

'It's 'ead's there, see, another push or two and it'll be through. I thought I'd get it over before you got 'ere.' Jess was torn between anguish for Melissa and pride in her own ability.

Disregarding the muddy ground, Alex knelt, positioning himself as if Melissa were lying on her bed and he standing at its foot. More to impress Jess than believing anything he carried would be called into use, he opened his bag.

'We'll soon have this over,' he smiled at Melissa.

She heard his voice, so steady and gentle. The familiar voices of the others hadn't penetrated her torment, yet his pierced through her barrier of pain. She heard it and, although the contrac-

197

tions tore her, she was strangely comforted. Melissa, always so lovely, but not tonight, not after all that these last hours had done to her. Plain or beautiful, her face went unnoticed. Alex had helped pull many a calf into the world when nature's path hadn't been smooth; lambing time was all in a day's work, just as sometimes he had to help a sow who couldn't drop the last of a litter. A young woman giving birth on the floor of the forest was outside his experience, but no one would have known it from his gentle confidence. Georgina felt she was seeing him anew.

'It'll soon be over,' his voice soothed, 'try again . . .'

'Hush dear, hush,' Patience whispered as Melissa's scream rent the air.

'There's no one to hear, only us.' He spoke without taking his eyes from the positioned head. 'One more try, that's it, here's the head . . . now again . . . as soon as the shoulders are there I'll be able to help you.'

'Oh . . . oh . . . oh . . . oh . . .' The long, piercing scream was unearthly, as unearthly as the moving shadows in the pale lamplight as sudden gusts of wind whipped through the branches.

From his damp perch amongst the trees on the far side of the grassy patch the cry seemed hardly human. John sat with his head in his shaking hands. She must be going to die . . . wasn't that what she'd warned him . . . this was his fault . . . not just for giving her a child, but for what he'd done tonight. What sort of a man was he? Thank God no one could see the way he shook, his whole body trembling as if with ague. What would Georgina think of a man who behaved like this? That's my *wife* out there, probably dying trying to give birth to the child I forced on her – and I'm letting myself wonder what Georgina is thinking about me, Georgina who is soon to marry Steven. Hark at Melissa, this isn't one of her hysterical tantrums, this is hell just as she'd known it would be. God, let her live. Punish me if You like, but for God's sake hasn't she suffered enough? Lunging from his uncomfortable seat he blundered blindly further into the wood in the darkness, ashamed of his own weakness as he clung for support to the slender trunk of a young beech tree and surrendered to the nausea he couldn't hold off.

When it was over, he stood with his back to the tree, breathless and exhausted. He'd done many things in his life of which he wasn't proud, but never had he been as low in self-esteem as he

198

was in those moments. The light from the lanterns around Melissa gave a warm glow, a welcoming from this distance. He became aware that her piercing yells had stopped, there was no sound except for the low-pitched voices of those around her and then the cry of a newborn child. It was over. The baby was born, Melissa was silent. That could only mean one thing . . . She'd told him and he hadn't believed. In his mind he seemed to see her, the lovely young girl he'd first known, the bride who'd been shocked and frightened by his lovemaking, then the pregnant and resentful woman sure that her life was soon to be over. That's what she'd believed even when she'd expected to be brought to bed with the child. To get away from him – was that why she had escaped into the night? No sane woman would do that, not even a frightened one. No sane woman . . . had he done that to her too? God forgive me . . . why should You? I don't deserve to be forgiven. If she's gone I have to live with the knowledge that I destroyed her.

Moving out from the shelter of the trees and undergrowth he looked across the open area of grass to the group; they were like a moving picture. Only Melissa was still, lying flat on the ground, all her fighting over, while Jess knelt at her side helping the man he supposed to be a doctor clear away the mess of childbirth. John ran his shaking fingers through his wet hair, trying to brace himself for what must come next. Patience was holding the baby while Georgina wrapped it in Jess's cape. They were careful how they folded the material around the little form, trying to ensure none of the damp outer layer contacted it. Then when they were satisfied, Georgina stooped to pick up the lantern she'd put at their feet.

It was as she held it high she caught sight of John and came to meet him.

Chapter Twelve

Biggs returned. In one hand he carried his lantern while under the other arm he bore an improvised stretcher in the form of the garden hammock, two long poles and, wrapped around all that, two blankets protected against the weather by an old waterproof cape he kept in the coachhouse for emergencies.

'Florrie's gone off on Miss Mellie's bicycle to fetch the doctor,' he called as he approached their pool of light. 'They'll go to the house first now that we've got something to carry the lassie home on. How's she doing?'

'Not doing,' Georgina shouted back. Thankfulness that it was over and Melissa sunk into exhausted sleep – that it might be unconsciousness she wouldn't consider – gave a ring to her voice, 'Not doing, but *done*. What did you find to carry her on?' His ingenuity added to their mood of hopefulness. They threaded the long poles through the mesh the length of the hammock then covered the criss-cross of knotted string with a folded blanket. In the lamplight Melissa's face had a waxen sheen, even her lips were drained of colour. The birth had been quick, leaving her weak and torn – but alive. It was with a feeling of thankfulness that John bent to gather her into his arms, thankfulness not just for her but for himself too, some of his guilt evaporated. One at each corner, Alex, Biggs, Jess and Georgina held the waiting stretcher.

Some inner warning must have alerted Melissa. Opening her bloodshot eyes she saw him in the flickering light, like a devil he seemed to loom over her. She wanted to scream, to struggle, but as happens in a nightmare she was powerless, the noise she made no more than an incoherent moan. She may have believed she was fighting him, but in truth her only movement was the threshing of her head from side to side.

'I'll lift her,' Alex said, 'you take my corner. I'm more used to lifting than you are.'

Dull, humourless, buttoned-up, nothing could alter that, but here was a side to his nature Georgina hadn't expected. Tact, awareness of other people's feelings, she'd not suspected they might be hiding behind the unbending politeness she was accustomed to. Without demur Melissa suffered him to carry her and lay her gently on the stretcher then cover her with the second blanket before he came to Georgina's corner and took it from her.

'You light the way, we'll come behind.' He laid his bag on the end of the hammock beyond Melissa's feet then their procession was ready to move off. Georgina went first, her lamp held high to cast its beam as wide as she could. Patience followed with the newborn in her arms and then the stretcher party, Biggs and Jess first, he bearing his share of the load with one hand and a lantern with the other, then Alex and John. Considering Melissa's state it was an optimistic party that confidently followed Georgina along tracks that to them (with the exception of Biggs) all looked remarkably alike. Already the black night sky was lightening to a deep grey and by the time they came from the shelter of the ancient forest to the lane and almost immediately to the gate of Kyneston, it was as if the supernatural gave them a sign, the first delicate colours showed a promise of dawn; somewhere below the far horizon the sun sent an ethereal light of pink and gold ahead of it.

And the final relief: the doctor's trap was already at the door.

Jess was in her element. With the others banished from the bedroom, only answering to the ring of the bell when anything was needed, it was she who helped the doctor as he made his examination and 'tidied the patient' as he referred to the necessary stitches. And it was Jess who gave the tiny and perfect baby girl her first bathe and dressed her in the clothes she had made sure were kept aired in readiness. Busy though she was, she had time to glance out of the window at the sound of the trap taking the vet home. To think that a vet had brought Miss Mellie's baby into the world, if she'd known at the time that that's all he was she would have stood her ground and not let him come interfering! She hoped Miss Mellie wouldn't be able to remember any of it too clearly. Perhaps she'd never see him again, he'd never come calling before so there was no reason he would now. But poor Miss Mellie, Jess's imagination raced away with her, awful for 'er it'd be to have to look 'im in the face and know she'd been treated no better 'un the farm animals what 'e's used to. Good job 'e's gone off 'ome before she comes to proper.

Gently she tended the tiny infant, marvelling that only hours ago it had been part of Miss Mellie. She'd seen brothers and sisters when they were as small as this, but never had she had this strange trembly feeling. 'Makes me ache all over. I feel like that with Miss Mellie sometimes. Ain't a comfy feeling, but I don't want nothing no different.'

'Now I think it's time for your husband to be allowed in. Only for a few moments, mind you, I want you to rest. Give the infant to its mother,' he told Jess, 'then come downstairs with me.'

'No . . .' Melissa breathed.

'She won't break,' the doctor smiled encouragingly. He remembered what a nervous and neurotic child she'd been, and tonight would have been strain enough on the most stout-hearted.

'No . . . won't see him . . . don't let him in . . . no . . .'

Concentrating on her post-natal care, he hadn't stopped to wonder what had sent her out alone into the night. She and her husband must have quarrelled. Poor child, this ought to be the most joyous moment – and so it would be. Once they were together with their baby the shadow of any misunderstanding would be lifted.

'You needn't sit up,' he took the baby from Jess and brought it to the bedside, 'just move your arm to make a nest for it.'

Perhaps if he'd called the child 'her' instead of 'it', the effect of his words might have been different. 'Her' implied a living being, a life apart from its mother: 'it' was no more than the thing she'd hated and resented all these months, even now 'it' was born she wasn't free.

With more strength than any of them realized she had, she pushed the child away from her. Eyes closed, she beat her clenched fists on the counterpane.

'I won't . . .' Her eyes flew open, the doctor was shocked by the fear and hatred he saw. 'Don't let him near me. Tell him . . . make him understand . . .'

'There, there, child. You just sleep.' Then, to Jess, 'Here, you take the child. I must go down and talk to Mr Derrick.'

'Send 'im orf, doctor, can't you. She ain't going to be easy till she knows 'e's gorn.' Jess always spoke her mind, no one understood Miss Mellie the way she did and she wasn't going to let them push her about. Give her a good sleep and she'd soon love this little angel – but as for the master, the sooner he was on the train and off back to London the better.

Downstairs the kindly doctor explained to John that it would be wise to give his wife a little more time before he saw her.

'This has been a traumatic experience for her, she's unnerved, poor child. It happens to a good many women. But it's a temporary thing, purely post-natal. I'll send Jess down with your daughter.'

Ten minutes later Jess brought the baby down to the drawing room. Georgina sent a message to the kitchen for everyone to come and meet her – after all they had all played their part in a night they'd not forget. Patience wept with unashamed joy at the sight of a creature so exquisite. Only Biggs and John were missing, the trap already turned out of the gate and on its way to Brockenhurst Station.

Alice spent most of the baby's first day at Kyneston, oblivious to Jess's resentment at the hours she waited patiently at the bedside while Melissa slept. It wasn't that Jess disliked Alice, how could she dislike anyone who so patently doted on Melissa? But she would have resented even the Angel Gabriel for pushing in front of her. In the first hours any attempt to introduce mother and daughter had been hopeless, but Jess had been sure that it would be *she* who would accomplish the miracle. She was wrong. That blind faith Melissa had always had in her aunt never changed. 'Aunt Alice says . . .', 'I'm going to talk about it to Aunt Alice . . .', how often Georgina had heard it through the years. Very real love for her niece must have heightened Alice's perception and helped bring about the miracle. Most of the afternoon she cradled the baby to her, that's how Melissa first saw her when she opened her eyes.

'My prayers have been answered,' Alice told her, 'you've come through your ordeal. And your baby is perfect – see, tiny fingers. A little girl, to bring joy to you as you always have to me.' What stopped her saying 'Cedric and me?' She didn't know, only that something did. 'I'm only an aunt—'

'Oh, no, you're more, you know you're more.'

'In my heart I'm your mother, this tiny girl's grandmother. Hold her, Mellie.'

But it wasn't that simple, even then Melissa pulled away, wouldn't look at the bundle of humanity that represented so much she loathed.

Another hour or so went by. Where Melissa had been lying flat she gradually moved to sit, propped by a nest of pillows. Jess came and went in the room, she brought food, taking control she forced Melissa to drink, regularly she relieved Alice of the infant to perform necessary acts for its comfort. When it cried she put the crook of her little finger to its mouth. And then, around teatime of that first day, she heard the newborn screams then silence as she came up the stairs to the bedroom. On opening the door she saw Melissa with the infant to her breast while Alice bent over them both.

Jess knew she ought to be thankful – but she was frightened. Oh Miss Mellie, don't look like that, like as if you're somewhere miles away from any of us, most of all miles away from that poor little soul what's not to blame for 'aving a father what used you so bad.

By evening Alice had gone home, the baby was back in its crib and Melissa gazing blankly at the ceiling above her. Her contact with her daughter hadn't touched her, she had found the light tug at her nipple distasteful but she'd been too far removed from it to care. Jess was busying herself putting away a pile of diapers she'd had around the fireguard in the kitchen.

'Mellie, dear, there's a caller to see you, it's Mr Graves. You know, the little girls' father.' Patience stood uncertainly in the bedroom doorway. 'I don't know what we would have done without him last night, we've so much to be grateful to him for. He wants to reassure himself that you are recovering.' Such a long speech was unlike Patience but she was frightened that, given a silence, Melissa might fill it with her refusal to see her visitor.

Jess frowned her disapproval. If one thing was geared to upset poor Miss Mellie it must be coming face to face with that vet man.

'That's kind of him,' Melissa answered. She hardly remem-

204

bered her saviour, only his firm, gentle voice that had pierced her terror.

'I'll bring him up.' And Patience was gone before there was time for a change of mind.

To Melissa he appeared as a stranger, only the voice was familiar.

'You don't think I'm intruding?' his uncertainty did more for her than any confident visit from the doctor could. 'You've been on my mind all day. I'm so thankful to see you looking better.'

She smiled, first the corners of her mouth, then her eyes. Could this pale, ethereal woman be the same as the girl he'd helped last night?

'It's like a nightmare,' she told him, 'you know how it is that when you wake you just know something dreadful happened but you can never remember exactly. I'm sure I ought to remember you . . . I know I was thankful when you spoke to me, that's the only thing that's clear.'

'And your daughter? She's none the worse?'

For answer her glance directed him to the crib.

'Ain't she just perfect?' Jess said proudly as if she claimed credit for such perfection.

'Indeed. I'm so thankful,' he added to Melissa in what Georgina called his buttoned-up voice. 'I have no wish to intrude on you, Mrs Derrick,' he must have been making enquiries for he'd certainly not had an official introduction, 'but I should deem it a favour if when you are feeling more rested I might bring Victoria and Becky to see the baby. I know they are often with Miss Rochester – but if you'd allow me to bring them myself I should appreciate it.'

'I'd like that,' Melissa found her mouth relaxing, almost smiling. 'Come when you like. Already I'm feeling better than I have for months. And Mr Graves – thank you – for turning out in the middle of the night and – well, for helping. I said it's like trying to remember a nightmare but, the strange thing is, as clearly as anything I recall how you drove away my terror.'

'You were very brave,' he told her.

No wonder she smiled, no one had ever called her brave.

After he'd gone she lay quietly with her eyes closed, giving the impression that she was asleep. She'd heard Georgina call him 'Mr Sobersides', but his formal manner put Melissa at ease.

Sobersides? He was no such thing. He was honest, kind, undemanding. Most men she'd met had left her in no doubt that they found her attractive and, before her experience of marriage and all it entailed, she had been excited by their mild flirtations. Alex Graves wouldn't know how to flirt, she felt comfortable with him. Of course he thought she was pretty – he would have been blind not to as she was aware – but that wasn't what had brought him here. 'I should deem it a favour . . .' she remembered his words, expressing his honest sentiment. When Jess wasn't watching she wriggled deeper into the bed, more content than she had been for a long time.

Then nature took over and she drifted into a sleep that was light enough that she heard the baby's yells, but deep enough that they had no power to disturb her. It was Jess who woke her.

'Come on, Miss Mellie, time you let her have another go. There won't be any goodness in what she takes, not for a day or two, but it flushes her out. Anyway we want her to get the idea.'

Melissa marvelled that poor skinny, plain Jess would be such a font of knowledge. She sat up and let her nipple be guided into the rosebud mouth, she held the bundle that was put into her arms. Instinct was the baby's guide, its cheeks were pulled in as it drew on her. Looking down at it her only emotion was distaste as memories crowded in on her; she shut her eyes as if to escape . . . she was back in the first weeks of her marriage . . . John . . . now the child he'd forced on her . . .

'I should deem it a favour . . .' A warm tear escaped her from under her closed lid.

Victoria was speechless, there was just no way of expressing what she felt at the sight of such a minute being, the tiny nails, the perfectly formed fingers like the curled petals of a flower.

'Can we see her feet?' Never shy, it was Becky who asked. 'Just to see how small they'd be.'

Jess unwrapped the shawl, and both girls knelt at her feet like worshippers at a shrine.

'Has she got a name, Mrs Derrick?' Victoria found her voice.

'No, I haven't thought. Perhaps I'll call her Alice after my aunt.'

Becky frowned.

'She doesn't look like an Alice. Mrs Griffin reads us stories of

angels, I 'spect you know about angels Mrs Derrick. I s'pose they
were people who've never been bad.'

'Mrs Derrick doesn't need to hear,' her father admonished her.
'But it's important.' The gruff voice wasn't stilled so easily.
'Mrs Griffin says that when a baby's born it's pure, just like the
angels. It's only the bad things we do like getting other people into
hot water or telling fibs that sort of stains us. So your baby hasn't
been stained. Silly though isn't it, angels all seem to be men. Yet
you'd think from the pictures in the book she reads to us that they
were ladies – they've got long hair and long sort of nightgowns.'

'That's more than enough please Becky.' Alex didn't raise his
voice, but his small daughter knew she'd reached the line that
mustn't be overstepped.

'You could call her Angela,' Victoria found her voice.

'Or Verity,' Alex came near to smiling. Then, seeing their
puzzled expressions, 'Verity means truth.'

'That's a splendid name!' Victoria agreed. 'Will you call her
that Mrs Derrick?'

'Take no notice of the child,' Alex interrupted. 'Alice is a
delightful name.

'I don't think so,' the gruff voice mumbled.

'Mrs Derrick, I apologize,' Alex's only change of expression
was a slight tightening of his mouth. 'I can't think what's come
over her.'

Melissa found herself smiling, just as she had on his last visit.

'Verity . . . Verity . . .' Melissa repeated. 'That's what she shall
be.'

And suddenly she'd had enough of their childish prattle, she
wanted them gone.

With mixed feeling Georgina delivered her last order of hats to
Madame de Bouverie's establishment in Christchurch. Working
for the London-born 'Frenchwoman' had been little better paid
than slave labour, but her work had been a challenge and since
she'd first started helping Augusta she had learned her trade well.
During the coming weeks she had far more to think about than
designing hats for the better-off of the county, she had to concentrate on her own wardrobe, to make her wedding arrangements
and see everything was in order for when Steven returned.

Rebuffed by Melissa, John had returned to his gallery. But he would soon be back, he hadn't even seen his daughter. Except for allowing the baby to be brought to her breast every three or four hours, Melissa left everything to Jess who was proving utterly capable. So probably by the time of the wedding John would have taken them all back to London. Anyway, Georgina told herself, that was nothing to do with *her*, her life was with Steven. And thinking about it she was aware of a tremor of excitement for her unknown future. She'd ride the oceans, she'd see far-away places, and always Steven would be at her side. Strong, dependable, laughing at the things she laughed at, fearless . . . 'soul of my soul' he'd called her, and wasn't that what he was to her too?

Melissa received news of the wedding plans with indifference. Indeed, she'd been in a strange state since the birth, impassive, disinterested. She gave herself over to Jess's ministrations, showed no impatience to stand out of bed, no curiosity about anything around her.

'It will be a quiet wedding,' Georgina told her, 'no wreath and veil. So there won't be a bridesmaid – or in your case a Matron of Honour – but Mellie you'll be well enough by then to be a witness, won't you? I can't be married without you being there to see me on my way.' She heard her voice as unnaturally jolly, as if that way she would pierce the stupor Melissa wrapped herself in.

'Aunt Alice says it'll be too soon for me to go out. You don't know what I went through.' Talking about it was unnerving her. A minute ago she'd looked relaxed, her hands folded in front of her on the counterpane. Like a doll who had been wound up she suddenly changed, the stillness gave way to uncontrolled twitching, her face, her shoulders, even her breathing was irregular as she clenched and unclenched her fists.

'Don't worry, then, Mellie. I'm not pushing you, if you're not up to it.'

'I'm not. Just leave me here. Jess understands, I'm safe with Jess.'

Georgina hugged her, she hoped the action seemed spontaneous and gave no sign of her own feeling of panic.

'You're safe anywhere, Mellie. And before you know it you'll be back in your own home getting a reputation of being the hostess of the season.'

'Are you telling me you want to get rid of Kyneston? Yes, that's what you want of course. What would Steven Howard want with a house in Hampshire? What would you want with a home at all? You're going to be a water gypsy.'

'I wouldn't sell my share of Kyneston even for the Crown jewels.'

Her words conjured up so many memories. There were more questions than answers in the silent look they exchanged: did Melissa love John enough to build a proper union with him? Why was Georgina running away from Kyneston? John . . . Steven . . . in their locked gaze so much remained unsaid.

Melissa's mouth was trembling, two tears rolled unchecked down her face.

'Wish we were still small,' she croaked. 'Wish it was like it used to be.'

This time when Georgina folded her into her arms it was certainly spontaneous. A married woman and a mother, but unhappy Melissa was still the child she'd been, the frightened, hysterical tornado craving admiration and attention.

'I don't like it, I don't like it at all.' As was her habit, when Mrs Biggs had something on her mind she took a walk to the coach-house to unburden herself.

'What's that you don't like, m'dear? Is it Miss Mellie that's worrying you?'

'Miss Mellie, fiddlesticks. That aunt of hers is upstairs sitting by the bedside again this morning. The way they make an invalid of the girl isn't giving nature a chance to set her right. No, it's not her, it's this wedding. Is he the right one for her? The girl's met no one – no young men of her own age. Captain Howard is handsome enough to turn her head, and I admit there's a romance about a man of the sea. But I don't like to think of her tossing about on the wild ocean, don't know how I shall rest easy in my bed when we get the autumn storms not knowing where she is. She's a country girl, the forest – that's the place for Miss Georgina.'

'Ah, you're right there. But she's got a mind of her own and always has had. Nothing you or me can do but give her our support.'

Adelaide Biggs pulled herself to her full height, then after pausing long enough to let him know the importance of her words she said, 'Now I'll come to what I came to tell you. Properly upset Effie was when she whispered to me what she'd heard. 'Just keep nonsense like that to yourself' I told her. And she will. Passing it on to me was one thing, but she'll not say a word to anyone else. Miss Georgina has always been the apple of her eye.'

'Go on then, what's she been telling you?'

'Walls have ears.' She moved closer to him, her head nodding, her brows pulled into an angry frown as she whispered in his ear.

'Bitch!' he breathed. 'Always has been and always will be.'

Alice had arrived earlier than usual on her morning visit to join Melissa in a 'glass of Madeira and a chat' as she termed it. In fact it was often a glass of Madeira – plus two Bath Olivers – and a comfortable silence while Melissa lay back on her pillows indulging in the feeling of safety and protection her aunt always gave her. And habit had formed that Jess had Verity to herself during the visit. The one-time nursery had been brought back into use and it was here that Jess reigned supreme. Even when Melissa was on her feet again she wasn't likely to pose a threat, she showed no more interest in her daughter after two weeks than she'd shown after two days.

It was seldom that Alice and Georgina came face to face, by common consent they didn't seek each other's company. That morning the clang of the front door bell had proclaimed a caller more than half an hour before Alice's usual time, just as Georgina was coming down the stairs, dressed to go out. So it had come about that Effie admitted Alice as Georgina reached the hall.

'You may go.' Alice had dismissed the maid without a glance, then to Georgina, 'I understand from Melissa that you've found yourself a husband, a seaman, the man John uses. Well, I wish you well my dear.' Transparently 'well' was the last thing she wished and 'my dear' far from being meant as an endearment. 'But it does raise doubts as to his motives. A carrier is a carrier, whether he drives a wagon over the countryside or gets tossed about on the seas. And Kyneston – even half Kyneston – is a prize worth taking.'

'Indeed it is.' Georgina's smile was dripping with honey, she gave no sign of the anger that raged in her. 'And of course you and Mr Sylvester are concerned, you've seen how easily one can be duped. But Steven is a very different man from John.'

'What are you inferring? How low can you sink with your spiteful jealousy? You've always been the same. I've made

210

allowances for your lack of grace, but I'll not hear aspersions of that sort and be silent.'

Georgina had shrugged her shoulders, hiding her anger behind an insolent smile.

'You mustn't worry on my account.' As if Alice had been! 'Captain Howard is the kindest, most honourable man I know.'

'And you've a wide experience of course . . .'

'No, I suppose I've no one to measure him against except for your husband and John.'

Alice twitched with anger.

'The man is a scoundrel, why else would he wheedle his way into your affections. Even that nincompoop Patience is in his clutches, not that it would take much to influence her, one smile from a man and she'd be his for the taking.'

'Mrs Sylvester, I'm sorry you find it so hard to accept that I am *not* being married for my inheritance. I've often had reason to be grateful for the way Father divided his possessions; after all, as I heard John and your husband agree on the evening he asked for Mellie's hand, half a house and no fortune can be more of a liability than an asset. But I pay my share in the running of this house, whatever you may think. For myself I don't touch a penny of Father's money, but what he left me brings enough to pay my half of the bills.'

'And like your mother before you, you disgrace the family name by working like some common seamstress. Well, this marriage will turn you into a water gypsy. Water or land, there's little difference. Just to look at that mother of yours told one she had Romany blood. Yes, you'll be happy, you'll be able to stop aping the lady. What's in the blood is what matters in the end.'

'How right you are. And thank God for it.' For Georgina that final 'thank God for it' had put an end to the conversation. There was nothing new in Alice's animosity, her views mattered not at all.

'And one more thing, young lady. Melissa tells me you want her to be witness at this hole-in-the-corner wedding of yours. And who do you think will be giving you away? Not Cedric, I promise you.' Even as she'd said it Alice had started up the stairs, determined to have the last word and sure that given the opportunity Georgina would strip her of the satisfaction.

211

From her listening post on the other side of the door that led to the servant's quarters Effie had gone to find Mrs Biggs.

'Not a word to a soul of what you heard,' the housekeeper had told her when the tale came to an end. 'If I hear a whisper of it I shall know it's come from your blabbing.'

'You think I would? Talking like that to Miss Georgina! I wouldn't repeat it to a living soul – only to you.' Effie sniffed appreciatively. 'Pity the silly old trout couldn't come in here and take a whiff of that wedding cake. We'll show 'em, Mrs Biggs, we'll let them see what we think of our Miss Georgie.' Then, as another thought struck her: 'But who do you reckon will walk her up the aisle? Not that she can't do without that old misery guts. But someone's got to do it. Do you reckon Mr Derrick will? Yes, that'll be it. He'll come for the wedding and by then Miss Melissa will be on her feet and ready to go home with him.'

Mrs Bigg's sniff could be taken any way she liked.

The doctor was satisfied with Melissa's progress, he said she could be allowed up, at first just an hour or two sitting out of bed and then a few days later dressing and venturing downstairs.

But she wouldn't budge.

'Come on, Mellie, you're going to get so weak.' Georgina had managed to persuade her to sit on the edge of the bed with her feet on the floor. 'I'll support you, just try and walk a few steps. Once your legs get going you'll want to be up and about. I've put the hammock up, why don't we get you out into the garden to lie under the trees.'

'No. I can't. I'm not better. The doctor's a fool. I'm still bleeding.' Just talking about it brought alive the horror, the pain she'd not been able to escape, then trembling with cold and fright how she'd felt the sudden gush of warm blood. 'I can't. You don't understand. No one understands.' There was no logic in what she said, only a need to match her mindless terror with the sound of her own voice.

'There's Mr Graves to see you,' Jess opened the bedroom door. 'Him and the girls, but it's Verity the little 'uns come for. I'll take them to have a peep at her. But do you want him, or shall I tell 'im you're having a sleep?' In her mind having organized the visitors, she looked more closely at the two sitting on the edge of the bed. 'Oh Miss Mellie, what's the matter lovey?' Then, like a terrier protecting some meaty morsel, to Georgina, 'You gone and got her upset again? Don't know how it is you manage to do it like you do. Come on, Miss Mellie, put your feet back into bed. You got a bit o' time before Verity will be ready for you, I'll tell him you're not up to having a visitor. He won't take it wrong, he'll understand. A real gent is Mr Graves.'

Propped again on her nest of pillows, the covers pulled almost to her shoulders, Melissa felt safe.

'Yes, he is. He's so kind, I've never known anyone so kind.' She wriggled deeper into the bed. 'Let him come up, Jess.'

'He comes nearly every day,' Georgina was puzzled.

'Sometimes he gets called too far away, he can't get back. But', a smile timidly touched the corners of Melissa's mouth, 'I think he always tries.'

'I bet you don't tell strait-laced Alice. Indeed!' And mimicking Alice's tone, Georgina's face took on an exaggeration of the hypercritical expression she has so often been treated to. 'It's unseemly! I would never have entertained a gentleman in my bedroom!'

'You're beastly about her. And don't be disgusting! When the doctor calls no one makes unpleasant remarks. And Alex – Mr Graves – did more for me than any doctor. If it hadn't been for him I wouldn't be here. Have you ever thought of that?' All too well Georgina knew the danger signal of the rising pitch of Melissa's voice. 'I was dying – you hear me, dying – just as I'd told you I would. But none of you listened, none of you cared. He gave me my life back. He was the first person to touch the baby, even before it was properly born. You think he comes to see me because I'm in bed, that's the way your horrid mind works. He doesn't think that way any more than I do. It's *you*. Your mind is full of filth. I won't listen. I don't want to hear . . .'

'Hush Mellie. You know I was teasing. I hear him coming.' But Melissa was in no mood to be placated, her fingers were tearing at the counterpane, her face was working, the storm cloud were about to break.

With a soft knock on the door Alex came in and in one glance took in the scene.

'Good evening Miss Rochester,' he lowered his head to Georgina with the solemn dignity she'd come to expect. 'The children have gone to the nursery. I'm sure they'll be delighted to see you.'

213

Dismissed in her own home! And even before she was out of the room he approached the bed where Melissa was looking at him in mute misery.

Georgina had called at the rectory to talk to Reverend Carter about the wedding. If he had any qualms he saved them until she'd gone, then shared them with his sister. He'd not met this Captain Howard so he had no right to criticize the arrangements, but he'd been fond of Georgina since she was a child and he feared she might be rushing into wedlock with the first person who had shown her any sign of affection.

'This is a very big step, Georgina my child. You have no father to guide you, forgive me if I overstep my brief. Any concern I have comes from affection of many years.'

Quick tears sprung to Georgina's eyes.

'Thank you, Rector. But I know I'm doing the right thing, honestly I do. I've never felt so – so comfortable – so much *me* – with anyone as I do with Steven.'

'He's a lucky young man, my dear.'

'Aunt Patience tells me you called to see Melissa,' she changed the subject with the first thing that came into her head. To agree with him that Steven was a lucky *young* man would have been less than the truth; to tell him that, lucky or not, he was nearer Patience's age than her own seemed like a betrayal of the person he was, ageless, strong, courageous, all the things a man should be.

Into the third week since Steven's departure, the wedding plans were well advanced. Georgina had been to Chadwick & Grieves to talk to Thomas Grieves, coming away with papers proving her legal adoption and a document showing her as half owner of Kyneston. In the larder, iced and decorated with marzipan flowers, her wedding cake was protected with a sheet of grease-proof paper; in her wardrobe (the ivory silk remodelled to a style she felt happy in with its fitted waist where a waist should be, it's high neck and leg o' mutton sleeves, a skirt that hung with elegant grace over her slim hips) her wedding gown was protected with a brand-new sheet she'd taken from the linen store. And on the stand in her workroom was her newly finished hat, a creation such as she'd never possessed – indeed it was an exaggeration of the models she'd designed for the local well-to-dos. And why not? It counter-balanced the simplicity of her gown, it laughed at sobriety, it seemed to say: 'Look at me, this is my special day, a day to remember, a day to make its mark.' It was a hat to cock a snoop at 'that Hapley Court lot and all their cronies'.

The morning after Steven's arrival they were to pay their visit to the rectory. His faith in a deity was as strong as any other man's who battles with the elements of storm and sea, but his attendance at church had been rare to the point of non-existent and the thought of going voluntarily to see the priest had never entered his head. But it was important he didn't fail Georgina, she seemed to set great store in this Reverend Carter and his opinions. He knotted his tie with extra precision, cleaned his boots until they gleamed, brushed his jacket before he put it on, then after examining the result carefully went down to where she was waiting in the doorway of the study.

'Everything's ready as you told me. The papers are there on the desk.'

Picking them up, he glanced through them.

She watched, waiting for some word of approval that she'd been efficient, forgotten nothing.

He looked up from the papers . . . to her . . . back again . . . then he dropped them on the desk, sinking to the chair, his hands clenching and unclenching, his face void of expression.

'Steven, what is it? Aren't you well?'

'Yes, yes . . .' he answered automatically.

'So what have I done wrong? Mr Grieves said everything was in order . . .?' Remembering her visit to her friend the solicitor she tried to keep the panic out of her voice.

Why did he look at her like that?

Chapter Thirteen

Why did he look at her like that, as if she were a stranger? What had she done? It must be to do with Kyneston, but she'd always told him the house was only half hers. For one wild second she imagined Alice's hateful innuendos had been right; but as the suggestion was born, so it died.

'What is it? Steven, say something – anything – but don't look at me like that.'

'Dear God forgive me,' he muttered, more to himself than to her.

'Forgive you for what?'

Coming to him she took his unsteady hands in hers trying to will him to meet her eyes. When he didn't, she dropped to her knees in front of him.

'You've got to tell me. Don't just sit there saying nothing. May He forgive you for what?' And again before she could stamp it out the memory of Alice was close, her face a triumphant sneer.

'This,' he nodded his head towards the top document, her birth certificate. 'Mother, Augusta Hawkesworth – Father, unknown.'

She recoiled from him as though he'd hit her. All her life she had been ostracized from local society, she'd learned to build a protective wall around her and had long since ceased to be hurt. But this wasn't one of those narrow-minded so-called gentry she scorned, this was Steven.

'You knew I was adopted,' she rasped, getting to her feet with more speed than grace.

'I didn't know this,' he pushed the birth certificate away from him. 'Marriage is impossible.'

'If that's how you feel, then I'm glad we've found out now

216

God forgive you, you say. He can if He wants to – but I won't. You're a narrow-minded bigot, like the rest of them!' There was so much more bubbling up in her mind to be hurled at him, but she couldn't trust her voice.

'No! No Georgina. Listen to me. Oh Christ,' he ran his fingers though his near-colourless hair, 'what have I done to you?'

'I'll tell you what you've done. Just in time you've stopped me making the biggest mistake of my life. I don't want to talk about it, Steven. I'd rather you just went. Now. You've been frank. I should be grateful.' She'd turned away towards the window looking out to where already Biggs had brought the trap waiting for their trip to the Rectory.

Then she felt his hands on her shoulders.

'I was hardly more than a boy when I knew Augusta—'

'You knew Mother . . . ?' Even as she said it the truth hit her.

'Georgina, you were born in 1886. It was the end of the previous summer she and I were together. Perhaps she saw me as a callow youth, that's what I must have been. She taught me to love. Now, don't you understand . . .? Father unknown. Unknown and unknowing. I'd no idea there was a baby. When I came back she'd gone, I never saw her again.'

'I don't want to know. If Mama had wanted to tell me she would have. Father – Mellie's father – he made me *his*.' But as she said it the full implications of their situation swamped her. Father had made her his daughter – but she was flesh of Steven's flesh, bone of his bone . . . soul of his soul. 'You're not my father,' she came near to hissing it. 'Just go away. Forget me as you forgot her.'

He didn't move and she hadn't the courage to turn and look at him.

'Shall I tell Patience or will you?' he asked after a moment. 'We'll have to explain.' He sounded helpless, as helpless as she felt.

'I tell you – Father was my father. There's nothing to explain except that we've changed our minds.'

'You don't want them told?' How gentle he sounded. She longed to turn to him for the strength she lacked, to the Steven who'd been her friend, the Steven she'd loved. May God forgive him, he'd said. And what about her? She'd led him to the pool, she'd intended them to make love . . . would He forgive her?

'Incest,' she said, ignoring his question. 'I've always known incest was a sin, but until now I've never known what it does to you. Please just go, Steven.'

Unprepared for his sudden movement she found herself spun round to face him, his hand under her chin as he willed her to look him in the eyes.

'Don't imagine you're the only one to suffer. I've been haunted by carnal lust – yes, carnal lust – for my own daughter.'

His words cut through her anguish and shame.

'It wasn't just that!' No, it was more. It was the feeling of rightness of being together. Into her mind sprang the scene at the Rectory, she heard herself telling Reverend Carter 'I've never been so comfortable – so much *me* – with anyone.' And his reply: 'Then he's a lucky young man.' Young man! But he wasn't, he wasn't young and neither was he lucky. Old enough to be her father. 'We were friends—' The croak in her voice silenced her as they looked at each other in dumb misery.

'Would you rather I told the Rector—?'

'I told you, I'm not telling anyone. You're not my father, you're a mistake I discovered in time.'

'And that's what I would tell him. Georgina,' he shrugged helplessly, the action saying more than any words. She stood stiff as a ramrod while he took her hands and gazed down at them, confused and shamed by his fantasies of the caress of those hands. What if he hadn't told her? No one but he need ever have known the truth. And just as he had every day of the weeks he'd been away, in his mind he saw them together, imagined her learning to accept and love a life at sea, imagining . . . He pulled his thoughts back from where they were going. He'd never known there could be such shame and self-repugnance; now, even now that he knew the truth, yet it was as a woman, a partner, he wanted her. Could she read his thoughts?

'Don't let's talk about it,' she was in control of her voice again as she withdrew her hands, 'there's nothing to say. When you've gone I'll tell everyone we talked about it – changed our minds—'

'You sound so calm. How can you be?' He gripped her shoulders, he had to touch her, to bring them together to share their shock and comfort each other. As if they could! 'I'll do as you say, I'll leave straight away. But this can't be the end. I've never been as drawn to anyone . . . you felt it too.'

'Not now.' Feeling her wriggling free of his hands, he loosened his grip. Then she heard the door close.

Steven had gone, gone from the room – and gone from her life. As if they mocked her, she remembered her dreams of what lay ahead of her, each day a challenge and an adventure because that's what everything was if she shared it with him. Try and think just of that, don't let your mind be pulled towards those other longings, lying in his arms, your body merged with his, destroying that other ghost. John. No don't think of John either. Steven's my lover and I wanted it, that's what I told him. Steven's my father . . . my father and my lover. Remember his hands on my breast, the tug of his fingers . . . my father.

As if it would take away her pain and confusion she picked up the bundle of papers she'd been so proud to have ready for him and thrust them into the desk drawer. Above all things she detested self-pity, she always had; yet what else could it have been that, as she relived her pride and eagerness, misted her vision with scalding tears she couldn't stem.

'I heard the trap go,' Patience hesitated in the open doorway. 'But my dear, what is it?'

'We talked. We're not going to be married after all. It would have been a mistake. We both knew it would.' Her sentences shot into the silent room.

Patience was out of her depth. More than that, she was ashamed of her immediate reaction to the news. Then she forgot herself in her concern for Georgina.

'Oh dear,' she muttered, 'and you'd been so looking forward to everything. Oh dear.'

'I thought I was. We should be glad we saw our mistake before it was too late.' She spoke it in a strong voice and was ashamed of the sob that caught in her throat on the last word.

'Selfish of me, and of no importance I know, but Georgina, I'm so glad you won't be going away. I wasn't looking forward to being without you.'

Two old maids together! Georgina bit back her spontaneous response. For some reason she didn't try to fathom, it was kindly, ineffectual Patience's sympathy that gave her courage the boost it needed.

'I'll go to the kitchen and tell Mrs Biggs,' she said. 'I suppose

Mellie has her aunt with her.' There were limits to how much she could tax her determination. 'You'll tell *them* for me, won't you. Aunt Patience, is my face all right?'

'Yes dear. And anyway you'd be entitled to a few tears. Oh dear, oh dear, what to do. Your beautiful gown hanging there ready – and Mrs Biggs is so pleased with the cake – oh dear me.'

'Marriage isn't about cakes and gowns, Aunt Patience. One day I'll tell you all about it. But not today. Just tell Mellie for me. Now for the kitchen – and then the Rectory.' Georgina stood up and squared her shoulders. She'd always prided herself in being mistress of her own destiny and if Fate had stepped in to queer her pitch then she'd fight her corner.

Battling had to be her salvation, it was the only way to try to escape from the torment. Incest, a sin she couldn't escape. Even committed in ignorance the sin was still there. It besmirched her memories, cast a shadow on the hours they'd spent together happy in each other's company. She'd led him to the isolated pool, she'd almost begged for him to make love to her, and wasn't that a sin? She wished he'd raped her, then she could have heaped the blame on him.

Crossing the hall on her way to the kitchen she stopped in front of the mirror as if she expected her appearance to bear witness to the revulsion she felt. The words of the marriage service pushed uninvited into her mind: 'With my body I thee worship', that's what he would have vowed in a few days' time. then the echo: 'I've been haunted by carnal lust . . .' Think of how it was when together – yes, together you and your father – reached the glorious moment of utter union – yes think of it, don't run away, think of it and then think of Mama and him. It was like that for them too, that's how you were conceived. 'She taught me to love'; oh, and she taught him well.

Patience came through the hall on her way up to Melissa's room.

'I'll ride straight to the rectory as soon as I've changed,' Georgina told her. 'Reverend Carter will be waiting. Can I leave you to explain in the kitchen after all.' It wasn't cowardice that decided her on the next move, it was a demand she couldn't ignore, as if this was the thing she had to do before she could move forward.

Upstairs, she collected clean undergarments and her riding

habit and carried them to the bathroom. Given the warmth of the June morning she knew the kitchen range would ensure there was hot water. As she stripped off her clothes she dropped everything except her gown into the linen basket then, naked, surveyed herself in the long looking glass. 'Carnal lust for my own daughter . . .' When her hands went to her breasts, instinctively she pulled them away. There was no logic in what she did, it was weeks since Steven had touched her. The previous evening when he'd arrived they'd walked in the gardens, he'd kissed her . . . now she rubbed the back of her hand vigorously against her mouth, but there was no way of wiping out how she'd welcomed the joy of being with him, feeling the strength of his hold, feeling the beat of his heart, knowing his desire was as heightened as her own. Desire? Carnal lust . . . She felt unclean to the very depth of her soul.

Climbing into the bath she rubbed the bristles of the long-handled brush hard on the tablet of soap, then on her body. Not an inch escaped its painful scouring. Bathing in the middle of the morning was unheard of, but then so was everything else about this day. When she'd scrubbed until her skin was red, she pressed the plunger to let the warm water escape and from the running tap rinsed herself in water so cold it took her breath away.

Ten minutes later she was riding towards the Rectory.

Telling Reverend Carter didn't present the hurdle she'd expected; but then she hadn't been privy to the anxieties he'd expressed to his sister about the quickly arranged wedding to a man none of them knew.

Georgina told him she and Steven had had time to rethink.

'He's a lot older than me you see, Rector. Twenty years or so. We get on so well, but—'

'Then my dear I'm thankful that you were given some sign that what you planned wouldn't have led to the happiness you deserve.'

'I don't, I don't deserve . . .' What a relief it would have been to unburden herself to her elderly mentor.

'Let the Lord be the decider of that. He has given you the strength to do what you see as right and, my dear, you will find there is a purpose behind all this. Your destiny is in another direction from the one you'd planned. Put yourself in His hands.'

'You make it sound so simple.' Then with something like her old smile, 'I expect I'm pig-headed, I don't like to think I'm not in charge.'

The Rector smiled indulgently. 'You think He doesn't know that? Our weaknesses and our strengths – and your "pig-headedness" as you call it may be a strength, you know – He understands them better than we do ourselves. I'll just slip outside and tell my sister you're here, perhaps you'll spare time for a little sherry with us before you go?'

Of course she realized he'd gone to prepare his sister for the change of arrangements, but she was warmed by their friendship. At the Rectory she had always known she was welcome.

Arriving at the gallery, John looked at the morning's post, immediately recognizing Steven's writing. The postmark showed that it had come from Poole. So he was home, probably by now they were married. Perhaps he'd posted it on his way back to the *Seahorse*, Georgina with him ready to go aboard. Putting off the moment of opening the letter he went from his small office to the main floor of the gallery. Forget Georgina . . . this was *his* world. Like a caress he moved his hand over the surface of a Queen Anne walnut table, until it came to rest on an epergne that stood at its centre. It was exquisite, for more than a century and a half it had graced the dining table in a manor house in Oxfordshire. Gently moving his fingers over the silver branches, each supporting its hand-carved crystal vase, he forced his mind on the epergne, not as a beautiful work of art, but as something that had been unchanged as one generation had replaced another around that dining table. Laughter, tears, happiness, family arguments, bereavements and heartbreak, through it all it had remained as perfect as the day it was made. Perhaps a wedding present to a couple long since dead, just as their own children would be and their grandchildren. No emotion was permanent, everything faded, passed away.

Reason told him that was true, yet he couldn't bear to think of the *Seahorse* leaving the dockside, taking her away. The epergne had lost the battle to hold him, defeated by memories both painful and precious.

Remember the times the three of us have been together, Georgina, Steven and me. Was she in love with him then? No, no, I swear she wasn't. Has she done this to get out of my life and Melissa's, thinking that without her we will come together? And we must. If Melissa doesn't soon agree to come of her own accord I shall have to go to Kyneston and insist.

Yet the thought of Melissa and the child (apparently his daughter had been registered Verity Alice) living in the house, her petulance, her hysterical outbursts that bordered on insanity (and if they did, who but he was to blame?) filled him with foreboding.

He'd come out into the main gallery to put off the moment when he must read Steven's news but, even there, no matter where his thoughts led him he saw no ray of light. So, carefully replacing the epergne, he went back to his little office and slit open the waiting letter.

'Your crates are safely aboard and I will hand them over on arrival in the usual way. However, I intend not to return to my home port in the foreseeable future, instead I shall be working off the eastern seaboard of America. That being so, the communication I invariably bring for you from your colleague on the other side of the Atlantic will have to be mailed.

'My congratulations to you on becoming a father.

'I remain, Yours aye, Steven.'

No message from Georgina, surely even after that last evening she could have sent a word of greeting. Had Melissa told her how he'd behaved? Yes, that must be it. And Georgina, what could she feel for him but contempt just as he felt for himself? Now she was gone, Mrs Steven Howard, not returning to Poole for the foreseeable future. Screwing up the letter he hurled it into the waste basket. He heard people come into the gallery but he made no move, Harold Rogers could deal with them. All his adult life it had been his goal to own an establishment like this, sure that however long he lived his knowledge would be growing, his appreciation never waning. Yet on that morning he looked around him and none of it had the power to touch him.

At Kyneston the tables had been turned. For months it had been Melissa who saw no hope in the future, now even though the baby didn't interest her and the thought of returning to John was a black cloud on her horizon, yet hope had been reborn in her. Each day she felt nearer to being her former self, each time she looked in the mirror (which she did frequently when she was on her own in her bedroom) her spirits rose. Why it should have boosted her own morale to know that Georgina's plans had gone awry she didn't ask herself. It was as if Georgina's cheerful anticipation, the excitement of her coming travels, had driven a wedge between

223

them, the more eager she had appeared, the deeper Melissa had been plunged into the doldrums of self-pity.

But with the cancellation of the wedding all that started to change.

About ten days after Steven's sudden departure, coming into the bedroom and expecting to find Melissa still playing the invalid even though Verity was more than five weeks old, Georgina was surprised to see her sitting in front of the dressing table. With a comb in her hand and, disturbed without warning, she was smiling at her reflection with satisfaction.

'Oh Mellie, you're feeling better, that's wonderful.'

'I'm going to get dressed today. When Jess had finished with the baby she'll help me.'

'Let me. Let's see what you're going to wear. Aren't you excited to think you can wear ordinary clothes again?'

'Thank goodness the fashion is for roomy bodices. I think my waist has gone back.' She stood up holding her nightgown tightly around her, 'See? Except for this . . .' She held her breasts with distaste. 'I feel like one of Old Silas's herd. Disgusting.'

'You look lovely, you know you do. How long have you been out of bed by yourself? You ought to have called. Don't your legs feel weak?'

Melissa giggled like a mischievous child. 'The truth is,' she confided, 'I've been getting in and out of bed for days when no one is here. I was going to get dressed and come downstairs to surprise you. But now you know, you can help me. Isn't this fun?'

Since Steven's unexplained departure Georgina had talked about him just once to Melissa, her story of a change of heart had been accepted without question but with a rush of real affection that had done much for Melissa's 'recovery'. She had grown up accepting that Fate treated Georgina less kindly than it did her; this put them back on the course they knew.

'Is John coming for the weekend? Is that why you want to be downstairs? Has he got a consignment to bring down?' It was as near as she could bring herself to come to asking his reaction to hearing that Steven had sailed without her.

'He hasn't been for ages, you know that. He writes asking me when I'm going back. In his last letter he hinted at coming to carry me back whether I was ready or not.' As she spoke she smiled at her reflection, well-pleased. 'But it's just talk. He's certainly not

224

coming this weekend. I think I'll wear blue. Open the wardrobe, Georgina, let's choose.'

She was like a child dressing for a party. Georgina suspected that during her period of playing the invalid she had spent plenty of time testing her legs, for this was never a person who had been confined to bed for weeks. And when the last hook was fastened she surveyed herself with satisfaction. It almost seemed a shame to waste herself at Kyneston . . . So what stopped her writing to tell John she was fit enough to come back? She left the question unanswered, just as she did that other one: what stopped her telling John that Steven had sailed without Georgina?

On the stand in the workroom was that masterpiece of millinery created for the wedding. For some young women in her circumstances it would have been a constant reminder of the unhappy ending to their dreams. Not to Georgina. Determined once more to be in control of her own destiny, she gazed at the hat. If she went to Mme de Bouverie and explained she wasn't going away after all, she was sure there would be work for her. Yes, that's what she must do. Having made her decision there was no running away from the empty loneliness that swamped her. She'd work, she'd even find satisfaction in Mme de Bouverie's praise; but she'd be afraid to look ahead and dream, afraid to hope. For where was the certainty in anything? Better not to have expectations than to leave herself vulnerable to hurt and disillusionment.

On the morning she set out for Christchurch, no one seeing her would guess that the material in her gown of pale apricot had been acquired by completely unpicking a ten-year-old model of her mother's. Setting off alone in her trap she looked every inch 'the lady of Kyneston', quite unlike the girls employed by Mme de Bouverie to work in the large room above the salon. She had two choices, either she could go towards Ringwood and then turn south onto the Christchurch Road, or she could approach through Lymington and along the coast. She chose the latter, her day well planned. First she would talk to Madame de Bouverie, then she would have lunch in the town. The idea of going alone to a hotel appealed to her, gave her the feeling of independence she craved.

It seemed she hadn't yet learned her lesson: one should never make plans and expect them to run smoothly. She didn't get to Christchurch, she didn't get beyond Lymington. It was as she

225

started up the slope of High Street that she noticed a sign in the window of a small haberdashery: 'To Let' and then the name of a local firm of house agents.

But this is madness, she told herself, it's not as if I've ever thought of running a business. I don't know the first thing about it. What a moment to remember Reverend Carter and what she liked to think of as 'his silly talk about everything happening for a purpose, just to make me feel better'.

Leaving her pony and trap with the stable boy at the coaching house she went inside to order a table for lunch at noon. The maître d'hôtel added to her confidence, he opened the door for her and bowed her out as if she were already a lady of importance – or at least the owner of a successful business. And from then on things snowballed fast. By teatime when she returned along the forest road towards Kyneston she had signed to take a lease on the shop from 1 September, ten weeks hence. 'Never make plans, don't take anything for granted ...' she warned herself as she resolved to keep her scheme a secret, superstitiously believing that to tell anyone, even Melissa, would be tempting fate. They thought her day was being spent in Christchurch, they expected her to bring home an order of work for Madame de Bouverie.

Georgina's secret was her own.

'All through this spell of lovely sunny days Georgina's shut herself away in that workroom of hers,' Patience's kindly face wore a worried frown as she sat sewing near where Melissa lay in the hammock. 'I expect she's right to keep busy, poor girl. She had such hopes. Now she gives herself time for nothing but work.'

'I can't think what joy she can get out of making finery for other people.' Melissa stretched luxuriantly, looking up through the canopy of young leaves to the blue sky. 'Georgina has always thought the world began and ended with Kyneston and the forest, I expect she would have been dreadfully unhappy being away so much.'

'I just wonder how they'll feel when they see each other – when he comes to collect John's next consignment, you know.' Then, trying not to let Melissa guess how much it mattered, she threw in a casual, 'But I suppose he'll only call to pick it up, he won't stay.'

'Has John sent anything?' Melissa would welcome a crate being brought by the railway wagon, a sure sign that John wasn't planning a visit. 'He usually writes to say when a crate is despatched.' Then he and the non-appearance of his consignment was forgotten as Alex rode up the drive. He gave no indication of having seen them, yet he must have looked towards the trees beyond the lawn, to the posts where the hammock was slung. It had been he who had first persuaded Melissa onto it, had held it steady while she hoisted herself in.

Florrie crossed the lawn towards them.

'Mr Graves to see you Mrs Derrick. I told him you were out here, but . . .' Her sentence drifted into silence, they'd all come to know Alex sufficiently well to realize that he wouldn't choose to intrude unannounced.

Melissa smiled, a smile not so much aimed at Florrie as born of her pleasure in what Georgina would scoff at as Alex's strait-laced adherence to convention.

'Ask him to come out, Florrie. And—' But she changed her mind and didn't finish the sentence. Only after the maid had disappeared, and as if the thought had just that second come to her, she said, 'Aunt Patience, would you be a dear and tell them to bring out some tea. Alex will bring the table across ready.' She didn't say in so many words that what she meant was 'tea for two' but, after a lifetime of being suffered rather than wanted, Patience didn't need telling.

Alex crossed the lawn towards her, on the way meeting Patience scuttling towards the house with her message and greeting her with the same courtesy as a moment later he bestowed on Melissa herself.

'I hope I'm not disturbing your rest?' he looked to her for reassurance. 'It's unusual for me to call at this hour, but I was passing on my way home from Rockford.'

'It's a lovely surprise,' the corners of her tightly closed mouth turned upwards into a smile, her eyes took up the message. 'They're bringing us some tea. Will you lift the table nearer, Alex. This is nice.'

He thought so too, or at least he thought so until he reminded himself that she was a married woman. She never talked about her husband and, as for the child, it might have no connection with her. Since her dreadful ordeal (and no matter how hard he tried he could find no logical reason for a woman in her condition wandering in the forest at night and in the rain when she should

227

have been in bed and asleep), nearly every day he'd called to see her, and that underlying tension he'd sensed at the beginning was gone. Yet she never suggested that she was ready to go back to her husband. One day soon she surely must, and bracing himself against hearing it he unconsciously pulled his mouth into a tight line and, if it were possible, sat even straighter on the wrought-iron garden seat.

When the tea tray was brought, thin cucumber sandwiches and slices of Mrs Biggs's sponge cake ('Miss Mellie always likes a nice piece of my sponge'), she lay back contentedly watching the deft way he handled the teapot. How neat he was, everything he did was orderly and circumspect, just as it was with Uncle Cedric. She felt safe, cherished. Look at the way he was transferring everything onto the table so that she could use the tray, then before he passed it being sure that her cushions were just right for her to sit comfortably.

From the window of the drawing room Patience watched them, wondering, sensing danger. And yet what danger could Alex Graves make? From Alice and from Melissa herself she'd heard how the young men had been drawn to her in London – and of them all she had chosen John. But something was wrong, something was badly wrong. If only he'd come, let her see him side by side with 'Mr Sobersides' as dear Georgina called Alex, then they'd go back to their own home and make a fresh start. No young girl, least of all pretty little Mellie with her moods and tantrums, could be attracted to anyone so devoid of fun and humour. Or had she put blind faith in him because it had been he who had helped her on that dreadful night? Certainly she had been different these last few weeks, even Alice had remarked on it. It was as if she had nothing to fight against. But did that mean she was ready to remember she was a wife and mother?

Patience told herself she was imagining troubles where they didn't exist. Alex Graves wasn't the sort of person to pose a threat to any man, least of all one like John. To be honest – and she wouldn't hurt Melissa by putting her feelings into words – she was of much the same opinion as Georgina. Oh, Alex was kind, and his little girls clearly thought the world of him; but he was a dry stick, his expression gave nothing away, his manners were impeccable but he had no charm.

Breaking the unspoken rule, she went up to Georgina's work-room.

'Shall I bring you a tray of tea, dear? All these hours of sunshine you shut yourself away in here, just so that that Madame de Bouverie can grow rich. 'Pon my soul, just look at all those hats! If you go on like this she'll be getting rid of all her other workers.'

'Come in Aunt Patience. Yes, you can see how busy I've been.' Georgina chewed her lip, tempted to take Patience into her confidence. Two things prevented her: one was the fear of tempting fate; the second was that she knew exactly how she meant to break her news to Mellie and Patience. So she put her needle down, smiled a welcome at Patience and suggested they should ring the bell and ask for their tea to be brought up to the workroom. Patience's face flushed with pleasure. She felt loved and wanted.

New habits were formed in the weeks of that summer. Georgina worked like a demon; the horses found their own exercise in the paddock, standing, sometimes trotting as if they knew what they were at, occasionally even noticing each other enough to take part in a communal gambol; Jess became increasingly indispensable; Victoria and Becky came to Kyneston at every opportunity, but now it was Verity they came to see, grateful to their father for being so willing to agree to their visits. Willing? Truer to say he was keen, promising to collect them to bring them home. Weeks passed bringing no consignment from John and, more important, he made no attempt to come to Kyneston nor Melissa to return to him in London.

It was towards the end of August she wandered unannounced into the bedroom where Georgina was getting dressed for their evening meal.

'I'm ready early, I thought I'd come in and wait for you.'

'I've only got my slippers to put on. You look nice, Mellie. Who would think you have a baby only three months old, you're back to being your old self.' Yet it wasn't true. Mellie's 'old self' had hovered precariously on the edge of an active volcano, these days there was a new peace about her.

At the compliment, the old Melissa would have preened herself as she viewed her reflection; today's model sat on the edge of the bed undecided whether this was the moment to take Georgina into

229

her confidence. That was what she'd come into the room for, but her confidence was floundering.

'Is something on your mind?' Georgina knew her too well to be fooled. 'You're ready to decide on the date to go back to London? Now that you've waited so long, don't go for another week or two, not until September, Mellie.' Then before she could be asked what was so special about September, 'You always used to say the summer was no time to be there, by September people are returning, thinking of the season.'

It took all Melissa's courage, but it had to be said. The letter was written, the reply received, it was too late to be persuaded to change her mind.

'I'm not going back to John. I've written to him and told him so.'

'But what does he say?' Bending to put on her evening slippers Georgina forced herself to ask it lightly. Did her voice give her away, how could Melissa not hear that every nerve in her body was alive with hope and excitement? He loved her, he'd told her so, his marriage had been a mistake. Soon he'd be free. No one would be hurt, not Melissa, not him . . . There is a purpose in all things, just like Reverend Carter had said. We don't always plot our own paths correctly, we have to learn to trust. What will John do now? Will he write to me? Will he come? One thought after another rushed in and out of her head in the seconds it took to fasten her slippers.

'He's really been very understanding. I dare say he's got lady friends enough to keep him occupied. "Lady", did I say!' she added with a shudder. She clasped her arms around herself, hugging her once-again-slim waist. 'All men can't treat their wives as he wanted . . . I can't tell you, wouldn't even know how to . . . so disgusting, humiliating.'

'Perhaps you weren't really in love with him.'

'Oh but I was, you know I was. And he can be so nice. Well, you think he's nice, you get on well with him. Anyway, he's been to see his solicitor. Lady friends or not, that doesn't give me grounds to divorce him apparently; it's only if I give him evidence that I'm – well, you know – with a man. And that will never happen. I wouldn't be so stupid, I know too much. You know Georgie you were lucky to see sense in time.'

'So, if you can't be divorced you will just stay married and live apart?'

'It seems so. I don't mind. I'm not making the same mistake twice. And as for him, he's only really interested in his silly pots and ornaments; apart from that he'll get what he's looking for better from a whore than a wife.'

'I hope you're wrong.'

'Do you? Well, it won't concern us either way. As for the money, that seems to worry him. You know it was mine that set up his gallery. He has no surety for a loan to pay me back, but I'm not concerning myself with money. I don't need it. And he is guaranteeing to pay half the profits into an account for me and then later, when the gallery is really established and the bank will give him an advance, he wants to repay me. But I'd just as soon he didn't.' There was something in the way she smiled that gave Georgina a stab of unease. 'I shall leave all the arrangements to Uncle Cedric, money matters are for men to consider, not us. But if he knows he's dependent on the help he had from me, it doesn't do him any harm. I don't see why everything should go his way.'

It seemed to Georgina that most things had gone Melissa's, but she bit back her words. John was free. Not free for another marriage, but free for the love they wouldn't attempt to deny. He'd not written to her when he heard that the wedding was cancelled, but then how could he when he'd been trying to persuade Melissa to come home to him? Now though there would be nothing to hold him back.

Each day she looked for a sign from him: a telegram telling her where to meet him; a letter; the sign itself was uncertain, but that it would come she was sure.

But days turned to weeks. She heard nothing. And just as she had when Steven had left her, so she concentrated all her thoughts on her new venture. As for Reverend Carter and his high-flown talk of God's purpose, hadn't she always known that there was only one person to map out her path – and that was *herself*.

231

Chapter Fourteen

Between the door and the top of the bow window of the shop front hung a sign, the gold lettering on a black background. 'Georgina of Lymington.'

'But what does it mean? Georgina? You mean it's yours?' Patience was out of her depth and, as if to bring back some sort of understandable normality, she added. 'This is Miss Trout's haberdashery. I've bought my silks here as long as I can remember.'

'Not any more, Aunt Patience. I almost told you when you thought I was working so hard for Madame de Bouverie. What do you think of it? Mellie?'

'A hat shop!' Melissa's reaction was being pulled in two directions and ending nowhere. 'It's exciting, better than working for that de Bouverie person.' But that was quickly swamped by the echoes of her aunt's caustic comments about Kyneston being treated as if it were an outworker's cottage. 'I'm thankful you didn't put *Rochester* on your sign. Aunt Alice will be displeased enough at this without having the family name over a shopfront.'

'You almost make me wish I had.' But Georgina laughed when she said it, much too pleased with the prospect of her new challenge to care one way or another about Alice Sylvester's displeasure.

'But that dummy in the window, surely she's dressed in your—' Patience swallowed her words just in time and finished the sentence with a lame, 'your own gown'.

'My wedding dress, or would have been.' Georgina believed hurdles should be recognized and surmounted and her wedding gown and the glorious creation she'd intended to wear on her head had presented more of a hurdle than she'd been prepared to admit.

Then had come the idea of using them as window display when 'Georgina of Lymington' opened its door for trade the following Monday. 'Don't they say that when the Lord closes one door he opens another – or in this case a window.'

Patience marvelled at her courage. Melissa was still less certain, surely there had never been a shopkeeper in the family and she did wish Georgina wouldn't make it so easy for Aunt Alice to find things to sneer at her for. One thing all three of them agreed on, the small bow window looked enchanting, surely it would catch the eye of every passer by: the dummy (wherever had Georgina acquired such a life-like model?) wearing the gown and hat, stood slightly left of centre. Right of centre was an artist's easel holding a board on which the signwriter had written a notice in perfect italics, not a few simple words to read in passing but long enough to make a reader linger. It declared that a lady's hat was a personal item, not something to be chosen from a window open to public view; another paragraph introducing Georgina as mistress of her craft, many models of which were to be seen inside, and who was prepared to discuss her clients' needs and design and make millinery to their order.

'But what a splendid idea,' here Melissa's enthusiasm was real. 'I hate hat shops, fancy buying something everyone had seen in the window.'

'Will there be sufficient trade, dear? Not everyone is rich you know, but everyone likes a pretty hat.' That from Patience.

'They won't all be expensive. But just because you can't spend a lot of money doesn't mean you don't want something special. I'll guide them into the sort of price they can afford I promise you.'

The shop opened on the first Monday of September. It was Melissa's idea that she should bring an Indian rug from Kyneston. The morning-room carpet looked much better without it, and it added a feeling of luxury and warmth to the salon. For that's what the little shop in the High Street was: a single room with a small English oak gateleg table and two upholstered chairs she had acquired from the local sale room and behind that, curtained off and private, two fitting rooms each with a gilt-framed mirror from the same source. On the first floor were two rooms, the one in the front she saw as ultimately being a workroom when she came to

233

the stage of employing staff; in the back one was a single-size iron bedstead, a marble washstand and a rail she'd fixed so that she had somewhere to hang her clothes. No sign of luxury here, the floor was covered with the worn linoleum left behind by Miss Trout, for she would have no need for it in the 'better land' which was where the neighbouring shopkeepers confidently said she'd gone; and as for her nephew who'd inherited her furniture, he'd known that the linoleum wouldn't have stood up to a move. For Georgina this was only emergency accommodation, for she intended still living at Kyneston. The boy at the coaching house further up the hill was glad to earn a shilling or two by looking after her pony and trap.

At the back of her mind, and despite all she had to think about in opening her own business, there was a confusion of hope and and excitement. Soon John would come. Not to Lymington, of course, for it was unlikely that Melissa would be writing to him. He would send a message to her at Kyneston, perhaps he would come to Lymington and meet her at the *Cork's Crew*, her imagination leaped from one possibility to another. All that was certain was that now there was nothing to keep them apart.

As autumn gave way to winter, 1908 rolled into 1909, she forced herself to face the truth. Yes, he'd desired her, safely married to Melissa he'd even professed to love her; but having no union with Melissa to hide behind turned it into a different situation. A woman who looked for nothing but payment left him free. What was it Melissa had said, that he would find more pleasure in a whore than a wife?

It was apparent he intended to sever connection with Kyneston. Melissa said that each month he made a payment into a banking account, sometimes more than others depending on his own income from the gallery.

'I don't concern myself with any of it,' she told Georgina. 'Now that I have a husband in name only, Uncle Cedric looks after my affairs again.'

She seemed remarkably contented, yet surely her life was more tedious now than it had been in the days she had fretted to be free of Kyneston and the forest.

Patience was a romantic, she always had been. Her life could hardly have been more devoid of romance, but nothing would ever change her. Reason told her the Knight Errant she'd trusted

234

in would remain a figment of her imagination but she had derived pleasure in delighting in 'pretty little Mellie's' marriage to John and, hardened to disappointment as she was, in the unexpected love that had blossomed between Georgina and Steven. When that had finished so abruptly she had been at a loss to understand the reason and, caring for Georgina as she did, had hoped that when he docked next time and came to collect John's consignment there might be a joyous reunion for them.

When she knew that Melissa's marriage was over in all but name she supposed that was why John didn't use Kyneston as a transmission point for his exports. But would Steven know that? She still clung to the hope that he might come. By winter, though, there was no longer any hope to cling to, the day to day routine of the house had to be sufficient. 'Romance' meant far more than the kindling of interest of a suitable man, it encompassed courage, confidence in the future – so for Patience it encompassed the opening of 'Georgina of Lymington,' and the excitement of watching the brave new venture make a place for itself.

Now that the days were shorter the children only came to pay homage to their adored baby when their father could bring them, but that was something he managed to find time for remarkably often.

'Now, mind if you have 'er on yer knee, you got to see she'd don't slip. Wriggly as an eel she's getting to be, bless 'er. Ain't she just the prettiest little soul you ever seen?' Settling Verity onto Victoria's lap, Jess knelt in front of them, rewarded by a smile that showed four milk teeth. 'And I tell you what, Becky, if yer sister minds her while we get the tea, you can be the one to give her 'er food. Mrs Biggs has made a junket for a special treat for her, but see if you can get her to chew on a toasted crust or two first, that helps her teeth.'

The nursery was a world apart from the rest of the house and, now that Georgina was so wrapped up in making hats for her special orders, the girls looked on their visits there as the highlight of their days. If she were old enough to think such things, Verity would have agreed with them. As soon as she heard their step her face would light with pleasure, she'd bounce on her small, thickly napkinned bottom with excitement.

Downstairs in the drawing room Patience presided over the teapot, Melissa's lovely face wearing an expression of sweet content, while Alex treated them both with unchanging and perfect courtesy. Although he was perhaps – perhaps, but not certainly, Patience considered as she sipped her tea and gazed at him – younger than Steven, yet there was a quality about him that had probably never known the joy of youth but would remain constant through the years. She speculated with vague interest, but with no increase in her pulse rate; there was nothing of the swash-buckling hero about the kindly vet, no gusto in the way he ate his thinly sliced, decrusted, egg sandwich even though he must have been in the fresh air working on some farm or other during the day. Patience's Knight Errant was a man of lusty appetite.

'Georgina dear,' Patience greeted her when she arrived home one evening in January, 'a letter came for you today'. Georgina's heart seemed to miss a beat. 'I thought you'd like to read it in the quiet so I put it up on your dressing table.'

He'd written! Just when she'd started to make herself believe she would never hear from him, he'd written!

But it wasn't John's writing on the envelope. This letter was from America.

At first I couldn't write, yet I couldn't put our knowing each other out of my mind. Perhaps even after all these months you will not want to hear from me. But, Georgina, I sincerely hope the time we spent together, the friendship that came so naturally, is a firm enough base for us one day to build on. When I left Poole my feeling was that I never wanted to return. But that is not so. I am working off the east coast of America, there is trade enough here. But it is not in my nature to leave my native land for ever. Roots are important. For the present time I intend to continue as I am, but my sincere hope is that, given time and space to adjust to what we discovered, we shall one day be ready to meet and form a new relationship, new and yet based on our very real friendship.

I often think of Kyneston. Will you give my regards to your aunt Patience. I hope I am not thought too badly of for the reason for my sudden departure.

Please write to me, Georgina. The headed harbour address will find me when I return here. I cannot ask your forgiveness, nor even hope for your understanding, but what I do ask – and ask fervently – is that you are prepared to look on me as your

236

friend. I do not propose to return to Poole until the day you tell me you are ready for us to meet and try to build a true, honest relationship based on friendship that I believe we both felt held exceptional qualities of understanding.

In hope I await your letter.

Affectionately yours, Steven.

That same night she replied to him, surprised how easy she found it to tell him about the challenge of 'Georgina of Lymington' and the success of its first months. It was impossible to think of him as a father, but natural to take up the threads of their very real friendship. Neither did she think of him as a lover, she almost wished she did. As long as she'd been with him, planning a life together, she had persuaded herself he had blotted out her feeling for John. But it wasn't true, it could never be true. John had gone even more certainly than Steven – but it wasn't in her nature to give room in her mind to empty dreams, better by far to concentrate on making sure that a tag inside a hat proclaiming it from the workroom of 'Georgina of Lymington' made it an item of pride.

It took weeks for letters to cross the Atlantic, then to await collection at the port address he'd given her. But once started, the flow became constant and steady; every week or two she would hear from him, and when he collected his mail there was invariably more than one in her handwriting awaiting him. That they were father and daughter was never mentioned, they wrote of everyday happenings. But strong foundations were being laid, one day they would be able to accept their relationship.

With the Atlantic between them, Georgina believed she was approaching the time when she could face the truth. She had her own reasons for deciding to share her secret: better to have it known and accepted now, than have the shock of it at the forefront of everyone's mind when ultimately he came home.

'Another letter from Steven, Georgina.' Patience couldn't keep her love of romance out of her expression.

'Aunt Patience, Mellie, I've never told you – I've been meaning to but – well, it wasn't easy at the time. The reason we couldn't marry – it wasn't that we quarrelled. When Steven saw Mother's name on my birth certificate, that and the date of my birth . . .' It was harder to say than she'd imagined, Melissa and Patience

237

watching and probably thinking, just as she had, that Steven had spurned her for her illegitimacy. 'I'm his daughter.'

There! She'd said it!

'Thank goodness you found out,' Melissa said as Patience was still too surprised to find any words. 'Imagine, you might have married the sort of man who would use a woman as he must have done Mama, then go off and leave her! I always thought he was a scoundrel!'

'He's no such thing.'

'No, dear, of course he isn't,' Patience found her voice. 'Poor Augusta . . .' For knowing his power of attraction more than twenty years later, Patience could well imagine how any young woman's resistance would have melted under his youthful charm. Georgina's father . . . now that they were writing to each other that must mean that they wouldn't lose touch again . . . for Georgina she was glad, of course she was for she'd seen how happy they had been together . . . one day he would come back to England, he would come to Kyneston. Patience had believed she'd overcome her dreams and her disappointment, but in those seconds hope sprang anew.

'I can see you couldn't marry him,' Melissa was saying, 'just imagine – your own father! But you wanted to sail with him, to travel the world, that's what you said. So, if you are his daughter, there was no reason why he couldn't have taken you.' She considered Georgina's life would have been much more comfortable and pleasant sharing a father/daughter relationship. Friendship, that was the most precious thing, companionship and the feeling of being someone special, being cherished. Her mouth curved into that secret smile as she followed her own private thoughts.

'*Your* father was *my father*, the only one I could ever have. I'm only telling you now because one of these days – he says not until I tell him I'm ready for us to meet as friends, but we've been writing for months, so perhaps soon – he will come back to England. And when he does I want you both to understand and to have got used to the idea. Now, let's forget it.'

Talking about it had helped. Meeting for the first time could never be easy no matter how long they waited, but it was a hurdle that they would surmount. And soon.

Every hat made by 'Georgina of Lymington' was different; the one thing they had in common was that she designed them all. But by the time the little salon on the High Street had been open six months she no longer actually made them all. The special orders were her own responsibility, she'd discuss with her client what was wanted, make suggestions, draw sketches and then, in her workroom at Kyneston, produce a finished article created to flatter and delight. But by that time, above the salon, the front room had been turned into a workroom and Esme Dawkins, an experienced milliner who'd married a local man and moved from Bournemouth, had been engaged. A month or two later an apprentice was taken on, Trudie Barnes, fourteen years old and with a head full of dreams of mastering her chosen craft and determination to match. And as trade increased there were plenty of nights when Georgina slept in the room behind the workshop, too busy to spare the hour or so it took to ride home. And another alteration to her original arrangement: because she often stayed away for a day or two at a time she no longer left the pony and trap to be cared for at the coaching inn. Instead, she travelled by bicycle, wheeling it through the salon and out to the yard behind. She had a standing arrangement with Patience: 'If I'm not home by eight o'clock don't hold back the meal, you'll know I'm not coming.'

During her first year of trading she was much too wrapped up in her own affairs to consider why it was that Melissa no longer flew into tantrums and made life difficult for everyone. If she thought about it at all it was to suppose that, being out of the house so much, she wasn't there to witness the scenes.

Cycling up the drive at Kyneston one summer evening she saw Patience dead-heading the roses, dumped her bicycle unceremoniously on the gravel and came over to join her.

'I was going to stay, but I couldn't. It's like that sometimes, Aunt Patience, no trees, no flowers, I think of Kyneston and the forest and just have to come home. Pedalling back through the forest to all this . . .' She nipped off a dead rosehead and dropped it into Patience's trug. 'Where's Mellie? Helping Jess with Verity?'

Patience shook her head.

'I wish she would. But, you know, she hardly glances at her. Unless Alex is here, then sometimes they let her crawl around on the lawn. No, Mellie is out. Alex has taken her with him on a call, out towards Beaulieu. A lovely evening for a ride in his new auto-

239

mobile.' Then, with a chuckle, 'The noise it made, great bangs when he started off, enough to upset the animals.'

'Good for trade,' Georgina laughed. 'Does he still come as often? She doesn't talk about him.'

Patience dropped her secateurs into her trug and gave her full attention to the question.

'He often takes her out with him. He calls and takes tea with us sometimes. Of course, this time of year the little girls can come and see Verity by themselves, they used to be his excuse in the beginning. Now he doesn't need an excuse. And there's no doubt how pleased she is to see him.'

'But he's so dreary . . .'

'Indeed, he wouldn't turn a girl's head. Or would he?' She bit her lip, her puzzled expression saying more than her words.

'Well, he'd not sweep *me* off my feet, that's for sure. Nor you, Aunt Patience.'

Arm in arm they walked towards the kitchen garden and the compost heap in companionable silence. It was only after the rose clippings had been disposed of that Patience went back to the conversation.

'When I think of the girl she used to be, her head so full of romantic dreams. Yet, she was never content.'

'Heads full of dreams don't make for contentment.'

'Something has given her a new – what is it? Is it peace? Can it come simply from the fact she has got rid of a marriage that brought her nothing but misery?'

'She hasn't got rid of it. She's not free, nor is she likely to be from what she says.'

'Ah well,' here spoke Patience the sage, 'a husband at a distance is no problem. It probably suits her better than having her freedom. If she were free she might think twice before she spent the hours she does with Alex Graves, as it is she knows he will get no romantic ideas about her.' At the sound of Georgina's guffaw she looked at her uneasily. To criticize her would be disloyal, but she couldn't help feeling that it wasn't the sort of retort a lady should make.

It was the Tuesday evening of the following week, the front door was locked, Esme Dawkins and Trudie both gone. The glorious summer weather had broken and rather than pedal home in the rain Georgina had been staying in Lymington since the weekend, sleeping on the none too comfortable second-hand bed. She had gradually transferred enough from her wardrobe so that the image she presented to her clients didn't hint at the make-shift arrangements upstairs.

Despite having a healthy appetite, she had no enthusiasm for preparing food that she would eat alone and hurriedly, with her mind on the work she intended to do now she had the workshop to herself. She surveyed the meagre contents of the gauze-fronted meatsafe she kept hanging on the north facing wall of the yard: the remains of a beef stew Mrs Biggs had carefully wrapped and laid in the basket of her bicycle two mornings before, three slices of ham looking tired, dry and with curling edges, a jug of milk and the cheese dish. Not exciting. She took the cheese dish and closed the door on the rest. Cheese and apple would suffice and then she would start work on the wedding hat she'd discussed that morning with the bride-to-be, daughter of a local solicitor who was to marry the young housemaster from Highbury Court, a school beyond Ringwood. Privately she considered it would take all the talent she possessed to give the unfortunately plain bride the sort of appearance she dreamed of; but Georgina enjoyed a challenge.

When she heard the jangle of the front-door bell, cheese dish in hand she started to go to open it. Then she changed her mind remembering how it had happened last night too and she'd looked out in time to see three small boys peeping from the end of an alleyway further down the hill. Satisfied that she'd answered their ring, they'd rushed off, shouting with merriment. Tonight they would be disappointed, she decided, smiling to herself as she pictured them peeping and waiting. As she went towards the stairs the looked across the empty salon and through the heavy net curtain that covered the triangular glass panes of the bow-fronted door she could see the shape of someone tall. It must be Lady Harcastle's man come for her hat, Lady Harcastle who was a friend of the hated Alice. She had a good mind not to open the door. But she stamped on her pride and pulled back the bolt.

'Georgina, I came as soon as I heard. Why didn't you tell me?'

For months she watched for him, listened for him. It was like living a dream.

'Tell you . . .?' she repeated. Still clutching the cheese dish she held the door open. John had come.

241

'I had a letter today by the afternoon mail. From Steven. All this time and I didn't know.'

Now the door was closed, he was taking the dish out of her hands and putting it on the salon's small gateleg table.

'Steven? What did he tell you?' She longed to touch him, as if only that way would she believe he was real, that she wouldn't wake and find him gone as she had so often.

'Read it.' He took an envelope in Steven's familiar hand from his inside pocket. 'Until today I believed you were married, I thought you were with him in America.'

'But hadn't Mellie told you?'

'She told me nothing. As soon as I read his letter I shut the gallery and caught the first train. Tell me it's what you want.' His hands gripped her shoulders, just as she'd dreamed, just as she longed for.

'You know it is.'

The envelope fluttered to the ground, whatever it was Steven had told him forgotten as he held her in his arms, so different from the demanding passion of the last time they'd been together. Now it was as if they'd come home from a long journey, thankful, thankful beyond all words. He moved his chin against her temple; she raised her hand to touch his cheek, to run her fingers through his hair. He was real . . . this wasn't a dream . . . they were here together, no one to spoil this blessed moment, only themselves in all the world. When his mouth covered hers she remembered that night in the stable loft, both of them straining towards the physical union they'd longed for. Tonight their lips clung, not with that frantic, driving passion, but with something nearer reverence. For them there was no urgency, the night was theirs, their lives stretched before them, nothing would part them.

Her evening was very different from cheese and apple followed by plain Dora Bishop's hat. Later he took her to the neighbouring coaching house; but not before they had covered the ground of the months (more than fifteen long months) since they had been together. Surely in all her life there had never been such perfect happiness. Later they would make love, both of them knew it and longed for it, the perfect culmination of their finding each other, but in the first hour as she got ready to go out to supper, there was so much to say. Was the gallery making its mark? Did he ship his

American cargoes out of London or was there some other company he used in Poole? How long had she been running her own business? Was she on her own or did she employ staff? Did she live there or had it been just Fate that had kept her working late this evening? The sort of interest any two friends might have shown, yet questions and answers had to be the way they bridged the gap of time, dispelled its loneliness, and filled them both with a deep sense of completeness.

Only then did she read Steven's letter telling John that he would shortly be setting out for Poole. He hadn't come until Georgina had told him she felt ready for them to meet: 'What we discovered was a great shock to both of us. Given time I trust we shall be able to make a new beginning, indeed her letters mean a great deal to me. The daughter I never knew I had, all the years that have been wasted. From our first meeting we felt drawn to each other, but never imagined the tie that bound us. Imagine my pride when she writes to tell me of the success she is making of her shop in Lymington.'

She passed the letter back to John.

'I thought you knew the marriage was cancelled. When Melissa told me she wasn't going back to London I was sure I'd hear from you, that you'd come. When you didn't . . .'

'All these months and not a day I haven't thought of you. There I was with my own gallery a thriving business, that had always been my goal. But what a hollow triumph it was. Ambition, shared ambition, that's wonderful. But alone it's nothing.'

'I know.'

'Get your coat,' he changed the subject. Like a child keeping its favourite flavoured sweet until last, he needed to savour his anticipation. They'd go to the inn, they'd sit amongst the bustle of activity and feel themselves to be part of it; yet all the time they would be safe in the knowledge that soon they would walk up the hill to the little shop and to the beginning of the rest of their lives.

The second-hand iron bedstead with its horsehair mattress was made for one – one who didn't look for too much comfort! That night neither of them cared that it sagged in the middle, a magic carpet couldn't have transported them to an earthly paradise more perfect than they found. They didn't want to waste an hour in sleep, greedy, insatiable, they shared love that touched them with the solemnity of a benediction, love that excited them beyond their dreams, love that was an adventure of sensual abandonment and love sparkled with joy.

Hearing wheels on the gravel drive, Melissa went to the window, her first thought going to Alex even though these days he seldom used the trap. Although the rain had passed over, the morning was dull and overcast, it wasn't the sort of day to expect him. If the weather was bright, lately he had fallen into the habit of calling in his motor car to suggest she should accompany him. She liked that. Never again would she encourage innocent flirtations of admirers as she had in her London season, never considering that the surest way to get burned was to play with fire. With Alex she could relax, he never bandied empty words, he never alluded to her appearance; yet with him she felt precious, held in respect.

But it wasn't Alex.

'No,' she whispered incredulously. 'He's not coming back, he knows I won't have him here. Aunt Patience, look, it's John. If I go upstairs, tell him I'm out. Tell him I'll never go back to him, tell him . . .' But her words dried up as, seeing her at the window, John raised his hand in greeting.

'I'll open the door before he rings, dear. No need for the maids to know. Oh dear, oh dear.' Patience scurried to the hall.

And a moment later John was ushered into the morning room while Patience hovered in the doorway uncertain whether to go or stay.

'Melissa, you look well. And the child? Verity?' He spoke too loudly, his voice filled the room.

'Oh, you must see her, she is such a darling,' Patience put in quickly as if the idea would ease the tension.

'Perhaps. Before I leave. And don't look so frightened, Melissa, I promise you I intend to leave.' Ah, that was better, he mustn't antagonize her.

'What have you come for?' She backed away from him. 'You've no right to pry on me, you don't support me, you can't tell me what to do. And Verity is perfectly well looked after – no thanks to you.' How often he'd heard her voice raise to that high pitch until the bubble burst in a storm of tearful abuse. Melissa was carried forward on a tide of fear that had no bearing on reason; John's expression gave nothing away; only Patience heard the threat of storm with genuine sadness, it had been months since

244

Melissa had behaved like this, yet in a moment all her newfound serenity could be stripped from her.

'That's not why I'm here,' John answered. 'Melissa I've come to ask you – beg you if you like – to give me my freedom.'

'You want *me* to . . . *you* . . . always it's what *you* want. How do you think you can divorce me? I've done nothing wrong. If I told the law that it was *my* money you used,' the sneer in her voice was ugly, '*my* money to buy your precious – precious' her words had to cut and hurt, '– old pots – lovely things, that's what you told me you loved—'

'I'll pay you back every penny.'

'You cheated your uncle, you cheated me, now you come crawling to ask me make you a free man. Well, I won't. You hear me. You will never have grounds to divorce me. And as for you, you can sleep with any whore you choose, and that's not against the law.'

'I'll agree to any tale you like to tell. If you go to a solicitor, tell him that my reason for coming today was to insist you come home with me; tell him that when you refused I physically abused you; tell him what lies you like to blacken my character and I promise I'll not dispute your word.'

She had been on a helter-skelter heading towards the release of tears and screams. His quiet plea held her back. For a moment she said nothing, he began to hope she might be prepared to agree. And when she spoke, her voice was as low and controlled as his own.

'Freedom? You may need to be free, but I am quite content as I am. Now you ask me to commit perjury. And why? Are you wanting to marry some paramour, perhaps you've found one with a fortune to invest. Is that it? You say you'll repay me, is that how you'll do it, with someone else's money?' Her heart was racing, not from fear, not even from anger, but from the rush of adrenaline that came from the certainty that it was she who held the trump card.

'Yes, I want to remarry. Not "some paramour" as you put it, not someone with a fortune. Someone I love and who loves me. Mellie, you don't want our union any more than I do. You can't be so mean-minded that you grudge someone else what you don't want yourself.'

She smiled that quiet, secret smile.

'Perhaps she ought to be grateful to me. I know more about you than she does I expect, I know that under that charming exterior you're no better than a greedy animal.' Careful, careful, she warned herself, stay calm, don't let him have the satisfaction of seeing you angry. What pleasure there was in hearing him beg and having the right to refuse. 'The law is as it is. Even if I wanted to, I couldn't divorce you for being unfaithful to your vows. If the tables were turned, if it were me with a lover, then you could win your freedom. But it's not me. I've not taken a lover.'

'Hardly likely.' Just as he intended, she heard his words as an insult.

Muttering a silent 'Oh dear, oh dear,' Patience backed out of the room. Neither of them noticed her go.

'Lay a finger on me and I'll have you thrown out, but it won't give you your freedom. Ask me to lie under oath and I shall stand up in court and tell the judge the truth, the whole truth and nothing but the truth. Now I think, John, you had better leave. Whoever she is, you can tell her that I don't believe in divorce.'

Coming within inches of her he raised his hands as if he would shake her.

'You know nothing about living, nothing about anything except your own stupid vanity. For Christ's sake why can't you start to grow up, find out what it's like to care about someone other than yourself.'

'I'd like you to leave. If you want to see your daughter I'll ring for Jess to bring her down.'

Turning on his heel he left her, went out through the hall without so much as a glance at Patience standing in the shadow of the passageway, climbed into the waiting coach and directed the driver to take him to Brockenhurst Station.

Chapter Fifteen

Melissa was smarting and angry from her interview with John. She'd come out the winner, but there was no satisfaction in it. She didn't want to live with him, looking back from this distance she marvelled that she could ever have wanted to. It wasn't just the physical demands, the lack of privacy; the truth was that she found his interests boring, and it hadn't taken her long to bracket his friends into the same category, most of them either in business or else besotted with antiques and objets d'art. Looking back from this distance in time she was glad that he hadn't given her a life crammed with theatre going, supper parties, dancing, all the things she'd hoped for. Now she was able to sweep aside the whole episode of marriage, all its misery, boredom, loneliness, physical abuse.

'Nothing's wrong, is it?' Alex asked her diffidently as he drove them towards Hamptons Farm where a sick cow awaited him. 'You look – worried?'

'I'm not worried,' she forced a smile as she assured him. 'I shouldn't even care for I'd never live with him again, but John came to see me this morning.'

'Very unsettling for you. Do you want to talk about it?'

She settled deeper into her seat, already being with him was taking away that dreadful feeling of pressure.

'You know how unjust the law is,' she said. 'Or perhaps you don't know. Why should you? I don't expect you've ever known anyone consider divorce.' Even then it was hard to make herself say it aloud. Her husband didn't want her, he wanted to get rid of her! 'John came to ask me for his freedom. There's some other woman, I suppose she's his mistress. But the law doesn't seem to care how men behave, so even if I wanted to I couldn't divorce him just for that.'

'What did he suggest?' How calm he sounded. Practical, unmoved yet as solid as a rock.

'I told him I would never give him grounds.' Alex made no reply, so she went on, 'Then he wanted me to commit perjury, to stand up in court and lie, to say that he had come to take me back to London and when I'd refused he had beaten me. To lie in court! Now you can see the sort of man he is.'

Just for a second Alex took his hand off the steering wheel and rested it on hers, a wordless expression of his understanding and sympathy.

'I deplore that as deeply as you do,' he agreed. 'But to give him his freedom would be to have your own.'

'Why should I care about that?'

'Tell me, is it for Verity's sake that you want to cling to your marriage? Do you think it will be easier for her to have parents married and living apart, rather than divorced?'

'Verity? He isn't a bit interested in her, you'd think he wasn't her father. Do you know, Alex, he didn't even want to see her.' It didn't answer his question, but he had a suspicion that Verity hadn't come into the equation.

'I'm glad.' He spoke quietly, for a second she wondered if she'd misheard him.

'I don't understand . . .?'

'I have no right to say this. Perhaps I'm being unkind to remind you of something you'd rather forget. But I remember holding her in her first moment of life, something I hadn't done even with my own daughters, and feeling that in some part she was mine. That was before you and I were even friends. Now I care for her because of that first affinity with her and I care for her because she is your child.' Then before Melissa had time to speak, he put his arm out to indicate to the empty lane that he was turning right and started up the track to the farm. 'Here we are,' and from the way he said it she knew he was drawing a line under what he'd told her.

Stopping at the entry to the farmyard he changed into tall boots, took off his hat, then his jacket and donned a green long-sleeved smock that buttoned down the front, took up his bag and went in search of his patient. Usually Melissa was anxious for him to come back, but this time she was glad to be alone. Verity . . . forget John, think just of what Alex had said . . . her daughter . . . he'd been the first to hold her . . . he felt in part she was his . . . he'd not even seen his own daughters in their first moments. Well, of course he hadn't, they would have been bathed and dressed, put in their mother's arms. But probably Verity wouldn't be here today if Alex hadn't helped her into the world – probably she wouldn't have been here herself either. How kind he was, she'd never known anyone like him. Dear Alex . . . The thought surprised her. Dear Alex . . . It was the truth, he was dear to her. Of course he was in love with her, not as she used to think of being in love. But that had been no more than the figment of her adolescent imagination. Now she knew about marriage. But Alex would never behave as John had, there wasn't a demanding, greedy streak in his gentle, unchanging nature.

She pulled her thoughts into check before they carried her too far down that track. But they jumped out of hand again. She wondered about his marriage, she imagined – no, she pulled herself up short before the thought formed. He was so gentle, so controlled. But he had two daughters. Melissa thought marriage had taught her all there was to understand; in truth she understood very little more than she had as the lovely bride who had walked up the aisle followed by her nunlike bridesmaid.

By the next day Indian summer had returned and, making the most of it, Patience, Alex and Melissa were having tea outside when Jess returned from her afternoon walk pushing the perambulator and with Victoria and Becky in tow.

'Look, luv, there's your mum,' she waved vigorously encouraging Verity to do the same.

'Bring her over,' Melissa surprised everyone, herself included, by calling. Peeping at Alex to see his reaction, she was well-pleased when his glance met hers. Verity, in part his. 'Run indoors and get us some more to eat, Jess, will you. And whatever Verity has. The children can all stay out here in the garden for a while, it's lovely in the sun.'

'Right-o, that'll give me a chance to hot up an iron and get a few of her things pressed. The girls'll keep an eye on her for you, won't you girls?'

Patience made an excuse to go in saying she had some correspondence to deal with. Melissa bit back the question 'Whoever to?' for no one ever wrote to Patience – or so she believed. But then Melissa hadn't seen the mid-day post arrive: one envelope addressed to Miss P. Sylvester. For a moment Patience had supposed it must have been a mistake. Then the wonderful truth had dawned. Steven had written to *her*, from thousands of miles away his thoughts had turned to *her*. Camouflaging the envelope within her bodice, glorying in the touch of the paper against her skin, she had hurried back up to the privacy of her room. By teatime she already knew his letter by heart, but she wanted to read it again.

Melissa told herself there was nothing unusual in taking tea out here with Alex but, in truth, today *was* different. Shrieking with laughter Verity crawled across the grass, the other two on all fours chasing her with more gusto than speed. Alex's solemn expression softened as he watched. Excitement, anticipation, what was it Melissa felt?

When they heard the rumble of wheels crossing the cattle grid onto the drive they looked at each other in a quick moment of shared regret that someone was arriving to disturb them.

'Ah, there you are, making the most of the sunshine,' Alice called as she climbed down from the trap. 'And there's my little treasure!' Years had marched on, but her greeting to Verity was much as it always had been to Melissa. Today her little treasure was much too occupied with her young friends, her squeals of excitement not boding well for Jess when bedtime came. 'May I join you? Good afternoon Mr Graves.'

With his never failing courtesy Alex stood up as she crossed the grass towards them, inclining his head in that characteristic movement.

'Mrs Sylvester, good afternoon.'

The atmosphere was changed, gone was that brief illusion of 'family'. And yet Alice was at her most charming, showing him that side of her nature she'd never wasted on Georgina, nor yet on Steven whom she considered a tradesman. Despite their tête-à-tête plus the children being over, Melissa was still enjoying herself. The truth was she could never be completely happy in any relationship she felt hadn't her aunt's approval. She only half listened to their polite but undemanding conversation (subjects such as whether he found it a great advantage to cover his rounds in an automobile, the children's enjoyment of their ponies, Alice's problems of keeping staff when 'these days young people are so fidgety and can't be content with quiet country life' and her envy of him for having a treasure such as Mrs Griffin, his agreement even though he stressed that Mrs Griffin didn't come under the general category of staff), letting their words wash over her just as she did the laughter of the children. That safe, warm feeling that the previous day's few minutes with John had so easily destroyed wrapped itself around her; the corners of her mouth wanted to smile.

Jess, born and bred a Londoner, was getting restive and with her restlessness came a feeling of guilt. She supposed it must mean that she loved Melissa less; she didn't dig deep enough to realize that what she'd loved had been Melissa's need of her, a need that now went no further than having her there to see to her clothes, arrange her hair. Never did they talk as they used to. Melissa didn't notice the change; Jess felt the fault must be her own because she could no longer look at her darling Miss Mellie and want just to be her slave.

It was November, another country winter almost upon them. This would be her third at Kyneston. To Jess the smell of rotting leaves, of autumn bonfires, the early dusk, the clothes that hung all day on the line and were taken in at night very little drier than she'd pegged them out in the morning, all these things crushed her spirit. She yearned for the bustle of busy people, she wanted to hear the cries of market traders, and, now that autumn had come, to smell chestnuts or potatoes roasting by street corners.

She'd come to Kyneston expecting her stay to be no more than weeks; that was more than two years ago. If I stay around 'ere much longer I'll be sitting on the shelf alongside that Miss Patience, she thought, viewing her reflection discontentedly as she tried on Melissa's newest hat, one that Georgina had made for her as a surprise present. 'Not that I want to go back 'ome, not likely. Suppose, truth to tell, what I miss is Miss Mellie. Her and me, we used to have good talks. But now all I got is Florrie or Effie – and I bet neither of 'em have ever been more than five miles from Kyneston in their lives – no, nor ever will, 'cos where is there to go stuck out here. Reckon they look on it as an outing to go to church of a Sunday and hear Ol' Man Carter tearin' 'em off a strip about how they should be living to make other people happy. Fat chance they'll ever get to do anything else but wait on folks and see they're happy, and if I don't buck my ideas up it'll be the same for me. Wish I could make 'ats like Miss Georgina. Slave labour, that's what I heard people say about girls who worked stitching. Slave labour my arse, what else is this, that's what I'd like to know. You'd think Miss Mellie would be fidgety to be off by now, pretty as a picture she is and all those parties and that waiting for her in London – but no, not so long as that vet hangs around after her. If you can call it being after her, I never seen him so much as give 'er a kiss. And I ain't missed anything for the want of watching out. She's not one for men though, I could tell that right from the start. Used to think her and me could make a nice home together and shut the door on the lot of them. Nowadays I can see it wouldn't work. Funny 'ow it is Miss Mellie and me don't seem close like we were. Is it because of that Mr Graves? Or it is me? Is it my fault 'cos I got itchy feet to be off?'

There was one person who had noticed a change in Jess, and that was Patience. Perhaps it was because she'd travelled the same road more than half a lifetime ago that she recognized the girl's fear that life was passing, moving on and she wasn't even aboard.

'November, yet it thinks it's springtime,' she smiled as she met the girl coming out of her nursery bedroom – for these days Jess used the nursery bedroom to be on hand in case Verity called out in the night.

'Reckon all the difference that makes is that the things I wash will blow dry so that I can iron them.'

'I was going to ask you a favour.'

'Go on then. What've I got to do?' Not so much as a smile.

Oh dear, the poor girl was down in the dumps.

'I wondered if you'd let me look after Verity, she'd be perfectly all right with me I'm sure. If you ride a bicycle – and all you young people seem able to – I wondered if you'd mind riding into Lymington for me. I want some embroidery silk, I can give you samples to match up. The stall comes to the High Street every market day, it's normally near the bottom of the hill on the left hand side. Georgina usually slips along to get me anything I need, but lately she hasn't been coming home so much. I could get Biggs to take me in the trap,' then with a quiet laugh that turned the clock back and made a girl of her, 'but to be honest I'm looking for an excuse to have charge of Verity for a day.'

252

'A day? Ain't that far to Lymington, Miss Georgina goes in and out as if it's nothing.'

'Too far for you to want to turn round and come straight back, dear. I tell you what I'd do if I were you, I'd go into Miss Georgina's shop and ask her if you can leave the cycle in her back yard, then you'd be free to have a good look round. I'd be so grateful to you. And – and please don't be offended – but I'd like to give you a shilling to buy yourself something or pay for a bite to eat.'

Jess's thin face lit with a smile. 'Bugger me,' she mumbled, forgetting herself in the unexpected turn of events, 'a whole day out, cor Lawks. I'd better get Verity up and 'ad her breakfast—'

'You make yourself pretty, dear. Leave Verity to me. The day will be a treat for both you and me too.'

For Patience, that's exactly what it was. For Jess it was more, it was a taste of freedom that jogged her out of her rut and made it impossible for her to wriggle back into it again. Her bicycling had gone no further than trying to get her balance in the stableyard or, once or twice when she thought anyone who mattered was out, up and down the drive. By the time she'd pedalled the four miles or so to Lymington her aching legs were nothing compared with her sense of achievement. From the top of the High Street she looked down the hill, both sides of the road flanked with the stalls of the Saturday market. The cries of the vendors were music to her ears. Next thing was to find the hat shop and get rid of her cycle.

The salon was empty when she went in, but at the clang of the bell she could hear Georgina coming down the stairs.

'Jess! Is something wrong?'

Jess grinned, she couldn't help it.

'No fear it isn't. Miss Patience, she's sent me off to buy her some silks for her sewing, she said to take one of the cycles from the shed. Then she said to ask you if I could leave it safe in your back yard – 'cos, you see, I'm on the loose all day, she's taking care of Verity.'

'Yes of course you can leave it. I shall be here all day, if the front door's locked just pull the bell.'

'Seeing it's Saturday I thought you'd be wanting to get off home as soon as you shut.'

'I'm staying here again this weekend, I'm very busy.'

'Nice in 'ere isn't it,' Jess looked around at the sparsely but

253

tastefully furnished salon, noting the arrangement of autumn foliage and berries on the small table. 'Fancy having a place like this, all your own, being a proper business lady. Is it hard, making hats? I suppose you got lots of book learning and that?'

Georgina heard the wistfulness in the question.

'When I started I was just a child, I wanted to copy my mother and let her see I could do it and make her want me in her work-room with her.'

She had always been irritated by Jess's over-familiarity with Melissa, yet here she was confiding something she'd never said to anyone.

Jess seemed to sense enough had been said.

'I better get the grid inside, we don't want some posh customer to turn up just when I'm wheeling it through do we.'

'Posh or no, we'd better get it out of the way. I'll hold the door open for you.'

Jess wheeled it through, carrying it carefully over the large Indian rug. Then she set off for her day of freedom, hats and busi-nesses forgotten. A friendly Londoner to the core, she was never lost for words. If a stallholder was busy then she passed by, if a stallholder was waiting for custom she stopped for a chat. The stalls lined the road, blocking out the view from the regular shops. But who wanted shops when there was the noise and activity of a street market? Certainly not Jess. She spent fourpence of her shilling on two faggots wrapped in newspaper. And she felt alive! Until now she hadn't really appreciated how dull her life had become recently and, perched on the edge of the low wall of the churchyard at the top of High Street, leaning back against the iron railings, she took stock of where it had brought her. She'd been so proud when she'd arrived at Kyneston, lady's maid to her darling Miss Mellie; the only fly in the ointment had been the visits from the master, but Miss Mellie soon despatched him; what if Verity had been born at home in their own bed? Ah, that's when things had started to change. Of course, Verity had been a consolation, Verity was a little love, but it wasn't natural to waste your life looking after someone else's baby. Any road, it was more than time that Miss Mellie took a bit more interest in her own daughter. It was all very well having her brought down when Mr Graves and his children were there, but when had she ever changed a napkin or got up in the night when the baby didn't settle? Never, that's

254

when. What if things had gone like they should, Verity born at home with the doctor taking care of things, then Mr Graves wouldn't have come into the picture. Instead of that, there he was putting his oar in, steering them off course. But it was no good grizzling about the way things were – they were as they were, so best to face up to it. She and Miss Mellie had been close as close. But not any more, now she was no different from any other nurse-maid, just someone who saved Miss Mellie having to be bothered with her own baby.

So what was she going to do about it? Wouldn't 'arf be good to go back to London, but if I turn up at home next thing I'll find myself looking after that brood. And I'm not doing that, buggered if I am!

As evening fell the market seemed to come to life. The familiar hiss of the kerosene lamps stirred longings that had lain dormant in her; each stall became an oasis of light and sound, an oasis of life.

But she couldn't put it off any longer, she must get back to Kyneston. The shop was in darkness when she pulled the doorbell, her bicycle had already been brought through the salon so that she only had to collect it and go. The only light came from the room above the shop. A workroom? But if that's what it was why was Miss Georgina dressed so smartly? Jess felt excluded, shut out.

It was the ride home that hammered the final nail into the coffin of her life at Kyneston. There was something eerie about riding through the forest at night, for what had been no more than dusk as the market traders had lit their lamps was already night in the forest. Every rustle in the trees threatened, the branches took on terrifying shapes, each moving shadow became a footpad. She told herself she was being a coward, she told herself that there was less chance of being waylaid out here in the country than there was in the streets of London. But even in the roughest area at home, she'd never felt gripped with fear like this. She thought with longing of the hazy yellow aura of gaslights in the London streets on this misty November evening, she imagined a cheery greeting from a passer by or even a wolf whistle from some cheeky lad. Pedalling hard she looked straight ahead.

She'd saved most of her wages since she'd been at Kyneston. In the beginning she had been gratified to see how the shillings added up. But no longer. Now all she felt was resentment that she'd had no chance to enjoy choosing what she wanted from the shops. Most of her clothes were Miss Mellie's hand-me-downs; and when her thoughts reached that point she was ashamed. But shame mustn't stop her. She was twenty years old. What was it Miss Georgina had said about learning to make her hats? She'd started when she'd been just a child. And here's me, pretty well twenty-one and got nothing to show for it but a bit of savings and a box full of Miss Mellie's cast-offs.

Patience had had a splendid day even if hadn't done much for Verity's routine. At eighteen months, the little girl was old enough to sense the day was special, she took her mood from Patience's. Being dressed wasn't something to be got through before she could be stood on her feet, it was a game.

'Here comes your head, peep-peep-peep-peep-o,' and together they laughed with delight. 'Now arms, one, here's your hand, and two here's the other. Now pop your peggies,' Patience cooed as she pulled the thick woollen leggings to cover the thick wadge of napkin. 'There you are, all done. Who's a pretty girl then?'

From the beaming smile Verity knew the answer just as surely as her mother had before her.

And that was only the beginning. They played together on the nursery floor, Verity laughing until her little body shook with hiccups at the antics Patience made Floss, her toy dog, perform. Then a walk through the forest tracks, determined to stay awake but in the end succumbing to the motion – and bumps – of the rutted path. Games at dinner time, another walk, teatime, a warm bath in front of the nursery fire, then cuddled close to the warmth of Patience's ample breast, lovely sugary milk from her bottle.

Georgina came home on the Monday evening. It didn't occur to anyone that if she'd spent the weekend working she could have done it just as well at Kyneston with the added advantage of having a comfortable bed to sleep in and someone else to put her meals in front of her.

She arrived while Melissa was dressing for the evening.

'Mellie, I want us to talk. I'll finish helping her, Jess,' she dismissed the maid.

'Jess knows how I like my hair. I want it to look nice, we've people coming. You ought to start dressing if you're to be in time.'

'People? You mean your aunt and uncle?'

'Not just them. Alex is coming too.'

'And to think I cycled four miles for that!'

Neither of them noticed the smile that twitched the corner of Jess's mouth.

'What do you want me to do?' she asked Melissa. 'Go or stay?'

'You'd better go. Miss Georgina does my hair quite well.'

With a shug Jess went.

'I want you just to listen. Mellie, you have told John you won't give him grounds to divorce you—'

'How do you know what I told John?' Immediately her old suspicions were on guard.

'I know because John told me. Don't you guess why he wants to be free? All the weekends I haven't been at home—'

'You mean you are the reason he wants to get rid of me! I don't believe it! You couldn't do that. You call yourself my sister, then you break my marriage.' The joy of having someone else to blame! Melissa climbed onto that helter skelter, her adrenaline racing. 'You don't care that he has a daughter, you rob a baby of her father!'

'You robbed Verity of her father. I had nothing to do with it. John was determined to make something of your marriage – but you – you treated him like dirt. You were no more a wife to him than you are a mother to Verity.'

Melissa flinched as if she'd been struck. 'You're unkind, cruel,' the first tears rolled down Melissa's face. 'You don't understand – he never loved me, I was just a possession, something to show off to his business associates then to use me – use me—' She bit hard on her knuckle stopping the wild flow of words.

'Then you'll be glad it's all over. You know you're glad. It was you who refused to go back to London. Mellie, he doesn't care how you blacken his name, you can say he beats you. None of the stigma will stick to you, he'll be the one to be spurned. And probably me too, but I don't care about that. You can tell them in Court that I am his mistress, that whenever he can he lives with me at the shop.'

'As if I could! Here, in our own district. I wouldn't do it anyway – but don't you understand what it would do to Aunt Alice and Uncle Cedric? Bad enough all these years that they felt ashamed on account of Mama – I didn't say *I* was ashamed, I said

257

they were' she added quickly, forestalling Georgina's retort, '– now you want me to bring a family scandal like this into the open to be the talk of every decent home in Hampshire.'

'So your answer is "No". I knew you'd refused John, but I thought when you knew it wasn't some stranger he wanted, it was *me*, I thought you'd understand. Mellie, it isn't a casual infatuation, honestly we need to be together.'

'It's unkind making me miserable when I'd been so looking forward to this evening.' She passed Georgina the hair brush. 'Of course I say "No". How can you behave like it? What happens if you get pregnant? It would be bad enough having an illegitimate child, but if people guess you've been to bed with *my* husband, think of the scandal. For goodness sake be careful, Georgina. He calls it making love, but there's no love in it. The way he behaves is disgusting.' Her pretty mouth turned down at the corners to emphasize her distaste. Then holding her head to one side, 'Brush more this way, can you.'

'I told you ages ago you ought to have been proud to be having John's child. I should have been – and so I should be now – but I'm not pregnant.' She remembered his going back to London after the announcement of his engagement to Melissa; she remembered that other time, after her morning with Steven by the lake (something she always pushed from her mind as soon as the memory stirred); and now the nights she and John had spent together, each time their union seeming like a fresh miracle, a perfect culmination to the harmony of their daytime hours. Yet Melissa, who had hated every moment, spoke as if becoming pregnant was all too easy.

'I knew you meant to steal him, ages ago when you used to spend so much time with him.'

'How could I steal what was never yours? John was my lover before he was your husband.' The words were out before she could stop them. 'You never loved him the way I do.' Defiantly her gingery brown eyes looked at the girl in the looking glass; blue eyes met hers with disgust.

Pulling away Melissa stood up. There had been plenty of quarrels over the years, plenty of tears and reconciliations. Ultimately nothing had had the power to make a permanent break in the bond that held them. This time they stared at each other in angry misery.

'You're disgusting!' Melissa said. 'Both of you.'

'You'd better get Jess to finish your hair. I shan't stay after all.' Then, making one last effort, 'Think about it Mellie. There's nothing to gain by hanging on to a marriage that's over?'

'You're so – so shallow! I made sacred vows in front of Reverend Carter and you expect me to treat them as if they meant nothing—'

But Georgina had gone.

'I had intended to be at home myself so that the children wouldn't arrive to find an empty house. Mrs Griffin would have postponed her trip had we thought an emergency like this would happen. I hate asking you Melissa but are you able to help me?' As straight as a ramrod, Alex stood in front of her, hat in hand. For nineteen months he had been her friend but none of his formal correctness altered.

It was a rare thing for anyone to look to Melissa for assistance. She'd taken it for granted that her path should be made smooth, someone always there to look after her. Now Alex was looking to her for help with his children.

'Of course I'll come. I'd like to.'

'Once I get to Milbrook Hall I shan't take long. There's no doubt I shall have to put the mare down, she's been badly hurt, internal injuries, she fell on—'

Melissa shivered.

'Don't tell me.'

His expression was tender as he looked at her, her eyes brimming with tears. He knew how frightened she was of horses, yet she could be moved to such visible pity.

'I'll drive you there before I set off.'

'No. Give me your doorkey, I'll go on my bicycle. I've plenty of time before the girls get home from the lessons. See to the poor creature as quickly as you can.'

'Bless you,' with that characteristic lowering of his head. 'Why don't you walk, push Verity. The girls would be so pleased. Then when Mrs Griffin gets home we could strap the perambultor on the back and I'd drive you home.'

'And stay to eat with us. That would be lovely. I'll tell Jess to get her ready straight away.'

It was a day of 'firsts': the first time over-protected Melissa had been treated like a normal adult and called on for help; the first time she had taken sole charge of her daughter; even the first time she had walked out pushing the perambulator. The afternoon wasn't all sunshine, there were plenty of bad moments mostly born of Melissa's incompetent handling of a situation so new to her: Verity's screams at her clumsy attempt at nappy changing – another first! – and the grizzles that followed when there was no sign of Patience or Jess and nothing familiar about the floor where she found herself planted.

When the girls arrived home to find no automobile outside the house, they were worried. How could they get in if he'd been called out? Although it was daylight outside, indoors it was gloomy already and before long the lamps would have to be lit. Uncertainly, expecting to find it locked, they turned the handle of the back door. It opened.

Verity listened, one finger held up as if to warn her mother to be quiet.

'Gir's,' she lisped, making for the passage and the kitchen on all fours for quickness.

And from there on, the children looked on this unexpected treat as a party. Party or family? Within minutes Alex returned. Melissa was aware of an atmosphere she had never experienced, comfort that came not from the surroundings but from the people, their pleasure in being together. For one mad moment she imagined there would be no Mrs Griffin returning in an hour or so to take control. It was decided to eat tea in the kitchen for, as in most houses, that was the best heated room in the house, the range glowing red enough for the girls to reach over the tall fireguard each with a toasting fork to hold bread to the bars. Toast, thick butter, homemade jam, such a simple meal but one Melissa would never forget.

There was no highchair so she sat Verity on her knee, a situation neither of them found comfortable.

'Here, let me take her.' How surprised Georgina would have been if she could have seen the natural way he handled the little girl. Clearly it wasn't the first time he'd eaten with a child on his lap. 'We don't want her greasy fingers on your gown.'

Verity lay back in his arms, lolling her head against him, gazing at him from this new angle then beaming to show two rows of milky white teeth in her pleasure at finding herself where she was.

260

'I like this,' Becky's gruff voice announced. She spoke for all of them.

That same afternoon the doorbell of 'Georgina's of Lymington' had jangled many times. Several clients had been ushered into the privacy of the cubicles to view themselves topped by creations designed specially for them, Lady St John Makepeace who came to place an order, and various locals who wanted to impress their friends at church on Christmas morning. In Alice Sylvester's eyes Georgina had disgraced the family by going into trade, she never mentioned her to her acquaintances. But those same acquaintances, well aware of the situation, had become regular clients, coming first out of curiosity and then because there was no doubt Georgina's idea of discussing what was wanted, making a design drawing, creating a hat to flatter, appealed to them. Add to that, let Alice say what she liked, Georgina had been brought up a lady! Georgina was very aware of the situation, secretly she laughed at their stupidity. Then there was Lady St John Makepeace, something of an eccentric who travelled from almost as far as Salisbury to Lymington to see her, leaving her chauffeur waiting outside in her automobile. On the social ladder Alice deemed so important, Lady St John Makepeace was just out of the Sylvesters' reach, stretch as Alice might. What displeasure it would have caused at Hapley Court if they could have seen the easy relationship between Georgina and her titled client. The wives of local tradesmen spent less on their headgear, they couldn't aspire to having hats made to order. But everything at 'Georgina's' was made to her design, even though those at the lower end of the price scale came from the workroom upstairs. No matter who they were or how much they could afford, Georgina treated all her customers alike, the butcher's wife was given the same courtesy as the titled lady. Hats were brought down for them to see and try in the privacy of a cubicle. 'Georgina's of Lymington' was no ordinary shop and no woman felt ordinary wearing a hat created there.

The afternoon had been busy. It was after four o'clock when the jangle of the bell brought Georgina downstairs again.

'I didn't write first. I only docked last night.'

Steven! Her first reaction was pleasure, the pleasure she had always felt on seeing him. Then their last meeting pushed between them. Neither of them had known how they would feel on facing each other. How could they know? They'd grown used to writing of their day-to-day lives; from a safe distance it had been possible to build on friendship and by-pass the love that had been rooted in it. Now, only feet apart, there was nothing to help them.

'I wondered when you'd be coming. John told me he'd heard from you too.' Anything to fill the silence. But as soon as she'd said John's name she wished she could recall the words. She'd told Steven about the shop, anecdotes of the day to day happenings there, she'd told him how often she stayed here and how busy she was, she'd told him that Melissa intended to remain at Kyneston and had refused to go back to London, she'd told him how Verity was growing up and how Patience doted on her, she'd reminded him about the Graves children and told him how they came to Kyneston at every opportunity to play with the baby and help look after her. But her letters had told him nothing of John, of John and her.

These first moments must have been equally difficult for Steven, for her remark went unnoticed.

'I've booked a room at the inn – left my things there.' Then with a smile that lit his face, 'Come on, then, show me everything. This is very smart – not the sort of place hard working seafarers are used to. And you, Georgina, you look – what is it? – grown up?'

'Is that a polite way of saying I've aged?'

They both laughed, not because anything was funny but because it was a brave pretence of being happy with the situation.

'Come upstairs. My sitting room doubles up as a workroom, this place is very tiny. But I want you to see for yourself what it's all like.' Ah now, that was easier. She *did* want him to see, she'd often imagined how proud she'd be to show him around. 'I can't shut the shop yet, I must wait until at any rate six, but I'll tell Mrs Dawkins and Trudie to put away their work and go home early, at least then we'll have somewhere to have some tea.'

She led the way up the narrow flight of stairs, divided from the shop by a curtain matching those at the cubicles, his footsteps heavy on the wooden treads. She'd known he would soon come, she ought to have been prepared. Yet there was a feeling of unreality about his being here, somehow in such a cramped setting he looked larger then she remembered, his complexion more weathered, his voice louder.

'An unexpected visitor,' she said as she led the way into the sitting-cum-work room, 'Steven this is Mrs Dawkins and Trudie, Captain Howard, a family friend.' Family . . . friend . . . yes, he was both those things. 'While I'm showing him around, I want you to pack up your things. There's nothing that can't wait until tomorrow.'

A tour of the premises couldn't take many seconds.

'Where do these stairs lead? Is there another room above?'

'No, I wish there were. It's just an attic, no window or anything. I keep my stock of materials up there, that's all it's any use for.' While she talked she lit the gas under the kettle, it was easier to keep busy. But in a minute or two the others would be gone, she and Steven would be facing each other over the tea table, nowhere to escape the thought that she was sure was as much at the fore-front of his mind as it was hers.

'You wrote to me that you sometimes stay here and sometimes go home. Why don't we do that this evening? Not to spend the night there, I told you I've booked a room at the inn, but it would be nice to see Kyneston and Patience.' He knew it should be for her to make the suggestion but, he reminded himself, Kyneston was half hers and she was his daughter. Surely that gave him certain rights.

'What a good idea. Much nicer than going to the inn to eat.' But would it be? She hadn't been home since her unsatisfactory scene with Melissa. It was no more than a fortnight, but because of the way they'd parted it seemed longer, this time the barrier between them insurmountable. Would it help to have Steven as a guest? Patience had had Biggs bring her to Lymington and had called at the shop but neither of them had mentioned John – nor yet Steven, and Georgina's mind had been so taken up with her own affairs that it hadn't entered her head that the visit had been based on the hope that there might be news of when he was expected.

Like a love-struck young girl Patience read and re-read her precious letter and it was on his '. . . before Christmas I shall be back in my home port and I hope you will find it in your heart to allow me to visit Kyneston' that she built her dreams.

As the clock struck six, Georgina turned out the gas in the shop and went into the tiny bedroom to dress. As long as there was action they could cope with the situation, or so she believed.

263

Steven went to the inn to change, then hired a cab and came back to collect her. She'd dreaded the ride along the familiar forest road to Kyneston, as familiar in the shadows of the lanterns as in daylight, but it was helped by the presence of their cabby, his outline silhouetted against the light from the two lamps just forward of his seat.

That romantic streak in Patience encouraged her to linger in her room, secretly smiling as she listened to the sounds from downstairs. She knew it was naughty of her, Melissa had a husband although you wouldn't think it from the way they behaved. In a minute she'd go down so that she'd be there ready when the gong called them to the dining room, but really it was lovely to hear Mellie playing the piano so prettily and, hark, the two of them singing a duet. With her door opened an inch or two she listened, smiling in delight not at the sound but at the thought of two young – was he young? – people in such a romantic setting.

Then the couple downstairs were forgotten as she heard the rumble of wheels and clip-clop of horse's hooves on the drive. It couldn't be Georgina, she always came on her bicycle. Crossing to the window she cast a glance in the mirror, something she would never have done at one time. How glad she was she'd put on her best powder-blue gown. She'd done it because she knew Melissa would want her to make an effort for Alex. But now even before she pushed the curtain a few inches to one side and looked out she knew who it was she would see. He'd come! Just as he'd written to her that he would!

Chapter Sixteen

In the kitchen panic reigned, panic that was touched with excitement. Mrs Biggs had prepared a meal for three, now suddenly within minutes of sending Effie to sound the gong the message came down that there would be five, Miss Georgina had come home bringing a visitor. That accounted for the panic. The excitement was added when Effie came back from putting more coals on the dining-room fire.

'It's him. Miss Georgina's Captain Howard. That's who she's brought home with her. I thought I heard his voice, so I made the excuse of checking if the fire needed mending in the drawing room so that I could make sure. And there he was – just as handsome as ever—'

'That's enough of that sort of talk. There must have been some very good reason Miss Georgina sent him packing like she did.'

'Well, you'd think it was Christmas already, the friendly feeling there is amongst them in there. Miss Patience looks like the cat who stole the cream and Miss Georgina is cheery enough. What do you reckon? Do you think you'll be getting another cake in the oven after all, Mrs Biggs?'

'What I reckon, my girl, is that it's no concern of ours. If you want to fill your head with something useful, get thinking how I can stretch this to make it enough for five.'

The answer was obvious. The leg of lamb that smelled so good and had been intended for the staff would have to go to the dining room; the game pie she'd made for three – or four at a pinch if Miss Georgina had turned up at the last minute – would have to be stretched for the kitchen. No chance of it going round, they'd each get no more than a sniff of it, and old Jack Hopwood needn't think

265

that because he and young Jim who helped him had been working out in the fresh air all day that meant they'd have a bigger share than anyone else. They'd have to make up with bread and cheese. Fancy that Captain Howard turning up again after all this time. Well, Miss Georgina was no fool. She'd made a new life for herself with that smart shop and all the work she seemed to get, and if she was as wise as Mrs Biggs thought she was she'd play hard to get.

Carving a joint was a man's job, that was Patience's opinion. But, although she'd never held a carving knife and fork until she came to Kyneston, she'd become quite adept in the last four years. In her imagination she heard herself saying: 'I think you should be the one to do this' to Steven, and him replying, 'I know you need no help, but if you'd like me to do it then, my dear, of course I will.' And why shouldn't she suggest it? After all, visitor or no, he was Georgina's father. But dreams had been Patience's companion too long for her to put the thought to the test, so she stood at the head of the table efficiently despatching the succulent leg of lamb.

For once Georgina was glad to have Alex with them, an outsider kept the undercurrents at bay. In fact, watching unobserved she wondered whether Melissa had forgotten all about their last meeting or whether pleasure at being with her dreary vet friend temporarily made it unimportant.

'Tell us about your trips, Steven,' she attempted to keep the conversation general, 'tell *us*' was so much easier to ask than 'tell *me*'.

He started to relate the tale of a storm while the *Seahorse* was heading south towards Rio de Janeiro, she let his words wash over her. All these months she'd tried to turn him into a father image, she'd believed she was succeeding. But had he been her father (no, not 'had he been'; he *was* her father), surely when he'd walked into the shop she would have hugged him, kissed him, shown her relief that he was safely home. Of course she was relieved, so why was she frightened of touching him? Just to raise her face to his, to touch his cheek in a daughterly salute, why couldn't she do it? The answer came almost before the question was formed: she was frightened of the ghosts; and he was frightened too. Perhaps he shouldn't have come back to England, not yet.

266

Vaguely she was aware that Alex was drawing him out to talk, asking him questions about the ports he'd visited. What a difference there was between the two men, Steven as strong as English oak – Alex as prim as a Victoria spinster. Look at dear Aunt Patience, her pale blue eyes alive with excitement. Poor Aunt Patience, all her enjoyment has to come from watching other people. Yet she looks truly happy – and really quite pretty in her own special way. And Mellie, she hardly takes her eyes off Alex Graves. She *can't* be in love with him, it's not possible. Out of the past came the memory of the letters she'd written during her season in London, not many letters for her days had been too full for her to want to waste time writing but, when she had, her letters had been one long description of her many admirers. A far cry from Mr Sobersides, yet as she gazed at him her face had that closed-in secret smile.

I'll speak to her again, perhaps before I go back tonight I'll have a chance. If she's smitten with our solemn vet an evening like this might make it just the moment for her to relent. And at that her own imagination took a leap forward. Under the table she crossed her fingers tightly for good measure as she silently begged, 'Make it work out right for us. I'm grateful for what I've got, for all the times he manages to get down to see me. But it's not like properly sharing a life. And all that pious nonsense she talked about making holy vows, she vowed to love him and she doesn't, she never has. Perhaps she loves old Sobersides. She can't! I bet a pound to a penny that he still wears a nightshirt – and a pound to a ha'penny that he'd never take it off.'

'Wake up, Georgina,' Melissa brought her out of her reverie, 'we're off to the drawing room. The men are going to have their port in there.'

Purposely Georgina hung back, letting Melissa and Alex lead the way, followed by Patience and Steven.

'Don't sit over there,' Steven said to Patience. 'Won't you come by my side on the sofa so that I can talk to you.'

There was no way of his knowing whether it was pleasure or embarrassment that gave her cheeks that sudden colour. When he held a hand towards her she did as he suggested, sure that they must all hear the wild beating of her heart. Since she'd left Hapley Court she had had many happy moments, but in all her life nothing could equal this evening.

Melissa went to the piano, Alex brought a chair to put by the side of the stool so that they could play duets. Georgina was the odd one out and for this she was grateful. The evening was proving less difficult than she'd feared. She loved the way Steven was being so attentive to Patience, almost as if he wanted to be seen and thought of as of that generation. She was glad, it helped her to try to gather together the shattered remnants of the paternal picture she'd been trying to create. The music ended, Melissa and Alex joined the others near the fire. Georgina noticed how often their eyes went to the clock on the mantelpiece . . . half past nine . . . ten minutes to ten . . . they heard the tightening of its spring as it prepared to chime then strike the hour, ten o'clock. At the first notes of the chime Alex stood up: time for him to go. He always left on the dot of ten o'clock. His farewells were courteous, one stage short of clicking his heels as he bowed first in Patience's direction and then Georgina's. He assured Steven how delighted he had been to make his acquaintance and he bid Melissa she shouldn't come out in the cold to see him off.

She went with him all the same. It was when she came back into the hall that Georgina waylaid her.

'Mellie, have you thought any more about what I asked you?'

'Don't be silly. I told you, I'm not breaking my vows. It isn't me who isn't faithful.'

'Being unfaithful means far more than going to bed with someone. I bet you think more of that boring vet than you do of John.'

'He isn't boring. He's the kindest person I've ever known. And I'll tell you another thing, he's a proud man. Every penny he has is his own because he works for it. Put the two of them side by side and then tell me who is to be admired.'

'You'll get your money back.'

'You've got more faith in him than I have. I wish I'd never met him. You and I have never quarrelled, not the sort of quarrel that matters, until he came between us. He's spoiled my life and he's trying to spoil yours too. I tell you he's rotten, he cheated his uncle, he pretended to love me until he got his hands on my money, and what does he get out of you? Don't tell me! I don't want to hear. And don't speak of him in the same breath as you do Alex. He's fine, honest, kind. I think he loves me, I'm sure he loves me. But love to him means something different. Do you know,' she tossed her head proudly, 'I've spent hours with him, just him and me when I've gone with him on his rounds. Once he touched my hand—'

'Hip-hip-hooray,' Georgina jeered but Melissa went on as if she'd not interrupted.

'– He's never kissed me, never tried to touch me.'

Georgina considered before she spoke, she wanted to understand.

'Mellie, don't you even want him to?'

Now it was Melissa's turn to weigh the question, probably consider it for the first time, then answer honestly.

'If it mattered a lot to him, then I'd be glad if it was me he wanted to make love to. But it doesn't. I'm sure he doesn't think about that sort of thing any more than I do. I wish you wouldn't talk about it, you bring everything down to that level. Alex cherishes me, respects me. And I respect him, care about him.'

'I'm going back to Lymington tonight.'

'Is Steven staying here?'

'No, he's booked in at the inn.'

Confident that she'd come out on top of the argument Melissa laughed, a laugh that was more like the conspiratorial giggle of their childhood and clearly told Georgina that she intended to give no more thought to John and his freedom.

'Aunt Patience is very cock-a-hoop this evening. I told you ages ago she had high hopes of the gallant captain. He's been buttering up to her ever since he arrived, I even heard him tell her how pretty she looked, her gown was the same blue as her eyes.'

'What nonsense you talk.'

'Don't spoil it for her. Is Biggs taking you?'

'No. Aunt Patience suggested we take the trap, we can leave it at the inn overnight. Steven will bring it back tomorrow.'

Melissa didn't answer, just raised her eyebrows with a teasing smile.

There was no moon, not a star to lighten the dark sky. Once away from the lights of the house they were alone in a blanket of night, nearly four forest miles ahead of them before they came to the open grassland and finally the outskirts of town.

Like Georgina, Steven wanted to escape the ghosts that lurked in the darkness of the lane. The two of them on horseback, the sheer joy of the gallop, he could see her clearly pulling ahead of him, turning to laugh over her shoulder . . . as if there'd been no woman before her he had fallen in love with her . . . he'd wanted to protect her, adore her, yes, just remember that . . . but it was only half the truth, he couldn't escape. You lusted for her . . . and afterwards, on that final trip when you were coming home to marry her, like a starving man you hungered for her. And now? God forgive me, my own daughter, and I want her as I've never wanted any other woman. She's here, only inches from me, if I reach out I can touch her. But I can't, I daren't. What if I did? What if I pulled her into my arms? I've tried all these months to forget, I thought I was ready to be with her. Talk, to talk about *anything* must be easier that sitting like this, conscious of each other – for it's the same for her, I know it is.

'Graves and Melissa seem very friendly.' His voice sounded unusually loud in the darkness.

'They are. It started because of Victoria and Becky I suppose – you remember Victoria and Becky?' She knew well enough he remembered them and, in any case, she'd often mentioned them in her letters. 'They adore Verity.'

'And Graves? Is he a regular visitor?' Not that he really cared.

'I suppose he is. Melissa seems to like having him around.'

'You wrote that she isn't going back to London. That hardly seems fair on John, a wife should be more than someone to visit at the weekends.'

She opened her mouth to tell him about John and herself, then bit back the words. Wherever they skated the ice was thin, neither of them was ready to touch on anything emotional. Perhaps tomorrow she'd tell him, it would be easier in daylight with a background of the bustle of the High Street.

'Your crew must be thankful to be back in Poole,' she moved the conversation in another, and safer, direction.

Upstairs in her bedroom Patience took off her gown and hung it carefully in the wardrobe, then came her stays, her petticoat. This evening when he'd told her how pretty she looked she had almost believed him – is beauty in the eye of the beholder? Sitting on the edge of her bed she folded her arms, hugging herself, her bottom lip caught between her teeth as her imagination carried her on a journey wonderful beyond belief.

All her life dreams had been her support, she had grown used to accepting that they never turned into reality. But this evening had been different. It hadn't been Georgina who had held his interest, no, it had been *her*. Thank You, thank You, she mouthed silently. Make me worthy, I beg you. And when he comes tomorrow don't let him look at me in the harsh daylight and see me as just a silly old maid. That's what frightens me. Yet it shouldn't have any power to frighten me. If I ask with all my heart, trust and believe, then You'll help me. It's so hard. Look at me in that looking glass, if he could see me now with my stays off he couldn't tell me I'm pretty. The reflection gave every appearance of agreeing, sitting there with her knees apart, her body sagging as she let her hands fall to rest on her plump thighs.

Turning round she slipped off the edge of the bed to kneel on the floor, her head buried in her hands on the counterpane.

Of all the miracles You've brought about, somehow, I don't know how, but somehow make him see in me what he wants. I know I've no right to ask it, I ought not even to think about it, but from that first day when he helped pick the apples he's been everything I've ever dreamed of. Please . . . please . . .

When she stood up she looked again at the mirror. She'd put her burden on stronger shoulders than her own and she expected already to see some visible sign that her plea had been heard. All she saw was a woman who'd left youth behind, her greying hair coming loose from its pins, a mouth that quivered with the threat of tears.

As if to bring the memory of the evening alive, she reopened her wardrobe, moving her hand on the silk of the gown he'd so admired. Tomorrow morning he'll bring the trap back, so pull yourself together Patience Sylvester. If it's a miracle you're looking for, what do you think this evening was? Now it's up to you to do your bit, get your rags in your hair and make the best of yourself.

With a head reminiscent of a porcupine she finally lay down – more gingerly than usual for tonight the knotted rags not only covered the top of her head but the back too; she'd have to be up extra early in the morning to coax the 'curls'. It must have been part of the miracle too that her mood of doubt had gone. Wrapped in memories of the evening and anticipation of the day to come, she wanted to lie awake. She tucked the pillow into her neck to

271

take the pressure off her knobbly head, conjured up a picture of the trap arriving in the morning – and before it even came to a halt with her meeting it at the foot of the front steps, Patience slept.

With the forest behind them Georgina drove the trap past the houses that edged the town and then came to the top of High Street. There was a light in the upper room at the shop, they both saw it at the same time.

'We turned off the gas,' Steven remembered them coming down the stairs lit only by the flickering candle. 'Would that woman who works for you come back in the evening?'

'No, it must be John.' She tried to say it calmly, but she couldn't keep the delight out of her voice. And why should she try? John and Steven were friends. Steven would understand . . . she wished now that she'd told him.

'What's Melissa's husband doing here at this time of night?'

'He's only Melissa's husband because she won't give him his freedom.' She reined in the pony. It was important that Steven understood before they joined John. 'He and I belong together, in my heart I've always known it even when I tried to pretend—'

'Pretend? What are you trying to tell me? That I was just a convenient means of escape?'

'No. You know how close we were – are. You know how easy it's always been for us to be together. I wanted to fall in love with you – oh, don't make me say it. It's so awful. You're my father, don't make me remember—'

'How can we forget?' With his hands on her shoulders he shook her. 'Perhaps I was wrong, perhaps Augusta had other men during that summer. Why shouldn't she have had others while I was away? I wasn't her first. There's no proof I'm your father.'

'Stop it! For months we've tried to get used to the idea – and you know it's true.'

'Then why do I feel like this about you?' She was unprepared for the way he crushed her against him. 'And that fop, Derrick, do you lie in this arms in the same way as you did in mine?'

Just as suddenly as he pulled her towards him now he released her, shielding his face with his hand. 'I thought I could look on you as my daughter, but I can't. I never shall. I ought never to have told you, if I hadn't you would have been my wife. You let

272

him come here to you, your sister's husband. For Christ's sake, what sort of a man would lay his wife's sister?'

He sounded like a stranger.

'What sort of a man would lay his own daughter?' she retorted.

He turned away. In the yellow light of the gas lamps she saw the way his hands were working. She hated herself for what she'd said.

'Steven . . . ' Timidly she rested her hand on his. 'We have to build on the start we made with our letters.'

He nodded without speaking.

'Walk on,' she started the pony forward again, going beyond the shop and turning into the yard of the inn. At that moment her mind was focused on the room above the shop where John waited for her.

'When we've handed over the pony and trap I'd like to come back to the shop with you,' Steven said as he handed her down.

'Tonight? It's very late.'

'I'll not keep you up long.' His words were friendly enough, it was his inscrutable expression that should have warned her.

He followed her into the dark shop groping blindly, half remembering where he'd seen the table and two chairs. Then she pulled aside the curtain at the bottom of the stairs and in the faint glow of light from above he saw her silhouetted. There was nothing rational in the emotion that gripped him, not even any coherent thought. His woman . . . his daughter . . . his love . . . no, not his, never his . . . she was running up the stairs, leaving him to follow, running into the arms of her lover . . . her brother-in-law. Fury, passion, jealousy fought with self-disgust. Poles apart as he and John were in interests and life-style yet they had always been friends, respected each other. Now he saw the younger man's sophisticated grace as foppishness, his aestheticism as evidence of his lack of masculinity. Half way up the stairs he watched as Georgina reached the narrow landing and hurled herself into John's embrace. Whatever his tangle of emotions had been before, now there was only one – blinding hatred.

'If I'd known you were coming we would have stayed here and waited. We went home,' she was saying.

'I knew that's where you'd be. When it got late I was afraid you'd not come back.'

273

'Afraid your journey had been for nothing.' At Steven's words, more accurately at the venom in his voice, they all three stood still as statues.

'I beg your pardon?' John kept his arm around Georgina.

'A long way to come to find the bed empty.'

'Stop it,' Georgina pulled away from John and stood between them. 'And Steven you've no right to say things like that, it's insulting – to John and to me too.'

'How could you think I'd insult you? But *you*,' he turned to John, 'you took advantage of the situation. If things had been different, if things had been as we believed, then she would have been my wife. And you, you treated your own wife like a piece of unwanted furniture—'

He got no further. With no warning they were thrown into darkness. Georgina was thankful for the interruption.

'I forgot the meter. The gas has run out. There's a candle in the sitting room.' She felt her way from the landing, the others following. 'Have you got a Vesta?'

A minute later the two men faced each other in the flickering light of one candle while she carried another along to the kitchen to feed pennies into the meter from the pile she always kept on the mantelpiece. She could only half hear them, she tried not to hear at all, Steven castigating John for walking out on his wife and newborn baby, John sneering at a man who could leave his pregnant mistress. She picked up the candle, but even then she couldn't bring herself to go back to them. She'd never heard either of them behave like this: John never lost his temper, and Steven had always been a rock of unchanging strength. They had to be stopped, once words were spoken they could never be wiped out and surely they had years ahead of them to be together – her father and the man that one day, please God one day, would be her husband. But hark at them, these men had been friends, she loved them both . . .

She went back into the sitting room where neither of them appeared to have noticed the hiss of gas that had been escaping since she fed the money into the meter, not even the strong smell of it. Shaken by a scene so out of character, perhaps she hadn't noticed either. Still carrying her candle she crossed to the bracket on the wall and was about to raise it to re-light the gas when a sheet of flame leaped from the fitting on the wall to meet her. She

274

ought to have been prepared, in normal circumstances she would have realized that the tap ought to be turned off and the window opened for a minute or two before she went near it with a naked flame. But nothing was normal about this night and in the instant that with a minor explosion light flooded the room, so she dropped her candle.

'Christ! Mind your skirt! Stand back, don't get near it,' Steven shouted at her.

'I'll get water,' John made for the dark kitchen.

When her helpers had been dismissed so suddenly at Steven's arrival that afternoon, the materials being worked had been put in a long uncovered cardboard box on the ground, and it was into one end of it that the burning candle fell. Some fabrics might only smoulder, be easy to extinguish. These weren't. Feathers, inflammable lining, and at the other end of the box a pile of straw shapes. In seconds, even before John returned with a bowl of water brought from the dark kitchen, the whole length of it was blazing, the flames already gaining a hold on the curtains.

'A blanket, get a blanket or towels,' Steven shouted as he tried to beat out the advancing flames with a cushion.

She did as he said but it was useless, she could see that as the yellow tongues of flame licked the cushion. He dropped it, stamping on it. Whatever they did, the fire beat them.

'I'll get them to fetch the fire tender, I know who to knock up.' There was no other way and already she was starting down the stairs.

Billy Timbrel, one of the volunteers who manned the fire-fighting tender, kept the ironmongery shop. If she went on foot, even running, it would take her five minutes to reach him so instead she fetched her bicycle from the yard and pedalled down the hill with all her might. Round the corner away from the High Street the road was darker, the gaslamps further apart, the buildings looked as though everyone had settled for the night. Certainly Billy Timbrell had, she hammered the door for what seemed like minutes although in fact it was far less before the upper window opened and his head appeared.

'We're on fire,' she yelled. 'It's Georgina from the hat shop. I dropped a candle.'

'I'll be there, lassie. You got your cycle I see, go on down to

Ernie Kilping, the last house, the one with the grass next. Tell him to bring the horse, I'll have the tender outside ready.'

She did as he said, thankful that Ernie Kilping was still up, his brass helmet in his hand almost before she'd delivered her message. Perhaps by now John and Steven were winning the battle, perhaps as she stood on her pedals for extra impetus as she went back up the hill everything would look dark, perhaps the only trace of the accident would be the acrid smell of lingering smoke.

One thing she'd overlooked in her dash to get help: she'd brought her cycle from the yard – and left the back door open; she'd pushed it into the street – and left the front door open. The draught had found its way up the stairs joining the battle on the side of destruction. Now, as she started back up The High Street she saw a small crowd on the opposite side of the road from the shop: from that distance they had a better view of the upper rooms.

But it wasn't the building Georgina thought of as, breathless and terrified, she refused to get off and push her bicycle. Let them be outside with the others, let them be in the crowd. Please, let them have got out. Please.

And then she saw them. They were a little away from the main cluster, Steven with a supportive arm around John's waist, John with his head buried in the crook of his arm against the wall. Only as she came near did she see how smoke-blackened they both were.

'Help's coming,' she panted. But one look told her no help could save the narrow building. She thought of the rickety twisting stairs to the attic, the store of material she kept there, material that was probably highly inflammable.

'John?'

'He'll be all right,' Steven told her. 'It was the smoke. Choking smoke. Georgina . . . all of it . . . everything . . . I'm so sorry . . .'

Her eyes stung with tears. Choking emotion she had no power to put into words as she raised her face to his and kissed his smoke-blackened cheek. The moment belonged just to the two of them, neither of them noticed John straighten up and pull himself free of Steven's arm. What was he doing out here? He couldn't remember coming down the stairs and out into the night air. Today he'd bought priceless porcelain from a sale in

276

Southampton, an early Ming lidded jar, valuable Japanese wares of the sixteenth century, an exquisite Minton vase. They were in the bedroom in a small wooden crate. Even with a gap in his memory he knew just where they were. The fire hadn't touched the stairs, he could get to the first floor, he could hold a handkerchief over his face . . .

'Where the hell's he going?' . . . 'Come back you damned fool' . . . 'You'll never get out alive' . . . 'Is there someone still in there?' House fires hold a morbid fascination, until that moment the neighbours who'd gathered had watched quietly. They felt sympathy for Georgina, but it was impassive sympathy. Although she'd traded for more than a year, most of the shopkeepers still thought of her as 'Miss Rochester from Kyneston, that nice house in the forest on the road to Ringwood'. And, truth to tell, there had been many a whisper lately about the comings and goings of the young man who seemed bent on risking his life.

John had only one goal as, his eyes stinging and the smoke that still filled his lungs making it almost impossible to breathe despite the handkerchief he held to his mouth, he took the stairs two at a time. His brain was incapable of clear-headed thought, he didn't question why Steven was close behind him. Reaching the landing he blundered on. Only a few minutes before he'd been almost unconscious as Steven had dragged him out, choking and retching. To go back in was madness, his reason hadn't fully returned or he wouldn't have rushed blindly into the burning building believing himself capable of fighting his way through smoke and fire.

By the time they came to the narrow landing the heat was intense, smoke made orange by the blaze was too dense for them to see each other even if they'd been able to open their stinging eyes. What an hour or so ago had been a sitting room was a blazing inferno, the ceiling plaster crumbled, the lathes crackling as they burned. Steven was guided to John by his choking cough and then by a heavy thud as he collapsed. As strong as English oak, that's how Georgina had thought of him; and he needed all that strength, strength of muscle and mind as, hardly taking in breath so determined was he not to succumb to the poisonous fumes, he dragged John's inert body to the head of the stairs. Another minute and they would be out of the heat, back in clean air. Even before the thought was born so it was killed, cast out by the sound of shattering glass as the sitting-room window exploded in the heat, sending splinters of glass into the street below. Like a fiend from hell a fire ball leapt across the landing enveloping them.

Outside the crowd heard the clang of the fire bell as the horse-drawn tender approached, they even heard the roar of the flames – but above it all, sending a shiver down every spine, was the unearthly cry of a man.

It was much later, already dawn was colouring the eastern sky. The fire was doused although the tender was still standing by, the air was heavy with the smell of lingering smoke and charred wood, but the walls between the little hat shop and its neighbours were of good solid brick and it had been contained. The first fire fighter had found John unconscious at the foot of the stairs; Steven's body, charred, lifeless and drenched with water from the firemen's hose as they'd fought their way up the stairs, had been found on the landing.

That was hours ago – hours or a lifetime? Georgina sat on the edge of John's bed at the inn. Fortunately the doctor had heard the fire bell and looked out of his bedroom window. So he'd been more than half prepared that he might be called out and had been there within minutes. A brief examination and he'd been able to reassure Georgina that no bones were broken, John's worst injuries were cuts and bruises to his head where he'd hit the wall as he'd been thrown down the stairs, singed hair and superficial burns to one hand and one side of his face.

He had been given some magic potion to ease the pain and help him sleep. And while he slept her own mind was a whirl of activity. Steven . . . how bitter and angry he'd sounded, yes and hurt too, she understood that now; and how far they'd still been from seeing each other as father and daughter. Now that he'd gone she wasn't afraid to remember the brief period of their love. Soul of my soul. So she had been, so she always would be. She closed her eyes as if to conjure up his spirit. Hardly daring to breathe she felt his presence . . . soul of my soul. What he'd done tonight he'd done for her. How much easier it would have been for him to let John go back alone. Wouldn't that have ended the relationship that had so angered him? So why had he followed John back into the building? There was only one reason. He'd done it because

278

he'd known she couldn't face a future without him . . . for that he'd given his own life. Greater love hath no man than that he lay down his life . . .

She moved from where she sat on the edge of the bed, turning to kneel, resting her head on the pillow by the side of John's.

'Where . . .?' He was waking. He put his hand to the angry swelling on his forehead.

'It's all over, the fire's out. Do you remember?'

He shook his head as if to waken his memory, then flinched at the pain. He seemed to have no breath to speak, his words were disjointed.

'The sitting room . . . Steven was there . . . you'd gone . . . he brought me outside.'

'You went back. Why? Do you remember why?'

Her words jogged his memory.

'. . . been to a sale. Bought – as if it matters – Georgina, your shop, it's gone.'

She nodded. She knew she couldn't hide from it, it had to be said.

'And Steven,' she whispered. 'You were both inside, he didn't get out.'

Looking at him she was suddenly frightened.

'Oh Christ, oh Christ,' his bruised and swollen face contorted as he started to cry, stifled sobs tore at his painful chest. 'It was my fault. I remember it now – going up the stairs – the smell, the heat – couldn't see him but I knew he was following – couldn't breathe. Suddenly, a wall of fire – oh Christ – he hurled me – he saved me – remember losing hold, falling—' His whole body was shaking, for a moment she remembered Melissa and the way she used to deal with her storms of tears. But this was different. She got off her knees and half sat, half lay on the bed, cradling him in her arms. For this Steven had given his life. This time when she closed her eyes she seemed to see him clearly, not the angry jealous man of a few hours ago, not the lover she'd expected to spend her life with, not the father figure she'd tried to create of him but the friend and companion who had been like a mirror of herself.

As John grew quieter she lay on the counterpane at his side and soon he was drifting back into a drugged sleep. Someone at the inn had produced nightwear for him, but she had nothing except what she wore. Later she'd have to go to Kyneston. She believed she was wide awake but, in truth, exhaustion was overcoming her. Somewhere between sleeping and waking she saw herself with Melissa and Patience, telling them that the shop had gone. And telling them about Steven. Only hours ago they'd been together, he'd been talking quietly to Patience as she sat with him on the sofa ... Patience, her homely face as radiant as a girl's. Georgina's eyes were wide open, sleep banished. Could Mellie have been right all the time? And had Patience read more into Steven's attention than he'd intended? Despite her own unhappiness, Georgina's mouth relaxed, almost smiled, even while her eyes stung with tears of pity for the aunt she'd grown so fond of. She couldn't destroy whatever dreams had put that expression on Patience's face. If she told a few white lies, let her believe he'd talked about her as they'd rattled along the lane to Lymington, even that he'd confided he'd intended to take the trap back to Kyneston so that he could collect her and take her to Poole to see the *Seahorse*, would that be such a sin? Again she thought of Steven, she knew just how his gingery-brown eyes would twinkle at their secret. And when she tasted the salt of her tears she knew they were for him, for Patience, for the end of all that 'Georgina of Lymington' had meant.

She'd go alone to Kyneston, perhaps after what had happened Melissa would be moved to agree to what they wanted. But even if she did, how could they start a new life together with the gallery founded on Mellie's money? It wasn't possible. They had to have a new page to write on. And if she didn't agree? Georgina drifted in that No Man's Land between waking and sleeping where dreams are touched with reality and reality slips into the realms of imagination.

They were children again, Biggs bringing them back from their lessons at the Rectory, Melissa huddled in the corner of the seat as far away as she could get, her face a picture of angry misery, then as they climbed down from the trap she pretended to twist her ankle. Only Georgina knew it was make-believe, only she knew that the shrieks and yells were to attract attention and sympathy. Imagination and memory mingled as she felt the weight of Mellie's trembling little body in her arms, the smack administered, the bellowing turned to quiet deep sobs of misery. She'd known the real cause of Melissa's 'bad mood' as she'd thought of it in those days had been that Miss Carter had given them a spelling test, she herself had been praised while Mellie had failed abysmally.

Another memory with the same dreamlike quality: Melissa surely the loveliest bride ever to walk up the aisle of the little church, herself in garb that was plainly stark, a few paces behind, there to serve but not to be admired. Mellie returning to Kyneston, unready for parenthood, unready to play the role of wife. Sleep lost the battle, again Georgina was awake.

How could Mellie have been threatened by *her*? Mellie was so lovely, she was the darling of everyone at Hapley Court, the *real* daughter of the house as the hateful Aunt Alice had never missed an opportunity of pointing out . . . there was no logic. Perhaps there never is, Georgina thought. No logic in who we love or why we love, no logic in the minor pricks that wound or the slights that have no power to sting. Poor Mellie, believing love was no more than being swept off her feet by the attention of a handsome and eligible man, even by the fact that he had a titled uncle. Mellie who'd run home like a hurt kitten – and now she finds that it's *me* John loves. So she fights, not against John, not even against me, but against her own feeling of betrayal. Perhaps she'll let me talk to her, perhaps I can make her see how unimportant the things were that used to worry her. But this isn't unimportant, this is *me* taking *her* husband and the locals (especially the sainted aunt) seeing her as rejected, that's how she thinks of it even though she doesn't want to live with him. So she'll probably still refuse. And if she does? Then John and I will live together, I'll change my name to his. From Hawkesworth to Rochester to Derrick, how strange when all the time I must have been Georgina Howard. What's in a name? Again sleep almost had her in its grip, she was riding through the forest to that gap in the trees where she had a view of the rooftop of Kyneston.

John made a jerky movement and cried out in his sleep.

She sat up with a start, suddenly completely awake, completely sure of what she had to do. Her beloved Kyneston, woven into her very being, every brick, every shrub and bush. She knew exactly what she must do. Was this how Steven had felt when he'd rushed after John to that burning upper storey? Greater love hath no man . . . But it wasn't simple self-sacrifice on her part, in part it was self-interest. She and John couldn't live bolstered by Melissa's

281

money. They had to have a clean page to write on, what they had must be what they earned. She would repay the gallery's debt with her half of Kyneston. That way they'd be free. But never to look on the lovely dark red brick of Kyneston in the evening sunlight and know that it belonged to her just as she belonged to it; never to ride into the forest on a crisp winter morning knowing that this was her world. How could she bear it?

This morning she'd tell Mellie what she had decided. And even as she thought it she knew the hurt she would inflict, Mellie would understand the sacrifice it would mean to her and believe that there were no lengths she wouldn't go to be free of her. Mellie, don't be hurt, try to understand. One day you'll know what it is to find someone you can't live without – then you'll see clearly.

How surprised she would have been had she known that was something that Alex – dull, boring Sobersides – had known right from the beginning.